DIE

IN THE

DARK

DAVE SIVERS

DAVE SIVERS

Dave Sivers grew up in West London and has been writing all his life. His books include the popular crime series featuring the Aylesbury Vale detectives, DI Lizzie Archer and DS Dan Baines. *The Scars Beneath the Soul* and *Dead in Deep Water* were both top three bestsellers in the Amazon Kindle Serial Killers chart.

In Ink, published in 2020, introduced DI Nathan Quarrel in a new series set in West Hertfordshire.

Dave lives in Buckinghamshire with his wife, Chris, and is a founder of the annual BeaconLit festival of books and writing.

To keep up with Dave's news and upcoming releases, subscribe to his newsletters at davesivers.co.uk.

Also by Dave Sivers

Archer and Baines
The Scars Beneath the Soul
Dead in Deep Water
Evil Unseen
The Blood That Binds
Too Long Gone

DI Nathan Quarrel
In Ink

The Lowmar Dashiel Mysteries
A Sorcerer Slain
Inquisitor Royal

Short Stories
Dark and Deep: Ten Coffee Break Crime Stories

For Bob and Janet

Comrades in crime

1

PC Darren Hayden was driving tonight, and he'd been messing about with the intermittent wipe since the shift had started at 10pm. It was drizzling again, that annoying kind of rain that is enough to reduce visibility but so slight that your windscreen wipers are screeching within a few sweeps.

The noise was beginning to get on PC Shari Patel's nerves. She liked Darren, but he was a compulsive fiddler and fidgeter. When it was her turn to drive, he'd be constantly bobbing around, either messing about with the air conditioning or retuning the radio. He couldn't seem to stop. Most of the time, she did her best to accept that it was just part of who he was and let him get on with it. But it depended how tired she was and how dull a night it was.

And tonight had been deadly dull. Like any urban environment, Aylesbury never truly slept, but some nights were definitely quieter than others. Fridays and Saturdays were inevitably the liveliest: with no work the next day, people stayed out later in greater numbers, had more drinks. Sometimes things kicked off, plus more people being out inevitably meant more houses were left unattended if the Buckinghamshire market town's lowlifes fancied trying their luck.

But Tuesdays? Tuesdays could be interminable. Sometimes it felt like a Tuesday night shift could be counted as busy if you picked up a person with dementia who'd gone walkabout and returned them home, or if you went to investigate a school whose faulty burglar alarm had gone off for the umpteenth time that week.

So far tonight, there hadn't even been any of that to entertain them.

Even the people they'd seen out and about in the early hours hadn't looked particularly suspicious. No cars weaving erratically over the roads, no one on foot staggering all over the pavement. No one lurking, looking as if they were up to no good. Just ordinary souls on the face of it, probably on their way home from somewhere or something more exciting than this patrol shift.

Shari glanced at the dashboard clock. 1.37am. Bloody hell. Four and a half hours to go.

"Next time we pass that all-night petrol station, pull in and I'll grab us a couple of decent coffees," she said. "My treat."

His serious expression softened into a smile. "Now you're talking my language, mate."

Already fantasising about skinny cappuccino with chocolate sprinkles, and maybe a muffin to go with it, she watched as he adjusted the speed of the intermittent screen wipe again.

"Give it a rest, please, Darren." She tried to keep her tone light.

"What?" He glanced at her.

"The wipers. You're never going to get it just right. Might as well just turn them on and off when you need them."

He sighed. "Christ, Shar, how many times have we had this conversation? I've told you, when you're driving, you can do whatever the hell you want—"

"Stop!" she yelled.

"Wha—"

"Stop! Stop now!"

He stood on the brake. Only her seat belt stopped her going head first through the windscreen, but she decided to berate him later.

They were passing a car park. The girl – no, young woman – seemed to have come out of nowhere, frantically waving her arms. If it had been left to Darren, they might have missed her. Shari lowered her window as the girl ran over.

"Oh, thank God! Can you come? It's my friend, my girlfriend – she's hurt." Wide-eyed. Voice panicky. "Her eye…"

"Where?" Shari was opening her door. So was Darren.

"Just over in the car park. Oh, quick! They might come back…"

"They?"

Just for the briefest of moments, Shari felt herself hesitating. There'd been the odd case – a dreadful one in Manchester in particular – where police had been lured into situations where they could be attacked. You never knew.

But you couldn't do your job if you let that kind of thinking get in your way.

She quickly looked the woman over. Athletic build. A mop of white-blonde corkscrew curls that looked messy and matted. There was a cut over her left eye and her lip was split. Even in the subdued light of a nearby street lamp, Shari could see that her white padded jacket was smeared with blood and dirt and her dark trousers were ripped in places. The jacket was open, and she realised there was a lot more blood on her yellow jumper.

"Take us to her," she decided. She turned to her colleague, who was now alongside her. "We'd best call it in."

2

The call had come a little before 3am. Detective Inspector Dan Baines had been beaten to the Aylesbury car park by Detective Sergeant Joanne 'Joan' Collins – hardly surprising when the DS was practically walking distance from here, whilst Baines lived some nine miles away in the village of Little Aston.

Baines had long since concluded that Aylesbury could be a bit of a Jekyll and Hyde. During the day, it was busy, like any town, the roads often rammed with traffic, people buzzing around heading for shops or cafés or restaurants. After night had fallen and most people had gone home, it became a world of shadows in which anyone – or anything – might be lurking.

Not that Aylesbury Vale was the crime capital of the Home Counties, let alone the UK or the wider western world. If you took a short drive or walk out into the countryside to take in the gentle beauty of the Chilterns, all rolling hills and green fields, it was easy to think this was one of the safest places on earth. On a summer's day, when the sky was blue with not a cloud to be seen, Baines thought there was nothing finer. But he knew bad things could, and did, happen here.

Joan stood almost dead centre in the car park, already closed off with blue and white crime scene tape, uniformed officers standing by to repel any inquisitive passers-by still abroad at this hour. The lighting was dim, the ground slick from rainfall that had mercifully abated, but he could still make out the dark smears of blood on the tarmac.

"The two women have already been taken away in an ambulance," Joan told him. "I've got all their details. One of them, a…" – she checked her notebook – "… Maisie Albright, was in a bad way. Slipping in and out of consciousness. Concussion at the least, and a very nasty eye injury they're worried about. The other's her partner, Lauren Black. The paramedics were anxious to get her checked out too, but she was lucid."

"You managed to question them? Before they were taken away?"

"Well, Lauren, yeah. They were walking back to their car after an evening with friends in a late night bar. They were holding hands and there were five lads hanging around. One of them started making homophobic remarks, Maisie gave them some lip back, and then it got really ugly. Five blokes on two young women? Not exactly a contest, is it?"

Her hands were curled into fists, and Baines could sense her simmering fury. Joan had encountered her share of racial prejudice, even before meeting Charlie and coming out less than a year ago. Things were supposed to be better these days, but he knew life wasn't always easy for a gay black woman.

"The bastards stole their bags and phones before they finally fucked off on foot," she continued. "Maisie got the worst of it, but Lauren managed to stagger into the road and flag down a police car. Sheer good fortune it was passing. Whether Joe Motorist would have stopped in the early hours, even though she was covered in blood... who knows?"

"Did you get hold of Lizzie?" Baines asked.

"Yeah. She said she'd get into the office early and to keep her updated."

Baines nodded. Not so long ago, it would have been Lizzie Archer here with Baines, but a lot had changed in the aftermath of events that had turned Aylesbury Vale Division upside down. Lizzie, Joan and Baines himself had all been given acting promotion initially, and all those steps up had subsequently become substantive.

It was all highly unusual. But then, so had been the circumstances. The oft-maligned top brass, to their credit, had recognised that what the division needed above all else was some stability.

He knew that adopting a more hands off position as Detective Chief Inspector had come hard to Lizzie; that she still itched to rock up at a crime scene and get a first-hand feel for the case. But so far she had resisted the temptation, allowing Baines space find his own way in his new rank.

He peered around him.

"I take it there are CCTV cameras?"

"Yep. Whether they'll be hugely helpful, who knows? I asked Lauren if she'd be able to recognise her attackers again, but she wasn't at all certain. It was dark, they were all wearing hoodies…"

He stifled a yawn. "Did you tell Lauren not to wash? And the paramedics not to clean under Maisie's nails?"

Joan rolled her eyes. "Yeah, yeah, Dan. We've all done this stuff before, you know? And, before you ask, CSI are on their way. Expect Phil to be grumpy. Poor old bugger needs his beauty sleep."

Phil Gordon was a crime scene manager, a Geordie with a dry sense of humour, but one who increasingly disliked early starts. If there was evidence here that would help them track down the men who'd carried out this attack, Baines would lay odds that Phil and his team would find it.

"Well," Baines said, "let's retrace our steps and get out of here for now. We don't want to be part of his problem."

They stood outside the crime scene tape, hands in pockets. Considering it was September, it wasn't too cold for the early hours. There was damp in the air, but at least there was a break in the rain for now. Baines hoped it stayed that way; there was nothing like rain for damaging or destroying precious evidence.

"So this Lauren," he said. "Lauren Black? Do you think she'll be up to making a statement sooner than later?"

Joan nodded. "I'd think so, yes. I mean, traumatised, no doubt, but bloody angry too. Once the medics have done with her, I'd imagine she'll be keen to help us catch these fuckers. I guess Phil will be dispatching one of his team to process her and, if they can, Maisie too. I know they both put up a fight. Let's hope there's DNA."

"And that at least one of the attackers is on a database," Baines agreed.

A dark van rounded the corner and drew up at the kerbside. Four individuals – two women and two men – climbed out. One of the men sketched a wave.

"Another early one," he remarked, the North East inflection in every vowel and consonant. "These wretched criminals have no consideration."

"Good morning to you too, Phil," Baines responded, grinning.

"Aye," Phil Gordon said more soberly, "well, it doesn't sound a good morning for those two poor lasses. Nasty bastards." He shook his head. "Anyhow, we'll get suited up and make a start. Attacking people just for what they are? It's not on."

He stole a glance at Joan, as if suddenly realising the added significance of his words to her.

"Well," he said, a hint of extra steel entering his tone, "we're going to do all we can to give you lot what you need to catch them."

"I know you will," said Joan with a smile. "You're the best."

*

Lauren Black had cuts, already forming scabs, and developing bruises on her face, as well as more scabbing across her knuckles. Yes, she'd fought back.

Otherwise, the doctors at Stoke Mandeville Hospital were as confident as they could reasonably be that the only other damage to Lauren was a couple of cracked ribs.

Maisie Albright hadn't got off so lightly, and was still under observation. She too had cracked ribs, but also probable concussion, a broken arm, busted nose, some missing teeth and, worst of all, an orbital fracture and real concern about her left eye. Specialists were investigating the latter, with at least some surgery likely to be necessary.

Although Maisie was in no state to interview, Baines and Joan had commandeered one of the hospital's small meeting rooms to take a preliminary statement from Lauren. They would want to talk to her again later, but Baines was anxious to gather as much useful detail as possible at this early stage.

The small room accommodated an imitation teak table and eight chairs. There was no space for any other furniture. The walls were adorned with a notice board displaying posters, both newish and dog-eared, and a formidable looking projection screen. A very helpful staff member had rustled them up some coffee from the café that smelled like the real deal, and a plate of biscuits. At what was still an obscene hour of the morning, both were very welcome.

"We were in the bar until it closed at midnight," Lauren said. "Then we stood outside chatting to our friends for maybe an hour."

"We'll need their details," Joan said. "Just for completeness."

"Sure. Now?"

"I'll remind you at the end."

Baines knew she would, too. Joan Collins was nothing if not efficient.

"So you'd have parted from your friends around 1am?" he asked.

"I'm not sure of the exact time, but yeah, give or take. It started to rain a bit, so we called it a night. Anyhow, the others live in the town and were walking home, but we've got a place in Stoke Mandeville. Not too far from here, actually." She grimaced. "How handy is that?"

"So your car was in the car park?" Baines prompted.

"Yeah. I was designated driver." Her smile was twisted, bitter. "The irony is, we wouldn't normally be out that late with work in the morning, but we were taking today off to have lunch out with Maisie's parents. It's their wedding anniversary. What a bloody awful present for them. I'll call them at a slightly more civilised hour. The docs assure me they don't need to come racing over in the middle of the night."

"Okay, so you walked back to the car park. Did you stop at all? Speak to anyone else?"

"No." She took a few sips of her coffee. "So we walked into the car park."

"Many cars there?"

"Only two or three, including ours."

"And the men, they were already there?"

"Yeah. Just hanging around. A couple of them were smoking. I think most of them had cans of drink. All in hoodies, with the hoods up. Talking too loud. Lots of raucous laughter." Lauren shook her head again. "I knew, I knew they were trouble. I'm not sure why. I started walking a bit faster, almost pulling Maisie, and she was like, 'What's the rush?' Maybe if she'd kept her mouth shut..."

"You had your car keys in your hand?" asked Joan.

"No. Stupid. Because I was holding Maisie's hand. I was going to fish them out of my bag when we got to the car. But as soon as Maisie opened her bloody mouth... Well, if they hadn't noticed us before, they did then."

"How far away were they?"

"Oh, I dunno. Not really close to the car, nor where we had to walk to get to it. But too close for comfort, know what I mean?"

"So what happened?" Baines asked.

"One of them's like, 'Christ almighty, it's a couple of fucking lezzas!'"

"Those were his actual words?"

"I think so. Pretty much. Then someone else said something about muff munchers, and I think there was even a wolf whistle. We should have ignored it. Got in the car, locked the doors and got out of there."

"But you didn't?"

She sighed heavily. "But we didn't. I love Maisie, but she's got this gob on her, and she can be stroppy too. She stops, turns round, and goes, 'Now, then, lads. Stop playing with your little dicks and put them away.'"

Joan snorted a laugh. "She said that?"

"It was so Maisie. I let go of her hand and said, quiet like, 'Shut up, Maisie, and let's get in the car.' But it was already too late. The biggest one, the one who said the lezza thing, rushes over and gets in her face. He goes, 'What did you say?' The others come over too. Some didn't seem quite so keen on

9

trouble, but they came anyway. It was like that scene in *The Lion King*, with the hyenas. It was like they scented blood."

Her hands were shaking now, tears rolling down her cheeks. She swiped them away.

"Maybe, even then, it might have been all right, but Maisie couldn't leave it. She never bloody can. She goes. 'Well, I can't see anyone else.'"

"And then what?" Baines already knew the answer.

"Then what? He just swings at her. Catches her right across the mouth. And I can tell he's not done, so I try to pull him off, and that's when the others join in."

"All of them?"

"I can't be sure," she admitted. "It's all a bit confused. It honestly felt like we were fighting for our lives. I box a bit – not serious, just for the exercise – and I was just swinging at them. I think I hurt them a few times, too, but it's all a blur really. Maisie went down first, then me. Lucky not to crack my head. I don't know if Maisie did or not. Anyway, they still weren't done. The boots went in a few times. Then it stopped."

"Stopped?"

"Yeah. Some of them were breathing heavy, and there was this silence, as if they were deciding what to do next." She was shaking, not just her hands either. Baines got up, slipped off his jacket, and draped it around her shoulders. Lauren Black had looked in control at the start of this interview, but now she looked as if she was coming apart.

"Do you want a break?" he asked softly.

"No, I want to get on with it. So I don't know how long this silence lasted. Probably not as long as I imagine. For a moment, I honestly thought they might rape us. Then one of them goes, 'That's enough, J. Let's go.'"

"J?" Joan mused. "Letter J, or the name Jay?" She spelt it out.

"Search me. Could've been either."

"And they left?"

"It was quiet for a few more seconds, then the one who started it just takes both our bags. We'd sort of lost them in the fight. They went off, laughing and joking about lezzas and how maybe they should have given us a seeing to. I waited until I was sure they'd gone, then asked Maisie if she was okay. But she was unconscious."

"So you decided to try and get help?"

"I didn't want to leave her, but our phones had gone with the bags. I managed to get up and get into the street. My legs were barely holding me up and everything hurt. I saw a car coming and flagged it down. I didn't think it'd stop, but it did. I couldn't believe it, when I saw it was a cop car."

She shrugged and then winced. "They were brilliant. Called an ambulance, did what they could to make us comfortable and, I guess, called it in with you guys."

"And DS Collins says you doubt you'd recognise them again?"

"Not likely, with the rubbish light and the hoods. The voices, maybe. Maybe bits of features, I suppose. Then again, maybe not."

"Could you tell if they were white or not?"

"I'd say yes. Oh, and accents. Most of them definitely southern. Probably local, but I could be wrong there. That J, though… maybe northern?" She wrinkled her nose. "Fat lot of use I am."

"Considering what you've been through, you've done great," he assured her.

"Will you catch them?"

He looked her in the eye. "I'm not going to make a promise I can't guarantee to keep. But we're going to give it our best shot."

3

Detective Chief Inspector Lizzie Archer's heart sank as soon as she walked into the briefing room. Not only had her boss decided to sit in on the meeting – something his predecessors had seldom done – but he'd already arrived and was sitting in the front row. What was worse was he'd put his slim-line briefcase on the seat beside him and was now removing it and indicating that he'd saved it for her.

She suppressed a sigh. Her predecessor, DCI Gillingham, had tended to sit at the back of the room and let the lead DI run the briefing. It was a practice she'd liked, and one she'd followed when she'd first replaced him. But she could scarcely snub her still quite new Divisional Commander.

Back when Gillingham, DI Steve Ashby, and the then Superintendent had all abruptly departed, it felt like a bombshell had hit the division. Archer had been made up to Acting DCI, then been made substantive in the rank, with promotions too for Dan Baines and Joan Collins.

Archer's advancement had been long overdue, a promotion she'd been on the verge of the best part of a decade ago, before an arrest had gone horribly wrong, shattering her life and stalling her highly promising career. It had taken a lot of hard work to recover the lost ground.

Even so, when that bombshell had first exploded, with everything still up in the air, an old and bold Superintendent had been parachuted in to hold the fort, and then Superintendent Josh Stowe had arrived a couple of months ago on a permanent basis.

He was thirty-three years old, looked younger, and was a product of the Direct Entry Superintendent Programme. Stowe had been a high-flying civil servant in the Home Office who'd seen police forces in action at close quarters and decided he could make a difference. Of the fourteen candidates on his programme who'd made the grade, he was not only one of the youngest, but also one of only three from the black and ethnic minorities.

He'd spent the first few weeks settling in, learning the lie of the land, attending a couple of courses and getting to know his new colleagues. In his early dealings with Archer, he'd been courteous, friendly and in listening mode. Yes, he'd sat in on briefings, but ostensibly as a learning experience.

"I'm the new boy here," had been one of his stock phrases as he eagerly sought the opinions of Archer and her team. There had even been the odd, perhaps unfair, rumbling that perhaps he would leave his teams to do all the work and then take the credit for himself.

But, after that honeymoon period, Superintendent Stowe had begun to flex his muscles. Nowadays, it felt like he questioned – even challenged – just about everything. And he seemed to have become a permanent fixture at briefings.

Half the time he had 'suggestions' – more like orders – for doing things differently, by no means all of which were practical. It made for some awkward situations in front of the team, and attempts to handle things in the privacy of his office met with dogged determination to 'try' his way first. Archer had soon learned that Josh Stowe wasn't a man who appreciated pushback.

"Give him time," Archer's next-door neighbour and lover Dominic Newman had urged more than once. "He's still finding his feet and wants to make his mark. You can't blame him for that."

Archer dropped into the proffered seat.

"Thanks again for your text," Stowe said.

She nodded. "You wanted to know if anything significant happened."

"Sounds like there'll be some press interest in this one. Should we start drafting a statement?"

Another thing she'd learned quickly was that the Super was not only media-savvy, but he relished opportunities to get in front of the press, especially if a TV camera was involved.

"We need to say something," she agreed. "A shout-out for anyone who saw anything."

"I'll speak to the press office."

"No need for that, sir," she protested. "We can get it sorted."

He looked about to insist, then gave the faintest of shrugs. "If you're sure. I'd like to see what we're putting out, though."

"Of course," she conceded, knowing whatever she ran by him would come back with his neat handwriting, in green ink, all over it.

She watched as colleagues drifted in. A few uniformed officers had already been seated when she walked in, and others continued to wander in, chatting quietly as they found seats. Finally Dan Baines arrived, with Joan Collins at his heels. Joan took a seat at the front, just across the aisle from where Archer sat, but Dan remained standing.

Archer found her feet and turned to face the room. "Okay, I think we're all here. This is a new case—"

But Stowe had risen a heartbeat behind her. "Actually, DCI Archer, I wonder if I might have a quick word?"

She felt heat rising to her cheeks, even though she didn't know why. "Of course, sir."

He stood in silence until she realised he wanted her to resume her seat while he spoke.

She sat.

"I just wanted," he said, "seeing as we're all here, to thank you all for a job well done with the Shenton case. Great result."

There were a few smiles. Nothing would undo what Cody and Dale Shenton had done, but at least they would be spending a long time locked away from decent people.

The cousins were a particularly vicious pair of burglars, who seemed to share the same psychopathic gene. Hideous excuses for human beings, their fathers were already under lock and key for violent crimes. What a family.

These two had targeted elderly couples in large houses, posing as couriers to persuade their victims to answer the door and then forcing their way in, securing the couple with cable ties. Then they would open their bogus 'parcel' to reveal a toolkit, which they would threaten to use on the wife unless they were told where money and the safe were.

One woman in her seventies suffered life-changing injuries when the cousins refused to believe the fact that the couple owned no safe. On another occasion, even when they had collected a decent haul of cash and valuables, they still mutilated the wife and kicked the shit out of the husband. And apparently enjoyed it.

If the physical harm they caused was terrible, the psychological damage was even worse.

The only good news was that, behind their crude methods lay pretty rudimentary brains, so it had only been a matter of time before they were caught, and the unanimous 'guilty' verdict had been a satisfying conclusion.

"That's what this job's all about, isn't it?" Stowe continued. "Getting scum off the streets. It's why we get up in the morning. But there's no rest for the wicked. No sooner do we put those two dangerous men away, than we've got new ones to catch." He nodded to Archer. "Over to you, DCI Archer."

She stood, waited for him to resume his seat, then finished introducing the new case before handing over to Dan Baines. He outlined the main facts, including the interview with Lauren Black.

The incident board behind him was bare at present. As soon as possible, photographs of the two victims would be added, as well as notes and other visual information.

"This was an innocent couple on their way back from a night out," Dan continued. "It's to be hoped this is an isolated incident, but we can't take that for granted. It's at least bordering on hate crime. So we need to catch these men quickly. Will, usual arrangement – everything comes through you."

"Yes, guv," DC Will Tyler said.

"And Will, can you see if any local bad boys called Jay or with the initial J might be worth looking at?"

Will nodded and scribbled a note.

"Jason, we're going to need to get hold of CCTV footage from the car park and I want you to locate other cameras within a sensible radius and grab footage from those too. See if we can find these guys and maybe plot the direction they came from. If we're really lucky, we'll see at least one with his hood down, or maybe spot them getting in or out of a car, with a view of the licence reg."

"On it, guv," DC Jason Bell, a red-headed Scot, acknowledged.

"Get Ibrahim to help you." Whether it was a CCTV tape or a computer hard drive, Ibrahim Iqbal – a specialist civilian officer – was the man to make it yield secrets it didn't know it had.

Finally, Dan turned to DS Amir Rashid, the latest recruit to his team.

"Amir," he said, "we really need to be asking around the area where this happened and seeing if anyone saw or heard anything."

"We're going to put out a press statement," Superintendent Stowe piped up, "appealing for people to come forward. And, by the sound of it, those thugs must surely have got blood on their clothes."

He was right. "Someone, somewhere, knows their son, or partner, at least got into some sort of altercation last night," Archer added. "Maybe they'll do the right thing."

"That'd be great," Dan acknowledged. "Meanwhile, Amir – I'm sorry, this isn't really DS work, but—"

"No worries," Amir said. "We all need to dig in, don't we? Shall I pick a few uniforms and get some door to door and stuff going?"

"Please." He looked around the room. "Is there anything else? Joan?"

"Shall I talk to DI Moseley's team? See if any of her cases might have involved the same bunch of men?"

"Yes, do that, and then report back to me. Just in case these charmers have got some form. It feels random, but I'm worried at how easily this escalated into some pretty nasty violence." He cocked an eyebrow at Archer. "Ma'am?"

He knew she loathed being 'ma'amed', and he only did it to wind her up.

"Nothing to add for now, Inspector," she said with equally exaggerated formality. "We'll need your input into this press statement. Otherwise, keep me posted and let me know when the next briefing is."

She went back to her office and sat behind her desk. She'd done her best to make this space her own. By the time events had moved DCI Gillingham to take his pension and, as the politicians had it, 'spend more time with his family', his once swanky executive chair had long since proved all style and no substance. A sagging, threadbare embarrassment, with one arm hanging off, it had been consigned to a corner, and she'd thrown it out.

She'd also brought in a couple of prints for the wall that added some cheer to a previously dour room. They featured lovers floating in the air, lively musicians and circus performers. Dominic had taken her to an exhibition of Marc Chagall's work and she'd fallen in love with the joy the Russian-French early modernist's work exuded.

On her desk sat a single photograph, of a girl and a boy: her brother's children. The rift between her and Adam was still healing, but at least they were in each other's lives again, and she was surprised to find she rather liked being 'Auntie Lizzie' – and Ruby and Luke seemed to think a detective aunt was a cool thing to have.

Despite the personal touches she'd introduced, she still found it hard sometimes not to think of this as Gillingham's office. She wondered how he might have got on with the new Super. Chalk and cheese? Oil and water? She suspected sparks would have flown.

There was a tapping on her open door, and she looked up. Joan Collins stood there, phone in hand.

"Come in, Joan."

"Just a heads-up, boss. Lauren Black's been released from hospital and she's gone home to collect some things for Maisie."

"That's good news. Any more word on Maisie?"

"Not so good. She might lose that eye."

"Jesus." It made her all the more determined to catch these people. "And how are you? A bit close to home, isn't it?"

"Yeah, I suppose so. Angry. But I need to channel that anger."

"Well, this case is top of our list right now. It could easily have been a murder enquiry." She leaned back in her chair. "Lauren's not going home on her own?"

"No, there's a Families Liaison Officer assigned now. Sharon Allen. She was going to drive her and help her pick up her car afterwards."

A nasty thought slid into Archer's mind. "You said their bags had been taken. I don't suppose their keys were in them?"

Joan nodded. "They were. So Lauren and the FLO are swinging round Maisie's mum's to pick up a spare set."

Then her expression changed, as if the same thought had suddenly occurred to her.

Her mouth fell open. "Oh, shit."

4

Joan had managed to get hold of Sharon Allen, the Families Liaison Officer, and get her to ask Lauren whether she or Maisie would have had anything in their bags with their address on. It seemed they wouldn't normally, but then Lauren remembered a letter from their broadband provider. She'd been carrying it around with her for days, intending to phone them from work about a new package.

Her worst fears realised, Joan had urged Sharon to get Lauren to hold off entering the flat until she got there. Then she'd called Dan Baines.

The flat was on the ground floor of a smart little block in an enclosed courtyard, within walking distance from the train station. Joan had slipped on latex gloves, taken the keys from Lauren, and let herself in.

Lizzie Archer had opined that the women's attackers would most likely just take money, phones, maybe credit cards and jettison the bags and their remaining contents. But it wasn't the case. At least Lauren had been spared seeing what had been done to her home for now.

"Bastards," Joan growled at Baines when he arrived. They were waiting outside the flat for the CSIs to turn up. "Why couldn't they just rob the place?"

Baines wasn't sure he'd ever seen her quite so angry, and he didn't blame her. He was also filled with impotent fury.

As Joan had feared, the Neanderthals who'd beaten the crap out of two young women had seen the letter with their address on it. The flat was now a crime scene.

Carpets and soft furnishings had been ripped with a blade. Clothes had been torn up. Sinks and the bath had been plugged and taps left running, so there was water everywhere. The contents of the rubbish bins had been thrown about. And even that wasn't the worst.

Underwear drawers had been dumped on the floor and pissed in. Someone had taken a shit on the bed. 'LEZZAS' had been painted on the bedroom wall in excrement. The stink hung over the room like a cloud.

Joan folded her arms across her chest. "Well, they don't seem to know much about DNA. Leaving us those piss and shit samples could be as good as writing their names."

"Don't get your hopes up," Baines cautioned. "We both know that healthy people rarely have any epithelial cells in their urine. But maybe we'll get lucky or there'll be shed cells in the poo. And then there's what might be under the girls' fingernails. But we'd still need the donors' DNA on a database."

"I'm hoping it'll be there. This is all so horrible. I'm finding it hard to believe this was a first offence."

"I can see why," Baines conceded. "Although it's possible it's just a shitty chain of events. Bunch of lads half off their faces on drink, maybe drugs too. What starts as a bit of name calling gets out of hand when Maisie answers them back, and then someone thinks it'd be funny to get into their place and trash it."

Joan looked sceptical. "Seriously?"

"You'd have to be pretty low on the IQ spectrum, I'll grant you."

"And vindictive. And homophobic to start with. This isn't just high fucking jinks, Dan. It's hatred. Pure, unadulterated hatred."

He couldn't deny that. "Let's see what CSI can find."

"They're still processing the car park, as far as we know?"

"Far as we know," he agreed. "Of course, the footfall in a busy car park can make it a swine of a scene to sift through…"

"You know what worries me most, Dan? Even more than us not catching them?"

The same thought had crossed his mind. "That they'll have got a taste for it?"

"And maybe found they like it, yes."

They fell into a gloomy silence for a moment.

Baines shook himself. "We're pretty sure they'd have come here by car, possibly straight after the assault. We'll need to check out local CCTV. Maybe we'll spot a car with a bunch of guys in the area in the right time frame. Maybe close by. There'll be VRNs to check, and we might even see some or all of them with their hoods down."

She nodded glumly.

He shook her shoulder. "Come on, Joan. This isn't you. There's a ton of work being done. Why shouldn't we catch them, and quickly?"

"I know." She smiled wryly. "I need to get a grip. I just keep thinking that could have been us. Me and Charlie." Her eyes narrowed. "Us and my extendable baton. And my pepper spray."

"Still five on two. Lauren and Maisie should have walked away."

Joan stared at him, stiffening. "Says the man," she snapped. She locked eyes with him. "Is that really what you think? Those arseholes can verbally abuse us but, if we give a bit of verbal back, then we're asking for physical violence too?"

It was like a slap, but he swallowed the retort that came to his lips. Her vehemence had taken him aback for an instant, but then Joan had grown up with racial abuse, endured more than her fair share of misogyny, and latterly had homophobia to contend with. Now this.

"No," he said quietly. "Of course I don't think that. I just think sometimes discretion's the better part of valour. For everyone."

She sighed heavily. "Yeah, it probably is." Her tone softened. "I shouldn't have snapped. Sorry. I'm letting this case get to me. I shouldn't, but I can't seem to help it."

"I'm pretty angry too," he said. "Look, how about you phone Jason and get him to add this area to his CCTV checks? Then, once CSI are up and running here, we can start knocking on doors."

"Yeah," she agreed. "Although it's a working day. Chances are, we'll be lucky to find any neighbours at home."

*

In the event, they did find someone at home, across the hall from Lauren and Maisie's flat. Lee Jackling was an IT consultant who worked mostly from home, doing business remotely apart from the occasional site visits for meetings or troubleshooting. About forty and a tubby 5ft 8in or so, he sported shaven hair, a blingy earring and a black Iron Maiden tee shirt.

"Last night?" He frowned. "Can't say I heard anything. What sort of time?"

He'd insisted they come in, but Baines had refused his offer of coffee, welcome though a drink might have been. The living room walls were adorned with posters confirming him as a serious heavy metal fan.

"Hard to be certain," Joan said, "but probably after 3am."

He shook his head. "I sleep with ear plugs. I'm actually a light sleeper and, being on the ground floor…"

Baines had been confident that, even if they hadn't bothered to investigate, someone would have heard five lads trashing a neighbouring flat. Somehow, he couldn't imagine them doing it quietly. The idea that maybe they had was all the more chilling.

"Mind you," said Lee Jackling, "now I think of it, I got up at some point to go to the loo. I can't be sure what time, but I'm usually up about 4am for a wee. I had a look outside."

"Why?" asked Baines.

"I dunno. I always do. Looking at the sky to see what the weather's like. Whether the sky's red. You know: 'Red sky at morning—'"

"And did you see anyone?"

"No. But now I'm thinking about it, there *was* a car I didn't recognise. A BMW. Maybe a 3-Series? I remember wondering whose it was."

"Was it gone by morning?"

"Yes. I normally get up around 7am. When I opened the curtains, I noticed it wasn't there. I supposed someone had a visitor. That's most likely all it was," he added. "What's this all about?"

"We can't really say at the moment, sir," said Baines. "Any idea of colour?"

"Bit tricky in the half-light. Dark, I think, but that's about all I'm sure of. Maybe blue, or black. Green perhaps."

"You're doing great," Joan encouraged. "I suppose the registration's too much to ask?"

"Sorry, but it is. I just didn't look."

There wasn't much else Lee Jackling could offer by way of assistance.

"Someone's going to have to come back this evening," Baines said, back in his car. "We need to speak to every neighbour to see if they saw anything, and whether that Beemer our Mr Jackling saw was there for a legitimate reason. And Joan, get onto Jason now. Tell him he and Ibrahim might be looking out for a dark BMW."

5

Archer sat at her desk, reflecting on a long, mostly unsatisfying day. The brightest news so far was that the hospital were at least reasonably confident that Maisie Albright's eyesight had been saved, although some reconstructive surgery on her orbital fracture would be necessary.

That was a relief. But any memory she might have had of the attack itself had probably gone forever. It was a kind of amnesia that often went hand in glove with head injury and concussion.

That meant that Lauren Black was the only real witness to the attack, and her recollections of the perpetrators' features were sketchy at best. Having initially thought she couldn't begin to describe them at all, she now thought she might recognise the ringleader, 'J' or Jay, if she actually saw him again – although, with the hoods, the poor lighting, and everything having happened so quickly, she couldn't be sure. Tomorrow she would work with a facial composite artist to do her best to produce a likeness, but no one was holding their breath for great results.

Archer was crossing her fingers that Lauren's memory was better than she knew, and that the young man had offended before, his image somewhere on police systems. Or that skin, faeces or urine samples that had been sent to the lab as a rush job would yield DNA that matched something on the national database. Or that, somewhere among the fingerprints collected from the flat would be sets that didn't belong, but which again had a match

Or maybe the tedious but essential work being done on CCTV footage would pick him out, ideally with the BMW they were also looking for. Evening enquiries with Lauren and Maisie's neighbours about the car had drawn a blank, reinforcing the likelihood that Lee Jackling had indeed seen the vehicle the women's attackers had arrived in. It was the best lead they had for now.

Meanwhile, DI Lara Moseley was checking back over recent months for any other complaints of aggression or verbal abuse around the town – and not just towards same-sex couples or women.

It was important to keep an open mind, she had stressed to Dan. It was always possible that anyone – gay or straight – who might have arrived at that car park at the wrong moment last night could have been on the receiving end of some insults; and that responding in kind might have been the catalyst for the horrendous violence that had followed. Young men off their heads, their inhibitions dulled by drink or drugs, could too easily cross a line.

But no one in Archer's department really believed it was like that. Not after the follow-up at the women's home. Not after the excrement graffiti on the bedroom wall.

LEZZAS.

There had been times in her career when people had amazed her with the good they had done. Days like this tended to depress her. She'd be glad to get home to Great Marston.

She smiled to herself. When she'd first transferred to Thames Valley from the Met, it had taken her a while to settle in Aylesbury Vale. Narrow country lanes, small market towns, and even smaller villages, all with their individual quirks and parochialisms, had seemed like a different world from the wall-to-wall concrete and, frequently, wall-to-wall traffic of London. Buying a house in a village had almost come as a surprise to her.

Now, several years on, the white gates, and the sign informing her she was entering Great Marston, with an entreaty to drive carefully, always gave her a warm, reassuring sense of homecoming.

And then there was Dominic.

Even since her friendship with Dominic had taken a more intimate turn, neither of them minded that there was no settled domestic routine. Had she had a more run of the mill 9 to 5 job, maybe they'd have taken the logical next step by now and moved in together. As it was, they kept their separate houses. When they spent the night together, it could be at either place. And a few things of hers now resided next door at Dominic's – a spare toothbrush, a couple of changes of underwear. Similar traces of Dominic had become part of her space, too.

There was also Barney, the ginger tom she'd gifted to him, but who was effectively their shared cat, and who divided his time between the two houses, doubtless getting plenty of double food helpings in the process.

Dominic had turned out to be one of the best things that had ever happened to her. His unconditional love and support had helped banish much of the self-consciousness she'd felt for years about the crescent scar on her cheek, inflicted with a broken bottle when she'd intervened in a drunken brawl in a pub. She still habitually went through the rituals of make-up and arranging her carefully cut hair to conceal it, but it seemed to matter less to her these days. If it didn't bother Dominic, then she wasn't going to let it rule her life.

She knew he'd be home tonight, and she looked forward to seeing him. She pictured his smile, the smile that always made dark days brighter. Maybe it was time to take that next step. Sometimes she wondered what they were really waiting for.

There was a tap on her open door and she looked up to see Dan standing there.

"News?" she asked, more in hope than expectation.

"Not really," he admitted. "It's getting on for 7.30, and I've told most of the team to go home and start afresh in the morning. Jason and Ibrahim say they want to spend another hour or so on the camera footage, though."

"Well, tell them not to overdo it." Some investigations were a marathon. Officers on their knees with fatigue on day two were no use to her.

"I have. An hour tops, I said."

"Fair enough."

"Right." He looked hesitant, then stepped into the office. "Actually, Lizzie... do you mind if I shut the door?"

She felt a little flutter of alarm. "Go ahead. This sounds ominous."

He broke into a grin. "Oh, no. Quite the opposite."

"Go on, then. A bit of good news wouldn't go amiss."

"We wanted you to be the first to know. We're going to have a baby."

She found herself gaping. "Oh," was her first response. "Was this, you know…"

"Planned?" His eyes twinkled. "Yep. Married at last, new house, new start, and it just felt right to have a child together. We're really excited. I mean, I know we're a bit, what's the word?"

"Mature?"

"Well, yeah, but we're not ancient, are we?"

She realised she was grinning too as she stood up, came around the desk and wrapped a hug around him. The news had come as a total surprise, but she found she really was delighted for them.

"That's the best news ever! When's it due?"

"March. We didn't want to tell anyone until after the first trimester."

"Do you know if it's a boy or a girl? Do you even *want* to know?"

"No, it'll be a surprise. We don't mind."

This happy man was a very different Dan Baines to the one she'd found when she'd first arrived in the Vale. Then he'd been touchy, distracted, haunted by nightmares from the past. Now, it seemed, he had dreams and plans for the future. It felt like the end really was in sight after a long, often dark, journey.

"Anyway," he said, "girl or boy, we hope you and Dominic will be godparents."

Joy leapt in her breast. "Really? Oh, I'd love to!" Then a thought crossed her mind. "I didn't think you two were particularly religious, though."

"True, but a christening just seems right to us. Besides, we thought it was high time you had someone to spoil."

The thought pleased her. She gave him another quick hug. "That one's for Karen. Tell her I'm thrilled, and I know Dominic will be too. And if you need anything, let me know. Will you be telling the others?"

"I'll get them together at some point tomorrow. We'll be telling the families tonight."

"Great." She mentally wished them good luck with Karen's parents. Her dad, in particular, had been weird about their wedding and only decided to attend at the last moment. But he *had* attended, so maybe he'd be pleased at the prospect of a new grandchild. Archer hoped so.

"I'll be off, then," he said. "See you tomorrow."

*

When Baines arrived home, he found an unwelcome visitor parked outside his house. As he swung his car into the drive, the door of the red Mazda MX-5 swung open and a pair of shapely legs swung into view.

She must, he thought, be around his own age – mid-forties. Yet the passage of time seemed to have made no impression at all on her personal style. Still the mane of blonde hair. Still the trademark skirts, if anything shorter than ever. Still that flirtatious flutter of eyelashes, that knowing look in those china blue eyes.

"Whatever you want, Claire, I'm not in the mood," he said, pressing the lock button on his key fob.

Claire King, chief reporter for the *Aylesbury Echo*, pouted. "Play nice, Dan. How do you know I haven't come bearing a lead for one of your cases?"

He turned and eyed her speculatively. "And have you?"

"Well, no. But I might have. I was at the press conference, by the way. Horrible attack on those two girls. I hope someone comes forward."

He sighed. "If it's inside information on the case you're after, you should know by now you're wasting your time here. Speak to the press office. Just because we happen to live in the same village…"

"I like your new place, by the way. I think it's good that you've moved on. Interesting that you didn't get right out of Little Aston, though."

"Not your business."

She lowered her eyes and nodded. "You're right, of course. I didn't mean to pry."

"Yeah, well." He turned towards his door. "Good night, Claire."

"Two minutes. Please?"

There it was, that familiar wheedling tone. There'd been suspicions more than once in the dim, distant past that her charms had wheedled indiscretions out of male officers who'd let the bulge in their boxers run away with their brains. These days, every introductory briefing to new recruits to Aylesbury Vale included a Claire King health warning.

Baines had never fallen for it. This wasn't the first time she'd doorstepped him. She was, if nothing else, persistent.

Yet he was curious, he admitted, at least to know what her angle was this time. He dropped his car keys in his jacket pocket, made a show of checking his watch.

"All right. Two minutes. It had better be good."

She moistened her lips. "Well. The fact is… I've got a book deal. With a publisher."

He was surprised. "Really? Wow! Well, good for you. But you didn't turn up here just to share your good news."

"It's about the Invisible Man."

He actually rocked on his heels. For the briefest of instants, the world seemed to turn monochrome, the dominant colour grey.

"You *what*?" he whispered.

"I know, I know." He didn't think the sympathy in her tone sounded fake, but you could never tell. "Look," she ploughed on, "it's well over fifteen years ago now."

He stared at her, initial shock turning to rising anger. "You think I don't know that? To the fucking *day*, Claire?"

She'd just talked of him moving on. And he'd thought, finally, finally, that he really was beginning to do so. The savagery of his response shocked him.

"And you what?" he heard himself barking. "You came here to tell me as some sort of courtesy? To maybe seek my *blessing*?" He locked his eyes on her china blues. "Oh, please don't tell me you're after some sort of endorsement. Or maybe an *interview*?"

"Dan…"

He was jabbing a finger at her now, barely in control. The space between them had somehow halved, although he had no recollection of closing the distance. "You write what you bloody well like, Claire. I can't stop you." There was a bitter, coppery taste in his mouth. "Eleven people died. Twelve, if you count…" he swallowed hard "…if you count Jack. Why can't you let the dead rest in whatever peace there is for them?"

She stood there, flinching, as if every sentence was a blow. When he ran out of words, she squared her shoulders.

"I'd be giving them a voice, Dan. Isn't that a good thing?"

"A voice?" He was incredulous. "A *voice*? Can you even hear what's coming out of your mouth? And why now, anyway?"

"Oh," she said, attempting lightness, "you know what the publishing world's like."

"Do I?"

"I've got to write it, research it, then there's the editing, the lead time for actual printing and publishing. We're looking at the book coming out in 2021." She paused, looking away. "The autumn."

"So…" He closed his eyes, doing the maths. "I never realised you were such a piece of work. The twentieth anniversary? Are you going to bake a bloody cake?"

She held her hands up, surrendering. "Maybe this wasn't such a good idea. But at least hear me out, now I'm here. You did give me two minutes, after all, and I've barely got a word in edgeways."

He really wasn't sure he hadn't heard enough. He felt like a healing wound had just been ripped open. Yet a part of him was compelled to find out just why she'd brought this to his doorstep. There had to be an angle. Claire King *always* had an angle.

"Get to the point then," he said, "and make it quick."

"Maybe you could invite me in?"

"Don't push it."

Brian next door had come out and was fiddling in his car. Having done whatever he came out to do, he slammed the car door, gave Baines a cheery wave, and went indoors. Baines wondered what he'd be saying to his wife about the blonde their neighbour was in heated conversation with.

"All right," she was saying. "Look, I meant what I said about giving a voice to the Invisible Man's victims. This won't be so much about him as about them. I think people should know them as the real people they were – six women and six children – not just twelve statistics. So yeah, Dan. If you could make some time to sit down and talk to me about Louise and Jack. I'm going to try to talk to the other fathers, too – well, most of them."

She didn't need to elaborate. Of six husbands and fathers whose worlds had been destroyed by the Invisible Man's brief reign of terror, four remained. Sam O'Bryan had taken his own life within a year of his wife's and daughter's murders. Richard Cutler had died of a heart attack two years ago.

"And I want to give a voice to those fathers, too," she was saying. "What their lives have been like. Where they are now."

He laughed hollowly. "I guess I'll be especially titillating, won't I? The man who married his dead wife's identical twin."

"The man who managed to find happiness again. I think it's a good thing."

Yet he knew not everyone would. He and Karen knew from bitter experience that not everyone was comfortable with the spouse of a murder victim finding solace with someone who looked, walked and talked just like the woman who had died.

Who was now carrying his child. What would an amateur psychologist make of that?

"You have a think about it," Claire said. "I can see I've really upset you. I didn't want to, and I'm sorry for that." She paused. "There's something else you should know."

His guts squirmed with suspicion. "Go on."

"Well, I can't not write about the case itself. The autumn of 2001 and what happened."

"Seriously? You think I'd talk about the case?"

"No, no. That wouldn't be right, not with you still serving, I know that. But still, I've got someone on board to help me with this, someone who was part of the investigating team at the time."

"Who?" Some pensioned-off copper who'd never got beyond Constable, looking for a few quid to help keep him in beer and fags?

"He was a Detective Sergeant. Your boss, I think."

His jaw actually dropped. *"Mac?"*

*

2001

Detective Constable Dan Baines sits on the pavement opposite his house, watching the uniformed officers still putting up blue and white crime scene tape around the property. Activity he's witnessed dozens of times before, never dreaming a day would come when it imported such personal significance.

It had taken a matter of minutes to discover that his life had been destroyed. Even through the rawness, the agony of shock and grief, he'd somehow known enough to remove himself from the scene. He'd already contaminated it, made the SOCOs' jobs that bit harder. He'd walked out, careful of what he touched, and made the call.

Now that agony has given way to numbness. He knows tears are pouring down his face and, every time he closes his eyes, all he can see is two-year-old Jessica Richardson and his beloved Louise, lying on his living room carpet, their heads swathed with the cling film that suffocated them.

The empty bed where his own son, Jack, should be.

He knows the Invisible Man's routine well enough. Since that first Friday, five weeks ago, when Emma Mahon was murdered and her daughter Chloe disappeared, the sequence has been as inevitable as it's been chilling. Chloe's body was found the following Friday, along with that of Martha Hallett, Chloe exchanged for Eliot Hallett like a changeling in a particularly grim fairy tale.

The pattern repeated every Friday, week after week.

And now that seven-day countdown clock has started for Jack.

Yet he feels nothing, as if it's all too much for him to process. He's dimly aware that, at least intellectually, there's still hope for Jack if they can catch the Invisible Man in time. But so far he's made no mistakes, and the flaky leads and tenuous suspects they've pursued so far have amounted to the square root of zero. And Baines finds that, even before the SOCOs have begun to process his home and the human tragedy inside it, he has no hope, no hope at all.

He knows in his heart that, seven days from now, it'll be someone else's wife murdered, someone else's child abducted, and his own funny, cheeky, infuriating, exhausting, but infinitely loveable Jack lying cold and dead on a stranger's floor.

He doesn't see how he can go on living.

He's barely aware of the person sitting down beside him, but then a strong arm encircles his shoulders.

"I came as soon as I could," intones that familiar Scottish burr. "I'm so sorry, laddie."

Baines nods, not looking at his boss. How many times has he told a grieving spouse or parent that he's sorry for their loss? He's even done the death knock twice himself in the course of this case, a case where he'd never dreamed he'd be the one getting the sympathy.

At least he knows DS Duncan 'Mac' McNeill is sincere, a man more than just a boss to him. A detective who came through the darker days of policing with his integrity intact, a mentor to him, almost a second father in some ways. A man who's known tragedy in his own life, who lives alone, but who never comes across as lonely.

In the time they've worked together, there's been talk of him coming to dinner, but it's never been arranged and now it never will be. The realisation breaks through that shell of numbness, provoking a fresh wave of grief, and he finds himself leaning into the other man's shoulder.

Heavy footsteps approach and a throat is cleared. "Sarge?"

They both look at the uniformed officer, tall, upright and awkward. PC Robin Watson.

"Not now," Mac says.

"But—"

"I said piss off." The Scot barely raises his voice, and there's no vehemence in his tone, yet the PC still gets the message. He shifts from foot to foot, nods tightly, turns on his heel and pisses off.

"Bloody Watson," Mac growls. He looks at Baines. "I suppose there was, you know, another doodle?"

Baines nods. Oh, yeah. Clamped to the fridge with one of the magnets Louise loved to collect: a crude sketch of a disembodied pair of spectacles and a smoking cigarette. The taunting calling cards had started after that lazy fool Watson had remarked to a colleague in front of headline-hungry journalists that hunting this killer was like looking for the invisible man – a reference to the way the killer apparently gained admission to his victims' homes with no sign of force or a struggle and left no evidence.

It's a golden rule: you don't feed a criminal's ego by giving them a nickname, at least not publicly. The next day, the maniac who was stalking the Vale had one, and the first of those sketches was found at the very next death scene.

What made Mac even angrier was that he himself had first used the words 'Invisible Man', a throwaway remark to Baines that Watson must have overheard. However furious Mac is with Watson, Baines knows he blames himself at least as much.

Baines looks the Scot in the eye. "We're never going to catch him, are we? Next week it'll be Jack, and he's going to go on and on."

Mac shakes his head, his mouth a grim line. "I'm not going to think that way, laddie. That way lies madness. We'll catch him all right. And, if I have anything to do with it, it'll be before next Friday and we'll get Jack back for you." He squeezes Baines's shoulder. "Don't give up hope, Dan. Don't you dare."

*

"You've got *Mac* on board?" Baines could scarcely believe it.

"Duncan McNeill, yes," Claire King confirmed. "He's living up in Scotland these days and working cold cases."

"Yes. I know."

Mac. It felt like a betrayal. Even before the Invisible Man came on the scene, Mac had already begun to grow weary and worn down by the evil people did to others. The horrors he'd seen. The ones who got away.

Louise Baines had turned out to be the killer's final victim, with Jack seemingly vanished into thin air. The killings had stopped and the trail had quickly gone cold. Baines tried to cope by throwing himself into work. Whilst the case was still live and ostensibly being worked, it had been gradually scaled down, and he knew they were now just going through the motions. One afternoon he found Mac sobbing in the toilets.

"This has finished me, Dan," he said, swabbing his eyes with loo paper. "You know I've been talking about jacking it in, taking my pension and going back to Scotland? Well, I can't do this any more. I just can't."

With untaken leave, he was gone within weeks. He and Baines had kept in sporadic touch for a while. Baines knew Mac was now somewhere near Aberdeen. He'd met a local widow with a young son and made her his second wife (his first marriage had been killed by the job). She'd died of cancer but he'd gone on to adopt Peter, about a year older than Jack would have been, as his own son.

These days it was just Christmas card exchanges, with a short note if there was any news. Baines hadn't known whether to be shocked or amused when Mac had revealed he was doing police work again. He'd actually phoned him, the last time they'd spoken. It seemed the local force had somehow got wind of a retired cop in the area and had approached him to help them with a couple of cold cases.

"I'm as surprised as you, that I said yes," he'd admitted in that soft brogue of his. "But you know, it feels like a second chance to get justice for victims. Does that sound corny?"

It should have, but it didn't. Maybe that was why the man had said yes to Claire King. Except…

"But he worked the case," Baines protested. "He can't just go blabbing to you about it. I mean, there are things that have never been made public. Police procedures we don't go broadcasting to the world. And it's still technically an active case…"

"I know all that," Claire soothed, "and so does Mac. My publishers aren't fools, Dan. Nothing will go in that isn't already in the public domain. Newspaper articles and the like. They'll have their lawyers poring over the manuscript and we'll run sections past your people if needs be." She fixed him with those blue eyes again. "Believe it or not, I want this book to do some good, not sensationalise a tragedy."

He sighed. "And what do you want me to say? That I think it's a great idea? Because I don't."

For years, Louise's death and the loss of Jack had taken a terrible toll on Baines, a toll that had – if anything – worsened with the passage of time. Only the support of Karen, more latterly Lizzie Archer, and an amazing counsellor called Tracey Walsh, had saved his sanity. There was even the odd day now when he hardly thought of the wife and child he'd lost at all.

He was no longer just marking time. The new house, and the news he'd just shared with Lizzie were an affirmation of that. He even seemed to be finally free of the last of the weird, persistent dreams he knew were connected to his loss.

"Look," Claire said for the umpteenth time, "Mac's coming down this week. Tomorrow, I think. Why don't you have a chat with him? I've got a feeling he thinks this could be cathartic. Maybe for you, too. And who knows? Maybe the book will shake loose something in somebody's memory, something they didn't think was significant at the time."

He found himself half-smiling. "That's Mac speaking. I still remember talking to him when I found out he was taking on this cold case stuff. One of the things he enthused about was the ways new evidence and new information can come out years later."

"It's true," she acknowledged. "He said that to me too. I know it's a long shot, but what if the book somehow unearths the key to solving the case?"

"It's a *bloody* long shot," he said. His stomach rumbled. "I need to get in. I phoned Karen when I was leaving work, and she was getting food ready." He half-turned away, then stopped, hoping he wasn't going to regret what he was about to say.

"Tell Mac if he wants to see me, to call me when he gets here," he said. "I may as well hear him out." And it would be good to see him, Baines admitted to himself, even if he didn't agree with what he was doing.

"I'll do that," she agreed. "Thanks."

"I haven't promised anything."

He went indoors then. As he closed the door behind him, he wondered what ghosts from the past were about to rise again. And what the consequences might be.

6

Much of Dan Baines's team's morning had been spent sifting through what they had, and trying to add to the sum of what they knew. Dan had deferred the morning briefing to 10.30am to allow more progress to be made before everyone came together to share. It made sense to Archer.

She arrived at the briefing room five minutes before start time and was pleased there was no sign of Superintendent Stowe. She knew he had a meeting in Oxford this morning – their paths had crossed in the corridor when he was hurrying for the stairs.

"I hope to be back in time," he told her, "but it might drag on. Bean counting stuff, I'm afraid."

"No worry, sir. We've got this."

"Be sure to let me know if our press conference has yielded any results."

Stowe had decided that he and Archer would front up the press conference. Archer had thought it should be her and Dan, or Stowe and Dan if the Super was determined to lead. Leaving out the lead officer on the case felt wrong.

But Dan had been fine with it. "It's not like we have much in the way of hard detail yet," he'd said. "I've plenty else to get on with. I'll fight that battle later, when I think I really need to front up to the flashbulb brigade.

She supposed he had a point, and she couldn't deny Stowe was good at it. He'd mastered the messages they wanted to put out, and he'd presented them engagingly.

"The victims happened to be a same sex couple," he'd said. "But we're not assuming the only motivation was homophobia. This was a vicious, unprovoked attack on two young women going about their business, and we can't assume it wouldn't have happened to anyone in the wrong place at the wrong time.

It could have been anyone's daughters, sisters, friends. Maybe anyone's sons or brothers. So we're appealing to anyone who might have seen anything, in the vicinity of either that car park or the victims' home, at the relevant times, to please come forward. The details are in your handouts."

Local TV news were there, and he'd looked directly and earnestly at the camera. "As a community, we need to come together when something like this happens, to make sure dangerous individuals are rapidly apprehended and brought to justice."

In Stowe's absence, Archer had been able to take her preferred seat at the back of the room and let Dan get on and run the session without having his boss constantly in his eyeline.

"First up," Dan was saying. "Jason, I know you and Ibrahim have been putting in a lot of hard work with the CCTV footage. You were saying you had something and nothing so far, but do you want to share?"

"Sure, guv." Jason Bell got up and walked to the front, a sheaf of papers under his arm. "We'll be putting what we think we've got on a separate file – or rather Ibrahim will – and we'll get it loaded up on the briefing room laptop, so everyone can watch it on the screen, if you want. But the good news, such as it is, is that we've got footage from the car park. You can see the whole attack. If they knew they were on camera, they didn't seem to care."

"And the attack?" Dan pressed. "It's as Lauren described it?"

"I'd say so, yes. Pretty horrible. It made me feel sick. Four men kicking two young women when they were down and defensive."

"Four? Lauren said there were five of them."

"Oh, there were, guv. But only four took part in the actual attack." He shuffled through his sheets of A4 paper, selected one, and attached it to the incident board, which was much more crowded than it had been at this time yesterday. There were photographs of Lauren and Maisie, both in happier times and post the attack, together with a selection of crime scene photographs. Notes had also been added, many of them questions that needed answering.

This picture was sickening enough. Archer didn't think you needed to see the whole film to get a sense of the brutality of the scene. Four dark-clad, hooded figures in a tight group. One with his leg drawn back to deliver another kick. Through the clump of legs, you could glimpse parts of the women they were meting out punishment to.

"Jesus," a female uniform near the front commented.

"So where's the fifth?" Dan asked.

Jason put up another still. The attackers had moved slightly, revealing a fifth figure standing slightly off from the rest of the group, hands in pockets.

The Scot indicated suspect number five for the benefit of anyone slow on the uptake. "This fellow takes no part in the attack. On the film, you can see him turning his head this way and that."

"Keeping lookout?"

"Maybe. Or maybe he doesn't want any part of it and he's also worried someone will come along. Just before the attack stops, you see him moving towards the others, moving his hands, as if he's appealing to them to pack it in."

"Lauren said someone said it was enough, and they should leave," said Dan.

"I might have something more on that," Joan Collins said. "You know I spoke to her again about descriptions and working with an artist?"

"Okay, we'll do you next. Jason, are there any shots of them with their hoods down? Any where you can make out faces?"

"No such luck. You catch a glimpse of bits and pieces of features. Ibrahim's going to clean some stuff up and work some techie magic I don't begin to understand—"

"Don't worry about it." Ibrahim Iqbal was seated next to the chair Jason had vacated. "That's what you keep me for. We can't have too many of you understanding the dark arts, or I'd be out of a job. Basically, I'm going to try a technique known as 'face averaging'."

"That's where you take multiple CCTV images and combine them into some sort of composite, right?" Dan checked.

"Yes. You start with a set of poor quality CCTV images, remove the variants – things like the angle of the head and the lighting – so all you're left with is the features that indicate the person's identity. In theory, you should be able to combine the images into a single, computer-enhanced composite. According to the experts, both humans and computer systems are better at identifying a face from an average image than from the original images."

"How hopeful are you we'll get anything useful out of that?"

Ibrahim shrugged. "We'll see. We're still going through a lot of other footage, trying to see if we can track their route through the town before and after the attack. Gaps in camera coverage aren't helpful, and they seem to live and die with those hoodies up, so I'm only going to get bits of pieces of features, I reckon. Unless we get really lucky and one of them smiles right into a camera."

"What about the girls' flat? Is that car park covered by a camera?"

"There is one," Jason said, "but it hasn't been working for months. The woman responsible for sorting it out hasn't got around to it."

"Marvellous," said Dan.

"There's one thing," Jason put one more image on the board. "This is them standing around shortly before the girls arrived. You can see a couple of them are smoking. On the film, you see them tossing the butts away. Phil Gordon's had a look at that bit of footage. He's gathered up every dog-end from the car park and marked where each one was found, so he should be able to connect the actual butts to the men who smoked them. Another source of DNA."

"Lots of DNA," Archer said, frustrated. "We need to get the lab's cage rattled."

Dan raised an eyebrow. "I did that just before we started. They've promised lunch time-ish, which isn't too bad, I suppose."

"You can also see the builds of the five guys in this one." Jason got back on track. "This tall one," he indicated, "seems to be the leader. He's the one who strikes the first blow."

"That chimes with what Lauren said," Joan Collins added. "She reckons he was quite tall. Maybe six foot. Quite well built. Bit of a sloucher. Northern-ish accent, she reckons, although she could be wrong about that. But considering how quickly it all happened, and the poor visibility, she's a good witness. I'll show you what she and the artist have got so far in a moment."

"As you can see," Jason resumed, "none of them are as tall as this J. This one's quite the opposite." He tapped another figure in the grainy still. "If J's six foot, this guy's maybe five three? And almost as wide. He's the one we think got them to stop the attack and leave."

"Again," Joan said, "that fits with Lauren's description. But as for the other three, not much to go on at all. All a bit medium – height, build, like in the picture. Oh, wait though. One of them, she said she thought his hoodie was a size or two too big. Hood falling down over his eyes."

"Must be this one." Jason tapped a third figure.

"I'd guess so. Apparently he kept grinning. She remembers it, because she thought it was a nasty grin and she noticed he had quite big teeth. She's going to work with the artist on that, but she says we shouldn't expect too much."

"We'll get to you in a moment," Dan promised. "But Jason, any clarity at all on these characters' movements before and after the attack?"

"Nothing so far you can take as indicating where they started from or where they finished up. In the centre, mostly just aimless meandering. At one point, there's obviously a bit of cat-calling at another pair of women. You can't really tell if they're an actual couple or just friends. They don't engage and the guys don't push it. This is about an hour before they get to the car park. But they were obviously looking for trouble."

"Any more on footage from the town?"

"Not so far. We're still looking."

"Did you have a chance to look for that car?"

"The Beemer? Yeah, we had a look at the roads near the flats where there were cameras. You'd be amazed how much traffic there is around Stoke Mandeville at stupid o'clock. We've clocked three dark BMWs so far, but we haven't had a chance to run the plates."

"Fair enough. I want names, addresses and driving licence photos. Give the numbers to Will to do that."

"Already got them," Will Tyler said. "First job when we finish here."

"Good," Dan said. "Anything else, Jason?"

Jason shook his head. "We'll keep you posted."

"Thanks, do that."

Jason headed back to his seat.

"So, Joan," Dan said, "You were going to talk about our artist and that likeness she was working on with Lauren. Any joy?"

Joan Collins rocked her hand from side to side. "Yes and no. They're going to try to refine it, but I've got a copy of where they've got to."

She walked up to the incident board and added another sheet of A4 paper. "You'll all be getting copies of this," she said, "and then copies of the final version, the one we'll be releasing to the press. This one's not so great, to be honest. White male, thin face, thin lips, pointed nose. No idea about the hairline, or the ears, because of the hood he was wearing, and Lauren couldn't describe his complexion."

"Looks a little like DC Bell," said a wag somewhere over to Archer's left, a few rows forward. Jason flipped a middle finger, and there was a ripple of laughter.

"J for Jason," the wag added, apparently encouraged.

"Very good," Baines said, "but let's keep focused, guys. Ibrahim, when you've done your face averaging thing, maybe you could pass the results on to the artist? I'm thinking—"

"—put the two together and see what that gives us?" The IT man nodded. "Makes sense. Imposing what we can scrape off the camera footage on what Lauren remembers. I'll give it top priority."

"Please. Now, Joan – when you were talking to Lauren again, did you get anything new?"

"No, nothing. I think she's been racking her brains."

"Maybe she happened to have heard any other names mentioned during the attack?"

"No. I pushed her on that. Just J."

"Okay." He sounded disappointed. "Amir? Any more luck with finding some witnesses?"

Amir Rashid riffled through his notebook. "Not much, guv, no. A woman with a flat in the centre, not far from the car park, heard what was probably the fight taking place, and admitted to hearing screams. She said she didn't get up and look out, though."

"You're kidding," Jason commented. "Women screaming, the likelihood of an assault taking place, and she stays safely tucked up? She could have called it in."

"Said it was none of her business."

"Hell's teeth." The Scot wrinkled his nose. "No wonder it sometimes feels like the bad guys are winning."

Archer privately thought that was putting it mildly. With each passing year, budgets and resources became more stretched and the blue line grew thinner. Meanwhile, random assaults like this one were just the tip of the iceberg. Organised crime in Thames Valley was becoming more organised, and Aylesbury Vale was no exception. Drugs, people trafficking, modern slavery. County lines and turf wars between rival gangs. Kids and vulnerable adults being used for the criminal ends of people without consciences.

It wasn't something to keep going on about. It wasn't going to help morale. But when members of the public couldn't even be arsed to pick up a phone to report two women taking a kicking, she wondered who the force was trying to protect, and whether it was worth the bother.

"Anything else, anyone?" Dan was saying, his gaze traversing the room. No one offered any questions or observations. "Okay, let's leave it there. We're not doing so badly. DNA, likenesses to go public with, suspect cars to check out. Let's hope something comes of it and we can start nailing these cowards."

People started to rise from their chairs and file out, some chatting, others checking phones. Archer waited for the room to start emptying out, checking her own phone for messages. When she stood up, Dan was loitering by the incident board. She walked over and joined him.

"I'm sure you're right," she said. "It won't take much for the whole jigsaw to come together."

"Fingers crossed. Actually," he said, "can we have a quick word about something else?"

She raised an eyebrow. "Another bombshell like last night?"

But he wasn't smiling. "Not like that, no. Maybe in your office?"

She sensed a tension about him. "Are you okay?"

"Sort of. It's just something you should know about."

"But not this case?"

"No. A much older one."

7

The three BMWs that Jason and Ibrahim had found on CCTV had yielded mixed results. One owned by a woman from High Wycombe in her thirties, the others by two Aylesbury men.

The woman, Hana Osman, had seemed the least likely to be involved in the assault, so Joan Collins had made initial contact by phone. Hana had driven over to Aylesbury around midnight after her mother had been taken ill. Reading between the lines, her father was as much use in a crisis as a chocolate sunshade and, since Hana's elder brother lived in Manchester and her other brother was working abroad, it had fallen to her to drag herself out of bed, spend half the small hours with her mother, dialling 111 and assuring herself and her parents that the terrible headache was nothing more serious than a migraine.

When the pain had started to recede, and Hana's mother finally began to accept that she wasn't dying, Hana had rejected the invitation to stay, preferring to go home and get some sleep in her own bed. She'd travelled mainly on the A4010, which took her close to Stoke Mandeville and Lauren and Maisie's home.

A quick call to the parents had confirmed the story and – not unexpectedly – eliminated Hana's car.

Of the two remaining owners, forty-nine-year-old Roy Barlow from Weston Turville also seemed an unlikely suspect, whereas Liam James Gunner, at twenty, was at least in the right age group. His address was a flat within walking distance of the town centre, which could be significant.

They'd checked his record on the Police National Computer and he was squeaky clean. It might just mean he'd never been caught. Besides, there was a first time for everything.

Baines and Joan Collins found him in the warehouse he worked at, on a small industrial estate just off the Bicester Road.

His BMW was in the car park. The manager seemed none too pleased to have two police officers turning up asking to speak to one of his staff, but he reluctantly offered his office, which was small, tatty and in need of a decent clean.

Liam Gunner turned out to be of average height and build, tacitly matching Lauren's description of three of the gang – but then so did maybe half the young male population. Floppy brown hair. Clean shaven. Soft looking hands. When he spoke, he proved to be much better spoken than Baines had expected. None of the multicultural 'Jafaican' dialect still in circulation among numbers of young people, and very few dropped Hs or Ts.

Being invited to talk to two detectives appeared to make him jittery, although Baines knew this didn't necessarily signify anything. Innocent people often fretted that they may have unwittingly broken some law, or that a mistake was being made that could land them in trouble. And Baines had also interviewed many a hardened criminal, guilty as hell, but cool as an ice cube.

When Baines asked him to account for his movements between two and four yesterday morning, he almost looked as if he suspected a leg pull. "In the morning? Are you sure you're detectives?"

"You've seen our ID," Joan pointed out.

"Yeah, but it could be…" He shook his head. "All right, then. I was in bed. Look, officers, I wish you'd tell me what this was all about. I work full time. I'm here from 8am. If I was out all night, I think I'd be asleep on the job by midday. Do I look worn out?"

"Maybe you've caught up on your beauty sleep by now," Joan said.

"I go to bed at 11pm. My dad owns this warehouse, among other interests, and I want to go into the family business. He's starting me out at the bottom, doing spells in different places. I'm also doing a degree by correspondence. I take it all very seriously. So no, I'm not going to run around in the middle of the night, doing whatever you're accusing me of."

A thought was stirring in Baines's mind.

"No one's accusing you of anything, Liam," he soothed. "We just need to eliminate you from our enquiries. We're interested in a BMW like yours that was seen in the Stoke Mandeville area in the early hours of yesterday morning."

"Well, it wasn't mine, unless it took itself out for a spin. I told you. I was tucked up in bed."

"Anyone vouch for you?" Collins asked.

"Nope. Just me. My parents live in Amersham, but dad owns a few properties, including the flat I'm in."

Baines wondered if Liam was actually paying daddy any rent. He also wondered whether the life mapped out in front of Liam was what the young man really wanted, or what his father had decided for him.

"What's this about?" Gunner wanted to know. "Do I need a lawyer?"

Baines smiled. "I don't know. Do you?"

The young man chewed his lip.

"Thing is," Baines pressed, "your car registration was caught on CCTV in the area. So if you weren't driving, who was?"

"I dunno." His eyes were darting all over the place. "It was right where I left it this morning. Maybe someone cloned it? You know, stuck my reg on another car?"

It was possible, Baines supposed. Except that it would have had to be pre-planned, and there was nothing about the assault that suggested premeditation.

"That's your story?" Joan said. "That it wasn't you driving your car around Stoke last night?" She paused for a beat. "Think carefully, Liam, because if we find you're lying, we're going to wonder why."

He looked about to cry. "All right. Yeah, it *was* me."

She folded her arms, as if she was holding something – maybe her rage – close to her.

"*What* was you?" Her tone was icy.

Baines was half-worried that he might have to hold her back, but he trusted in her professionalism.

"Yeah," Gunner said again. "It was me driving around. But that was all I was doing, honestly. I get jumpy and I can't sleep. So I go out driving and it calms me. Stoke Mandeville, you say?" He shrugged. "Maybe. I don't really know where I went. It was pretty aimless. It always is."

Joan tapped her foot. "Seriously? So why did you say it wasn't you?"

He turned crimson. "I was scared. Police turning up questioning me. Obviously a young guy with a nice car like mine has been up to no good. Saying it wasn't me was the first thing that came into my head. I'm sorry," he mumbled.

"Do you have a mate who goes by the name of J?" Baines asked.

"What? Who?" He was really flustered now. "I don't think so."

"You don't know who your mates are?"

"I've hardly got any mates." He bit his lip. "Look. Most of the friends I had have gone off to uni, but Dad didn't want that for me. He reckons the school of hard knocks was good enough for him and should be fine for me. I'm only doing a degree at all because Mum talked him into it."

"So who do you hang out with?"

"I have a quick drink with some of the guys I work with on a Friday night. That's about it. I usually spend the weekend with my parents. What with that, the job and the course, I don't exactly live the social whirl, Inspector."

"How do you feel about same sex couples?" Joan threw in casually. "Especially lesbians?"

"My parents aren't too keen. But I'm not so narrow minded. I don't feel anything about it, really. It doesn't hurt anyone, does it?"

Baines thought the whole story sounded so lame, it was almost plausible.

"We'd like to take a DNA swab from you," he said. "If that's okay?"

Just for a moment, the young man looked anxious again. Then he shrugged. "Swab away."

They spoke to some of his colleagues before they left. Yes, Liam had been in yesterday. No, nobody had noticed him looking especially tired.

Back in the car, before he started the engine, Baines asked Joan what she made of Liam Gunner.

"Not sure," she said. "Almost too good to be true, in a way. If his life is what he claims it is, it sounds like a bit of a sad existence to me."

He knew what she meant. "Maybe a bit *too* sad and frustrating? Did he have an outlet for whatever feelings he might have about that?"

"Like going out queer bashing? I guess I wouldn't rule it out. We've got his DNA, of course."

"We have. Although I couldn't see any scratch marks on him."

"True," Joan agreed. "Did you see the way he hesitated when we asked for the sample?"

"I couldn't decide if he was just spooked by the very business of being questioned by police and then having a sample tested, or whether he actually had anything to hide."

"Or even something more calculated? Working out whether we're likely to have his DNA before he consented?"

"Not that we actually needed his permission."

"He might not know that. But he's probably like a lot of people. Thinks he knows all about forensics from the TV. Knows he didn't pick up any scratches in the course of the assault. Knows it wasn't him who left his piss and shit in the girls' flat. Thinks a DNA sample will eliminate him."

"It can't do that," Baines said. "But it might not incriminate him, either. Okay, we might as well go and see Mr Barlow."

*

Roy Barlow managed a supermarket in Aylesbury. He was maybe 5ft 9in, neither chubby nor skinny. Average. But he looked, if anything, a few years older than his forty-nine, and the top of his head had probably been a stranger to hair for a long time. They turned up in his store out to the west of the town and he showed them into his functional but tidy office.

"Now, how can I help you?" he asked, all smiles. "Can I offer you a coffee?"

Baines was tempted, but he doubted this would take long enough for the drinks to cool.

"That's kind, but no, thanks. We're investigating an incident in the early hours of yesterday. Wednesday morning?"

Barlow frowned. "Okay."

"Can I ask you where you were between, say 2am and 4am?"

The other man smiled. "Funny you should ask. I had to nip over here during the night, probably around that time."

"What on earth for?"

"I'm on medication at the moment, for a bad back, and I'd stupidly left it in my desk drawer. I thought I could get through the night without it, but you know what it's like. I kept worrying I'd need it, and I couldn't sleep. In the end, I decided I might as well come and get it. It's only ten minutes. But what's this about? What sort of incident?"

Baines ignored the question. "Can anyone confirm that?"

"Well, I disturbed my wife getting in and out of bed."

"What route would you have taken?" Joan asked.

"My usual route to work. Out of the village and a loop around Stoke Mandeville."

It added up, but Baines wasn't quite ready to let it go.

"Does anyone else have access to the car?"

He frowned now. "What am I supposed to have done?"

Baines smiled. "Honestly, sir, we're just eliminating vehicles like yours from our enquiries. Just humour us."

Barlow nodded. "Fair enough. Well, I mostly drive it. My wife might drive home after an evening out. We have a designated driver rule. It's not always her." He flashed Joan a smile. "She likes a glass of wine too. But she has a Toyota she uses most of the time."

"And no one else has access to it? Any kids at home?"

"Not at the moment, no. Our daughter's living in Watford with her partner, and our son's away at uni. Edinburgh, actually." He sounded proud.

Baines pressed him. "No one else at all?"

Roy Barlow shook his head. "No one."

They thanked him and left soon afterwards.

"I'm thinking, out of our three car owners, I'm liking young Liam Gunner, if anyone," said Joan, back at the car. "I mean, I don't see middle-aged Mr Average with a bad back being out at some ungodly hour, sporting a hoodie, with a bunch of yobs in search of trouble."

"What did you think of his alibi?"

She shrugged. "What, getting up in the middle of the night to drive over here and get his back medicine? So bizarre, it must be true. Mind you, I think I'd just take some ibuprofen or paracetamol."

"My dad has back trouble," he told her. "Normal stuff doesn't touch it." He looked at her. "Maybe we should just run his story past the wife?"

*

The Barlows owned a Georgian style house in a quiet close. Amanda Barlow had probably been rather beautiful ten years or so ago. She was still an attractive woman, Baines thought. Shoulder length hair with coppery highlights, soft brown eyes, and a figure she kept in trim. A gym bag in the hall suggested she worked at maintaining those good looks.

"I don't understand," she said in a tasteful, almost too perfect, living room. Baines took in the family photos. "You spoke to Roy. What can I tell you that he didn't? Unless you didn't believe him?"

"Just routine," Joan said. "Have you spoken to Mr Barlow, since we saw him?"

"Yes. He phoned to say you'd been at the store asking him questions. He thought it would amuse me – my hubby, the suspect. He didn't say you'd be coming here. What's it all about? *Are* we suspected of something?"

Baines decided to open up a little. "You may have heard about a nasty assault on two young women in the town early yesterday morning. We think a car like your husband's might be connected. We're trying to rule it out."

"I see. Yes, I heard about it. Awful. What's this town coming to?" She gave her head a sorry shake. Baines didn't think a great acting career awaited her, but whether this was simply faux concern by someone who didn't really give a rat's arse, or something more sinister, he couldn't tell.

She folded her arms. "Inspector, there must be lots of black BMWs around these days. I mean, once upon a time, a nice German car was a bit elite. A real statement. Nowadays, there are BMWs, Audis and Mercedes everywhere."

"What about your BMW? Where was it last night?"

"I gather Roy told you. He popped over to the store to get some medicine he left behind. One of these days, he'll forget where he left his head."

"You won't mind if we just have a look around?" Joan said.

The smile froze on the woman's face. "What for? Don't you need a warrant?"

"Do we have to get one?" Joan was all wide-eyed innocence. "This is just routine. I promise we won't make a mess."

Amanda Barlow rolled her eyes. "Honestly, I'd have thought you had better things to do with your time. But go ahead."

The house was immaculate. Lounge, dining room, high-end kitchen, utility room and downstairs loo at ground level; four bedrooms, two of them en suite and the smallest kitted out as an office, plus a bathroom with jacuzzi tub on the first floor. Nothing out of place. Or so Baines thought until they were headed back to the station.

"Tell me if I'm reaching," Joan said, "but did you notice the duvet in the third bedroom? The son's room when he's home from uni?"

"The duvet?" There was a slow cyclist ahead, pedalling hard and making little progress. Baines put his hand on the gear lever to slow down, then remembered for the umpteenth time that his two-week-old Kia Sportage was an automatic. He was beginning to regret the choice already. It didn't quite feel like 'real' driving. "What about it?"

"Well," Joan said, "I'd say the lovely Amanda's obsessively tidy. Everything a bit too perfect. In the other bedrooms, the duvets and pillowcases looked like they'd been ironed in situ. Not so much as a wrinkle. In the son's room, it was all very neat and tidy too, except the bed linen looked less perfect. As if the bed had been made carefully enough, but after someone had slept in it."

"Maybe the last time the lad stayed over, it was just the one night, and she's in no hurry to launder it."

"Really? Because I'd bet it'd all be in the washing machine before he reached the end of the road."

The cyclist turned off and he pushed down on the accelerator. "You're thinking he's actually staying there?"

"I don't know. Maybe. I'd like us to check with his university and make sure he's been there. And I clocked him in some of the photos in the lounge. I'd be interested in what Ibrahim's imaging techniques come up with."

He nodded. "Make the call. I actually think it *is* a reach, but let's make sure. Let's check whether the Barlow boy has any sort of record, too. And let's see what CCTV footage we can get from the dad's store. Make sure he really did go there. But honestly? I think you were right first time. I'm much more interested in Liam Gunner, to be honest."

"Yes. Lonely lad, under dad's thumb. His whole future mapped out, with no say in it. What if he meets a couple of guys by chance, gets invited out on the lash and decides to slip his leash for once? How keen would he be to be accepted?" she mused.

"He's had a few beers too many. Maybe something else, too. They're larking around in the car park…"

"… and, when two girls turn up, holding hands, it starts to turn ugly quite quickly." She nodded. "Question is: does he stay out of it, or does he join in, eager not to disappoint his new best friends?"

"Exactly. Maybe he didn't do any actual violence or, if he did, it could have been half-hearted. It would explain why there were no obvious scratch marks on him."

"Or," said Joan, "maybe he'd be first to put the boot in, wanting to prove himself."

"We've got nothing on him," Baines said, "and we can't rely on Ibrahim to come up with anything good enough to be stone cold proof that he, or young Barlow for that matter – what was his name?"

"Zack, the mother said."

"Zack Barlow. We need to dig more on both those young men. Let's hope we get lucky with DNA."

"We've got to get something," Joan said. "Some sort of lead. I really want these people, Dan."

8

Archer sat in her office, her chair swivelled so she could look out the window. The view was an uninspiring one on the best of days, and this wasn't the best of days. The sky was an indifferent shade of grey and a brief spell of light drizzle hadn't long passed.

She had a lot on her mind. The horrendous assault in Aylesbury was by no means the only case her people were investigating, although certainly the worst. Lara Moseley's team was trying, with little success so far, to stem a series of distraction burglaries around the villages, and Archer herself was liaising with opposite numbers across Thames Valley and neighbouring forces on the ongoing, ever spreading issue of 'county lines' organised crime.

But her thoughts kept returning to Dan Baines and what he had told her this morning.

A few years ago, Dan had been headed for a meltdown, and she had seen the effects with her own eyes. He'd finally opened up to her: how for years he'd suppressed his grief over his dead first wife and his lost son – and how the price of that suppression was now being paid in dreams and waking visions of Jack, in the shape of the teenager he would have become if he'd lived.

Or if he was still alive.

Archer had given him an ultimatum. He'd agreed to have counselling – and it seemed to have helped. The periods when he seemed to be only half-there were now just a memory. It had been great to see him grow, and he richly deserved his promotion to DI.

She really hoped Claire Bloody King and her bloody book didn't undo all that progress. She'd gained the impression that reopening that door was the last thing he wanted

Interestingly, and surprisingly, it seemed Karen's reaction had been quite different. She thought it would be good for Dan to see his old friend after all this time, and had even insisted that they have him to dinner.

Archer knew her colleague didn't exactly have a lot of friends. She and, by extension, Dominic, were probably the people he was closest to besides Karen and his own family.

Karen's circle was wider, with a couple of girl friends from work, and she'd surprised both Archer and Dan himself in recent months by joining Little Aston WI, roped in by a woman from the village shop.

Louise Baines had been one of the WI's youngest members and well loved within the village. When Karen had moved in with Dan, they'd feared the same negative reaction that they'd received from Karen's parents: the notion that Dan was somehow trying to replace his dead wife with a carbon copy.

It turned out they couldn't have been more wrong. WI members who remembered Louise were delighted to have a little piece of her back, but at the same time they seemed genuinely to accept Karen as a person in her own right. She was soon getting involved with things like the cake stall for the village fete, a sponsored tidy up around the village, and the WI book group.

And she dragged Dan along to quiz evenings and other fund raisers. Once or twice, he'd even helped out where a bit of male muscle was needed in setting up for events.

"I seem to have become a WIMP," he'd said to Archer one Monday morning. She'd looked at him, puzzled. "WI Male Partner," he explained. A couple of times he'd ended up in the pub with a couple of fellow WIMPs. Archer hadn't been overly surprised when they'd opted to stay in the village.

But Dan believed it wasn't just the opportunity to meet up with an old friend and mentor that lay behind Karen's enthusiasm. Just because they were getting on with their lives, that didn't mean Louise and Jack had been forgotten, nor that the couple had any sense of closure. There were so many unanswered questions.

Why had the Invisible Man targeted young mothers with two-year-olds? How had he selected his victims? Why had he stopped after Louise's death?

What had become of Jack?

"She hasn't said as much," Dan had confided to Archer, "but I think she agrees with Claire. After all this time, she thinks it might be worth giving the tree one last shake. And that a cold case expert like Mac might just be the man to do it, and maybe get some answers."

"And what do you think?" she'd asked him.

He'd been silent for a couple of beats, then sighed heavily. "Me? I honestly don't know. I can tell myself I'm only looking forward these days, but I know that's not entirely true. I still catch myself looking over my shoulder. And that's probably a good thing. Trying to close the lid on what happened didn't work so well, did it? But I'm scared, Lizzie, if I'm honest. Maybe what I'm most scared of is actually learning the truth and finding that it's even worse than the not knowing."

Archer could see both sides of the coin. The chance, however slim, of some sort of answers. A renewed threat to Dan's mental wellbeing. She guessed Superintendent Stowe would make a long speech about Balance of Risk. That was okay when you weren't talking about someone you cared about.

"Boss?" Will Tyler's voice interrupted her thoughts.

She looked up. He stood in the doorway. "Hi Will? Everything okay?"

"Could be more than okay, actually." He came in. "We've had a response to the media appeal and I thought, since Dan's out chasing down this Beemer…"

"What have we got?"

"There was a similar incident in the town about a month ago."

"What, a homophobic attack? And it wasn't reported?" Dear God.

"No, no." He held his hands up. "Not an attack as such. These young women decided not to stick around and ran for it. Luckily the guys who were cat calling didn't follow. But it sounds like it might have been the same group. Four or five guys in hoodies, one distinctively tall with, the women think, a Brummie accent."

"Our victims said Northern."

"An easy mistake to make if you're scared. I'm guessing phonetics isn't the first thought in your mind when you're trying not to get your head kicked in."

"Fair point," she conceded. "And this was where?"

"They were crossing the Market Square around midnight. The lads were hanging around the Charles Compton Statue. Holding hands, like Lauren and Maisie. As soon as the 'lezza' comments started, they sensed it could turn ugly and just ran. It sounds like they chose wisely, or we might have two nasty attacks under investigation."

"I agree it's a possibility." She drummed her fingers on her desk. "This is Dan's case, but I assume he'll want to take statements from them and see if there's any CCTV footage. There must be, mustn't there?"

"I'll find out and, if there is, I'll get hold of it. And I'll see when they can come in and make those statements."

"Good. Thanks, Will."

"One thing, boss. If it was the same guys…"

"…they could do it again. I agree," she said. "We really do need to find them. Or, sooner or later, someone will end up dead."

*

The two women who'd come forward – Nicola Scott and Abbie Brooks – were eager to help, and came in that same afternoon to make their statements. It left the team all but convinced that they were lucky not to have suffered a similar fate to Lauren and Maisie, and that they had indeed been taunted by the same pack.

But their statements, and the follow-up work, had so far yielded little in the way of hard leads. Footage from the CCTV cameras covering the Market Square had, infuriatingly, been deleted just two days ago, under data retention policies, and further questioning of Liam Gunner and Roy Barlow had seen them both not only sticking to their guns but becoming agitated about being questioned a second time – although Barlow's original alibi for the night of the assault was looking a little flakier.

When Joan first pressed him and his wife over the less-than-immaculate bed in their son's room, he'd initially ridiculed the notion that such a small thing was even worth thinking about. But Joan wasn't a woman to be put off by a little bit of ridicule. The Barlows started subtly backtracking and then Roy admitted, yes, perhaps that was the night he himself had slept in the bed. With his back trouble, he kept fidgeting to get comfortable, so he'd moved into the son's room out of consideration to Amanda.

"So," Joan had said with a tight smile, "when you told us earlier you disturbed Mrs Barlow getting up in the night, that wasn't strictly true, was it, sir?"

"Oh, for God's sake. She's a light sleeper. She wakes up if a pin drops two miles away. And, for the record, I never said we were in the same bed."

But Baines was sure the man had avoided their gaze. And, Baines realised, for a man with a dodgy back, he seemed to be moving surprisingly freely.

Back at the station, Baines contemplated two owners of cars of interest whose stories had changed. Liam Gunner's tale of aimless driving felt so lame that he almost believed it, whilst there was something decidedly shifty about Roy and Amanda Barlow. Roy had grudgingly given up a DNA swab for checking against samples recovered from Lauren and Maisie, if only as a precaution. He had also put a chase on Liam Gunner's sample.

Meanwhile, phone calls to Edinburgh already indicated that the Barlows' son, Zack, really had been there all week, but Baines decided to invest in an EasyJet flight from Luton for Jason Bell in the morning to poke around, question him in person and take a sample from him too. It was almost certainly a waste of time and money, but Baines knew from experience that sometimes the most solid of alibis turned out to be built on sand.

All in all, it had been a frustrating day. Just before heading for home, he phoned Duncan McNeill, to check when his old colleague would be coming down and to extend Karen's dinner invitation. Despite his misgivings about Claire King's book project, and the Scot's role in it, he had to admit he'd missed hearing that accent, and the warmth in Mac's voice couldn't help but boost his spirits.

Mac was driving down tomorrow, Friday, and would be delighted to come to dinner, although he politely refused the offer of a bed while he was in the area.

"That's kind, but young Claire's already bought and paid for a hotel. West Lodge?"

"On the London Road. I know it. About four miles from Aylesbury town centre."

"Aye, nice and convenient."

Baines closed the call looking forward to seeing Mac again after all this time and wondering if he should adjust his thinking about Claire and her book. Whatever his personal feelings, he couldn't deny that the Invisible Man had been a long time ago now. It was a wonder no one had already made a TV drama about it.

Maybe part of moving forward was accepting that the past never went away, however much you might like it to.

*

Joan Collins arrived home to find Charlie in the kitchen, stirring something in a pot that smelled delicious, the aroma of mingled cloves, cinnamon, ginger and nutmeg transporting her back to her childhood.

Caribbean cooking was still big in Collins' family, but the culinary gene had passed her by. Charlie, on the other hand, loved getting busy in the kitchen and exploring new recipes. She loved Collins' mother's cooking and now several Caribbean cookbooks sat on the shelves, Craig McAnuff and Levi Roots rubbing shoulders with Gordon Ramsay, Jamie Oliver and Mary Berry.

Collins had phoned ahead to say she was on her way, and Charlie had promised to rustle something up for when she got in. Now she looked up from the stove and smiled.

"Hello, you."

"Hello yourself." Collins felt a familiar rush of affection.

"You've just about got time to get out of those work clothes and pour us some beers."

Collins grinned at her. "Is that all? I mean, shouldn't I put something else on?"

Charlie looked her up and down. "Well, it might be nice if you spent the rest of the evening starkers. I guess I'd feel overdressed and obliged to join you."

"I could help you with that."

"I'm sure you could. But maybe we should wear a few bits while we eat, or we won't be able to concentrate on this lovely, lovely dish I'm creating."

"Fair enough. See you in a sec." She turned around.

"Hey, lady," Charlie said. "Aren't we forgetting something?"

Collins turned again, walked up to her, and leaned in for a kiss. The hint of spices played with her lips and tongue.

"You've been tasting the goods," she said when they broke away.

"As any decent chef must." Charlie was wearing a black apron with 'Head Chef' emblazoned across the front in red letters. Collins had one that said, 'Kitchen Slave'. "Go on. Get changed."

Collins stole another kiss and headed for the bedroom, wondering – not for the first time – how she had managed before this woman came into her life and made her complete. Blonde and fair-skinned, Charlie was a cool beauty with a mercurial temper that could flare hot when something really got to her, but which was over almost as soon as she got whatever was bugging her off her chest. Like all couples, it wasn't always sweetness and light, but the making up after a rare falling out could be very good indeed.

The chicken, rice and beans were delicious, possibly even better than Collins' own mother's version. When she had finished eating and was sitting back drinking beer from the bottle, Charlie looked at her appraisingly.

"You look tired. Case getting to you?"

Like her colleagues, Collins made it a rule not to discuss details of the cases she was working on with her partner, but Charlie knew she was involved in the car park assault.

She nodded. "It's funny. I'm usually capable of distancing myself. Even when race is involved, I can stay objective. I don't know why I've let myself get so angry about this one."

Charlie took a swig of beer. "Maybe it's because it's still quite new to you. This, I mean. Us."

"Being gay?"

"Well, yeah. I mean, I knew when I was more or less a kid. You know I'd had relationships before you."

Collins did know that. While she was still figuring out why dating guys never seemed to work for her, Charlie had lived with a partner for a while, but it hadn't worked out. For Collins, the pieces had only fallen into place when she'd met the woman who now shared her life.

"You might be right," she admitted. "Maybe a bit like those reformed smokers who become the most avid anti-smoking advocates?"

"Not the analogy I'd have gone for," Charlie said with a laugh, "but maybe. Anyhow, you should channel that anger. Make sure you get those nasty bastards off the street sooner than later."

"You know, that's what I love about you. Face and body of an angel. Mind of a sage. And you're right." She shrugged. "Let's not talk about it any more."

"Agreed." Charlie smiled slyly. "So let's talk about my birthday tomorrow. You'd better not be late home."

"I'll do my best."

"It'd better be better than that. So where are you taking me?"

Collins still hadn't booked anything. She kept meaning to, but there was always one more task…

At least she'd got a present: a delicate silver brooch in the shape of a sunflower. She hoped she'd chosen well.

"Is there any dessert?"

"Changing the subject?" Charlie shook her head. "No, there's no dessert."

"No?" Collins gave her a sidelong look. "Then it sounds like it's time for that starkers thing you mentioned."

"Oh, yeah. I seem to remember you said you could help me with that."

"If you help me."

"Well," Charlie's voice was husky, "one good turn deserves another."

9

Baines had left the house feeling rattled by a familiar dream that had returned to haunt him. A dream that had once plagued his sleep almost nightly, but had not done so now for the best part of a year.

A house on a cliff, looking out over a beach. A pale face at an upstairs window. The images fading fast as wakefulness came upon him, the face never quite distinct, but the house always the last to fade.

He knew it was somehow to do with the Invisible Man and the family he'd lost. The face at the window might even be Jack. There had been times when he'd – stupidly – believed it was important. That, if only he could remember the dream, he'd find a key to Jack's fate there.

He'd even started keeping a pad by the bed and had trained himself to roughly sketch any lingering details of the house before they blew away like smoke. Every now and again he would sit with his sketches and try to make a composite picture of the house, but he was never confident that he'd captured anything remotely resembling it. Nor did he have a clue as to how he'd ever find it if he had.

If it even existed. Which, chances were, it didn't.

In his craziest moment, he'd entertained the notion of working his way through every inch of Google Earth until *The House* jumped out at him. But common sense had prevailed. He'd have been better off chucking a needle into a haystack and then searching for it, one blade of hay at a time.

He'd thought he'd finally left the dream behind. He supposed its sudden return must be connected to Claire King, to Mac, and to that damned book. But it had still unnerved him. It felt like a doorway back into some of the darkest recesses of his mind had been opened a crack. And that, if he re-entered, his sanity might not survive this time.

Swiping his pass and entering the station, he forced himself into professional mode, reaching for calm, for focus on his job. At best, two young women had been attacked and the perpetrators needed to be brought to justice. At worst, there was a group of predators out there, preying on female couples. If that was the case, then sooner or later someone might get killed.

As he hung his jacket on the back of his chair, he spotted a sticky note on his computer screen: Lizzie Archer, asking him to drop by her office. He found her behind her desk, coffee mug in one hand, pecking at her keyboard with the other. She glanced up, tapped a couple more keys, took a sip of coffee, and set the mug down.

"Grab a seat, Dan," she said. He parked himself in the chair opposite her. "Just a heads-up," she told him. "We've had a complaint."

"Complaint?" he echoed, a stab of alarm in his guts. What was he supposed to have done?

"Nothing to worry about." She waved her hand airily. "Liam Gunner's daddy has set his solicitor on us. Seems to think we're harassing his little boy."

"What?" Alarm turned to irritation. "It's all been routine so far. We've been to see him, we haven't dragged him in here – although I might, if they start that lark..."

"Chill," she said, smiling. "They're just trying to get us to back off, but I'm wondering why. An over-protective father, or a son who protests just a little too much?"

"I always thought that 'driving around' line was a bit feeble. Maybe it *was* his BMW outside Lauren and Maisie's when they were broken into."

"Maybe. Let's just park it for now. I'll have a word with the Super, but I'm sure he'll agree: we need to send a short, simple response, rejecting the harassment complaint and pointing out that we're merely expecting little Liam to help us with our enquiries like a good citizen. God, I hate these people with a bit of money who think they can bully their way through life. If you need to speak to him again, make him come here and do it under caution. We can be tough too."

Baines returned to his desk. He had barely settled in when Ibrahim Iqbal appeared at his side.

"Morning, Dan. I thought you'd like to see how we're doing with the pictures of those suspects. You'll remember I was going to try to do some composite imaging?"

"And feed it over to the artist, right?"

"Yeah. Well, we've done both, and here are the results."

He put two sheaves of paper on the desk in front of Baines and tapped the one on the left.

"These are the best composites we can manage, while these," he tapped the sheaf on the right, "are the artist's work, taking what they produced with Lauren and enhancing it from actual details in the facial averaging."

Ibrahim started to flip through them. "You'll see most of them are pretty useless. Lauren didn't really see or remember much of most of the gang, so the artist's impressions were speculative; and, frankly, the CCTV footage hasn't got us any further forward."

Baines nodded, seeing what he meant. The faces looking out at him were really not much better than the crude 'identikit' images that had been the height of sophistication back in the sixties. The technique had given way to 'photofit' before Baines was born, but he'd seen some of those old-fashioned, now sometimes laughable, attempts to produce likenesses of persons of interest.

Often, they could have been anybody. Which about summed these up.

"So we shouldn't hold out much hope?" Baines felt a stab of frustration.

"I wouldn't go that far," Ibrahim said, smiling. "I've saved the best until last."

He removed the penultimate images, leaving two likenesses side by side in front of Baines.

"This is the tall guy we think goes by 'J' or 'Jay'," he said. "We got some good points of reference from the camera footage and you'll recall he was the one Lauren saw the most of."

The face looking up from the sketch bore a resemblance to the computer-generated likeness, but had some real life about it. It was reminiscent of the original drawing, but Baines's gut told him it was more accurate.

"We've given him a shaven head," Ibrahim said. "Bit of a cliché. Obviously, we don't know."

Baines nodded. Sharp features, thin lips with just the hint of a sneer. Eyes narrow, but somehow intense and angry in their gaze.

"Those eyes," Baines said. "Is that done for effect?"

"No," Ibrahim replied. "If you look at the composite, you'll see his eyes really do seem to be like that. A tad scary, right?"

"Right." Baines focused on both the pictures. "How many copies do you have?"

"Only a couple for now. Those are for you."

"Get a set to Joan and I'll ask her to see Lauren – and Maisie, if she's up to it – and see how good they think those images really are. If they're as good as we hope, we can flood the media with them. Although it'll probably bring out a lot of time wasters."

"And maybe someone who really does know who it is."

"Fingers crossed. Oh," he added, "and text a copy to Jason. He's off to see young Zack Barlow."

*

Jason Bell always found it a little strange being back in Scotland. His Glaswegian accent was as much a part of him as his red hair, a physical trait apparently carried by about thirteen per cent of his countrymen due to a gene mutation; he still looked first for the Glasgow Rangers score on a Saturday afternoon; and he had family in Scotland's second city, whom he saw at the odd wedding or funeral. But the south of England had been his home for long enough now that the country of his birth exerted no emotional pull on him. Landing at Edinburgh airport didn't invoke that lump in his throat that he knew some of his exiled kin felt when they found themselves back on Scottish soil.

Not that there was any reason Edinburgh would have invoked much in the way of nostalgia in Bell. Growing up, he'd had the rivalry between Weegies and Edinbuggers drummed into him by his mother in particular. He'd never been entirely sure where it came from, but she was firmly of the opinion that the people of Edinburgh, with their posh, 'pan loafy' accents, imagined themselves more refined, and higher up the social scale than they actually were. "All fur coat and nae knickers," was her verdict.

"Edinburgh boys used to come to Glasgow for a laugh and go home in stitches," was the adage his dad and granddad had trotted out more times than he could remember. Two of the gentlest men Bell had ever known, implying that Weegies as a species were tough customers, prone to violence.

The reality these days was that the controversy was more likely to be about football and architecture than any pathological hatred.

And Edinburgh certainly had its share of fine architecture, Bell couldn't deny that. The taxi ride from the airport had taken less than half an hour and then he was at the sixth oldest university in the English-speaking world, rated one of the ten best in Europe.

Zack Barlow was studying Art History, and Bell found him at the College of Art, an impressive 18th century building overlooking the Grassmarket, a historic market place and event space in the Old Town, but also a one-time place of execution. On a visit to the city in his teens, Bell had seen the memorial near the former site of the gibbet commemorating over 100 Covenanters, hanged between 1661 and 1688 – 'The Killing Time', a period of conflict between the Presbyterian Covenanter movement on one side, and the government forces of Kings Charles II and James VII – the latter also being James II of England and Ireland.

The image Ibrahim Iqbal and the artist had cooked up had arrived on his phone and, just as he was getting in the taxi, Joan had confirmed that Lauren and Maisie both thought it was as fair a likeness of the ringleader in their assault that anyone was going to get.

Even allowing for that rather lukewarm endorsement, Zack Barlow was an immediate disappointment: tall enough, and with the right sort of build, but facially nothing like the man in the sketch. Nor did he have a Northern or Birmingham accent that Bell could detect. But he was determined to go through the motions. He still had reservations about his father's explanation as to what his car had been doing in Stoke Mandeville the night of the attack.

"Tuesday?" Zack nodded. "Yeah, I was in the Wee Red Bar."

"Which is?"

"Ah, sorry. Yeah, it's on the Lauriston Campus. There was a gig on."

"Can anyone vouch for that?"

"Well, I went with a bunch of mates. I can give you their mobiles, or try and get them here, if it's easier." He gave Bell a speculative look. "Yeah, you're here about that nasty thing in Aylesbury, right? My mum called me. Said the police might be in touch. And you say you're Thames Valley, yeah?"

"Yeah. I mean, yes."

"I thought you were local when you introduced yourself. The accent…"

"Glasgow. But not for a while. Anyhow, the mobile numbers will be fine. It's a while before my flight back to Luton."

Zack took out his phone, fiddled with it, then started copying numbers onto a fresh page of a pad retrieved from his backpack. A few minutes later, he ripped the page out and handed it to Bell.

"It was a homophobic attack, is that right?"

It was in the public eye by now, so Bell didn't see the point in being cagey. "It certainly looks that way." He looked the young man in his limpid brown eyes. "How do you feel about that?"

Zack grimaced. "Pretty bloody angry."

"You've nothing against gay people then?"

"Not hardly. I'm gay myself."

"Okay," Bell said. "I didn't speak to your parents myself, but I don't think that came up."

"It wouldn't. They don't know, and I'd like it to stay that way."

"Fair enough." He'd been one of the first people Joan Collins had told when she'd got in a relationship with Charlie and finally accepted the truth about her sexuality. He hadn't told her, but up to then he'd liked her enough to wish they were more than friends. Had been summoning the nerve to ask her out. Yet he'd covered his shock well, and somehow found himself pleased that she'd found someone.

It had taken her longer to pluck up the courage to tell her parents, fearing they might disown her. He understood that, but still wondered what might lie behind Zack Barlow's remark. "Any reason why you haven't told them? I mean, it's not my business…"

"I'm not saying they're homophobic. We just don't talk about that sort of thing in our family." He hesitated. "Look, it's not my story to tell. If you really want to know why, ask my mum. But it's nothing to do with your case, I can promise you that."

"I do want to know," Bell persisted. "We'll decide what's relevant."

"Then ask mum. But don't betray my confidence, fair enough?"

"We'll try not to. No promises. Meanwhile, I'll follow up with your mates. Oh, and I'd like to take a DNA swab."

Zack rolled his eyes. "Really? You've got a bunch of phone numbers there that'll alibi me."

"Call it belt and braces," Bell said. No one was going to say he wasn't thorough.

10

The doorbell rang just after 8pm. Baines had just opened a bottle of red. He set it down on the kitchen worktop and went to open the door.

Mac stood on the step, juggling a bottle and a bouquet. For all the years that had passed, he hadn't changed much. A bit thinner on top, a few more lines, perhaps. He must be pushing seventy, but he obviously kept himself fit and in shape. He wore a grey leather jacket over a navy jumper and a check shirt – a change from what had almost been his uniform back when they'd worked together: plain dark grey suit, white shirt, striped tie.

Baines felt the corners of his mouth bending upwards as his old friend beamed back at him.

"God," Mac said. "It's so good to see you." He gestured with bottle and flowers. "I'd shake your hand, or even risk a wee manly hug, but…"

"So come in and put those down."

His burdens safely parked on the hall table, the Scot wrapped a quick bear hug around Baines, then stepped back and examined him.

"Hmm," he appraised. "A few wee strands of grey, but pretty well the same man, young Daniel. What's your secret?"

"Not so young any more. I was – what? – twenty-seven last time you saw me. Mid-forties now."

"Aye, well, you're still a wee bairn to me. I feel ancient some days."

"How's your son – Peter?"

"He's great. Didn't get the A level grades he needed for uni, so he's left school. He's working in a hardware store for now, but looking for something better. And how's the lovely new Mrs Baines?"

"Yes, sorry. She's in the kitchen. I think she's at a critical point with the meal. Come and say hello."

Mac picked up his gifts and followed him into the kitchen, where Karen was stirring a sauce, her face tight with concentration. It was an expression Baines loved, and one he could remember seeing on Louise.

His old colleague halted in the kitchen doorway, mouth agape.

"Karen, this is Mac."

"Hi," she said with a quick glance round. "Sorry, I can't leave this, but it's lovely to finally meet you. Dan's told me so much about you."

Back in the day, this would have been a cue for Mac to make some crack about trusting she'd heard nothing good about him, but he merely shook himself. "It's great to meet you too."

"You okay?" Baines checked.

"What? Oh, yeah. It's just this kitchen. It's so great. And huge. You must get lost in here after the old one."

Baines took the bottle from him and popped it in the fridge, then put the flowers on the side.

"Look at these, Karen."

She looked round. "Oh, they're gorgeous, Mac. You shouldn't have."

"I'll leave you to put them in a vase," Baines said. He winked at Mac. "I never do it right."

"We never do, laddie."

"Why don't you get our guest something to drink?" suggested Karen. "Then you boys can sit in the lounge and not watch me cocking up the cooking."

"Take no notice," Baines said. "She's a great chef."

Mac opted for a Diet Coke. Baines got himself a beer, poured a smoothie for Karen, and ushered the other man into the living room.

Mac looked around before sitting down. When the couple had moved, they'd got rid of some furniture, kept what was in good nick and would fit in with Karen's grand design, and splashed a fair bit of cash on new stuff. Baines had to admit that his wife had a good eye for style. He loved this room.

"This is a great house," Mac said. "You must be delighted."

"We are."

"You know, it gave me a shock for a moment, seeing Karen. I only met Louise maybe three times, and I knew they were identical twins, but I couldn't believe how like her she is."

"And I thought you were overawed by the kitchen."

"It's amazing. I mean, I know I only ever saw the old one in the crime scene photos, but…" He faltered. "Och, there I go with my mouth. That's the last thing I intended to bring up tonight." He grimaced.

Baines felt a rush of sympathy. "It's okay. We're really moving on now. Or we were, before Claire King and this book." He sighed. "Karen thinks it's a good thing. That we might even get some answers this far down the line."

"Aye, well, it's really not what Claire's engaged me for, but I must admit I'm tempted to do a bit of poking around, revisit the odd suspect and some of the victims' families." He sipped his Coke. "Would you mind?"

Baines leaned back in his chair. "I honestly don't know, Mac. There's been some pretty dark times since…" He swallowed, surprised how readily the emotion came back. "I tried to seal myself off from what I was feeling, and that didn't work so well. I've confronted it and finally come to terms with it. I've even let myself accept that Jack is dead. So a part of me still wants to know who the Invisible Man is, or was. Why he did what he did. What became of my boy. Another part wonders what good any of that knowledge would do me."

Mac nodded. "I get that."

"And there's another thing." He hesitated. Did he really need to share this?

"What's that, laddie?"

What the hell? "Karen's pregnant."

For the second time, Mac's mouth fell open. "Really?"

Baines frowned. "Well, that's not quite the reaction I was expecting."

The Scot laughed, stood up, stepped over to Baines and squeezed his shoulder. "No, no, it's fabulous news. I'm delighted for you both. You just took me by surprise, that's all. I mean, you're no spring chicken…"

"Well, cheers for that."

"You're welcome. No, I suppose I assumed… Oh, Danny boy, that's brilliant. I should have brought champagne."

"Wine is fine. We like Malbec." He sighed. "Mac, why *did* you agree to work with Claire King? Really?"

"It's a fair enough question. I suppose that case still haunts me too. You know it was the last straw for my police career. I couldn't do it any more."

"Yet here you are doing cold cases."

Mac sat again. "Here I am doing cold cases. I suppose the difference is, by the time I get my hands on the files, they're historical. To me, at least. If I can close the odd case, get some justice served – well, maybe that makes up a bit for the ones that got away." Another sip. "Can I ask you something?"

"Sure."

"It's delicate, but it's been eating away at me."

Baines put his beer down. "Spit it out, Mac."

"Well…" He licked his lips. "Those sketches, those so-called *calling cards*." He made it sound like the vilest of obscenities. "They only started after that fool of a Watson as good as christened our killer 'The Invisible Man', right?"

"You know it's right."

"He was taunting us. That's what we thought."

"What's your point?"

"My point, laddie, is this. We could never work out how or why he was choosing his victims. Oh, all the women were brunettes, but the kids were a mix of boys and girls and not a bit alike, apart from their ages. Yet his last victim is the wife of one of the very cops he's been taunting. The only one with a child the right age."

"Yes. It's crossed my mind." Often, in the worst of times. "I've wondered if I was the ultimate taunt."

Mac slapped a meaty hand on his thigh. "Ultimate. Exactly. I've also thought about it a lot. We always wondered why he stopped. Was he dead? In prison? But what if it was more simple?"

Baines stared at him. There was an intense light in the Scot's eyes. He remembered that look from their working together days, when an important truth about a case was dawning.

"Don't you see?" Mac persisted. "Whatever sick itch the bastard was scratching, he couldn't top that. Striking at the very team that was hunting him. And after that, what better way to take the piss than for you to never see your son again?"

The tears fell unexpectedly, ambushing him like a bushwhacker on a lonely road. Baines swiped at his eyes, angry with himself. He was supposed to be past all this. Yet, the moment Claire King had broken her news to him, he'd known it would come to this.

"Ah, hell." Mac stood, shuffled his feet uncertainly. "The last thing I wanted was to upset you."

"No." There was a lump in his throat. "No, you're all right. We were always going to be talking about this. Although I must admit, I thought I could handle it." He swallowed, composed himself as best he could. "But you seem to be suggesting it was more personal in my case?"

"Or the whole bloody thing was in some way personal." Mac took a hesitant step towards Baines. Faltered. Stepped back and sat down. "I'm sorry."

"No, it's worth a think. We rather got into the mindset that it was all a bit random. But of course, that was never quite right. Stay at home mums with toddlers, who were around on a Friday. Quiet locations where he wouldn't be observed coming and going. The regular Friday pattern. And seemingly getting into the house with the minimum of disturbance."

"It all took a great deal of forward planning, we knew that much. But again, with you…"

"You really think he broke the pattern to target a copper's family?"

"Maybe. Or maybe he didn't know you were a cop on the investigation until the story broke. Maybe it was getting lucky in that way that made him decide he couldn't top it. Made him decide to stop and make Jack disappear."

The coldness that had been stealing over Baines suddenly erupted in hot fury as he saw the logic. There had been times before when he'd longed to have the Invisible Man helpless in his power for a couple of days. Fantasised about torturing him until he gave up the truth about Jack, and then torturing him some more anyway.

He'd thought those emotions had been banished. Now he realised they'd been locked away, just like he'd locked away so many other feelings.

He drew a deep breath. "Whatever digging you do, Mac, I can't be seen to be involved. But if there are ways I can help that won't come back to bite us, let me know. The worst that can happen is I end up no worse off."

Was that really true?

Before he could say more, Karen appeared in the doorway, all smiles.

"Dinner's on the table. I hope you're hungry, Mac."

11

When the trilling of her phone crashed into Lizzie Archer's sleep, the first thing she did was answer it. The second was to remind herself where she was, something she frequently needed to do nowadays. Dominic's. He slept on beside her, oblivious.

"Archer," she said softly.

"Boss?" Will Tyler.

"Will. What time is it?"

"Sorry, boss, just after two, but I thought you'd want to know. Joan's been attacked."

The news jolted her. "Joan *Collins*?"

"In the town centre last night. She was found not long after eleven."

"Found?" Panic warred with professionalism. Joan was more than just a colleague. "Where? What happened? Is she all right?"

"It's bad, I think. She's in Stoke Mandeville, in some sort of coma."

"Oh, Christ. Is she going to be all right?"

"They don't know. They're doing tests."

"Is she in intensive care?"

"No. Apparently she's breathing unassisted, but she's been put in a room on her own so they can monitor her more easily."

She was aware of Dominic stirring, sitting up to look questions at her, but all she could see was Joan's face, her ready, infectious smile.

She forced herself to get some sort of a grip.

"Is Charlie with her? Is *she* all right? Do we know what happened?"

Some grip, right? Questions were still tumbling out of her.

Silence on the line.

"Speak to me, Will."

"Well, that's the thing, boss. We can't locate Charlie."

"What do you mean, can't locate her?"

"Exactly what I said. She wasn't at the scene, she isn't at the flat, and she isn't answering her phone."

She swung her legs out of the bed. "Is the scene secured? Where she was found, I mean?"

"Uniform are there now. As far as I can make out, Joan was found unconscious by a passer-by."

"Where, exactly?"

"Just off the Buckingham Road. She'd probably been on foot. There's a cut through between the centre and their home. She's mentioned it. It's not much more than a mile. The couple who found her dialled 999 and stayed with her. DI Moseley was notified as the duty DI and she contacted me in the first instance. I said I'd let people know."

"So does Dan know? Jason?"

"You're the first I've called. They're next. Should I call Amir, too? I mean, I know he's relatively new—"

"Call him. He's part of the team. What's being done about informing the families?"

"I'm going to get someone at High Wycombe to inform Joan's parents and then track down Charlie's. I think they're in Oxford."

"They are," Archer confirmed. "So who's at the scene now?"

"Uniforms, as I said, and DI Moseley is on her way."

"Good. I'm heading over too, if you give me the precise location." Dominic was already handing her a pad and pen. "Get Dan to meet us there. Then call Jason. He's close to Joan, so ask him if he knew what her plans were for last night. Then get me an update from the hospital, if you can. Where are you?"

"Leaving for the station as soon as I've made those calls."

She jotted down details, thanked Will and ended the call.

Possibilities swirled around in her head, none of them good: a repeat attack by the gang that had beaten Lauren and Maisie just a few nights ago? A mugging gone wrong? A targeted attack on Joan by a villain with a grudge?

And, underneath all that, somehow even more worrying than Joan's condition: where was Charlie?

*

Archer and Baines lived roughly equidistant from the location where the unconscious Joan Collins had been found. Baines knew Lizzie had been the first call Will had made, so he wasn't surprised to find her already there and talking to Lara Moseley and uniformed officers.

Baines himself felt shattered. Mac had finally departed just after midnight, and the call had come barely an hour after he'd climbed into bed, his head full of the Invisible Man and bad memories.

But he was ignoring his tiredness, even if he couldn't stifle his yawns. This was one of their own. It felt very personal, in the same way that Mac's suggestion that the Invisible Man had deliberately singled out the Baines family felt incredibly personal.

The narrow, one-way road had been cordoned off at both ends. Baines knew it wasn't much used by traffic, unless there was a hold-up nearby, but he'd worked in the town long enough to know pedestrians often used it as a shortcut southwards from the town centre towards the flats where Joan lived with Charlie.

Baines knew that Charlie was a lawyer, specialising in domestic abuse, and that the couple had met outside the town's court building, an accidental collision that had somehow led to coffee, an exchange of phone numbers, and a blossoming relationship. A disaster causing serious damage to Charlie's block of flats had seen her moving in with Joan sooner than they might have expected, but Baines always got the impression they were very happy together.

He knew Charlie sometimes moaned that her partner was more wedded to her job than to her, but that was the case with so many police relationships. Not everyone could hack it, but so far this couple had stayed the course.

Lizzie finished her conversation and came over to join him.

"Well, it's not quite like Tuesday night," she told him. "Not a hail of blows and kicks. I mean, we'll need proper medical opinion, but it seems likely she was struck in the face, fell, and hit her head."

"It doesn't rule out this 'J' and his mates though, does it?" he observed. "I mean, Maisie was punched. If Joan was knocked out in the fall…"

"I agree. Still, we need to keep an open mind. Entertain the possibility that it might not be them."

He knew she was right. He'd snatched at the notion that, this time, a friend and colleague had caught the eye of a bunch of homophobic thugs. He knew better than to make uninformed assumptions, and he knew better than to allow such an assumption to narrow his focus.

"Do you think Charlie's been taken?" He realised that, in his concern for his colleague, he hadn't given much thought to her partner's fate.

"We don't know that for sure. The most hopeful scenario is: they were attacked; Charlie got away; Joan didn't."

"Thin," he remarked. "Why didn't she call us? Where is she now?"

"I agree it's thin, even with an open mind. Much more likely that whoever hurt Joan has got her."

"They've got her." He agreed. It was the only thing that made sense. "Maybe – whoever it was – didn't mean to hurt Joan quite so badly. They got scared and abducted the only witness."

"Could be," she agreed. "Or maybe they didn't give a damn about Joan but had something worse in mind for Charlie."

It was exactly what he'd feared himself.

"Has Joan ever opened up to you about any of the abuse she's had?" she asked.

"A bit. Not very specific."

"Well she did to me, just once. She's black, Dan. She's used to racism. Since she's been with Charlie, it's been homophobia too. Well, one time, she got the double whammy."

"Which was?"

"A black woman with a blue-eyed blonde? These particular morons made a few remarks as they went past, holding hands. Then one of them said something about it being bad enough for black men to be taking 'our women'" – she made parenthesis with her fingers – "without their dykes doing it too. What if some bastard wanted to take out Joan and then show Charlie what a man has to offer?"

He grimaced. "Pretty twisted. But you've got a point."

"We need to find her, Dan. And time might not be on our side."

12

"Right," Archer said, "this is what we know."

It was a Saturday, no overtime had been allocated, and people doubtless had plans. Yet the briefing room was crowded. As soon as they heard what had happened to Joan Collins, pretty well everyone had dropped everything and come to the station, eager to roll up their sleeves and do whatever was required.

Lara Moseley was there, even though she'd handed the case over to Dan. Superintendent Josh Stowe was there, looking ridiculous in loud yellow trousers and a pink and grey Pringle sweater. He'd been at the fifth hole when Archer had phoned him at 7.30am as a courtesy to put him in the picture. His clubs were still in the car. He was grim-faced and had declined the opportunity to make the opening observations he was usually so fond of.

"No," he'd said, "let's just crack on. And treat me as a resource, Lizzie. I can make a phone call or chat to a witness, just like anyone else."

He'd soared in her estimation at that moment, although she thought perhaps a non public facing role might be best in that get-up.

As detectives and uniforms had assembled, there had been little of the usual banter, gallows humour or general chit-chat. The atmosphere was shock and anger. Joan was family and so too, by extension, was Charlie.

So Archer outlined what little was known so far. She knew everyone would be anxious to know about Joan's condition, but she chose her words carefully.

"She's in a coma. I spoke to the doctor handling her case, and it's too soon to say how long that'll last. It could be a few days or weeks. It can last for several years, but that's rare."

"Years?" Jason Bell echoed. He was uncharacteristically pale, fear for his friend naked in his eyes. He'd already been asked if he knew what Joan's plans for last night had been, but he had no idea, other than it had been Charlie's birthday.

"They treat a coma as a medical emergency, Jason, but let's not panic yet. Apparently the majority of cases last from days to weeks. So let's hope she wakes up sooner than later."

The doctor had also warned her that, if the patient's condition didn't change after an extended period, it might be reclassified as a persistent vegetative state. And, if that state lasted for months, Joan would be unlikely to wake up at all. But she wasn't going to say that. She was trying not to think about it.

She could hear whispers, see worried faces. People had their heads together.

"Listen up." She raised her voice a level. "It's worrying and upsetting, but she's in good hands. The best we can do for Joan is to do our jobs. We need to find out what happened and if – as seems very likely – someone is responsible, we need to bring that person to justice."

She paused, moving closer to the board behind her. "But, even more urgently, we need to find this person." She tapped the picture of Charlie, stuck there alongside one of Joan. The latter's photo was from her police ID, looking serious. The blonde woman beside her was smiling, vivacious.

"Charlotte Elaine Ward, known to most of us as Charlie. Joan's partner. We're supposing she was with Joan when she was hurt. She's not at home, she's not answering her mobile. We have to be concerned for her safety. She might well have been abducted at the time of the incident." She was trying hard not to call it an attack, although it was difficult to imagine what else could have happened.

She briefly scanned the board, which also contained pictures and information relating to Lauren Black and Maisie Albright.

Maisie was apparently doing well. Her post-traumatic amnesia meant she was actually doing better mentally than Lauren who, according to the family liaison officer, was having nightmares and flashbacks. She was apparently scared to go home, even when it was eventually released by CSI. It no longer felt safe to her.

Lauren had been shown pictures of both Liam Gunner and Zack Barlow in the hope that they might jog her memory.

"I just don't know," she'd admitted. "Might be, might not. All I can say for sure is, neither of them is J."

Archer turned to address the room again.

"We're treating this as potentially linked to the assault on Tuesday night, at least for now, although we need to keep an open mind. But we certainly need to go back over some of the suspects in that case. Any thoughts?"

Jason Bell lifted an index finger. "I've not had a chance to feed back from my trip to Edinburgh yesterday. The Barlow lad, Zack, said homosexuality was something 'not discussed' in his family, but he refused to elaborate. Said we should ask his mum. But we're already thinking his dad's story about why his car was caught on ANPR in the Stoke Mandeville area on Wednesday morning feels a bit fishy. And now we've got this from the son. Who, by the way, is gay himself, but his parents don't know."

"You're thinking there's a homophobic streak in the family?" asked Dan Baines. The Black and Albright case was still his lead, and so now was Joan's. But he hadn't argued when Archer had said she'd run this briefing.

Jason turned to face him. "We've been assuming it's a reach for the dad to have been involved with a bunch of young-ish gay bashers, but he's also the right height and build for one of them. And we all know assumption is the mother of all cock ups."

"You and I had better see the parents again," Dan said. He looked at Archer. "If that's okay?"

"Yes. Lara, could you and Amir go and see Liam Gunner? In fact, better still, bring him in. His dad's brought his lawyer into it, so we'll make it official."

Lara Moseley smiled. "My pleasure. And don't forget daddy is a bit of a property tycoon."

"True. Maybe the boy has Charlie stashed in one of his flats or houses." Archer checked her list. "Will?"

"Yes, boss?" Will Tyler said.

"I want to know if there were cameras near where Joan was found and within, say, a mile radius. I want the footage yesterday. Ibrahim, as soon as we've got it, anyone not doing an urgent job can help you look through it."

"Got it," Ibrahim Iqbal said.

"And Will, chase those bloody DNA samples. I want a rush on them."

"I took a swab from Zack Barlow, for what it's worth," Jason said, "although I'm as sure as I can be that he was in Edinburgh on Tuesday night."

"Has it gone to the lab?"

"Yes, but—"

"Chase that, too, Will." She glanced at the Super. Rush jobs were expensive.

"Whatever it costs," he said. "We want it yesterday. Day before yesterday would be even better."

Somehow, that raised a chuckle.

"In fact," he added, "leave that with me. DC Tyler can concentrate on the CCTV."

"Thank you, sir." Pleased with the support, she scanned the room. "Can someone get round to Joan's flat? Make sure Charlie's not found her way back there, then knock on doors. See if anyone knows when they went out, where they were going, that sort of thing? Sue and Dean, I think."

PCs Sue Dyson and Dean Barker were two of the best in the station when it came to door-to-door enquiries.

"On it," Sue said. Dean gave her a thumbs up.

Archer checked her list one more time. "I think that's it, unless anyone can think of anything I haven't covered?"

"There was DNA under the other victims' fingernails," Jason Bell said. "Any chance we'll find any on Joan?"

Archer shook her head. "CSI have already processed her, and no such luck. The thinking is she was taken by surprise and never even knew what hit her."

Jason's nose wrinkled with disgust. "Fucking cowards. I'd like to—"

"We all would," Archer said softly, "but we need to try and put those feelings aside and just do our jobs. If we let ourselves be blinded by anger, we'll mess up, and that's no use to anyone."

*

Baines's phone rang as he was crossing the car park with Jason. When he saw Mac's name on the screen, he was tempted to reject the call, but he decided he ought to take it.

"Sorry, Mac," he said, "but this needs to be quick."

"Sorry to interrupt your Saturday, but I thought you'd like an update. The other men whose wives and kiddies were murdered? I've managed to get in touch with the three who are still alive."

"Uh huh." Baines pressed unlock on his key fob and motioned to Jason to get in the Kia.

"Turns out James Hallett has remarried and moved to Cyprus. I got a number, but he insists he doesn't want to reopen that part of his past."

Baines was both interested and curious, but the job in hand was urgent. "I'm in the middle of something, Mac. One of my team was attacked last night. Can I get back to you?"

"God, I'm sorry. Yes, yes, of course. Are they okay?"

"Not really. Look, nothing's been released yet, but she's in a coma and her partner's missing, possibly abducted."

"Oh, bloody hell, Dan. You crack on then. It's just that Neil Mahon and Mark Richardson have both said they're happy to help, and I wondered if you'd like to tag along when I talk to them."

"I would, but later, maybe. I kept in touch with both of them for years, but it's fizzled out a bit of late. I know Neil's still local. I might be able to make it to Neil's with you later on, but I don't know when I'll be free. Getting to Surrey, where Mark's living now, might be a bit trickier," he said ruefully, torn between present and past. "I'll do my best."

"No, I understand. Look, why don't I see them both for now and let you know how I get on?"

"Fair enough. Cheers, Mac. Gotta go."

He hung up, still conflicted, but knowing he'd done the right thing. Joan would rightly expect her colleagues to be putting every ounce of energy into finding Charlie.

Still, as he got behind the wheel and started the engine, ghosts from the past crowded into the car: Emma and Chloe Mahon; Martha and Eliot Hallett; Lindsey and Noah Cutler; Jill and Kelly O'Bryan; Sally and Jessica Richardson; and, of course, Louise and Jack Baines.

"You okay, Dan?" Jason asked. He realised he was just sitting there, gripping the steering wheel too tight. He willed the ghosts away, fresh fears for his mental health surfacing.

"That wasn't bad news, was it?" Jason persisted.

"No. No, nothing like that. Just an old friend stirred up some unpleasant memories. Sorry."

He put the car in drive and pulled away.

*

As the briefing had dispersed, Archer realised that the one person she hadn't allocated a job to was herself. Even the Super had picked up a task, using his rank and muscle to get the DNA results on a fast track.

Her late father, who'd retired as a uniformed sergeant, had been convinced she'd go far, but she remembered him saying there was nothing better than feeling a collar.

She had to admit that, at times like this, she knew exactly what he meant.

She knew she'd been identified as potential Chief Constable material at the Met, before her injury and disfigurement, and her transfer here. She'd worked so hard to put the trauma behind her, to get her career back on the rails, and to make DCI. She still had ambitions, although she knew her chances of ultimately getting to the top were slim now.

But sometimes she wished she could get out from behind her desk more often and do a bit more of what she did best: making arrests, questioning suspects; the blood hot in her veins when someone fled and she gave chase. More than once, she'd run them down and wrestled them to the ground. There was a real satisfaction in snapping on those cuffs.

She'd always known that, the higher up the tree you rose, the further you'd become removed from all that. Mostly she was fine with it. Today she just felt frustrated.

By the time Liam Gunner came in with his lawyer, with his father also in tow, Archer had made up her mind to follow the interview on the monitor.

Liam's father, Andrew Gunner, had the smug air of a man used to having it all his own way, and the bloated face and body of a man used to having it all at the dinner table.

His disdain at seeing Lara Moseley and Amir Rashid – a woman and an Asian man – on the other side of the table was unmistakeable. After everyone had identified themselves for the recording, he'd actually asked if anyone else – presumably a white male – would be joining them. He'd rolled his eyes when answered in the negative and Lara politely asked him if he had a problem with her or DS Rashid.

"Course not." His lip was curled into a sneer. "I'm sure you have to keep your quotas up."

"Good to hear." Her smile was saccharine, her tone liquid honey. "You won't mind staying then, even though you're not part of this interview and you're only sitting in as a courtesy. But if you stay, those will be your last words, are we clear?"

He stared at her. "You what? I—"

"Are we clear?"

"I suppose so."

"I'm not sure I care for your tone, Inspector," said the solicitor. Chris Sitwell was an equally bloated Tweedledee to Andrew Gunner's Tweedledum.

"Noted. Let's get on, shall we?"

"Get on with what, though? My client has already been questioned twice about his and his car's whereabouts on Tuesday night, and he has co-operated. What more can there possibly be to say?"

"Oh," Lara said, "this isn't about Tuesday. Well, we might get back to that but, at the moment, we want to talk to Liam about last night."

"Last night?" Liam squeaked.

"What about last night?" Andrew Gunner protested. "What are you trying to fit him up with?"

Lara simply folded her arms and looked at him. He subsided like a punctured zeppelin.

"Mr Gunner is correct, though," Sitwell persisted. "It does rather appear that, for some bizarre reason, some vendetta is being conducted against my client. Not content with harassing him in connection with an incident on Tuesday night, now you seem to be trying to connect him to something that happened last night. It sounds as if you've got it in for my client and are trying to pin any and every crime on him."

Lara continued to sit with her arms folded across her chest. Amir was mirroring her.

Sitwell eyed them uncertainly. "Well?"

"I just wanted to be sure you'd finished," said Lara, and she yawned theatrically. "If you have, we can get on. I'm sure your time is Mr Gunner's money."

"So, Liam," Amir said, unfolding his arms and leaning slightly forward, "would you like to give us an account of your movements last night? Especially between, say, 10pm and midnight?"

"I was at home. I went to the pub with some guys from the warehouse after work, had a couple of drinks – just a pint and a Diet Coke, seeing as I was driving. Got home about seven, had a pizza out the freezer, watched a bit of TV and went to bed about eleven. Exciting, right?"

"And no one else was using your car?"

"No. Unless someone took it for a joy ride and then brought it back."

Archer saw him glance at his father with a smirk, seeking approval for his weak joke. Gunner Senior was too busy scowling at Amir to even notice. She wondered what other prejudices he might harbour. And whether he'd passed them on to his son.

"So CCTV won't show it out and about in Aylesbury at the times in question?" Amir asked. "And you won't suddenly remember that you went for a drive?"

"I was at home."

"Of course," Lara added, "your flat's just a short walk from the centre. Maybe you were out on foot. Maybe you met your mates in the centre and one of them had his car or van with him."

"Do you know where Charlotte Ward is, Liam?" Amir put in.

"Who? No. Who's she? I keep telling you. I was at home."

"Inspector," Sitwell said, "badgering my client will get you nowhere at a great rate of knots. He'll just keep telling you he was at home last night, unless and until you produce a shred of evidence to refute that obvious fact." He took off his expensive-looking glasses, appeared to inspect the lenses for dirt, then slipped them back on. "So, unless you have anything else for Mr Gunner, I think this fishing expedition is done. Unless you mean to charge him."

"Not yet," Lara said. "But I'll have the names of the people he went drinking with after work."

Sitwell inclined his head. "Within twenty-four hours."

"Now, please. A woman is missing. We're trying to rule Mr Gunner out of our enquiries. We don't have time to waste."

"And yet you waste my client's time when you could be out—"

"Oh, for Christ's sake," Liam interrupted him. "Just let me give her the names."

"Watch your tone," his father growled.

"But she's right, Dad. Why waste time? The sooner they leave me alone and start actually finding this woman, the better." He looked at Amir. "Can I borrow your pen, and a piece of paper?"

Amir obliged and Liam began writing.

"I'm minded to file a complaint," Sitwell huffed.

"Knock yourself out," said Lara, the saccharine smile back.

Liam returned the paper and pen. "So can we go now?"

Lara terminated the interview, a decision Archer supported, but she found herself in two minds about the suspect as she watched him leave. Maybe, out of genuine compassion for the missing Charlie, he was prepared to stand up to his father and lawyer to be helpful, the quicker to be eliminated from the enquiry.

Then again, perhaps he was simply eager to give Lara something and get out of the station before she tripped him up.

Either way, she strongly doubted that the names on the piece of paper he'd handed to Amir were going to amount to anything. She also doubted that Chris Sitwell's threatened complaint would materialise, at least if there was a chance of this going away.

Still she wondered. She trusted in her instincts that Liam's father was a racist and a misogynist, but it was harder to tell whether the son – most likely under his father's thumb in most respects – was cut from the same cloth.

He'd told a stupid lie about his whereabouts when the flat in Stoke Mandeville had been wrecked. He'd said it was panic. But was it?

13

Roy and Amanda Barlow were at home when Baines and Jason Bell called. Both expressed surprise, although no obvious resentment, at a further visit from the police, especially when Jason confirmed that he'd been to see their son and that Zack's alibi appeared to check out.

Baines had invited Jason to lead the questioning.

"So what brings you back?" Roy asked, standing in the living room with his arms folded.

"Just some routine, sir," soothed Jason. "Can you account for your movements last light?"

"Last night? Why?" He didn't wait for an answer. "We went to the Waterside Theatre with friends. Go West and Paul Young. Amanda likes them. I've never understood why."

"I was about eleven when they were big," his wife said. "Some of the first CDs I bought. No harm in a bit of nostalgia."

"I can show you the tickets and the programme," Roy said. "Give you the names of our friends, if it'd help. But I thought it was Tuesday night you were interested in."

Jason ignored the implied question. "When I saw Zack in Edinburgh, we had an interesting chat about homosexuality and homophobia. He gave me the impression it's a taboo subject in this house. I wonder why."

"We've nothing against gay people *per se*, if that's what you're wondering," Roy said.

Baines watched as Jason looked at him unblinkingly, then turned to Amanda. She was looking at the floor and wringing her hands.

"He specifically said I should ask *you* about it, Mrs Barlow."

She looked up. "He didn't tell you?"

"Obviously not," Baines said, fed up with dancing around, "but *someone* had better explain, before we caution the both of you, bring you to the station, and maybe drag your son down from Edinburgh to join you. We've had two young women assaulted, one put in hospital. We had another attack last night that's seriously hurt another woman, who happens to be a police officer. We've got your car unaccounted for—"

"I told you—" Roy Barlow began.

"All right!" Amanda cut across him. "All right," she said again, quietly. "I'll tell you. But it's nothing to do with these attacks. It's like Roy said in the first place. He went to the store."

"Right." Baines didn't think he believed that. "So what's this thing we have to ask you about?"

"My sister," she said, eyes on the floor again. "Cath. I still don't understand. She had a lovely husband with a good job, a nice son. Beautiful house. Then, ten years or so ago, she upped and abandoned her family. Left them for a *woman*."

Roy cleared his throat. "Can you imagine the effect on the whole family? I mean, when I said we've nothing against gay people, that's true, so long as they're not doing any harm. But we don't subscribe to that crap about it being in any way natural. It just *isn't* natural, and that's all there is to it. And Cath did hurt people. It nearly killed her husband and son. The humiliation. I mean, another man would have been bad enough..."

"So we don't talk about it." Amanda raised her head and looked a challenge at Baines. "It's too hurtful. As far as I'm concerned, my sister's dead. We don't talk about her, and we don't talk about... *it*."

Baines didn't know whether to be annoyed or amused. This was the 21st century, and this woman was talking like a Victorian maiden aunt. No wonder Zack hadn't come out to his parents. Presumably they'd disown him too.

"What about her husband and son?" Jason asked. "How angry are *they* now?"

"Not angry enough to go out attacking random lesbians, if that's what you mean," said Roy. "Besides, they live nowhere near here."

"So where do they live?"

"Wolverhampton," Amanda said. "It's where Gus – my brother-in-law – is from. He and Cath met at uni, and that's where they made their home."

"Has Gus or the son been down recently?"

"If they have, they haven't been to see us."

"They certainly haven't been driving my car," added Roy.

Baines wondered again whether Roy Barlow might, against the odds, be running with a nasty crowd that had started attacking gay couples, and providing transport when needed. Maybe the whole crew were older than Lauren and Maisie appreciated.

He was half-tempted to impound the BMW for the CSIs to take apart, but he knew this conversation wasn't evidence of anything other than a resentment against women who weren't what the Barlows saw as 'natural'.

But he was suddenly very interested indeed in the DNA test results. And the CCTV from the store.

*

With nothing hands-on she could do, Archer's itchy feet got the better of her. She left a message for Dan with Will and then headed off for Stoke Mandeville Hospital.

She showed her ID, explained who she was, and was shown into a small office. She waited about ten minutes and then was joined by Dr Gupta, a harassed looking middle-aged man.

"How is she?" Archer wanted to know.

"Poorly still. But, to be honest, I'd say the prognosis is hopeful. She's showing some purposeful response to stimulus, and starting to make sounds."

"She's talking?"

"No. She's not forming words yet, and she isn't opening her eyes. We're monitoring her closely, but there's definitely some improvement on when she was first brought in."

"And her parents are here?"

"They're spending as much time with her as they can, when we're not needing to check her over or administer treatment."

"And are we any wiser about what happened to her?"

"Not really. Her nose is broken, and everything we can see is consistent with her being hit in the face. We're still pretty sure she was knocked down and struck the back of her head on the pavement, but that doesn't really tell you anything useful, does it?"

"Hardly your fault. Thank you for what you're doing for her. Where are Joanne's parents now?"

"The nurse packed them off for a coffee. They needed a break."

Archer had never met Mr and Mrs Collins, but she'd seen pictures of them, Joan showing around snaps taken on family occasions: her mum, round and smiley, her dad slightly more serious. She found them in a corner with their heads together, half-eaten pastries in front of them. Joan's dad had at least drunk most of his coffee. Her mum had barely touched hers. They both looked tired and drawn.

She introduced herself and asked if she could sit down.

"Please," said Mr Collins, indicating a spare chair. His wife simply stared into space.

"I just wanted to see how you were holding up," she said, "and to assure you we're doing all we can to find Charlie and to catch whoever hurt Joan – Joanne," she corrected herself.

"Thank you," Mr Collins said. "Have you any idea what happened exactly? The doctors aren't saying much."

"It's early days. When Joan – sorry, Joanne—"

"We know you call her Joan. It's fine. And we're Paul and Sarah."

She nodded, committing the names to her memory. "Call me Lizzie, please. We're hoping, when Joan wakes up, she can tell us more."

"They say, with a head injury, she might not remember what happened."

"We'll have to see. There's a lot we can do in the meantime."

"You need to get her Charlie back," Sarah Collins said, suddenly animated. "She can't wake up and Charlie not be there. That girl means everything to her." She smiled a sad smile. "The first time she brought her home, she hadn't told us she was gay. She'd only really accepted it herself after she met Charlie, and she was afraid of what we'd think. But you know, we weren't surprised. Well, maybe a little."

"All we ever wanted was for her to be happy," added Paul. "You can see Charlie makes her happy. That's good enough for us."

"We're doing all we can," Archer said again. "We're following quite a few leads. But can you think of anyone who might want to hurt Joan or Charlie?"

"Well," Paul said, "I suppose in your job you must make some bad enemies. It's something I try not to think about. But otherwise, no. Joanne and Charlie are lovely. Very nice, hardworking girls."

"Especially Joanne," Sarah said. "You shouldn't let her work such long hours, Lizzie. She shouldn't neglect Charlie."

"I'll tell her that." As if that would make a difference to Joan's work ethic.

"I'd better get back to the office," she said. "I just wanted to see how she is."

Sarah squeezed her hand. "Thank you for coming to see us."

At the café door, Archer turned and raised a hand in farewell. But they were already staring off into an uncertain distance.

*

Back at his desk, Baines was finding it difficult to settle, his mind more than a little overloaded. From the moment Karen's home pregnancy test had told them they were to be parents, all the natural excitement and apprehensions of an expectant father had been constantly on his mind, whether in the background or the foreground. Now his head was also full of worry about both Joan and Charlie, and he was desperate to get a solid lead on the homophobic attacks.

At the same time, Mac's determination to go beyond helping Claire King fact-check her book, and to actually poke around in the case again was more distracting and intriguing than he'd like it to be.

He kept telling himself that the case was dead. That, having spent so many years coming to terms with what had happened to his family, the last thing he needed was to raise his hopes that new leads might be unearthed after all this time.

And yet.

And yet that chapter in his life was being revisited whether he liked it or not, and he couldn't ignore it, nor help wondering how Mac was getting on. He decided to send him a text, asking the question. Back came the response in less than a minute. Neil Mahon really wanted Baines there if he was going to talk about the case again.

Baines sighed, agonised for a few moments, then responded: *After work? Not that I know when that will be.*

Mac: *Sure. Will check with Neil.*

As he put his phone down, Will Tyler came over. "Guv, do we know when our next catch up meeting will be?"

"I'd imagine as soon as Lizzie gets back. Why, anything urgent?" His mind raced. "Any luck with CCTV?"

Will shook his head. "Not so far. No cameras where Joan was attacked – wouldn't you know it?"

Typical. "What about any footage in the surrounding area?"

"Yeah, Ibrahim and some others are still poring over what we've got on that. Looking for dark BMWs, for figures who might look like Lauren and Maisie's attackers, and anything else that might be significant."

"Have they had a chance to review the supermarket footage?"

"They didn't say. I'll ask. But we might have something else—"

Archer breezed in. "Right," she said, "briefing in fifteen minutes. Will, can you spread the word?" She frowned. "Sorry, I interrupted you."

"This might be good timing," Baines said. "Sounds like Will might have some news."

"Good news, I hope," she said. "Dear Lord, we could do with it."

"Well, I wouldn't go that far," said Will. "But you asked Sue and Dean to talk to Joan's neighbours?"

"Yep. Anything?"

Will looked awkward. "Look, it's probably nothing, but they called it in for me to log. It seems the party walls in those flats aren't the thickest. I don't think they're paper-thin, anything as bad as that—"

"But?"

"But you can hear if the telly's too loud. Or if voices are raised."

Baines digested this. "You're saying voices *were* raised?"

"And not for the first time. This is the immediate next-door neighbour, obviously."

"But you mean like a shouting match?" Lizzie wanted to know.

"Maybe. Some sort of row, anyway."

"But all couples row." Baines was anxious not to make too much of something that might be no big deal. "I mean, could they hear what was being said?"

"I don't have that sort of detail," said Will.

"Perhaps we should get it then. But seriously? I can't imagine those two coming to blows."

And yet...

Baines wondered again if they were focusing too much on the men who had attacked Lauren and Maisie when it came to Joan and Charlie. Maybe they needed to take a serious look at other possibilities. But Charlie as perpetrator? Could he really see it?

"We never know for sure what goes on behind closed doors," Lizzie said. "But even if they did have a row, even if it got a bit ugly, how does Joan end up unconscious in the middle of town?"

"The neighbour heard the front door slam ten minutes or so later."

Lizzie's brow furrowed. "So did they both go out?"

"That isn't clear. Sue asked. But the same neighbour keeps a spare key for them, and they do the same for her. Sue and Dean borrowed it and let themselves in. Nothing untoward and no sign of Charlie. So you have to think, either they went out together, or first one went, then the other followed later."

"But the neighbour only heard the door once?"

"So it'd seem."

She scanned the room. "Where's Jason?"

"Helping with the CCTV footage."

"Can you grab him for us, Will?"

As he departed, she sank into the chair next to Baines's desk. "What do you think?"

"I'm pretty sure it's nothing," he said. "But I suppose, as you say, what happens in private…"

She nodded, looking troubled. "Let's just suppose for a minute that they have just a simple enough domestic tiff. Maybe they were already planning to go out, so they go anyway, then the row re-surfaces in the street, probably on the way home."

"Or," he added, slipping naturally into the brainstorming that was such a part of his working relationship with her, "maybe only one of them goes out, maybe in a huff, maybe just to cool down…"

"Or to let the other one cool off. Either way, the remaining partner follows at some point…"

"…finds them. They row again…"

"…it gets overheated," Lizzie said. "Physical. Maybe even it's Joan who strikes the first blow. Whatever. It's her who ends up going down, striking her head…"

Baines raked his fingers through his hair. "See, there you start to lose me. Surely Charlie calls an ambulance?"

"You'd think. But who knows? What if she thinks Joan's actually dead? That she's killed her? She panics…"

"I'm not buying it," he persisted, wondering who he was trying to convince. Because he had to recognise that he didn't know Charlie anywhere near as well as he knew Joan.

Will returned with Jason Bell in tow.

"Any more luck with the CCTV?" Lizzie asked.

"A blank so far," Jason said. "I mean, you see people, but none look like the guys we're looking for. A couple of dark BMWs too, but not one of the registrations we spotted on Wednesday morning in Stoke Mandeville. We're still looking though. I need to get onto that supermarket stuff too."

"Okay," said Lizzie. "Look, here's the thing. You know Joan and Charlie better than any of us. What I'm wondering is, do you know if they ever row?"

He looked confused. "What's that got to do with anything?"

"But do they?"

"All couples row. I'm sure they do too. Why?"

Lizzie's eyes narrowed. "Jason, I'm not asking this for fun, and I'd appreciate you not beating around the bloody bush. It's a serious question. It could be important."

He blushed to his red roots, a much rarer sight these days than it used to be. "I wouldn't call it rowing, exactly. But Joan sometimes feels guilty about her long hours. I think Charlie moans about it occasionally. You know how it can be, especially when you're on a case. Plans can go out the window. It can be hard sometimes, especially..." He tailed off. "Oh."

"What?" Baines demanded.

Jason looked troubled. "I just remembered. I think I told you it was Charlie's birthday yesterday. I think they had plans. But you know how focused she gets at work..."

"She stayed fairly late again, didn't she?" said Baines. "What if she forgot?"

He imagined Charlie, pacing the flat, ready to go out somewhere, only for Joan not to show, not even to call. "She might be so mad she wouldn't even chase Joan. Maybe seething when she finally came home." He met Lizzie's eyes. "It's possible, I suppose."

But Jason was shaking his head.

"What's possible?" he said. "That it got ugly and violent, and Joan ended up in a coma? And what? Charlie legged it? That's rubbish, with respect."

"Can you be sure?" Lizzie said quietly. "One hundred per cent?"

"Look, I know Charlie. Even if they did have a bit of a falling out, that's light years from what you're suggesting. No, those gay bashers are still the ones I've got my money on."

"But how well do you *really* know Charlie?" Lizzie asked him. "You were the one who said, 'Oh,' when you suspected Joan had forgotten her birthday."

"I know," he said. "But only because you were asking if they might have argued. I still can't see it. Sorry, but I can't. Look, Charlie's someone who can get a bit stroppy sometimes, but violence? To Joan? Christ, Charlie *handles* domestic violence cases. She's passionate about it."

"There's a first time for everything," Baines suggested. He hated this train of thought, but knew it had to be pursued.

"Even if something like that happened," Bell said. "You're suggesting Joan's unconscious and Charlie would just leave her, go into hiding? I don't think so. She'd try and help her. Call an ambulance."

"Maybe not if she was panicking," Lizzie persisted. "Panic makes people do stupid, irrational things. And then they can't always see a way back. Maybe she's somewhere right now, trying to screw up her courage to hand herself in, fearing prison, the end of her legal career..."

"Let's say that's how it happened, Jason," Baines said. "Suspend your scepticism for a moment. Where might she be now?"

He looked about to argue some more, then closed his mouth and his eyes. Baines could hear the cogs go round as he tried to think.

"Well," he said, "not with her parents. It's pretty clear how worried they are. They've got a couple of friends in the Vale that they see. Lawyers that Charlie's worked with. Would they hide her, bearing in mind this story's already made the news? Risk their own careers?"

"Do you have their details?" Baines asked.

"No. I've heard a Marcia mentioned, and a Rupert. Maybe there's an address book at the flat, or the numbers are in Joan's phone. I suppose we do have her phone?"

"Yes," Will confirmed. "Unlike Tuesday's attack, her bag wasn't taken."

"Actually, she had an ex, too," he said. "Somewhere in Oxfordshire, I don't know if they kept in touch..."

"Jason, get someone to get into her phone and see if any of those numbers are there. If not, get that key off Sue Dyson and see what you can find at the flat. Anyone else she might go to?"

"Her car's still outside the flat," Will said, "so that rules out her having driven anywhere."

"If I was on the run, I wouldn't take my car," Baines said. "Too easy to find me with ANPR."

"There are trains," Lizzie said. "They'd have still been running. Walk or get a taxi to the station. Get a train into London, and then the world's your oyster."

"What about her parents?" Baines said. "Who spoke to them? Where are they again?"

"They're in Oxford too," Jason supplied.

"If she phoned them in a state, they could have been here picking her up in less than an hour," said Will. "Mind you, they've been allocated a local Families Liaison Officer and, by all accounts, they're worried sick…"

"That needn't signify anything," Lizzie said. "There are enough cases of people making tearful public appeals for the safe return of a loved one, or for bringing their killer to justice…"

"…when the person making the appeal is the killer," Baines completed. "Or is harbouring the missing person for some reason."

"Will," Lizzie said, "can you get onto our Oxford colleagues and ask them to search the parents' home? They need to stress that it's just routine. We don't want them claiming harassment when their daughter is missing, and then the worst happens. And let's find out if they happen to know where the ex is."

It was the first time since the search for Charlie had commenced that anyone had voiced the possibility that she might be dead.

Lizzie's face fell, as if she herself had just realised what she'd said. "Three possibilities: she's dead already; someone's holding her; she hurt Joan herself and is on the run. And the clock's ticking."

Almost three-quarters of missing persons were found within twenty-four hours but, as time went on, the chances of them returning home safe became slimmer. Often, the first seventy-two hours were crucial. But this was unlike the majority of missing persons cases, where the individual failed to return home as expected. Here there was the added dimension of the attack on Joan.

All three of the scenarios Lizzie had listed had the potential for a bad ending. If Charlie was still alive, but being held somewhere, what was happening to her? Would her abductors eventually release her? Or was she living on borrowed time?

If Charlie herself was responsible for Joan's injury, what was her state of mind? Was she at risk of harming herself?

Baines doubted they had the luxury of anything like seventy-two hours. He feared it could already be too late.

14

Charlie's parents, Denise and Alan, were even more sceptical than Jason about the violent row scenario, but they had no problems about their home being searched. They didn't care what it took to eliminate fruitless lines of enquiry and focus down on more promising leads. They were scared, but doing their best to hold it together.

Asked about other people in her life who might hypothetically shelter her, they volunteered that Marcia Powell was probably her best friend, going back to school days. They had heard Rupert's name mentioned, but hadn't met him.

Marcia, and Charlie's ex, Vicky Weaver, were still on their Christmas cards list. Despite the breakup, their card exchange with Vicky had continued. The last card had included a change of address.

"She was lovely," Denise said. "We never did find out why they split up. All Charlotte ever said was it was just one of those things."

Lara Moseley and Amir Rashid had headed into London to see Marcia, while Baines and Jason had driven over to Headington, where Vicky had a bedsit. The suburb overlooked Oxford from the top of Headington Hill. The area had hit the headlines in the late nineties when a 25ft fibreglass sculpture of a shark ripping into the roof of local broadcaster Bill Heine's house had been erected, causing great local controversy.

En route they contacted the local division, just to notify them they were coming onto their patch, and they found DC Steve Ashby waiting for them outside the sizeable terraced house where Vicky now lived. Ashby had been a DI at the Vale, but had left under a cloud and been demoted. Since transferring to Oxfordshire, he'd moved in with DS Amy Petrescu, a one-time lover of Baines's and still a friend.

Ashby and Amy had met when she'd joined Lizzie Archer's team a couple of years ago on temporary detachment, and the relationship had been good for him. Even so, seeing Ashby again was an awkward moment for Baines, who'd had no choice but to play a part in his demise. But if his former colleague, once the prickliest of characters, harboured a grudge, he concealed it well.

"Amy and I both like Joan," he said. "We can't do much to help, but I'm happy to be a point of contact for whatever you need over this way."

It turned out that Vicky Weaver rented a room in the house, and they found her at home. She looked early thirties, perhaps a little older than Charlie. Dark hair framed a pleasant, heart-shaped face that smiled easily. She spoke to other residents who were in the communal kitchen, and they withdrew, closing the door to give them privacy.

The kitchen looked tired and neglected. Baines had also noted that Vicky's housemates looked a few years younger than her. She offered drinks and set about making them.

"So Charlie?" she said with her back to them. "What's she done?"

Baines gave her the briefest summary of what had happened. She turned around.

"You think she's been kidnapped?" The smile had left her face. "Oh, Christ."

"That's one possibility we're looking into."

"What else could it be?"

"We're just trying to build up a picture of Charlie," he said. "Anything would help. You last saw her when?"

She frowned. "It must be over a year now."

"You lived together?"

"For about six months."

"What was Charlie like as a partner?"

Vicky smiled fondly. "She was lovely. She could be intoxicating, actually. The whole thing was a bit of a whirlwind." She shrugged, the smile fading again. "Maybe we should have taken it a little more slowly. Got to know each other better."

Baines recalled how quickly Joan and Charlie had moved from dating to co-habiting. It was an arrangement born of necessity after Charlie had been rendered homeless by a gas explosion in her apartment block; but then moving in with Joan hadn't been her only option, and they'd not been seeing each other for long.

Still, from the outside looking in, it had seemed to be working out. Baines would have said they were happy.

"So what went wrong?" Jason prompted. "If you don't mind me asking."

Another shrug. "We just found we liked different things. I'm quite sporty, she isn't. She can be pretty work-centric."

"So you turned out not to be compatible?"

"I suppose so, yes." Her face clouded. "And she did rather like her own way. I realised she was stifling me. I tried to put Charlie first, but she also put Charlie first. There was no room for me."

"So what happened?" Jason asked softly.

"Oh, we talked about it like adults, agreed it wasn't working for either of us. So she went back to her parents while she was looking for somewhere else. I stayed on in the flat we were renting, but it was a real struggle to cover the bills on my own, and then I was restructured out of my job." She grimaced. "So this is the best I can afford until I get back on my feet. Sharing a bathroom and kitchen."

The kettle turned itself off with a click and she turned to attend to the drinks.

"You described her as stifling," Baines said. "I have to ask you, was she ever aggressive or violent?"

"I wouldn't say that. I mean, she had a bit of a temper sometimes, but don't we all?"

She turned to face them again, a teaspoon in her hand. "As I said, she liked her own way."

"So she never hit you?"

Her eyes widened. "What? No! Well…" she seemed about to amend that, then shook her head. "No, not really."

"Not really," he echoed. He exchanged a quick glance with Jason. "What does that mean?"

"It was just the once. My fault really. She just sort of lashed out."

"What was it about?"

She shook her head. "It's not important. I did provoke her, and she was immediately sorry."

Baines was troubled. How many times had he met domestic abuse victims who blamed themselves? Whose abusers were always contrite afterwards, only for the next time to be that little bit worse?

"And it didn't happen again?"

"It was over soon after that. To be honest, maybe her hitting me was part of that. I found I was walking around her on eggshells. Trying too hard to please her. Looking back, maybe I'd have lost myself in the end." She looked sad. "I still care about her. I hope she's okay."

"Let's change the subject," Baines said. "Let's say Charlie wanted to disappear for a while. Any idea where she might go?"

Vicky frowned. "What do you mean?"

"Apart from her parents?"

"But… what are you saying? Why would—"

"If you could just answer the question?"

She turned back to the drinks. "Well, I don't know. There's her best mate, Marcia, I suppose. Marcia Powell. Another friend, Rupert Scott. I don't know if she still sees either of them. But I still don't get it." She came over with two mugs. "You said she'd been abducted?"

"What I actually said was, it was one possibility. We're trying to keep an open mind."

She picked up the remaining two mugs, brought them over. Set one down in front of Jason, then leaned against the worktop with her hands wrapped around her own drink. "That's just crazy. You can't think she attacked her girlfriend and did a runner? What I said about her hitting me. That was just one of those things."

Baines found himself wondering if Vicky was still in love with Charlie. And there is nothing as blind as love.

"Her new partner is one of our colleagues," he told her. It would be on the news soon enough.

"A policewoman?" Vicky raised her eyebrows. "And she's the one who's been assaulted? How badly?"

"I can't go into details."

"But she's going to be okay?" She took a sip of her drink. "I'm not being funny, but you're wasting time here. What you're suggesting... no. Whoever attacked your colleague has got her. You should be out there looking for her."

"We are. That's why we're here, Miss Weaver."

She sighed. "If you seriously think someone's harbouring her, by all means check out my broom cupboard of a room, and you should look at Marcia and Rupert. But you're wrong."

They duly saw her room. It was small but incredibly neat and tidy. There was, unsurprisingly, no trace of Charlie. They left Vicky with cards, and she promised to contact them if anything occurred to her.

"Thanks for the liaison, Steve," Baines said at the cars.

He waved the gratitude away. "It's for Joan. I hope she wakes up soon. What did you make of that?"

"Troubling," Baines admitted. "I wonder if any of us knows Charlie as well as we thought we did. I got the sense that Vicky was playing down Charlie's aggressive streak. She and Joan *were* heard rowing. And, if she did it once..."

Jason scowled. "I'm still not buying it."

"I wish I could be as certain as you."

"Well, keep us posted," Ashby said, pointing his key fob at the Audi. Amber lights flashed as it unlocked. "Anything else we can do..."

"We'll be in touch. Love to Amy."

*

The day moved on in a whirl of activity. Both Marcia Powell and Rupert Scott had been interviewed and their homes searched with their co-operation, but with no more trace of Charlie than had been found at Vicky Weaver's.

Jason Bell continued to deny there was anything in the notion that Charlie was responsible for what had happened.

"That Vicky," he'd argued. "The relationship ended easily enough. That's not like most of the domestic abuse cases we come across. And, from what we saw of Vicky, I'd say Joan's a stronger character. I can't see her taking that sort of shit from a partner."

But Baines, much as his instinct had been to agree, had found himself nagged by a little twinge of doubt. If Charlie was prone to lashing out at the person she was supposed to love, there was a first time in any relationship. What if the first time with Joan had been Friday night?

At the same time, it had been established that Andrew Gunner's property holdings were in the name of a self-contained company: two flats and four houses. All were currently tenanted, which at least appeared to rule out the possibility that Charlie was being held in one of them.

Meanwhile, frustration continued over the tests on DNA recovered from Maisie Albright and Lauren Black. Even with pressure from Superintendent Stowe, the best the lab could promise was by lunchtime tomorrow. It seemed that a combination of holiday, illnesses, a couple of resignations and the sudden death of a technician from a heart attack had left the lab short-handed at the same time as it was experiencing a spike in demand for both urgent and routine testing.

Charlie's family had come over to Aylesbury to make a TV appeal with Stowe and Lizzie. The usual stuff:

"Charlie, if you're watching this, we love you... please get in touch with us, or with the police, and let us know you're all right... If you're holding Charlie, we're begging you to do the right thing and let her go..."

Their terror was palpable and reminded him horribly of that feeling he'd had when Jack had first disappeared. His grief at losing Louise had been bad enough, but the waiting and wondering about his son's fate had been even more horrific.

It was as if everything that was happening this week was designed to rip open a wound he'd told himself was healing.

There'd been a time when most of the 'Invisible Man Widowers', as one of them – Baines couldn't remember who – had styled them, had kept in regular touch. With Neil Mahon, the contact had lasted until about three years ago, when Baines had started receiving counselling and stopped calling him. But, with Mac's return to the Vale, and Baines almost inevitably being drawn into the work he was doing, the memories had begun to unspool in his mind once more.

Emma Mahon had been the Invisible Man's first victim. Neil had returned home on a Friday evening to find her body on his living room carpet, her head encased in cling film. Of their daughter Chloe, there had been no trace.

This was before the taunting 'Invisible Man' doodles had started to appear. They'd had no idea a serial killer was at large in the Vale. All Baines and his colleagues had known was that a woman was dead and her daughter was missing. Some suspicion had even fallen on Neil.

Then, the following Friday – precisely one week later – everything had changed. Martha Hallett was dead, the identical method of killing, her son Eliot nowhere to be found. Only, this time, Chloe Mahon's still, small body had been left alongside Martha's, killed in the same way.

Neither the CSIs' work, nor the post mortem, had unlocked a single clue as to where Chloe had been, nor what had happened to her, since her abduction. She had died at, or around, the time of Martha's death. Cause of death: suffocation. The killer had left no vestige of himself behind. Only then had the true extent of the nightmare stalking Aylesbury and its surrounding towns and villages begun to reveal itself.

The horrendous death of a beloved spouse. The simultaneous murder of one child and the disappearance of another. The agony of waiting, then, seven days later, hope extinguished for one husband and another plunged into the same week-long ordeal. It seemed the worst form of cruelty.

Neil had once said their loss had left scars on his soul, but Baines had always felt that was an understatement; for him, the agony seemed to be felt at an even deeper level, leaving scars beneath the soul that would never truly heal.

It was gone 9pm when Baines finally left the office. The case had worked itself to a standstill for now, and Lizzie had ordered everyone home for some rest and a fresh start tomorrow. All personal plans for Sunday were cancelled. In the meantime, the skeleton crew manning the phones overnight were fully briefed should anything happen.

In the station's car park, he took out his phone, thought about texting Mac, and then decided to phone instead. The forecast was for rain, and he sensed it wasn't far away.

"Dan! I was on the verge of giving up on you."

"I've just finished for the day, if you still want to see Neil Mahon. Or perhaps you've already been."

"No, no, laddie. He said he wanted you and so I've been waiting to hear from you. He said any time, however late, was fine. Do you remember the address?"

Baines did, even though he hadn't actually visited Neil at home for maybe eight years. What estate agents back in the day would have described as a 'detached executive home', on an estate full of very similar houses.

The grief had taken each of them in slightly different ways. Baines had channelled all his energies into work. Sam O'Bryan, of course, had killed himself.

Neil had gone on living, but living for Emma and Chloe, with nothing left for himself. The house had been like a shrine to them both, and he had vowed to keep Emma's beloved front and rear gardens as beautifully as she herself had.

"I'd hate to think of her looking down and seeing it all gone to rack and ruin," he'd said.

Judging by the front garden now, he was still keeping that promise.

His appearance was a shock when he opened the door. He was around Baines's age, mid-forties, but he looked nearer to sixty. His hair, once dark, wavy and immaculate, was now grey, untidy and in dire need of a cut. His face was pale and heavily lined. And he was stick-thin, as if he could do with several good meals.

Even his voice was feeble. Baines wondered if he still held down his good job on the corporate ladder.

"No," he replied as he shuffled around the kitchen in a wrinkled shell suit and worn-out carpet slippers. "No, they let me go in the end. I couldn't hack it, you see. I suppose I was lucky, though. Emma and I both had our lives insured, so I was able to pay off the mortgage. I've done bits and pieces since. Shop work. It's okay. I see people."

Baines couldn't help wondering how joyous an experience being served by this sad figure could be.

If Neil Mahon had let himself go personally, the almost Stepford-Wives neatness of the front garden was a theme that continued into the house. Absolutely nothing out of place. Not so much as a pen lying about. Every cushion looked plump and perfect. Baines had a fleeting mental image of the man never sitting down, for fear of disturbing the perfection of the seats, and never putting anything down on the gleaming coffee table, keeping hold of a book and magazine and returning it to its designated place the instant he had done with it.

The thought both chilled and saddened him.

Pictures of Emma and Chloe were everywhere.

"You'd best sit down, and I'll get us some drinks," he said. Mac looked around the Ideal Homes lounge and headed for an easy chair.

"Sorry," said Neil. "Maybe that sofa there?" He indicated an olive green two seater.

"Of course," Mac said genially, veering off.

Baines followed him. When he sat, he felt that the contact of his backside was sacrilege to the perfect seat. He even fancied his host winced.

Neil took drinks orders and disappeared.

"Jesus," Mac whispered when he was out of earshot. "The poor sod. But this is what grief can do to a person." He looked at Baines and grimaced. "Sorry, Dan. You'll know all about that."

Neil returned with a tray. On it were three mugs of coffee, each on an individual mini-tray, and three plates, each with three biscuits carefully arranged. Baines suddenly realised he hadn't eaten since a snatched sandwich at around 2pm. He devoured a biscuit, carefully holding the plate underneath it.

"It's good to see you, Dan," Neil said as he took the easy chair he'd steered Mac away from. "DS McNeill says you've remarried and have a baby on the way. That's great."

Baines shot Mac a look. He'd actually told Neil in his last Christmas card that he was married again, but the news about the baby wasn't Mac's to share. And *DS* McNeill? Was Mac letting him think he was still in the police?

"You're looking well, too," Neil went on. He clasped his hands together. "So this is all about the case. It's being reopened?"

Baines looked at Mac again, who avoided his gaze.

"Not as such, no," he said. "I think maybe *Mac* here didn't make himself clear. Technically, the case has never been closed, but he's no longer on the force. He's acting as a consultant on a book about the case, and I think he's interested in just hearing from people who were involved."

"Technically, that's right," Mac said, a little too smoothly for Baines's liking. "I retired a few years ago, but I still work on cold cases, so I guess the person writing the book thought I'd be ideal to fact check for her. And you never know. You'd be amazed how new information can shake loose years after the event, for all sorts of reasons."

"You think I've got new information?" Neil half-sobbed, half-laughed. "You don't think I've spent every day since it happened, going over and over it, trying to decide if I should have seen it coming? You think, if anything had occurred to me, I wouldn't have reported it?"

"I'm absolutely sure that's the case," Mac said. "But humour me. Can you, to the best of your memory, run us through the couple of weeks leading up to your wife's death and your daughter's abduction?"

Neil Mahon sat statue-still, his face a blank. He could have been on the verge of tears, or about to attack Mac physically. Or maybe both. Baines wished to God they hadn't come.

And then Neil shrugged. "Why not? It'll do me good to talk to someone about it, instead of just talking to myself. Not that there's much to tell. Weekdays, I went to work. The early train to London, the late train back, all except Fridays, when I made a point of getting away before five. The weekends immediately before... *it*... were just the usual. The supermarket. The park. I washed the car, mowed the lawn. Took Chloe out while Emma did some baking. It was just our routine. Nothing unusual."

"And – I know you must have gone over and over this, but – no one hanging around, acting suspicious? No strange cars? No unexpected callers at the door? No funny phone calls?"

"No. To all of the above."

"And Emma? What did her weeks look like?"

"That was all routine too. It all revolved around Chloe. Pre school classes. Parent and toddler. Kids' art and craft classes, which Chloe loved..." He paused and swallowed. "There were a couple of other young mums she was friendly with, and they used to take the kids and meet up for coffee on a Tuesday afternoon. She'd do a little shop at the supermarket on a Wednesday, so the vegetables were that bit fresher..."

Baines's gaze stole to a photograph on the wall of the three of them. Judging by Chloe's likely age in the snap, it was probable that it had been taken not long before her murder. Three people in a rural setting, laughing for the camera, Neil and Emma hunkered down beside their daughter. A normal family, with normal, almost dull, existences, utterly destroyed by an evil that had never been unmasked.

"I'd almost forgotten all those kids' activities," Mac was saying. "I think we did some sort of roadshow that year, talking to the parents about home security."

Neil gave a faint smile. "I think you're right. Yeah, the parent and toddler group. How ironic is that? Didn't do much good, did it?"

'Outreach' had been big that year, in schools, and in the homeless and drug using communities. He remembered the hopeless but genial PC Watson's hand shooting up to volunteer for a gig no one else had fancied. Anything to swan around. But his good looks and easy charm had at least made a good impression on Louise's group.

"And she never said anything in the weeks before her death that gave you any concern?" Mac persisted.

"Well, there was that guy in the kids' shop in Milton Keynes," Neil said. "What was his name?" He snapped his fingers. "Kevin Bray. I never liked his manner, or the way he looked at Emma. You know, Dan, quite a few of us Widowers felt the same. Including you, as I recall."

It was true. Every family that had fallen victim to the Invisible Man, including Baines's, had shopped for toys and children's clothing in the store at one time or another. Most – although not all – remembered the tall, skinny, pale-faced assistant whose gaze was a little too intense, who never seemed to blink when he spoke to a woman, and who was just a little too over-familiar, talking to customers who'd never met him before as if he'd known them for years.

"But the investigation left him in the clear," Baines reminded him. "He was off work on some of the days in question—"

"Three, I seem to recall," Mac added. "But he was at work the other three days. Rock solid alibis."

Neil Mahon nodded. "So, unless he could be in two places at once, Bray was just a weirdo."

"No one else?" Mac prompted.

Neil let out a long sigh. "There was no one else I could think of then, and I've racked my brains, God knows how many times, since. I've simply no idea who would have wanted to hurt Emma or Chloe. If I did, I'm not even sure I'd tell you."

"How do you mean?" Baines demanded.

"Prison's too good for him. I think I might deal with it myself. If I was sure. I'd take him when he least expected it. I'd use a knife. I've dreamed what I'd do to him if I had him helpless for a few days. Scared myself with what I might be capable of." He gave a shaky laugh. "Of course, we're just talking here."

It wasn't the sort of thing one should say to a police officer, but Baines knew he'd had a few of those fantasies himself. He suspected most of the Widowers must have, at one dark time or another. But fantasy was different from fact.

Well, wasn't it?

There wasn't much more they could ask or Neil Mahon could tell them. Outside, a light drizzle had set in. They wanted to talk before heading for the cars, but Neil stood on his doorstep, evidently wanting to see them off.

"You go in, laddie," Mac said. "We'll be chatting here a while."

Neil shrugged. "Fair enough. Have a nice weekend."

They watched the door close behind him.

"Nothing new there, was there?" Baines said.

"No," Mac agreed. "You know, I'd forgotten Robin Watson's outreach thing with the toddler groups. I wonder what happened to him. Is he still around?"

"Not in the Vale. Last I heard he was somewhere in Oxfordshire. He finally made sergeant."

Mac raised an eyebrow. "I wonder who he had to screw for that. Anyhow, maybe I should try and have a word with him."

"We did ask him at the time, didn't we? Whether he saw or overheard something on his travels."

"True enough, but maybe something might seem more significant to him now? It's worth a phone call, at least."

"You're right. I'll try and find you a number."

"I got down to Surrey, by the way. Saw Mark Richardson. Same story. He mentioned Kevin Bray, too. You know, I might try and check out those alibis of Bray's, for what it's worth. And there were those two other guys we looked at: Ollie Carter and Antony Creed."

"Is it even worth it?" Baines wondered. Like Bray, they'd been fleetingly of interest, but neither of them had achieved serious suspect status.

Antony Creed was a convicted sex offender living in the same road as the Mahons. He'd groomed a fifteen-year-old girl and been caught taking her on a ferry to France. But there was no evidence that any of the Invisible Man's victims had been sexually assaulted in any way. The profiler who'd been brought in, and who Baines had opined was a waste of money, breath and time, had insisted that most serial killers obtained some sort of sexual gratification from their crimes; but it wasn't as if this killer's victims bore any resemblance to the girl Creed had targeted.

Plus he'd been with his probation officer when the Hallett and Richardson homes had been hit and in Leicester with his parents the day Lindsey Cutler and Eliot Mahon had been killed.

Ollie Carter was a courier whose patch took in all six of the addresses where the Invisible Man had struck, but he was only known to have delivered to the Mahons, Cutlers, O'Bryans and Baineses, and he had been on a short break with his wife in Liverpool on the day Martha Hallett and Chloe Mahon had died.

"You're right, of course," the Scot conceded. "I'm sure it'll be a waste of time. To be honest, between you and me, I feel I'm getting paid for this whole trip under false pretences. The lassie Claire could have just sent me her manuscript to look over."

"She'll be on shaky legal ground, won't she, if she mentions Bray, Carter or Creed in the book without their agreement?"

"I'm no lawyer, but I'd imagine so. And what's the point of even mentioning them, when they were such dead ends?" He shoved his hands in his pockets and sighed. "I get the impression that Claire's a bit bored with the *Echo*. We all know it's getting tougher and tougher for provincial papers to make a profit."

"You think she sees this book as a stepping stone onto bigger, better things?"

"Maybe serious investigative journalism, aye," Mac said. "Maybe the nationals, maybe even into broadcasting. She hasn't actually asked me to poke around in the case again, but there have been subtle hints. Books like this… they really need a hook. All those Jack the Ripper books and what have you? There's always a theory about who he really was."

"Dangerous in this case," Baines remarked. "Especially if she fingers someone who's still alive. They could sue. Or something nasty could happen to them. Remember when the case was live?"

How could they forget?

No one had ever been arrested, but names had somehow found their way into the media with catastrophic results. Kevin Bray had paint stripper poured over his car. Excrement through the letter box. 'Murderer' spray-painted on the front door. Even after Bray was exonerated, the torment went on for several years, 'no smoke without fire' theories abounding, and even notions of an accomplice did the rounds, even though the man was known as a strange and awkward loner.

The mother Bray lived with had died that year, and he'd made a formal complaint, claiming that the publicity and its consequences had hastened her demise. Nothing had come of that.

It was a similar story for Antony Creed. Police visits to his home had shone a spotlight on him, dragging his past offences back into the light. He'd been forced to leave the area when it became obvious it was too dangerous for him to remain.

Only Ollie Carter had never received any publicity – nor, on the face of it, should he have.

Baines remembered his old boss, DI Britton, a mentor as Mac had been, feeling bad about Kevin Bray. He'd had more limited sympathy for Creed, but what Bray had gone through had left a bitter taste in the mouth.

"Still," Mac said. "Can't do any harm to go through the motions, so long as I'm discreet. Who knows? One of them might have a story they've been longing to tell. I'd like to justify this jolly somehow, lovely as it's been catching up with you."

"You'd have to track them down, first," Baines pointed out.

"Och, already done that."

"When?" Baines sighed. "You decided to rattle their cages before you even came down, didn't you?"

Mac at least had the grace to avoid eye contact. "Well, no, but I thought I might. You can trace anyone if you know how." He hesitated. "As a matter of fact, Kevin Bray's dead. Cancer. So nothing's going to hurt him. But apparently his old boss is still at the store where he was working at the time."

"I want nothing to do with this," Baines said, his vehemence surprising him. "And you should be very careful, Mac."

Mac smiled, but he looked disappointed. "Always, laddie. Always."

*

Baines was finally on his way home, dispirited. This was as bad a time as he could remember for years. He wished Claire King wasn't writing this book. He wished Mac hadn't got involved. And he wished the Scot wouldn't keep drawing him back into the case, wasting his time with ghosts from the increasingly distant past when he should be channelling his energy into people who needed him here and now. Yet, at the same time, fanning faint flames of hope for a breakthrough against all the odds.

The dreams were already returning. He hoped it wouldn't get any worse.

Despite the late hour, traffic was sluggish through the centre of Aylesbury, and he found himself in a barely moving line of cars. Rain slid down his side windows and kept his wipers busy. The traffic lights had turned red, but it barely mattered.

To his left was the Odeon cinema. Across the road to his right was the Waterside Theatre, whose architectural design, apparently inspired by the Chiltern Hills and surrounding woodland areas, had divided the crowd when it had opened. He thought of the child growing inside Karen and imagined them taking her or him to cartoons at the cinema and panto at the theatre.

The lights turned green. As he waited to move, he glanced over towards the theatre again.

And he froze. There was a roaring sound in his ears.

Through the rain, he saw a young man standing, waiting to cross the road. Even before the face registered, something about the stance hit Baines like a lightning bolt. Then he stared at the face. A face that had, a couple of years ago, been haunting his dreams and his waking hours. Older, a little more mature, but unquestionably the same face. A little filled out, but then the ghost of his dreams always seemed to age in real time. If he was wearing the usual Queen's Park Rangers football shirt, it was underneath a black leather jacket.

Oblivious now to the traffic around him, the vehicle behind him honking, he stared at the teenager. Part of him wanted to get out of the car and go to him. Part of him knew that, if he did that, his sanity might snap, maybe irreparably this time.

Besides, it couldn't be Jack. Because he knew in his heart that Jack was dead.

Well, didn't he?

He realised he was holding his breath. Let it out in panicked pants. A bus rolled in front of the apparition and stopped, obscuring it from Baines's view. When it moved on, the figure had gone.

Behind him, horns were hooting furiously. The man behind him was leaning out of his window, shouting and gesticulating. Baines raised a hand in apology and moved off.

He realised he was shaking. And badly scared.

This couldn't be happening.

Not again.

15

In addition to the appeals by Charlie's parents, yesterday's press conference had also included a request for the public to check garages and outhouses. It was extremely unlikely she was hiding in such a place, but it was important to cover all the bases.

Last night's rain had continued into the morning. Potholed roads and blocked drains conspired to create big puddles and mini-floods on her way into work. One road flowed like a shallow river. Nevertheless, Archer was at her desk by 8am.

Half an hour later, Phil Gordon walked in.

Normally, if he wasn't wearing a white CSI suit, Phil would be in a jacket and smart trousers. Today he wore a pair of baggy jeans and a Newcastle rugby shirt.

"Fancy dress day?" She gave him a smile of studied innocence.

"Don't start," he retorted. "I came in on a Sunday out of the goodness of my heart, specially to help bully those DNA results out of the lab, and I've got them."

"In that case, you can wear a leather corset and thigh boots, for all I care," she grinned.

He winked. "My secret is out."

"So does it take us any further forward?"

"Aye, I think it does."

All thought of further banter evaporated. "Tell me. Please."

He pulled up a chair. "So we had the DNA recovered from the fingernails of Maisie Albright and Lauren Black. And we had swabs from the owners of two BMWs we were interested in."

"James Gunner and Roy Barlow, yes."

"And Barlow's son, Zack."

"And we've got a match?" Her pulse quickened.

"It's not quite that simple, but we've certainly got something interesting. Not a direct match to either of them, but a familial match. For young Zack, in fact. Not for his dad, so someone on his mum's side. About twelve and a half per cent of the DNA is a match…"

"Suggesting what? A common grandparent, right?"

He smiled. "Very good. So we're looking at a first cousin of Zack's"

"So one of our suspect's parents is presumably Amanda Barlow's sibling."

"Full marks."

And Amanda's sister had run off with another woman, leaving her husband and son devastated.

And angry?

*

"You told us only yesterday that your brother-in-law and nephew lived in Wolverhampton and hadn't been near nor by lately," Baines said. He and Jason Bell had returned to the Barlows' home and were questioning Amanda Barlow under caution. He'd had a good mind to drag the pair of them to the station in handcuffs, but he was anxious not to waste the time.

If the lie had slid easily off her tongue before, now she at least had the grace to avoid their gaze as she confirmed the story she'd told.

"But that wasn't true, was it?" he said. "Because he was here on Tuesday night. Was, in point of fact, one of a bunch of thugs who beat the crap out of two young women who hadn't done anything to deserve it. Possibly the ringleader."

"I told you," she protested, "no."

He outlined the DNA test results to her. "So does Zack have any other cousins who might have happened to be in the area on Tuesday?"

"No. There's only Julius."

"Julius?" he echoed.

"Christ," Jason said. "Poor sod. No wonder he goes by 'J'."

"Surname," Baines demanded.

"Mullins. But he wasn't here," Roy protested.

"Evidence says otherwise," said Baines, angry now. "Listen. There are all sorts of things I can charge you both with, starting with perverting the course of justice. That's a maximum sentence of life in prison." He thought of Maisie Albright, whose recovery could take a very long time; Lauren Black, her sense of personal security, even in her own home, shattered, the full psychological consequences of her ordeal as yet unknown; Joan, still in a coma; and Charlie, God knew where. "And it could easily come to that. So I suggest you start helping yourselves right now."

The Barlows were shooting each other anxious glances now.

"Let's start with last Tuesday night," Baines said. "Or early Wednesday morning, actually. Because we can place him in a car park in the early hours, carrying out a vicious, violent assault, and we can place your BMW in Stoke Mandeville around the time he and his mates drove over there, used the girls' keys to let themselves into their home, and wrecked it for them."

"We don't know if he was the one who actually shat on their bed or pissed all over their underwear," Jason added. "But he was there all right."

"And we'll prove it was your car if we have to reduce it to component parts," said Baines.

"Oh, for Christ's sake," Roy Barlow said to his wife, "just tell them, Mand."

"I can't," she whispered.

"Then I will." He'd gone pale. "Look, yes, okay. Julius was here at the beginning of the week. He spent a bit of time with us when, you know, when his mum left, and he made some mates in the town."

"I'll want their names," Baines said, "but go on."

"Well, he comes back sometimes, when his dad's away on business, for a visit and to see his friends."

"How old is he?"

"Eighteen. Nineteen in a few weeks' time."

"So he was here Tuesday?"

"He came down Sunday. He was going to stay all week, but – oh, just tell them, Mand!" He looked pointedly at her.

She started to cry. "It's not his fault. He was such a sweet little boy. But he changed after what my sister did. Seeing what it did to his dad... I knew he was going off the rails, but I didn't, or wouldn't, see how badly. And those friends he made here..." She wiped her eyes. "I don't know who his friends are at home, but this bunch are a bit weak, I think. He's a bit older than them, and he's very much the leader of the gang."

"You've met them?" Baines checked.

"Only a couple of times. They hero worship him. Laugh at all his jokes. None of them are true friends who'll stop him doing something he shouldn't."

"Amanda loves him," said Roy. "She's been the nearest thing he's had to a mother since his own mum abandoned him. I've seen it for about two years. He's a very angry young man, and he hates gays in general, and lesbians with a passion. Even so, even I didn't realise how bad it had got until this week."

"Tell us about Tuesday night," Baines prompted.

"He went out," Amanda said. "Said he was meeting his mates. When he wasn't back by midnight, we went to bed. He was often out really late. I supposed he was at one of his mates' houses, or just hanging out. He has his own key.

"I woke up, it must have been just after four. I realised I'd heard a car door slam. I got up and looked out the window, and Julius was standing on the drive, by Roy's car. On the driver's side. After, it must have been a minute or two, he walked up the drive and I heard him letting himself in.

"I went back to bed, and I must have drifted off, because the next thing I knew, I was awake again and there were noises downstairs. I looked at the clock, I remember. It was about ten to five. Roy sleeps like the dead, but I got up and came down. I found Julius trying to fathom out how to use the washing machine."

"He was doing his washing at five in the morning?" said Jason.

"And swearing to himself. He went all quiet and kind of furtive when I appeared. Said his clothes had got a bit dirty. It seemed odd, but I was up now, so I thought I might as well help him. I was worried he'd just chucked everything in together, so I started taking the things out. He really didn't want me to. When I got them out, I could see why. His jeans, his tee shirt, his hoodie were all covered in blood. Then I saw the scratches on his face."

"So did you ask him what had happened?" said Baines.

"Of course. Oh, first of all he started giving me some obvious nonsense about tripping over. Then he admitted he'd got into what he called 'a bit of bother'. What kind of bother, he wouldn't really say. Said there'd been a misunderstanding with some idiots. I didn't believe a word of it. But I helped him with his washing."

"Did you tell your husband?"

"In the morning, yes. I was so worried he'd got himself into some sort of serious trouble."

"The last straw was my car," Roy said. "I looked out the window and it was there on the drive, but I knew there was something off. I suppose I'm a creature of habit. I always leave it in more or less the same place, and more or less central. This was just wrong."

"Wrong in what way?"

"Oh, not far enough up the drive and at a funny angle. I went out and looked inside and there were brownish smudges on the driver's seat and one of the back ones. I guessed then that he'd come in at some point, taken the keys out of the bowl in the kitchen and basically stolen my car."

"Borrowed," Amanda insisted.

"Let's not start that again," he said wearily. "You borrow with permission. You steal without it. I wouldn't have given him permission. He's not insured to drive it."

"So you questioned him?"

"Oh, yes. First he tried denying it, then he started getting angry, asking why I was making such a big deal of it. I'd already guessed those marks were blood. Oh, they're leather seats, so it washed off easy enough."

"Have you had it cleaned since?"

"No."

"We'll need to take it away for examination." Baines would be surprised if just washing would have removed every trace of blood from the upholstery. Even more surprised if it wasn't Lauren's blood, or Maisie's. Or both. Maybe Joan's too, but something about that was niggling him. "So what happened next?"

"Roy threw him out," Amanda said. "Told him to pack his bags and drove him to the station before he went to work."

"Amanda didn't agree with me," said Roy. "She's always been soft on him. Too soft."

"His mother walked out on him when he was just a little boy," she pushed back. "You might be messed up too, if that had happened to you."

"Yeah, yeah. I know all that. I do. But we can't condone him just waltzing off with my car, we can't condone him getting into who knows what trouble. He was going to finish up bringing the police to our door." He looked at Baines. "And he has."

"Can you maybe save your recriminations and bickering for later?" Baines said. "Because this is serious stuff. You've both lied to us, quite deliberately. Helped him conceal evidence. You'll say you were covering for a family member who's had some problems, but it won't wash. We're looking into a serious assault on Tuesday night, and another on Friday night."

"He wasn't here Friday night," insisted Amanda.

"Are you sure about that?"

"She told you," said Roy. "I drove him to the station myself."

"Did you actually see him get on a train?"

"Well, no…"

"So, for all you know, he got straight on his phone to his mates and arranged to stay with them."

"I doubt it."

"But you don't know. I want his friends' names and addresses."

"We don't know where exactly they live," Amanda said. "We don't know their full names, either. There's a Kyle, a Harrison…"

"Ryan, I think," Roy added. "Aaron? No, Ethan, that's it."

"I met Harrison a couple of times," said Amanda. "He seems a nice lad, but I could imagine him being easily led."

"What about surnames?" Baines could feel his frustration growing. "Addresses?"

"Sorry. Oh, wait. Kyle's name is Evans. He lives in Granville Road. Our cleaner lives near him and knows the family. She doesn't like them."

He thought fast. Something told him if Julius Mullins knew he'd been rumbled, he'd run. And, if he knew where Charlie was – if she was even alive – that could be very bad news. But the chances were, if these two were simply left alone, told to come to the station later and make a statement, they'd be straight on the phone to him.

"You know Julius's address in Wolverhampton, obviously?"

"Obviously."

"Okay," he said. "So I want that, and then I'm arresting the pair of you on suspicion of perverting the course of justice."

Roy Barlow stared at him. "You're joking."

"Do I look like I'm joking?"

In fact, although Baines had enough to charge them with something, and so had justification for arresting them, his main aim was to stop them contacting Amanda's nephew while they went through his mates and also had his own home checked for signs of him. It could be a tortuous enough process, without him being forewarned. He might go to ground.

"DC Bell will call up a squad car to take you to the station," Baines said. "I'm going outside to make a couple of calls. You two sit tight."

"We need to make some calls too," Amanda said.

"Later," said Baines. "Leave your phones alone for now. I wouldn't want to have to cuff you."

"This is outrageous," said Roy.

"So were your lies to the police," said Jason Bell. "Think yourselves lucky we're being so reasonable."

16

In the event, Julius Mullins hadn't been so hard to track down. What was more, he wasn't at home in Wolverhampton, but crashing in Aylesbury with one of his mates. Kyle Evans in Granville Road had been easy to find, and his father – who was 'known' to the police and didn't want them around longer than necessary – had leaned on the teenager to point Amir Rashid and PC Sue Dyson towards his friends. They found Mullins at the first address they visited.

While they stood at the front door, an overweight young man by the name of Harrison Dunning denying all knowledge of his mate's whereabouts, a half-naked figure suddenly hurtled down the stairs, ran right at them, shouldering Dunning aside, and attempting to barge past Amir and into the street. Amir grabbed an arm, Sue casually stuck out a foot, and the fleeing youth obligingly tripped over it, landing heavily on a rain-soaked path.

As he lay there groaning in nothing but his pants, Amir cheerfully read him his rights.

"Now don't embarrass us all by getting in our car like that," he said. "We'll let you back inside to put some clothes on, so long as you're quick about it."

Now he sat across the table in an interview room, next to a grumpy duty solicitor who'd clearly hoped for a quiet Sunday.

Archer had decided to make an exception to her 'hands off' rule and conduct the interview herself, along with Dan Baines. She'd started to explain, but he'd held up a hand to cut her off.

"I get it, Lizzie. It's fine, really. This is about one of our own."

The resemblance between Mullins and the likeness created from CCTV images and Lauren Black's sketchy impressions was striking. Archer was as certain as she could possibly be that this was the piece of garbage who'd started the attack on Lauren and Maisie. But had he also been at the heart of what had happened to Joan, and – most important of all – did he know what had become of Charlie?

Meanwhile, the other lads were also being rounded up. Harrison Dunning and Kyle Evans were already in custody, and Ryan Lumley and Ethan Dixon should be joining them soon. Resources had been allocated to interviewing each of them as quickly as possible. Archer suspected it was already too late for Charlie, but she'd been missing for over thirty hours; if there was any hope at all, every second counted.

If they'd been involved. There was nothing she could put her finger on, but something didn't feel quite right.

Archer showed Mullins the likeness, told him how it had been created, and invited him to confirm that it was him.

He reached for cool. It wasn't something he could easily pull off, sitting there in a rumpled tee shirt and a pair of ripped jeans, his hair shaven to the scalp and a formidable pimple on his nose that Archer tried not to stare at.

"Yeah," he said with an attempt at casual that was undone by the tremor in his voice. "Yeah, I'll give you that. It does look a bit like me." He continued to study the picture, probably to avoid looking at his interrogators. His Midlands accent was strong.

"Come on, Julius," Dan urged.

"J," he said quickly. "I prefer J. Julius is a shit name. My shit mother's idea."

"You don't care for your mother?" asked Archer.

"I ain't got no mother. She walked out on me. She's a filthy lezza."

"You don't like lesbians?"

"Who would? Not natural, is it? Why? Are you one?" He grinned at her, a little cockiness mingling with his nervousness.

"And you dislike them enough to beat them up when you can find them?"

He lolled back in his chair. "Didn't say that, did I?"

"No," Archer agreed. "You didn't say that."

"So let's talk about Tuesday night," Dan said. "Actually, let's talk about the early hours of Wednesday morning. You and your mates were hanging around the car park in Aylesbury town centre, right?"

"If you say so." He didn't bother asking which one.

"Answer the question, please. Yes or no."

"So what if I was? Not a crime is it?"

"No," Dan said, "but a crime was committed. Two young women just walking to their car. Verbal abuse, then an unprovoked physical attack. Grievous bodily harm."

"Really?" Mullins shrugged. "We must've gone by then."

"Oh, please," Archer said. "You're not helping yourself, *Julius*." She drew the hated name out. "Okay, so this is what we've got. We've got DNA recovered from under the fingernails of those brave young women who put up a fight against five men who beat and kicked the crap out of them—"

"There's no need for that kind of language," objected Mullins's brief.

"Shit," Archer said, locking eyes with him. "I'm so sorry I said crap. Five men who beat the shit out of them."

The lawyer sighed.

"That DNA is a familial match to Zack Barlow, your cousin," she continued.

"So maybe it was Zack that done it."

"No. It's the DNA of a first cousin of his. We're pretty sure it matches yours. We're also pretty sure we'll recover traces of the women's blood from your uncle's car, which was almost certainly outside the women's home when their attackers trashed it. And, if we get lucky, we'll find yet more of the same blood on the clothes you tried to wash when you got home. Washing doesn't necessarily destroy DNA, Julius, did you know that? It depends on the temperature, the length of the wash, the fabric. I'll bet we'll get something off that hoodie on the back of your chair. And something from that flat, of course."

"Why not make it easy?" pressed Dan. "Save us all a lot of time and grief?"

"We're pulling in your mates," Archer added. "Do you suppose they're all going to deny everything? Or do you think maybe they'll sell you out, hoping it'll play better with the court?"

His eyes narrowed. "Look," he said. "They asked for it, all right? Fucking lezzas, parading around like normal people, and then gobbing off at us."

"Really?" Dan made a big show of thumbing back through his notebook. "That's strange. I've got here that they were minding their own business, you gave them some verbal abuse, and one of them just gave as good as she got. Isn't that what happened?"

"All they needed to do was get in their car and piss off." Julius Dunning didn't look so casual now. Archer thought she was seeing his true, very angry face. His brief had a hand on his arm and was whispering in his ear. Whatever advice he was offering wasn't being taken. "But she had to answer back, didn't she?"

"And that's your justification for putting them in hospital?" Archer shook her head. "A little bit of verbal? One of them nearly lost an eye."

"And you weren't done at that, were you?" Dan added. "You stole their bags. When did you get the idea to break into their flat? When you saw the keys? Or did you hope you'd find keys and their address in the bags? Was that why you took them?"

"It was just a laugh."

"A laugh," Dan echoed.

He scowled. "When I first found out what these lezzas do to each other... the thought of my mum doing that with another woman... it made me want to throw up. It's bloody disgusting."

"Not like shitting on someone's bed, right?"

"And this was what?" Archer said. "Payback? Punishing two strangers because your mother had hurt you?"

He shrugged.

"So did that give you a taste for it? Maybe you started looking out for more female couples to punish. And you found one on Friday night."

He stared. "What you on about?"

"Oh, come on. You must have heard it on the news."

"I don't listen to the news. Boring crap. All about how we still haven't done Brexit. I dunno why we bothered voting to leave. Fucking foreigners still coming over here and taking the piss."

"Friday night," Archer persisted. "Two more women attacked in Aylesbury. One's in hospital, the other one's missing. So where is she, Julius?"

"Where is she, J?" Dan asked, more softly. "Is she alive? You're in trouble now, but it doesn't have to get any worse."

"I dunno what you're on about," Mullins said. "Nothing to do with me."

Archer thought he looked confused. Was he was simply a better actor than she'd given him credit for?

"Chief Inspector," the duty solicitor finally decided to get more directly involved, "you can't start accusing my client of everything that happens on your patch."

"No one's doing that," Archer responded, "but when we have two similar incidents in less than a week, we have to wonder if there's a connection. Now, your client doesn't seem to be denying the serious assault on Maisie Albright and Lauren Black any more. If he's also responsible for what happened on Friday night, now's his chance to do the right thing."

"And I'm telling you I weren't there!" Mullins raised his voice. "It weren't me. Yeah, yeah, my aunt and uncle chucked me out when they knew I'd been in some sort of trouble and borrowed the car. He dropped me at the station but, soon as he'd drove off, I was on the phone to Harrison. I wasn't ready to go back and him and his mum are pushovers. He said I could crash there for a few days."

"And Friday night?" Dan pushed.

"Nah, didn't go out. We stopped in, playing Call of Duty. Harrison's mum'll back us up."

"His dad?"

"Long gone." He grinned, not a pretty sight. "At least he didn't run off with a bloke."

"We'll see what your mates have to say about that," said Archer. "See if they recall being out and you being with them. If it doesn't stack up, we'll wonder what you're hiding, even if they don't actually admit to what happened on Friday."

"For the moment, we're charging you with GBH," said Dan. "It's a maximum of five years plus an unlimited fine."

That wiped the smile off his face.

"Look." Suddenly he was just a scared teenager. "It just got out of hand. She should have shut up."

His solicitor laid a hand on his arm once more. "I really don't think you should say any more."

"I think he's said more than enough," Archer said, "with regard to Tuesday night. He needs to reflect on what he really wants to say about Friday."

*

Outside the interview room, Dan sagged, looking suddenly pasty.

Archer touched his shoulder. "You all right, mate?"

His smile was weak. "Yeah, yeah. Just tired. Didn't sleep much last night."

"Yeah," she said, "I'm worried about Joan and Charlie, too."

"Yes, that's part of it. And there's…" He looked at her. "Actually, can we have a word?"

They went into her office and closed the door. He sat opposite her and licked his lips.

"I need to tell someone," he said. "I think it's happening again."

"'It' being…?"

"The dreams, for a start. And last night, in town, I'd swear I saw him again."

"You mean Jack?"

"I suppose so. Yes. I mean, it was just like the other times. Suddenly there he was. Then he was gone. I guess it must be this bloody Claire King book, stirring it all up again. I can't tell Karen, not with the baby, I can't lay all that extra worry on her."

"But surely she'd want you to?"

She was feeling a twist of different emotions: sympathy, and worry too, about her friend's mental health; and a more selfish concern that he was going to go sick in the middle of a case where she needed him like never before.

"I'm sure she would," he conceded, "but pregnancy after age forty is considered high enough risk as it is, despite all the advances in technology. I'm not chancing it."

She thought he was wrong, and that Karen might not thank him; but she knew when his mind was made up.

"How can I help?"

He half-laughed. "You can't. It helps just to have told someone. I guess this is a heads-up that I might need more counselling. Just as I thought I'd done with all that."

"Whatever it takes."

"I know that. And don't worry. I'll see this case through before I do anything about it. I owe that much to Joan."

"I'm here any time you need to talk," she said. "Don't go bottling it all up again."

"I won't. I promise."

There was a brief, not uncomfortable silence.

"So what do you think about the boy Julius?" she asked.

"I think he's a piece of shit, but a sad one."

"But about Friday?" she pressed.

"Call of Duty? Thin, don't you think? I wonder what his mates are saying."

"But if his alibi seems to be holding up?"

He looked grim. "We'd have to look closer at his mates, I guess, but I don't know. He's got a definite axe to grind when it comes to gay women."

She leaned forward, elbows on her desk. "So what are you saying? That the other three wouldn't have attacked Joan and Charlie without him?"

"Not quite. It's possible one or more of them enjoyed what they did to Lauren and Maisie. Or our boy Julius isn't the only homophobe in the gang. But I'm a long way from convinced. We know at least one of them took no real part in Tuesday night's assault and urged J to stop. Say J and Harrison *were* playing video games together. That'd leave just two of them taking on two women. And one of those women is Joan."

She couldn't resist the smile. "Her self-defence skills *are* pretty damn good. But we know she was struck in the face, fell down and hit her head. A lucky punch?"

He shrugged. "Got to be something on those lines." But she thought she saw her own doubt reflected in his eyes.

"I mean," he went on, "yes, we've imagined an attack where no one was supposed to get killed, and then Joan's lying there, looking like she might be dead. Maybe Charlie can identify them. So why not just kill her as well? Why abduct her? What are they going to do? Keep her prisoner forever?"

"We know panic leads to bad decisions, Dan. Say they think they killed Joan by accident? Killing Charlie in cold blood to silence her is a different thing altogether. So maybe take her away while they decide what they're going to do about the mess they made."

"But take her where?"

"I can't see them having a property stashed away," she agreed.

"That aside," he said, "my real worry is that it won't take long for whoever did take her to realise they *can't* keep her forever, and then there's only one real option."

He frowned. "Or…"

"Go on."

"What if that's not what happened? What if it's a natural – for them – escalation from Tuesday? They had a good time trashing the victims' homes, but they've done that. So this time, they decide to take one of them and, I don't know, gang rape her."

"And then what? After that? Never mind where they do it. What do they do with her when they've finished with her?"

"Nothing good." He looked grim. "I guess we can't rule it out."

"Okay." She still wasn't convinced. "So we've got good interviewers working on them. If there's a hint of their involvement, they'll draw it out. If I'm not satisfied, then you and I can have a go at them. But if it's not them? And it's not a tiff between Joan and Charlie gone wrong?"

"I still can't see that. It's been over thirty-six hours now. She's not stupid. She'd have come to her senses by now and turned herself in, don't you think?"

"And we've been monitoring her phone and credit cards. None of them have been used. I agree. It doesn't ring true."

"Nothing does," said Dan. "We're missing something."

17

Down here, time seemed to pass interminably slowly. Every time she pressed the button on her Fitbit to illuminate the screen, she was astonished at how little time had passed since the last time she checked.

4.07pm on Sunday. Over forty hours – just over a day and a half since a carefree birthday night out had turned into her worst nightmare. Forty hours of not knowing whether Joan was alive or dead.

She'd seen this place, in all its cold, wet, and dirty glory, by the light of her captor's head lamp when she'd first been brought down here, forced to struggle down a metal ladder with her hands secured in front of her, a terrifying experience.

Now her left wrist was handcuffed to a thick metal ring set in the concrete floor.

The floor, awash with water, was also strewn with rubbish. By one wall stood an old metal table, badly rusting. Two filthy plastic chairs lay on the floor near to it, like dead soldiers. The only other furnishing was a rotting cupboard with its doors hanging off, containing a few bottles covered in dust and mould and some plastic packages whose contents were unidentifiable horrors that might once have been food.

And there was a rat.

A couple of times when she had turned on the torch she'd been left, it had been horrifyingly close, its beady little eyes glinting in the torch light.

At least, she hoped it was the same one. She devoutly wished she'd never read James Herbert's *The Rats* as a teenager, during her horror phase. The idea that there might be hordes of the nasty, sharp-toothed little buggers down here, just waiting to emerge and devour her alive, wasn't helping her situation.

It was tempting to keep the torch on, but she had no idea how long she was going to be down here, nor how long the battery would last. And she hadn't seen her captor since Friday night.

For all the horror and trauma of that evening, at least she'd taken some comfort when she'd been handed a bottle of water and a cereal bar, as well as the torch. More bottles and more bars had been placed on the wet concrete floor. At the time, it had at least given her some reassurance that she wasn't intended to die of hunger and thirst down here.

That reassurance had proved short-lived.

Those provisions had actually been placed well out of her reach. Even at full stretch, straining her unrestrained arm, they were so far away that they may as well not be there. And now she guessed that the real purpose of the torch was so that she could see the food and drink she needed, tantalising and taunting her, knowing they were denied to her.

Being simply left in the dark, terrified by the scrabbling of the rat – or *rats*, please God, no – would have been bad enough. This had been infinitely crueller.

There was a bucket within reach, which she'd worked out pretty quickly was her toilet. There was a door set in one of the walls that she thought might lead to an actual toilet but, again, it might as well have been on the moon.

Fortunately, that bucket had made her situation at least a little less dire than she'd first feared, because she'd found another use for it. By itself, the bucket didn't extend her reach by much but, with the addition of the leather belt cinched around her waist, she found she was able to drop it just beyond the bars and bottles and scrape them towards her. It was painstaking work, especially having to hold the torch clamped awkwardly between her teeth. The metal casing felt awkward in her mouth and tasted unpleasant, but she'd finally pulled all those precious supplies to where she could easily reach them.

It had felt like a small triumph, even though, not knowing when – or even *if* – her captor would come again, she'd still be forced to eke out her meagre provisions, with no idea as to whether there would be any more.

That bucket had initially given her some hope, that the person holding her would be coming to empty it. But she'd soon wondered if that hope too would prove false. Certainly, it was something she was no longer counting on.

So she was eating and drinking sparingly.

One of those pieces of what she'd always considered useless information, stored away in her mental filing cabinet, was how long a human being could survive without water: an incredible three to four days. She was relatively young, kept herself reasonably fit. She fancied she might have been able to last the full four days, maybe longer, on that 330 ml bottle of water, even though she had consumed perhaps a third of it before realising that it was effectively all she had.

Another fun fact she knew was that she could probably last three weeks or more without food. But that wasn't really an issue if she didn't get fluid.

Dehydration and pangs of hunger were already taking a toll, urging her to take more water, more nourishment. She had to steel herself to deny those cravings. She'd wept a lot at the start of her ordeal, until she had realised that every tear she shed was costing her body precious moisture. Since then, she'd done what she could to hold them back. When they threatened, she concentrated on her breathing, inhaling and exhaling slowly and calmly. She moved her eyes around and blinked back the tears to try to prevent them from spilling out.

One thought that had occurred to her quite early on was that she knew in theory how to pick a handcuff lock. She'd seen Joan's cuff keys, of course. They'd looked pretty basic, and Joan had said they were universal, so any cop could undo any handcuff. More importantly, Joan being Joan, she'd researched her kit, discovering that handcuff design actually hadn't changed much since 1912. She'd also looked into ways of picking the unsophisticated lock. There was plenty of guidance on the subject on the Internet, something Joan bemoaned but accepted as inevitable.

She'd shown Charlie how relatively easy it was, using a paper clip, bent into a shape that could mimic the action of a key pressing against and releasing the cuff's locking mechanism. Charlie had even given it a try herself, and had succeeded after a little perseverance.

She had no paper clip now. She'd wondered if she might try using the point of her belt buckle as a lock pick, but it was too wide to even fit into the lock and, in any case, too hard to bend into any sort of shape.

Meanwhile, she was damp and uncomfortable, shackled to a wet floor with restricted movement. Her throat, raw from yelling in vain, attested that either no one came by this place, or it was soundproof or both. But it clearly wasn't watertight. The recent rain had either got in or was feeding some sort of nearby stream that found its way inside. Either way, there was an inch or so of water on the floor. Indeed, she was pretty sure there was more than there was when she'd first been brought here. Maybe an inch and a half deep. Unable to stand, she was obliged to either kneel, sit or lie in it. She felt sodden, which made her colder.

That couldn't be good.

She'd slept on and off, drifting away when tiredness, and maybe despair, had overwhelmed her.

She had to believe her captor would return, perhaps to give her another bottle, another cereal bar. But they'd given no indication they would. Indeed, they'd said next to nothing at all, ignoring her questions and pleadings.

Perhaps it was all about power, showing her who was in charge.

Or perhaps they'd never come back, taking a sick pleasure in the thought of her dead body rotting, being gnawed at by rats, her skeleton being found years later.

No. She mustn't think like that. She'd be insane long before she was dead, if she thought like that. Even if her captor had no intention of returning, she had to believe that someone out there was searching for her. She had to believe that Joan was alive, less badly hurt than she'd seemed, and looking for her. She was the police, after all. She'd find her.

It was tempting to stretch out and go to sleep, but she knew better than that. It would be the first step towards giving up. It was Sunday afternoon, and she needed to be awake, keeping normal hours in these entirely abnormal circumstances.

She needed to amuse herself, and think positive thoughts. Thoughts of Joan. A memory came to her: the two of them dancing around Joan's flat and singing along to 'Me!' by Taylor Swift. Charlie had been a Taylor fan from the start, Joan a more recent convert, and this track had somehow become 'their song'.

Suddenly they were there together again.

"I promise…" she whispered, faltering on that first line. Then, in her mind, she seemed to hear Joan singing with her, her slightly deeper timbre supplying the harmonies, encouraging her to raise her own voice. The louder and stronger she sang, the more like a small act of defiance it felt.

By the time she hit the chorus, Charlie was belting it out, her voice echoing off the walls of her prison.

18

The one positive to have come out of the day was that Julius Mullins and his miserable little tribe had all been charged with the vicious assault on Maisie and Lauren. It had given the women some comfort. For Lauren, at least a little of the fear of returning home had receded, even though that wasn't happening any time soon. The locks had all been changed, family had rallied round, and the insurance company had turned up trumps with a promise to replace, repair and redecorate, erasing all traces of the outrage that had taken place there.

There was a good chance that the youths would plead guilty to the charges, sparing the women the ordeal of giving evidence in court. They would get justice. Baines hoped that, given time, the physical and mental wounds would heal.

Mullins and the others continued to deny any knowledge of, or involvement in, Joan's injury or Charlie's disappearance. And, although no one was talking openly about it, the feeling that this wasn't going to end well was almost palpable.

Plans were already being drawn up for more searches of woodland and other potential body dump sites. Superintendent Stowe was supportive of the plan and even threw in a few suggestions, although he had cheerfully pointed out that a killer determined to get rid of a body could take it anywhere in the country. Charlie's remains could even be in the North Sea, for all they knew.

It was getting on for 10pm when Baines arrived home.

"Well, you look shattered," Karen remarked. "Will you want much to eat at this time of night? I mean, you need something, but you don't want to go to bed on a full stomach, either."

He flopped on the sofa. "Don't worry. I'll get myself a bowl of cereal and a banana in a minute. How are you?"

"So-so. Bit tired. I think the bump's starting to show and I'm going to have to get bigger bras."

He looked her over. "I think you're right about the bump. Bigger boobs, you reckon? That's a bonus!"

She rolled her eyes. "Talk about one-track mind. Anyway, I had a chat with Mum and Dad, which was nice. The prospect of a grandkid seems to have really brought them round."

"Good," he said. "I'm glad."

"Any developments? How's Joan?"

"Making progress of sorts, according to the doctors. She's speaking, apparently – that is she's sort of saying words. They're completely unintelligible, but they reckon it's a good sign. Showing more response to stimulus too. They're hopeful she'll wake up soon, but less optimistic that she'll remember anything about the attack or the attackers. So chances are it won't help us find Charlie."

"Do you think she's dead?" Karen could be blunt sometimes.

He sighed. "Honestly? I still have some hope, but I think now that it's more likely than not we won't find her alive."

"Oh, poor Joan."

"But we're not writing her off yet."

"And what about Mac? Anything new from him?"

"I don't know. I've got a few missed calls from him. Texts and voicemails too. I need to catch up with him."

"So why haven't you?"

Should he tell her what was scaring him? That the dreams had returned? About that vision? He knew how she'd worried about him back when he'd been on the edge of a breakdown. Now was the time to protect them both. And their baby.

"It's just been one of those days," he said, knowing it sounded hollow. And, despite the fears he felt, he also remained hopeful that something would turn up. The conflict and indecision were tearing him apart.

"Why don't you call him now?" she suggested. "I'll make some tea and get you that cereal."

He knew when he was being handled.

"Yeah. No time like the present. I still think the end product will be a fat zero, but I guess you never know." He took his phone out. "Okay. Go and get the kettle on."

She smiled. "Good choice."

As she headed for the kitchen, he speed-dialled Mac's number. Every single time it had appeared on his phone screen today, he'd had the same feeling of trepidation he was feeling now. Butterflies fluttered in his stomach.

"Danny boy! Where have you been?"

"Sorry, Mac. Pig of a day."

"Any progress with your missing lassie?"

He ignored the question. "So how can I help?"

"Well. You remember I told you how things can change in a cold case. The passage of time, altered circumstances?"

"Yep."

"So here's the thing. I tracked down those suspects we looked at back when the case was live. Bray, Carter and Creed."

"Anything?" He couldn't deny a slight twinge of interest.

"Well, as you know, Kevin Bray's dead, but his old manager absolutely insists she remembers checking and double checking the rosters for the times of the murders. She's one hundred per cent certain he was at work on three of the dates. I also double checked with the hotel in Liverpool where Ollie Carter claimed to have been staying when Martha Hallett and Chloe Morris were killed. When Eliot Hallett was taken. I thought that'd be a busted flush with data retention rules being such a thing, but they're old school and keen to help the police..."

"You said you were the police?" Baines felt his hackles rising.

"Not exactly. I reminded them of when I was working the case, and they sort of assumed."

Baines sighed. He'd almost forgotten how much Mac had always had his own way of doing things.

"So was he there or not?"

"Oh, he was there. No, it's Antony Creed who's interesting. The sex offender?"

"Yeah. But he had strong alibis too."

"Aye. In Leicester with his parents one time and with his probation officer for a couple of other killings. The rest I don't recall. Home alone?"

"Something like that. I think. No one to corroborate for him, as I remember." As if every detail wasn't etched on his brain.

Baines wondered where this was going. "Still, even if you discounted the parents vouching for him, a probation officer's pretty watertight."

"Except, now she isn't. Watertight, I mean."

Baines's pulse quickened, his attention finally captured. "She's saying she lied?"

"I know it's Sunday and it's late, but can I come round?"

"I think you'd better."

*

"It turns out Antony Creed's probation officer, Carol Eustace, was having an affair with him around the time of the killings," Mac said. "In fairness, they were both single people, but it was all totally unprofessional, obviously."

They were in Baines's living room with a pot of black coffee in front of them. Karen had left them to it and gone to bed. He knew she'd be sitting up reading, waiting to see what he had to say.

"You're telling me," Baines said. "Surely she'd have been in trouble if the probation service had found out."

"Doubtless. But they didn't. Then he asked her to marry him, so she left the service. They left it a discreet interval."

"So she lied for him?"

"He did have appointments those days, but now she says he skipped them. They weren't the only ones. She claims he always gave her some cock and bull story she didn't entirely believe about having to sort out some family trouble and asked her to cover for his absence. She said she was under his spell, thought he was a reformed character. That *she'd* helped reform him. She trusted him, and she thought she loved him. She didn't want him to be in hot water for missing his appointments."

"Okay," Baines said. "So why is she telling us this now?"

146

"Well, they did get married, but it didn't go well. He started behaving violently towards her, especially sexual violence. Rape fantasies, increasingly degrading acts that he frightened her into. The last straw was when he tied her up and put a plastic bag over her head."

"He did what?" A sort of sick excitement twisted in his guts.

"I know. Not quite cling film, but the similarity is there, don't you think? Anyhow, she left him. He tracked her down and stalked her, but she found strength and support from some friends. Ended up with a divorce and a restraining order. Now she admits she has her doubts about any of the stories he gave her when she covered for him. It's been on her conscience, but she was scared of getting into trouble."

Baines forced himself to think. "But what about the so-called family trouble? And the visit to the parents?"

"Useless trying to verify that now. Dad's dead, and Mum has dementia big time. She doesn't even know she has a son, much less what he was doing when."

"And the parents wouldn't have been the soundest of alibis anyway. Nor, as it turns out, was a woman who was in love with him."

"Exactly. If we believe Carol Eustace, he has no real alibis at all. Home alone, with his parents, with his girlfriend. A man with a history of sex offences with an interest in suffocation." He looked Baines in the eye. "What do you reckon?"

After all these years, Baines found that he hardly dared hope this was what it appeared to be. A long way from a conclusive case, but a real and credible suspect. He ran the information through his mind a couple of times. Mac drank his coffee, leaving him some thinking space.

"Right," Baines said finally. "What I think is that we should definitely have a word with our Mr Creed. I find myself wondering though. I see why she might have lied at the time, but she'd know better than most what a serious offence that is, especially given she knew the case we were investigating. When she broke up with him, she could have come and told us the truth then, but she didn't. So why does she cave in and spill the beans now, as soon as you ask her a few questions?"

Mac smiled slyly. "You wound me. Didn't you know how very persuasive I can be?" He poured himself more coffee, waved the pot at Baines, who took a swig from his mug before holding it out for a top-up.

"No," Mac continued, pouring, "I asked her that. As I said, it seems it hadn't sat right with her, not once she'd realised what kind of man he really was."

"So did she think he might be the Invisible Man?"

"I don't think she was sure he was. She just wasn't sure he wasn't any more. She said it was a call she'd been half-expecting for years. She'd been dreading it, but hoping for it too, and it was a relief to finally get it off her chest. To be honest, I think he might have been dominating her right from the start."

"See, that's where it doesn't quite ring true for me. I remember you and me interviewing Creed. I think maybe someone else spoke to Ms Eustace. But my recollection is he'd formed an attachment to an underage girl he tried to take away with him. I don't think he actually did jail time."

"Not quite true. He'd been in custody for about six months when it came to trial. But the judge was lenient. Gave him eighteen months suspended plus probation, which is where he met the lovely Ms Eustace."

"I remember him. A bit pathetic and creepy. Not exactly Mr Charisma. How could he weave such a spell over a woman in her position?"

"Damned if I know. But love is blind, laddie. We both know that. Maybe she just imagined she saw something in him. Or maybe she saw saving him as a project, and he played up to that. Hell, maybe he was planning a series of murders already and thought a probation officer in his corner would be a useful thing."

"Maybe," Baines acknowledged. "It leaves a load of questions, though. Like how did he choose his victims? How did he get in and out of their homes undetected?" He swallowed a lump in his throat. "Why did he stop... when he did?"

"As to the first question," Mac said, "how he chose them? I still think those parent and child groups Robin Watson gave those talks to are worth a look. Maybe someone will remember Creed hanging around. Did you ever get a number for Watson?"

"No. Sorry. You know what it's like." He hated that he'd not followed through, but he'd completely forgotten.

"Och, don't worry. You thought he was in Oxfordshire? I'll find him myself."

"No, hold on." Baines picked up his phone and called up a number from his contact list. He texted it to Mac. "Give her a ring. DS Amy Petrescu. She'll be able to find him for you." He tapped out another text, this time to Amy, warning her to expect the call.

Mac checked the number on his own phone. "Thanks. But what I want to know is this. Don't you think it's worth asking Antony Creed all those questions? Officially, I mean?"

He thought again about the bad timing but, then again, would there ever be a good time?

"Yes," he said. "Yes, I think we should talk to him. I'll speak to my boss in the morning."

19

Monday morning. Over fifty hours since Charlie Ward disappeared. The very last thing Archer needed to hear today was a reason to divert resources into Dan Baines's resurrection of the Invisible Man case. She'd known from that first moment he'd told her about that damned book that it would spell trouble, and she wasn't wrong.

During her time at the Met, it had been the national media that they'd all been on edge about. Sure, the local rags could be a nuisance, but they could also come in handy as a conduit with the communities they and the police served. Even colleagues here in Thames Valley and in neighbouring forces spoke of the local press with ambivalence.

Everyone understood that bad news stories sold papers. So it was never a real surprise when police fallibility hit the front pages, whilst the product of months of hard work, leading to an arrest, a conviction, making the streets a little safer, seemed to get less space – squeezed onto page seven or eleven.

But no one else seemed to have a Claire King.

Behind the pretty face lay a sharp mind, and underneath the skimpy clothes the heart of a crusader beat. But Archer wouldn't be surprised if Dan's suspicion that she was bored with the *Echo* was accurate. Oh, she might make editor one day, but why wouldn't she yearn for something more? It might explain why she dug so much deeper and pushed so much harder than the average local journo. Maybe she was trying to build a portfolio that would eventually get her taken seriously in the sectors she so wanted to move on to.

It was hard to believe that this book wasn't part of such a strategy.

Archer knew Dan had always been immune to Claire's charms, and he might well have flatly refused to have anything to do with her project, had his old mate McNeill not been brought into the picture. The bloody man had gone way beyond his fact-checking brief, as Claire had almost certainly hoped he would, and now he'd found an inconsistency in one of the suspects' stories.

She should be pleased that there was a potential lead in this case that meant so much to Dan, but the timing was terrible.

And yet.

Could she really just put it on a back burner until Charlie was found, dead or alive, or they were finally forced to scale down a search that had run out of steam and ideas?

The latter was a long way off yet, and she prayed it wouldn't come to that. But she knew that in the meantime there was the risk that Antony Creed would get wind of his alibis unravelling. If he really was the Invisible Man, the author of at least eleven deaths – almost certainly twelve, including Jack Baines – he could attempt to flee the country.

Dan sat patiently across the desk from her, knowing better than to interrupt her train of thought.

She sighed. "Okay. We need to get him in and question him about what he was really doing those times when he skipped probation and his girlfriend covered for him. But you can't be part of it, Dan."

He inclined his head. "I know that."

"Good, because you absolutely can't. I'll put Lara and Amir on it. And I'd better get hold of the case files."

"You know access to them is controlled? Because of all the stuff that was never put in the public domain?"

"Yeah. The last thing you'd have wanted was serial confessors or, worse still, a copycat. Then or now. But I have access. The old boss told me whoever sits in this chair always has access. Don't worry, I'll keep the files to myself. Even you won't get to see them."

She studied his face. "Are you okay? Only you look exhausted. This Joan and Charlie thing is demanding enough, without all this other crap. Any more dreams and visions?"

"I dreamed of Jack last night. Usual thing. Not *my* Jack, the Jack I remember before..." He'd spoken to her before about the day his family had been destroyed. It was rare for his voice to crack as it did now. He paused for a moment. "Sorry. Anyway, this is a fantasy Jack about nineteen or twenty, the one I imagined I saw the other night. He wears a leather jacket."

"He's still ageing in real time in your dreams then?"

"Yeah, all part of the wish fulfilment my counsellor reckons is part of my problem. You remember when this started he'd be a kid, playing football with me in our garden? Well now we're having a pint together. The Old Swan in Cheddington, unless I'm mistaken. And you know, it all adds up."

"In what way?"

"My dad wasn't big on going for a beer, but him and Mum came over soon after Lou and I got married, to see what we'd done to the house. We'd redecorated, got a bit more furniture than we started out with. Out of the blue, he suggested we went for a pint. We'd tried a few pubs in the area, including our local, of course, but I quite liked the Swan, so I took him there. Now I'm dreaming of being there with my own son. Which, by the way, I'd probably love to do now, if he was alive."

"Jesus, Dan, call your counsellor and make an appointment. Do it now. That's not a request, by the way."

"Yeah," he said. "Yes, I will. I'm still not telling Karen though. But then maybe we're on to something with Creed." He smiled, a little crookedly. "Just imagine if he breaks down after all these years and confesses. Maybe he'll even tell us what became of Jack."

"Dan, don't get too many hopes up, not yet. And let's not jump our fences. All we know is what the woman who used to be his probation officer has told Mac. It could all be true, but it doesn't mean he did the murders on the days she covered for him. And yes, I know serial killers can get some sort of turn-on out of killing their victims, but it still seems a bit funny to me that a man like Creed, who systematically seduced a young girl, would have women in his power and not do anything to them sexually."

"Not impossible, though. The actual killing is a different sort of thrill."

"I suppose. Then again, this Carol Eustace may be spinning a fantasy of her own. We need to keep open minds, that's all."

"Sure," he said. "Can I watch the interview on the screen?"

"If you think it's a good idea."

"I don't know about that. But I think I need to."

"Okay. I'll get him picked up. Meanwhile, we're no nearer a breakthrough over Joan and Charlie. I mean we've charged Julius and his gang with the assault on Lauren and Maisie."

"That's a start. At least those two will get some justice."

"Yes, and that's good. But there's still not a shred of evidence that they were even out in the town on Friday. And two of the five offenders reckon they were really upset about what happened on Tuesday night. It was only peer pressure and fear of Julius that stopped them from walking away. As it is, they insist they were virtual bystanders in the violence and what was done in the flat afterwards."

He nodded. "And we believe them, don't we?"

"I do, actually."

"Me too."

"I think it'll be a very long time before they willingly venture out with that particular group again."

"So basically, we've got nothing." He frowned. "I said yesterday I thought we must be missing something."

"And aren't we?"

"Yes, but maybe not in the sense I meant. I was thinking maybe there was something we'd seen or heard but not picked up on."

"Something we overlooked?" She'd been thinking much the same. "And now?"

"Now I'm fearing it could be something we haven't seen at all. Like – I don't know – some random person hearing about a homophobic attack and thinking it's a good idea. Some racist who just doesn't like seeing a mixed race couple, especially a same-sex couple. Someone from Joan or Charlie's past we don't know about."

"We've spoken to their parents," she said. "Their friends. Charlie's ex. None of them is aware of anyone specific who'd wish them harm. Although obviously, they're both in jobs with the potential to piss people off. No trouble at work that anyone knows of…"

"Charlie handled domestic violence cases," Dan pointed out. "That must put her in contact with some nasty pieces of work. No aggression, no abuse, no threats?"

"Amir and Jason spoke to a fair few of her colleagues over the weekend. And, of course, a bit of that, but not recently."

"What about an abusive husband or partner who loses access not only to the woman he's been using as a punch bag, but to his kids as well? And then a period of mounting resentment until something snaps?"

She examined the idea. "I suppose it's possible. The 'snapping' thing doesn't sit with me though. He'd have to decide to take revenge on Charlie, maybe follow her home from work, then attack both her and Joan. One man against two women, one of whom is Joan, who's no pushover."

"I don't know," he said. "Joan can certainly look after herself, but all the thinking is that the attack came out of the blue, catching her off guard."

"But then he just abducts Charlie and holds her somewhere? No, that all smacks of a plan to me, not snapping. And why now?"

"Something changed? Or how about this? A recent client's other half shows no emotion: no anger, no threats. Precisely because he *is* calmly planning what he wants to do to this bitch of a lawyer. Maybe he's holding her because she's a substitute punch bag for the partner Charlie took away from him."

Archer cocked an eyebrow. "You've got a really sick mind, DI Baines."

"I've seen some sick things, DCI Archer."

"All right. Take Jason and visit Charlie's practice. Ask some more questions on those lines and see if there's anything that sounds worth a follow up."

"You said I could watch the Antony Creed interview."

Friendship and professionalism warred inside her for a moment. "Sorry, Dan, I haven't the manpower to have you kicking your heels waiting for that to happen. This thing about past clients was your idea and I need you to run with it. If you're back in time for the interview, all well and good. Otherwise, you'll have to make do with the recording."

"Fine," he said, a little sulkily. Then, "Sorry, Lizzie. You're right. But if we get no leads from Charlie's firm, I'm not sure where we go from there."

It was exactly the thought that was gnawing at her insides.

"I think," she said, "that we'll have nothing left except to hope Joan wakes up soon. And that she has some memories of the attack."

"And if she doesn't?"

A desperate fear of failure washed over her. "Honestly? I don't know."

20

"I'm really sorry, Inspector," said Ivan Wright, Managing Partner of Wright Farleigh solicitors, "but you must know we can't just talk willy-nilly about our clients. There's data protection, legal professional privilege, and then there's the clients themselves. Domestic abuse survivors often carry the mental scars for years after they get away from their abuser. Some spend the rest of their lives looking over their shoulders. Some behave as if they're still being controlled for years, still feeling they need permission to do things most of us don't even think about. Like popping to the shops, even going to the loo in one case we had. I can't just—"

"I get it," Baines said. "But I'm not asking for clients' names, not even their exes' names yet. This is Charlie Ward, we're talking about."

"I know that." Wright was about fifty years old, dapper in navy chalk stripes, pink shirt and a navy tie with pink polka dots. He still had a full head of dark hair, with waves that might have been sculpted. And he looked troubled. "Charlie is a very valued and very well-liked member of our team. She's hard-working, caring and professional and also great fun to work with. She's made domestic abuse cases her speciality over the past year or so, and she's passionate about it."

"So why can't you help us?" Jason Bell asked, clearly irritated. "You know she's missing. You know time's of the essence. Doesn't that matter?"

"Of course it matters, Constable. Don't you think I'd hand over all her files in a heartbeat if I could? If it would help?"

"Look," Baines said, making his tone conciliatory. "I understand the problem, Mr Wright, I really do. But maybe we can take this one small step at a time, and see where it gets us?"

Wright had dropped everything when Baines had called ahead, and had opted to meet with them in the rather grandly named 'boardroom', basically a narrow room containing two tables pushed together with chairs around it. There was a smaller table with a coffee machine and a basket of catering packs of biscuits. The pictures on the wall looked like one of the office juniors might have gone out and grabbed the first three random prints they could lay hands on: a landscape, an abstract and a portrait of a Spanish senorita.

His colleague and fellow senior partner, Tara Farleigh, had said little so far. Now she spoke.

"That can't do any harm, can it, Ivan? We know where to draw the line."

She was neat in a black suit with a white shirt blouse. She wore a plain gold brooch at her throat. Her name suggested posh education, hockey sticks and horses, and fancy apartments in the Knightsbridge area. Tara Farleigh might have had all those things, but her accent was pure London East End.

He looked uneasy. "I suppose. All right, let's see how we get on."

"You said she'd been specialising in domestic abuse for about a year," Baines said. "How did that come about?"

"She asked us, didn't she, Tara?"

"That's right. She'd just split with her partner and she was looking for a new challenge. We weren't sure at first, but she's very good with the clients."

A thought fleeted across Baines's mind. "Who was dealing with those cases before? How did they react to her taking it over?"

Wright smiled. "I see what you're getting at. But Charlie didn't really take it over as such. The truth is, we had no real specialist. People dealt as required. That was sort of her point. More cases were being brought to us, and she argued that we needed some real expertise, rather than the scattergun approach we'd been taking."

"And the clients were comfortable with her? Most of them must be in a pretty bad place when they come to you."

"They are. She seems to elicit their trust, and she's very supportive."

"And generally, how do the alleged abusers react to her?"

"Are we straying into individual cases?"

"Not yet. Just generally."

"Well, she doesn't always see them," Farleigh said, forestalling her colleague. "In court, of course. If there's any out of court dialogue, it's more often through their solicitors, if they have them. But there's the odd session where both parties are present at a meeting. It can vary, from what Charlie's told me. Turning on the charm, trying to seem like the last person on earth who'd hurt or control their wife or girlfriend. A couple have overstepped that mark and more or less flirted with her." She laughed. "Not only is it counter-productive, but obviously they're barking up the wrong tree."

"Aggression?"

"A few."

"Anger directed at Charlie?"

"None that really fazed her, I think. There was one who made a big deal of her, in his view, encouraging his partner to leave him and seek injunctions against him just to make money for the firm. He said they could have worked things out, if she hadn't interfered. This, by the way, a man who beats the crap out of the woman he's supposed to love, then says he'll never do it again. But there's always a next time."

"Yep," Baines said. "We've seen some of that. One or two have ended up as murder cases."

"And there was the one, quite recently, who called her a dyke bitch."

"Really?" Jason interjected. "But how did he know that?"

Tara Farleigh shrugged. "Well, the client knew. Charlie makes no secret of it, and she chats to clients to put them at ease. I think this client went back to her abuser twice after getting up the courage to come to us. She left him in the end, but she might well have told him Charlie was gay."

Baines processed this. Was it relevant? Would Charlie's sexuality make the man even angrier at her?

Maybe. But the leap from there to the events of Friday night was a big one.

"Have any abusers in Charlie's cases actually gone to prison?"

"I don't think so. Ivan?"

"No. I think there was a suspended sentence. Some restraining orders. Probation a couple of times. You must know, Inspector, that, while coercive control is now a specific offence, domestic violence isn't. A perpetrator could be charged with assault, maybe rape. You lot take it more seriously than you used to, but charges and convictions are still falling."

"And has she ever helped a victim to disappear, to get away from their abuser?"

"She might put them in touch with refuges early in a case, if they need to escape their home. It's down to the police to deal with ongoing behaviours like stalking, breaching restraining orders."

Baines chewed his lip. "You know, we really do need the names of those men who showed anger towards Charlie."

"I can see that." Wright looked distressed. "But if we reveal their names, we're effectively identifying their victims too. Plus, if you go questioning them, it could stir everything up again, possibly putting our clients in fresh danger."

"But *we* could contact them, Ivan," Farleigh suggested. "The clients, I mean. Explain the situation. Seek their consent."

"Yes," he said. "Yes, I suppose we could do that."

"How long's it going to take?" Jason sounded frustrated.

"I'll get on it right away," Farleigh said. "But I'll have to remind myself which cases they were, then it's a matter of getting in touch. I can't promise how they'll react."

"But," Jason spluttered, "criminal investigations trump data protection."

"They do," Ivan Wright agreed, "but legal professional privilege is a different matter."

"Let's not do this," Baines said, giving his colleague a pointed look. Then he turned his attention back to the lawyers. "Seek those consents, if you would."

"We'll do our best," Farleigh said, "but I wouldn't hold my breath for a breakthrough. Charlie's tough. I didn't get the impression she felt especially threatened, or scared. I think she would have said so."

"Understood," said Baines. "But can you do better than your best?"

She inclined her head. "I'll give it a go."

*

Archer didn't know what she was expecting Antony Creed to look like. She knew nothing of the man himself, other than what she'd been told about him.

She didn't know whether to expect a grubby little pervert, or a handsome, charismatic character. Creed turned out to be neither. Not especially good-looking, but not bad looking either. Evidently uncomfortable being questioned at a police station, but that wasn't unusual. Slightly underweight, but otherwise unremarkable in almost every way.

Except for the eyes.

There was a staring intensity there, plain to see even on the monitor, as Lara Moseley and Amir Rashid started their interview with him. He'd asked for his solicitor to be present, and a boy who looked like he'd just discovered shaving now sat next to him. His suit reminded her of a school uniform his parents thought he'd grow into one day.

Outside it was raining again, and it looked like it had set in for the day. Fat raindrops slid down the window of the room from which Archer was watching the proceedings. The interview room had no windows and she knew that, on days like this, it could feel especially airless and oppressive. That was why it had been chosen. To put some extra pressure on Antony Creed.

"First of all," Lara said, "thank you for coming in."

"I wasn't exactly given a choice," he said, a rough rawness to his voice. "What's this all about?"

"I want to take you back to 2001," she said. "I'm sure you'll remember that. There were a series of murders—"

"Oh, for heaven's sake!" More exasperation than anger. "Really? After all this time?"

"You were questioned."

"It was routine. I was on the local sex offenders list. You had to look at me, I get that. I had alibis for the dates and times of the murders. They were horrible crimes, but nothing to do with me."

"Inspector." The boy solicitor had a surprisingly deep voice. He could probably sing bass baritone. "I must ask why my client is being questioned now in relation to a case that's getting on for twenty years old, from which he was eliminated."

"Yes," Lara agreed. "The thing is, it turns out those alibis may not be as sound as we were led to believe. I was really sorry to hear about your parents, by the way, but obviously we can't now double check their recollections of you being with them on any of the occasions in question. And we know there were some occasions where you had no alibis at all."

"It's my ex, isn't it?" Creed said. "What lies has she been telling now?"

"Let's just say her memory isn't what it was."

"She's lying. She can't help herself. She's not right." He leaned forward. "The thing is, Inspector, she obviously got some sort of crush on me when I was on probation. At our last appointment, she suggested we go on seeing each other as friends."

That was different to Carol Eustace's account that the relationship had started while he was her offender.

"Well," he continued, "her idea of friendship... nothing was off limits. She was into some pretty filthy sex, you know? Like, really kinky. Once, she—"

"I don't need the details at this stage, thank you," Lara said.

Archer could see his eyes were fixed on the female DI. Was he watching to see what effect his words were having on her? It wouldn't be the first time she'd thought a sex offender was getting a buzz out of describing sexual acts to police officers, especially to women.

"Well, anyway," he said, "for someone with my delicate mental health – it was like she cast a spell over me. When she said she should quit her job and we should get married, I couldn't refuse. I mean, have you met her?"

Lara shook her head.

"You wouldn't dream what she was really like. She seems so ordinary. You wouldn't dream she was so depraved. She liked being tied up, me pretending to rape her. But it was only when she told me to put a plastic bag over her head that I managed to draw a line."

Either Creed was very clever, and was making Carol Eustace out to be the instigator of the behaviour she'd complained about. Or Creed's ex-wife was a malicious liar.

"So what happened?" Amir prompted.

"She got angry that I wouldn't do it. I realised then that I was being used, and that I wasn't really in love with her at all. I asked for a divorce. She refused at first, but when I proposed we do it amicably, without her nasty little foibles having to become known, she went along with it. But I remember her parting words."

"Which were?"

"She said if ever she could do me a bad turn, she wouldn't hesitate."

"What did you make of that?" Lara asked.

"At the time? Not much. I thought it was all talk. But, seeing as we're here and talking about 2001, I'm betting she's walking back on those alibis she gave me when you were failing to catch the Invisible Man. Just to drop me in the shit."

"And herself too," Amir pointed out. "Lying to the police is a serious business."

"Of course it is." Creed sighed heavily. "But I'm betting she's told you *I* was the pervert in the relationship, that *I* controlled *her*, that she felt she had to lie for me. Those appointments? Of course I kept them."

"Let me get this straight," Lara said. "She goes along with an amicable divorce so no one will hear about what you call her depravity?"

"Yep."

"But now she's happy enough to talk about all that stuff, but to try and blame it on you?"

"That's about the size of it." He leaned forward again, lowering his voice. "You have to understand, Inspector, she's a pretty sick woman. I begged her to get professional help, but she wouldn't hear of it. If she's got worse, she might even believe the bullshit she's telling you."

He sat back. "Like I say, I'm a changed man. Life's different for me. Pretty lonely, actually. I long for a normal relationship, but how will I find one? I mean, there's dating apps, and some of them screen for registered sex offenders, but quite a few free ones don't. But I don't feel comfortable using them without being honest about my past and, let's face it, it's a bit of a turn-off, isn't it?"

He shook his head, a sad gesture. "See, that was the thing about Carol. She already knew my history. I didn't have to hide it from her. Now I see that it was my history that attracted her to me. Instead of appreciating that I had problems and really needed help, she thought I was as twisted as her."

"Hang on, though," Lara said. "You did have help. You had counselling sessions. Therapy. Did courses. I thought all that was supposed to have worked?"

"Ah, but it did work, Inspector. That's the irony. All that really did help me change, and that was down to Carol for arranging it. But the more I changed, the more her sick games disgusted me. In the end, I couldn't even get an erection without her lending a hand, so to speak."

He smiled at his own little joke. Putting images in his interviewers' minds and doubtless enjoying the idea of them not being able to help but see them.

"As I say," he concluded, "the decision to divorce was mutual."

A man who liked to play games, Archer thought. The Invisible Man had liked games, too. The calling card sketches left at the murder scenes. And the whole ritual around his crimes. The murder method, suffocation with cling film, had to mean something to him. And why did he take the children away, only to murder them along with his next target?

"Are you sure it was mutual?" Lara asked him.

"That's how I remember it, yes. Why, what's happened? Did Carol seek you out with these lies? Or did you have some reason to check my alibis out? Has new evidence come to light? I can't see what, given that I'm innocent."

"Then you're going to have to help me out," Amir said. "You seem to be saying she's unbalanced. That she decides to drop you in it, but waits until now?"

He shrugged. "What do I know? I suggest you speak to Carol again, but really push her. See if you think her story adds up."

"Detective Inspector," the solicitor said. "Have you any further questions for my client? because this is sounding like you're trying to clear up some of your old cases and clutching at straws. It seems he was only questioned as a formality in the first place, and now, years later, when he's rebuilt his life as best he can, you're harassing him again on the word of a vindictive ex-wife."

Archer found herself troubled. She didn't like Antony Creed, but that didn't make him a serial killer. And he was right. They needed to tread very carefully before they went too much further purely on an alibi recanted by his former spouse. Unless Carol Eustace could prove he didn't keep those probation appointments, and they could turn up evidence that he was elsewhere, ideally in the vicinity of at least one of the Invisible Man's victims at the relevant time, the whole line of enquiry was thin, to say the least.

They needed to have another word with Creed's ex.

As if reading her mind, Lara brought the interview to a close. "We'll take a break while we make some more enquiries," she said.

"You're releasing my client?" the boy solicitor demanded.

"Not just yet. We have twenty-four hours. But we'll speak again as soon as we can."

He looked about to object, but Creed languidly raised a hand, forestalling him.

"Anything for the forces of justice," he said. "And it would certainly be nice to see *you* again, DI Moseley."

Even on the monitor, Archer could see the way he fixed that intense gaze on Lara, as his lips curved into what he presumably thought was a flirtatious smile. The effect was chilling.

But that wasn't nearly enough to build a case with.

21

The exclamation sign on Charlie's Fitbit told her that the battery would need charging soon. Although, in reality, she knew it would still last several hours, the thought that she could lose her one means of keeping track of the time alarmed her. It was bad enough being hungry and thirsty. She wasn't sure why knowing how long she'd been here was so important to her: it just was.

How often had she laughed at Joan for wearing a watch on one wrist and her Fitbit on the other, just so she could tell the time if the Fitbit battery failed. Charlie used her phone as backup, but Joan maintained that phone batteries could die too. She'd had the last laugh. Charlie's bag, with her phone inside, had been taken from her, of course. How much simpler it would have been to get rescued otherwise. She had no idea where she was, but the GPS on her phone would know. A quick call to the police and they'd be here in no time.

The police. She'd call Joan first, of course. But would she, could she, answer?

In her mind's eye, Charlie could see the woman she loved falling, hear the sickening crack as her head hit the pavement. Herself screaming Joan's name before a hand had clamped over her mouth. The threats that had been frightening enough to silence her.

The image made her parched mouth feel even drier.

She took a water bottle from inside her jacket and helped herself to a sip. She'd stashed her food and water there because the water on the floor was definitely higher than it had been, and she'd been concerned that it would ruin the cereal bars and maybe even float some of her water bottles away.

What provisions she had, she intended to keep.

The risen water level concerned her, especially since she had shone the torch around the walls and seen what looked suspiciously like a tide mark. This cell was maybe nine feet from concrete floor to concrete ceiling, and the line – which admittedly didn't look particularly recent – was a bit more than halfway up the wall. Maybe as much as four or five feet. With her wrist cuffed to the floor, that was definitely a lot higher than she would be able to raise her head.

And it had rained a lot recently. She could tell when it was raining, because she could hear the water running somewhere, wherever it was getting in, like a tap turned on.

Still, she told herself, it must take a lot of rain over a sustained period for the water to rise to the level of that tide mark. And it must be able to escape somehow. She supposed it must have risen to that level only as the result of some sort of rare flash flood. Surely it would take a sustained torrent of biblical proportions to cause that?

She refused to scare herself with the possibility of drowning down here. She had enough to be scared about already. Like whether her abductor intended ever to return.

It was the middle of Monday now. Two and a half days into her ordeal. She was still eking out her supplies, making them last as long as possible. So she was desperately hungry and thirsty all the time. Her mouth was dry and sticky, her lips feeling parched and cracked. She felt light-headed, with a gnawing sensation in her stomach. Her head ached constantly, and was getting worse.

It didn't help that sleeping was already almost impossible, even though she was tired to the marrow of her bones. She was terrified that she would end up in a sleep too deep to awaken from, face down in the water, and drown. The best she had managed was some sort of drowsy wakefulness, on her knees with her palms braced on the floor.

And she couldn't remember when she'd last felt the urge to pee. In one way, that was no bad thing – using the bucket in her constrained state wasn't exactly easy, and there was neither toilet paper nor washing facilities. Yet she knew she was getting badly dehydrated. She was going to have to start drinking more, which would deplete her clean supplies more quickly.

She had managed to scoop water from the floor into an empty water bottle, and she thought she'd continue doing that. It might be one positive aspect of the water ingress into her miserable environment. She knew it couldn't be clean and she didn't really fancy drinking it, but she supposed she'd drink anything if it came to it.

She wasn't singing any more. She continued to run through songs in her head, but she'd got to a point where singing out loud sapped her strength. Just one more resource she needed to conserve.

But, whatever lay in store for her – even death itself – there was one thing she wouldn't allow this nightmare to do.

It wouldn't break her.

She had learned to be strong a long time ago. She'd fight to survive with everything she had. And, if she died, she'd go out with strength and dignity.

22

Baines had barely returned to the office when his phone rang.

"We're still working our way through Charlie's case files," Tara Farleigh said, with little preamble, "but we have two ex-husbands so far that you might be interested in. I've spoken to both the clients, and they're willing to speak to you."

"Great," he said. "Thanks. Go ahead."

Ten minutes later, he looked in on Lizzie.

"I've got a couple of names," he told her. "Men who were aggressive with Charlie over domestic abuse cases she handled. One's a Jeffrey Cunningham, but I think we might easily cross his name off."

"Why's that?"

"He's no longer in the country. He's working in Vietnam at the moment. Some sort of tech consultancy. Obviously, we need to check that he's there now, and has been there the past few days, but…"

"Get Will to look into that," Lizzie said. "And the other?"

"Edward Smithson. Nasty case, by the sound of it. Controlled his wife Heather's every movement. He also put her in hospital three times. You can imagine the bullshit explanations she gave for that before she finally left him. Fortunately her sister's no fool, realised what was going on, and helped her find the courage to do something. She's living in Wales now, under a new name, but she's willing to help us if it stops anyone else being hurt."

"And is this Edward Smithson still in the country?"

"Bedford, by all accounts."

"Really? That's, what?"

"Less than forty miles away. You can probably drive it in under an hour if you put your foot down."

"Speak to the local cops."

"Jason's already on it. He's going to ask them to find him and invite him to have a little chat with us, but make it clear that it's not really an optional invitation."

"Good. If he can't account for his movements on Friday, maybe we're getting somewhere."

"Maybe. How's Lara getting on with Antony Creed?"

"A lot of pushback. Says his ex has got it in for him. That all the abuse she's complained about was instigated by her."

"Are we buying it?"

"Honestly?" She rubbed at eyes that had dark smudges underneath them. "I can't really see it. We're holding him for now, although his brief is hopping mad about it and uttering dark threats. Carol Eustace is coming in, and we're going to have to test her retraction of Creed's alibis. But in the end, even if we can drive a coach and horses through his alibis for the murders, it doesn't even begin to show that he did them. He's pretty creepy, and I wonder – to say the least – if he's changed his spots. None of that's enough."

"You were going to let me watch his tape."

"Later. I told you, Dan. Charlie's our priority. Trust me, we're taking this Creed thing seriously."

He quelled the frustration rising inside him, knowing she was right. "No, that's fine. Any change with Joan?"

She smiled. A cautious smile, but still a smile. "Yes, actually. Sorry, I should have told you. They say we shouldn't get carried away yet, but they're quietly optimistic. She's opened her eyes a couple of times in response to sound, she's speaking more normally, but still confused, and she's withdrawing from contact designed to irritate her. These are all good signs, especially after a relatively short space of time since her injury."

Despite her warning, he couldn't resist the surge of hope.

"She's speaking? Can we start talking to her? See what she remembers?"

"Not yet. When she seems properly orientated, they might let us have a few minutes with her, but we mustn't push her too soon."

"Fair enough," he said. "I'll focus on this Smithson character for now."

*

Archer swallowed the last bite of her chocolate bar and washed it down with a mouthful of Diet Pepsi, rueing, not for the first time, the horrible eating habits she tended to adopt when her work life became especially hectic. Dominic had once offered to make her lunch boxes, but she'd graciously declined, partly because the notion made her think of her mum and school days, partly because she knew she ought to jolly well make her own sandwiches.

But her shopping habits were often as bad as her eating habits. The last time she'd galvanised herself to throw something together that she could eat at her desk, she'd found that the potential makings included stale bread, mouldy cheese and some sort of vegetable that was in the midst of a sci-fi-like transformation into something nameless and horrific.

So on a good day it was a shop-bought sandwich and a smoothie. On days like this, whatever unhealthy crap the vending machine had to offer. Maybe it was time to take Dominic up on that offer after all.

Dan Baines would be in Bedfordshire by now, speaking to Edward Smithson. As soon as Will Tyler had notified the local force that their colleagues in Thames Valley wanted to interview the man in connection with a serious attack on a police officer, they'd moved fast to invite him to their station for a chat.

Meanwhile, Carol Eustace had come into the station and Archer was watching the monitor as Lara and Amir set about questioning her. They were in the same room that had hosted Antony Creed earlier on.

Archer's overwhelming impression of Carol Eustace was 'round'. Round face, round spectacle lenses. Bobbed hair that made her head look football-shaped. Round figure. There was what Archer supposed she'd describe as a latent prettiness about her, but it was almost as if she'd gone out of her way to adopt a plain look. Archer could think of a few reasons why that might be.

"So you spoke to an associate of ours recently," Lara began after the formalities. "Former Detective Sergeant McNeill. Concerning your ex-husband, Antony Creed."

Eustace looked bemused. "*Former* detective? I don't think he made that clear." Her eyes narrowed behind her glasses. "What's going on?"

Archer was irked, but not surprised. Baines had as good as said he thought his old friend was being deliberately vague about his status as he went about his research.

"Oh, nothing to worry about," Lara said airily. "He's doing some private research, but obviously what you had to say was of interest to us. So we've spoken to Mr Creed and, perhaps unsurprisingly, his description of your marriage is rather different to what you told Mr McNeill."

"In what way?"

"Suppose you just tell us what you told Mr McNeill. Remember, you're here voluntarily, but I should warn you: if you're now saying you lied back in 2001 to protect Mr Creed, that's a serious matter. It's only fair to ask you if you'd like a solicitor present."

"Am I in trouble?" Carol Eustace blinked. "To be honest, I'm not sure I care. I was a fool at the time, but the way he's treated me since…" She hesitated. "All right. If we're going to do this, we should do it properly. I think, yes, I would like a solicitor."

"We can find one for you," Amir said, "or maybe there's someone you have in mind."

"I know who I'd like," said Eustace, "but that's not possible right now, I don't think."

"No?"

"No. You see, my solicitors are Wright Farleigh. You guys are looking for the person I would have asked for. Charlie Ward."

*

Bedfordshire Police Headquarters was in Kempston, a dormitory town for the county town of Bedford. The building was in Woburn Road, a big oblong expanse of terracotta-coloured brick. A local DS had sat in as Baines and Jason Bell interviewed Edward Smithson.

Baines knew what the man had done to his wife, but he was normally professional enough to distance himself from his feelings towards a suspect. Yet something about Smithson made Baines loathe him in less than a minute. The man was way *too* charming. He declared himself happily remarried and denied having ever abused his first wife, Heather.

The mask had begun to slip when he'd spoken of Heather and Charlie 'stitching him up'. He'd referred to them in matter-of-fact terms as 'those two bitches', and also said that Charlie 'had dyke written all over her face'. He'd even implied that something inappropriate and unprofessional might have been going on between client and lawyer, something Baines didn't believe even for an instant.

Baines would cheerfully have punched him in the mouth, and he could tell that Jason's feelings were similar.

The trouble was, the man might have a dislike of Charlie, but he had a pretty unshakeable alibi for Friday night. Had he simply said his new wife would vouch for him, Baines would have questioned the validity of her testament; the chances were that Smithson had moved on from one controlling relationship to another and she would say black was white if he told her to.

But no. It turned out he was currently captain of his golf club and had been at a club dinner on Friday night, along with sixty or so other people. He'd even made a speech. By the time the party had broken up and Smithson had been heading for home, Joan was already at the hospital.

On the face of it, the exercise had been a colossal waste of time, other than to eliminate yet another potential suspect.

"We're getting nowhere," Jason had opined as Baines drove away. "We keep unearthing people who might have had it in for Joan or Charlie, but they can all prove they were elsewhere at the time. Maybe it's not that at all. Maybe they ran into a different mob."

"But then why would they abduct Charlie?"

"Maybe they wanted to take them both, to have some fun with, but Joan put up a fight. Only there were too many of them. She's knocked out, so they just take Charlie. Or they take her because she's a witness. Or maybe they actually left them both for dead. Charlie comes to, but has some sort of amnesia and just sort of wanders off."

"But then, where is she now?" Baines overtook a slow-moving Fiat. "Amnesia or no, people don't just vanish off the face of the earth."

"I know that." The Scot was silent for a while. "What if she ran into the wrong kind of person? Some predatory animal who spots a vulnerable woman and sees an opportunity?"

"I suppose. But that would mean she walked the streets until your sex fiend picked her up, without encountering a single CCTV camera."

"Unlikely, I know, but not impossible."

"Suppose it happened like that." Baines thought they might as well play the scenario out. "How do we narrow down our suspects? I mean, we've gone through local sex offenders who might have the right sort of form, and it didn't get us very far."

"Someone new, then," Jason suggested. "First offence. Maybe someone who's fantasised about grabbing a woman off the streets. Perhaps he's even planned it all out in his mind, including where he'd hold her. Then he sees this opportunity. In fact," he continued, "she might not have even wandered far before he encountered her. Not far enough to get caught on camera."

"Big coincidence."

"I know." He went quiet again. "But, you know," he said, "Lauren Black emerging from that car park the other night just as a squad car rolled by was quite a coincidence. They do happen, Dan. We've still got CCTV from the surrounding area, and of course the initial focus was on people who looked like what we now know are Julius Mullins and his mates, or one of those BMWs we were interested in."

Baines shot him an appreciative glance. "You know what, Jason? You might just have a point. She wanders away, dazed and confused, straight into the arms of someone who persuades her to get in his car. Ring through to Ibrahim and see if he's still looking over that footage. We're interested in *any* cars in the right place at the right time. Every single owner will need questioning."

Jason already had his phone out. "You really think there might be something in it?"

"I think it's still a long shot. But maybe a long shot is what we need."

He was approaching a pedestrian crossing on his way out of town. He saw a young man approaching, clearly intending to cross, and he rolled to a halt. As the figure stepped off the pavement, he looked Baines's way and raised a hand in thanks.

Baines was transfixed as he took in the leather jacket, the dark hair.

The face.

He blinked and the features seemed to shift. Then the man was across the road.

Not Jack. Nothing like the Jack he knew from dreams and visions gone by, nor the young man he'd taken for Jack the other day.

He remembered the days after Louise had been killed and little Jack had been taken. In the street, in the supermarket, at a bus stop, he'd see a mother with a small child and, just for a moment, his heart would leap. The first time, in Tesco, he'd been so convinced that he'd believed he'd just had a bad dream. He'd rushed up to them, scaring them, the joy on his lips dying as he looked into the eyes of a stranger, a woman pushing her child behind her and backing away from this now sobbing madman.

And then those years when he'd started to see phantoms of grown-up Jack, in dreams and awake. In his heart, he supposed he'd known full well it wasn't real, but a small part of him still entertained the hope that it meant something.

Dr Walsh had shown him that what it actually meant was that he'd never properly acknowledged, or dealt with, his grief. And, in the absence of a body, he'd so hoped his son was still alive that his mind had constructed the person Jack would have grown into, ageing in real time until, thanks to the therapy he received, the visions had ceased and the dreams had faded away. There had been that strange new dream of a beach and a hilltop house, but that too had passed.

Or so he'd thought.

A car horn sounded.

"Um," said Jason. "We can go, Dan."

As he released the brake, he realised he was shaking badly. His foot skittered over the accelerator.

No, no. Jason couldn't see this.

With the brake off, the automatic transmission was already moving the car forward. With an act of will, he calmed himself, at least enough to get his foot on the pedal and increase his speed.

"Sorry," he said weakly. "Woolgathering."

Jason had his phone to his ear. "Hi, Will, it's Jason," he said. "Yeah, yeah, on our way back… Yeah, I'm afraid I've got another little job for your list… Well, we can't have you getting bored, can we?… It's about CCTV…"

Baines let the DC's words soothe him. He wondered how Lara Moseley was getting on with Antony Creed. He'd been hardly daring to hope that Mac really was onto something, yet now he found himself praying that it was so. That Creed would break down, confess, reveal the truth about Jack.

And that he could finally find some lasting peace.

23

Carole Eustace's solicitor had arrived. Eyeing him on the monitor, Archer sighed. Other people felt they were getting old when the policemen started looking younger. With her, it was solicitors. Antony Creed's man had looked about thirteen. This girl looked barely eleven. But there was a flintiness in her eyes that said eleven going on fifty.

"Very well, Detective Inspector," she said to Lara Moseley. "Let's get this over with. It seems to me that this is a very unsatisfactory state of affairs. It appears that an ex-Thames Valley officer, who in fact is no longer serving, asked my client to reiterate what she told you way back in 2001 about her interactions with a Mr Antony Creed. Believing this to be an official enquiry, she decided to be frank about her relationship with Mr Creed at the time and to admit that her memories might have been hazier at the time than she had realised."

"I'm sure the retired officer's status was a simple misunderstanding," Lara said smoothly, "and it doesn't really matter for practical purposes. He rightly reported the conversation to us, and that's why we're here."

"Yes, but based on information my client imparted under a misapprehension."

"With respect, I don't see that it makes any difference. Your client thought she was telling the police, and now the police know. All we're interested in is properly verifying or otherwise Mr Creed's movements on dates when Ms Eustace previously attested that he was attending probation appointments with her."

Eustace looked at her lawyer, who nodded.

"Well," she said, "I think Mr McNeill may have misunderstood. See, all I meant was, I can't be *sure* whether I gave an accurate account of those dates in 2001. I mean, I wouldn't have *knowingly* lied…"

Lara's hand slammed down on the table. "Can't be sure? Didn't knowingly lie? You categorically told the police, in the midst of a multiple murder investigation, that he was in appointments with you at the time of at least two of those murders. Mr McNeill says you told him you lied about that. Which is it?"

"Mr McNeill can't have been listening."

Archer felt herself seething. If she'd been in Lara's shoes, she'd have struggled not to roll her eyes.

"So what are you saying now?"

"You have to understand. When I first knew Antony, he made me feel sorry for him. I suppose, I've always been a sucker for a lame duck. He begged me to get him help, and I thought I could support him in his rehabilitation. But somehow, I developed feelings for him. I should have withdrawn from his case, but I didn't. I thought he felt the same. So, when he skipped the odd appointment, I cut him some slack and covered for him."

"And now you're saying that was what you did when the police asked you to confirm his alibis?"

"It was a long time ago. I can't say for sure now whether he kept those particular appointments or not."

Archer's mouth went dry. This, or something like it, was what she'd been afraid of.

"Oh, come on," Amir cut in. "This wasn't him being a bit late getting away from the barber's, or going to his mum for tea and losing track of time. You're seriously saying you might have covered for him in the context of a murder enquiry and then forgot?"

She stared at the tabletop. "The truth is, I suppose, maybe I wanted to get back at Antony and went a bit too far. Our relationship moved fast, too fast with hindsight. I allowed myself to be blinded to the kind of man he really was. It was only after we were married that his true character began to emerge. Squalid, degrading sex. Violence…" She was blushing.

"Would it surprise you," Lara said, "to know that Mr Creed's position is that you instigated those practices?"

Eustace looked up and smiled. "To use an old cliché, he would say that, wouldn't he?" She shrugged. "Anyway, there was only so much I could take. I left him and, when he came after me, I said I'd get a restraining order and do all I could to get him back in jail. To my surprise and relief, he backed off. He didn't even contest the divorce. But it was a difficult period in my life. Perhaps that's why, all these years on, those memories are hazy. Sorry for the confusion."

"We might well come back to that," Lara said. "But, for the moment, may I change the subject?"

Eustace looked at her solicitor.

The young woman folded her arms. "All right. For now. Let's see how it goes, though."

"So," Lara said, "when you decided you'd like a lawyer, you said your first choice would have been Charlie Ward."

"That's right. But she's missing, isn't she? Is there any news? I liked her."

"So what dealings have you had with Ms Ward? I know she wasn't with the firm at the time of your divorce, so you must have used her later. She's a domestic abuse specialist, so I'm wondering…"

"Yes," Eustace said. "After the divorce, I gradually got my life back on track. There were even days when I didn't think about him. Then he suddenly started turning up again. About a year ago. Maybe less. Trying to talk to me. Sending me notes. Saying he was sorry and wanted to start again. I don't know what his agenda was, but I made it clear I wasn't interested."

"But he wouldn't take no for an answer?"

"No. So I consulted my lawyers and Wright Farleigh put Charlie on the case. She was very good. Sent him letters setting out exactly what would happen if he didn't leave me alone. Non-molestation orders, maybe even restraining orders, with the risk of jail if he breached them. It worked. He backed off."

"And did you get any sense of how he felt about Ms Ward?"

"I don't think they ever met, but he wouldn't have liked it, and he wouldn't have liked it coming from a woman. The truth is, I don't think he likes women full stop. He turns on the charm, but it's a game he plays." She hesitated. "You think he might have had something to do with her disappearing? I know he's not right, but…" She made a face.

"What?" Lara pushed.

She looked troubled. "When the divorce was happening, he didn't like my lawyer at the time. She was a woman. He said lawyers were paid busybodies, poking their noses in other people's private business. And he said women lawyers were the worst. And that, one of these days, she'd piss off the wrong person."

"Did you see that as some kind of a threat?"

"I thought it was just words, but still… you could tell how angry he was. Thinking about it now, I suppose Charlie's warning letters… he might well see that as a threat by a woman. He wouldn't take kindly to it."

Archer felt her stomach muscles tensing.

"But," Lara said, "do you seriously think he might go after her?"

"Honestly? I just don't know. There were times, towards the end of our marriage, when I didn't think I knew him at all, let alone what he might be capable of. It scared me."

"We know where he lives," Lara said. "But do you know if he has access to any other property? Say another home, a lockup garage?"

"Oh, my God." There was stark horror on Eustace's face now. "You really think he's got her, don't you?"

"Please. Don't go discussing this conversation with anyone else. We're just asking questions. So is there anywhere?"

"Well, I wouldn't know, is the honest answer. Until he tried to get back into my life, I hadn't seen him for… it must be well over ten years. I didn't exactly invite him to tell me all about his life since we broke up. But he's never had a lavish lifestyle. When we were married, I was the main breadwinner, yet he wanted to control our finances. Tell me what I could and couldn't spend."

Lara turned to Amir. "DS Rashid, anything to add?"

"One thing," he said. "Say for argument Mr Creed is the one who abducted Charlie Ward. You say it's a year since his dealings with her. Why wait so long?"

She seemed to mull this over. "All I can say is, he lets things fester. For all I know, he's spent all this time building resentment and then decided to do something. But I'm speculating really."

"All right," Lara said, "I think we're done for now."

"What about, you know, the confusion over those appointments?" Carol Eustace asked.

Confusion was a good word, Archer thought. Carol Eustace should have been a politician. Even now, every word she said had to be treated with caution.

"We'll see," Lara said. "We might need to talk to you again about that."

*

"We can just hold onto him for now," Archer said. Lara and Amir had joined her in her office. "The clock's running, but we've plenty of time before we have to charge him or release him."

"Let's talk about the Invisible Man case first," Lara said. "Back then, presumably the police would have checked out his home. Remember, the killer was holding small children for a week between their abduction and their death. If we were investigating that now, we'd search his house and try to find out if there was anywhere else he might have been keeping them."

"I've called for the case files," Archer said. "But Dan and his old buddy must remember."

"Still, it's pretty obvious he's not a man of property now. I know not all employers are entitled to check criminal records, or even ask about them, but I'm sure his record must limit his job options and his earning power. I wouldn't be surprised if even that one bedroom house he rents in Cumbria Park puts a strain on his finances."

"We should still search it," Amir said. "Maybe he's keeping Charlie drugged. And maybe he's inherited somewhere else. Are his parents still alive?"

"We need to question him again," said Archer.

181

"Of course," Lara said, "we're only looking at him for Charlie because of what Carol Eustace said. I'm beginning to think it would be one hell of a coincidence if it turned out he was responsible."

"It would. But it all needs checking."

"And the alibis back in 2001?"

Archer massaged her temples. The weather forecast was predicting that this rainy spell would end briefly and then there would be thunderstorms and heavy rain. The aching in her head suggested as much. Either that or she should cut back on sugar.

"I just don't know," she admitted. "Did Ms Eustace retract them to get back at him, or did he really miss those appointments? Either way, did she then realise she'd be getting herself into trouble and start obfuscating? Because the one thing I'm not buying is this 'confusion' malarkey. She's not going to give him alibis – true *or* false – for high profile murders and then just forget. Damn. We've got a guy who might just be the Invisible Man and who might just have abducted Charlie. Or neither."

24

"Oh, yeah," Antony Creed said. "I can tell you where I was on Friday night. You wouldn't believe the social whirl I live. It was cocktails with the Queen, dinner with Ed Sheeran, then an exhausting night of passion with three nubile movie starlets. I filmed the whole evening on my phone, so the time stamps will confirm it all."

"I'd really appreciate it if you took this seriously," Lara said.

"Yeah, well, I wouldn't mind being taken seriously myself. I made a few mistakes when I was younger and they follow you around the rest of your damn life. Some psycho starts running around killing women and kids, and who gets interrogated? Antony Creed. My ex decides to drop me in the shit by lying about my probation appointments, and who gets dragged in and branded the liar? Antony Creed. Now this. What am I supposed to have done on Friday?"

"Inspector," the boy solicitor protested, "how can my client's movements on Friday night possibly be relevant to events in 2001?"

"I just want a simple answer to a simple question," Lara said.

"All right, then," Creed said, only slightly less aggressively. "I finished my shit job around five, called in at Tesco on my way home to pick up some bits – and yes, I've got the receipt. Then I went home, did myself a Tesco curry ready meal, and watched shit TV until about midnight. Then I turned in. So what?"

"But you've no one who can vouch for you?"

"No more than any sad bastard who lives alone, no. Can you give me a hint what this is all about?"

"Does the name Charlotte, or Charlie, Ward mean anything to you?"

"Should it?"

"She was Carol Eustace's solicitor last year, when you were stalking your ex-wife."

"Oh, her? The one who sent me those letters? I never met her, but I assumed she was a glorified ambulance chaser, contacting me out of the blue, saying I was stalking Carol. Accusing me of all sorts of nonsense and threatening me with court action if I didn't stop."

"You deny harassing Carol?" Amir asked.

"I'd moved on after the divorce. I was well shot of her. I still don't know what her game was, suddenly making those accusations. But no one ever believes the man, do they? And no one believes someone can change. Yes, Carol helped me turn things around, but it turned out she was the abusive one in our marriage."

"Let's get back to Charlotte Ward," Lara said.

"If we must." He looked bored.

"You say you never met her."

"I've no idea what she looks like."

"She's been on the news."

"Yes? I never really watch it. So what's this lawyer lady been up to?"

"She's been missing since Friday night."

Creed recoiled. "Whoa! Don't tell me you're trying to pin something like that on me. I told you. I never even met the woman."

"Her photograph is on the firm's website. Easy enough to identify her from that, wait outside their offices, follow her home…"

"Inspector," the boy solicitor interjected, "I thought we were talking about the Invisible Man murders. Now we seem to have gone off track."

"Not really," Lara said. "We see a clear chain of events here… the new doubts over Mr Creed's whereabouts when the murders were committed; his marriage to, and divorce from, the woman who gave him those alibis; his subsequent stalking of her; and the intervention of a solicitor who's now missing herself."

"And that's all theory and supposition," the lawyer retorted. "Where is even a scintilla of evidence for this fantasy?"

"We'll find it if it's there," Amir said.

"We will," Lara agreed. "We're getting a warrant to search your house," she told Creed. "Would you like to save us some time and trouble by giving us permission?"

"Sure," he said. "Done. Search away. Knock yourselves out. I've nothing to hide."

"My client has the right to be there when you do that," said the solicitor.

"I don't suppose you're in a hurry to release me?" Creed said.

"Not just yet, no."

"Then I might as well stop here. Try not to make too much mess, please."

Archer felt a prickle of doubt.

"What about other properties?" Lara asked.

"Oh," sneered Creed. "Do me a favour."

"I was thinking maybe a lockup garage, or perhaps an allotment shed."

"Do I look like something out of *The Good Life*? And a garage? I can barely afford the rent on my home. I won't be able to do that, by the time you lot have finished making me look bad. If this gets back to my boss…" He sighed. "That business with Carol's solicitor and those ridiculous letters was a long time ago. If I was going to do anything to her, why would I leave it so long?"

For a man being confronted over some serious crimes, he seemed almost too confident. Did he know there was nothing to find because he was innocent?

Or because he'd made damn sure there wasn't?

"Whoever the Invisible Man was, he was careful," Lara said. "A planner. The sort of person who'd maybe spend a long time planning a revenge." She folded her arms. "I'm going to ask you outright, Mr Creed. Do you know anything at all about the attack on DS Joanne Collins—"

"Joanne who?"

"—and the disappearance of Charlotte Ward?"

"No," he said. "I don't even know who this Joanne person is. None of this is anything to do with me. That's the honest truth."

*

Baines arrived back at the station to be told Lizzie Archer was keen to see him in her office. She didn't go into detail, but asked him if he could get Mac to join them.

"Can't you give me a clue what it's about?" he'd pressed her. "Have there been developments?"

"I could," she said, "but there's a lot going on and I don't want to waste time having the same conversation twice."

Baines had known better than to argue, and now he was back in her office with Mac and Lara.

"Thanks for coming in," Lizzie said to Mac, "and thanks for unearthing a possible lead for us."

"Did it lead anywhere?"

"We're really not sure," said Lara.

"You spoke to Carol Eustace earlier," said Lizzie. "What did you make of her? By which I mean, how much store did you put by her story that she lied about him keeping those appointments?"

He stared into space, the contemplative look Baines remembered well from their old working partnership settling on his face.

"I was surprised," he admitted. "All those years she kept it to herself, apparently through a nightmare of a marriage, a divorce and beyond. Then I show up and she spills the beans just like that, knowing she could land herself in trouble, as well as him. But then you find that sometimes. If it had been on her conscience all that time, maybe all she needed was that extra little push."

"Well, she's backpedalling now, saying she's 'all confused' about what happened and when. Did she happen to mention to you that he started harassing her again a little more recently?"

He pursed his lips. "No."

Baines looked from Lizzie to Lara. "She said that? I don't get it. If that's true, why wouldn't she have threatened to retract Creed's alibis at that point, to get rid of him?"

"She chose the legal route," Lizzie said, "and, by all accounts, her brief made a good job of scaring him off, or so she thought. But this is where it gets potentially messy. Her brief was Charlie Ward."

Baines's stomach flipped. "You're joking."

"Look at my face. Is this me joking?"

"When was this?"

"Maybe a year ago," Lara said. "Maybe just after Charlie got into domestic abuse. Carol Eustace thinks he has a problem with women in general, and certainly female lawyers. She's still using Charlie's firm, and the lawyer she came in with is going to check the exact dates. But certainly time enough for the resentment to fester. I made the point that the Invisible Man was almost certainly a planner, and taking his time could be a hallmark."

"But hang on," Baines protested. "If it's part of a plan, why attack her when she's with Joan? That makes no sense. Why not get her on her own?"

"You got me there. But then no solution's going to hang together perfectly. Amir's meeting Phil Gordon and his team at Creed's house, along with Natalie Chen." Natalie was one of Lara's DCs. "If there's evidence there, I'm betting they'll find it. If there's any indication he has access to some other building where he might be holding Charlie, they'll find that."

Baines was finding it difficult to keep his mind from reeling. Was the nightmare from his past about to collide with their current case?

"This is all very well," said Mac. "And say he is responsible for the attack on your officer, and for her girlfriend disappearing. It doesn't necessarily make him the Invisible Man. And if he is, why stir Carol Eustace up all those years later, when he's relying on her for his alibi?"

"He'd have expected her to keep quiet about lying, if that's what she did," suggested Lizzie. "He might even have thought it gave him power over her."

"It didn't keep her in the marriage," Lara observed. "Although, even then, they disagree on who was abusing who."

"Here's the thing," Lizzie said. "And it might just be common ground between the two cases. Dan, Mac, you must have looked at the time for somewhere he might be keeping the children, if he was the killer."

"Aye," Mac said. "If he had anything, we never did find it. Och, a couple of neighbours mentioned an old camper van he used to own, which they hadn't seen for a while. We wondered if he'd moved it somewhere secluded and was keeping the kids there."

"You asked him about it, of course?"

"I remember," Baines said. "He claimed it had been stolen."

"Did you believe him?"

"We did wonder at first, but then it turned up burnt out on a hillside, before the killings had stopped. If it had been afterwards, it would have looked a bit more suspicious. I remember the CSIs sifted through what was left of it and reckoned there had been booze and drug paraphernalia. Most likely kids had been using it as a den."

"It really was old," Mac added. "I remember, forensics established that the locks were crap. The mileage had gone round the clock once and was well on the way to its second full tour. He'd only reported it to us to get a case number for his insurance. Reckoned whatever they paid out would be more than it was worth."

"Did you consider he was being clever?" Lizzie wondered. "Maybe he had somewhere else, and swapped, just in case he came under suspicion."

"Of course we did. If there was anything else, we never did find it. And then the killing stopped. Even now I can't see why Creed would have stopped there, if it was him. Serial killers don't, unless something happens to stop them."

"Like other outlets for whatever is driving them, for example," Lara said. "Like finding a partner to abuse maybe?"

Mac looked at her, nodding. "Maybe, maybe not. The research on why serial killers stop, or pause, is far from conclusive. But remember, we had Carol Eustace alibiing him at the time. We had no reason not to believe her, so it made everything else *he* said look more plausible. If that's unravelling now…"

"Of course," Lizzie said, "there's no reason to suppose he's holding Charlie alive anywhere. We have to face that. But if she's buried somewhere, maybe we can get clues from soil samples on his shoes. And we need to keep in mind this is all speculation. But let's say, whatever reason he had for killing women and children, he stopped doing that and channelled his emotional energy into abusing Carol Eustace instead. And now, maybe, his violent propensities have surfaced again in the attack on Joan and Charlie. That leaves a gap between the divorce and now."

The whole conversation was making Baines feel queasy. They'd questioned Creed back in 2001. His alibis checked out. Yes, they'd wondered about the camper van, but vehicles got stolen all the time. All they were left with was a local sex offender whose previous offences hadn't even come close to murder.

Had he slipped through their fingers? They'd first questioned him before Louise was killed, he remembered now. They heard about the van later. Maybe he'd decided to ditch it just in case. Maybe, if they'd pushed harder, Louise and Jack would be alive today.

Yet Lizzie's words penetrated that feeling of dread.

"You're suggesting there should have been more offences after the divorce," he said, "after he lost his outlet. Well, maybe. Or maybe he bottled it up for as long as he could. When he couldn't cope any more, he went looking for his ex-wife again."

"Then Charlie thwarts him," Mac said. "He's angry. So he decides to go after *her*."

Baines swallowed. Once again, in his mind's eye, he was in his living room, two still bodies on the carpet in front of him: Louise and Jessica Richardson.

"You know, the thing with Joan and Charlie isn't completely out of whack," he said, forcing himself to think past the emotion that threatened to engulf him. "The Invisible Man would leave one victim for dead and abduct another – her child, someone she loves. Here it's Joan left for dead and Charlie taken. So maybe there's something in his psychology that works that way."

There was a knock on Lizzie's office door. Will Tyler let himself in without waiting for a response.

"Can't it wait, Will?" Lizzie said. "We're in the middle of something."

"Sorry, Lizzie, boss, but you'll want to hear this." He was smiling. "Joan's properly woken up. The docs say we can see her."

25

"You gave us all quite a scare," Archer said.

She and Dan were sat at Joan's bedside. Archer was holding her hand. She still looked washed out, and the nurses had warned the detectives not to over-tax her.

"Sorry about that," she said. "I still can't make any sense of how I came to be in here. The doctors aren't telling me much. They say it's Monday. That I've been out nearly three days. They just say I had a fall, but it must have been some fall. But Charlie hasn't been in since I came round." She searched Archer's face. "She's all right, isn't she?"

"What's your last memory before you woke up and found you were in hospital?"

Joan closed her eyes. For a moment, Archer thought she'd drifted off to sleep. Then she opened them again. Her smile was weak, but also grave.

"Lizzie, this is me you're talking to. I might be in here and feeling like shit, and my memory might be shot to pieces, but I still know all the tricks. Like answering a question with a question. Now where the fuck is Charlie?"

Dan cleared his throat. "Joan, we think you were attacked on Friday night, in Aylesbury."

"Attacked? What? Both of us? Oh my God, Charlie—"

"We need you to be calm and focused," Archer said. "Do you remember anything about Friday night?"

"I'm not sure I remember Friday at all. Today's Monday, right?" She grimaced. "Yeah, yeah, I just said. But what about Charlie? God, it was her birthday. I hadn't booked anything. I was going to. I suppose I must have, if we were out."

"You had a receipt from La Salute in your purse." An award-winning, family run Italian restaurant in the centre of town. "We think someone hit you. You went down and banged your head.

You were in a coma, but they think you'll make a full recovery."

Joan was agitated now. "But what aren't you telling me about *Charlie*?" Tears fell. "She's dead, isn't she?"

"She's not dead," Dan said. "Not as far as we know."

"But what does *that* mean?"

"She's missing."

"Oh, no, no, no…" She blinked away the tears. "Oh, Jesus, there was that case we were working on. The two women? Laura and…?"

"Lauren and Maisie."

"Homophobic thugs. That's it, isn't it? They attacked *us* this time."

"We don't think so. We got the men who did that, and we're pretty sure it wasn't them who attacked you two."

"Then…" She closed her eyes again. "I don't understand."

"Is it possible you guys had a falling out on Friday?"

"What?" Anger, then confusion. "I doubt it. I mean, if we did, then I don't remember that either. But even if we did, it would never come to blows, if that's what you're wondering. Oh, yeah, we have the odd row. I get moody and distant. She shouts a lot. Then one of us – usually me – makes a cup of tea and we move on."

Her voice was getting fainter. "You can't think she hurt me and then did a runner. I can't begin to tell you how ridiculous that is. No, someone's got her." She opened her eyes. "What day is it today?"

"Monday," Dan volunteered.

"Yeah, course it is. Oh, sweet Jesus. How many days is that?"

"Three."

"Yeah, I said, didn't I? Right." She swung her legs round, pushing down on the bed with her hands. "I'm coming in." What little colour remained in her face drained away. "Oh, dear…"

"Joan, don't be silly," Archer said, helping her get her legs back on the bed and straightening her covers. "You've still not fully come round. The doctors are as sure as they can be that you're going to be okay, but you need lots of rest. Let *us* find Charlie."

"Yes, but you haven't, have you?" she whispered. Then, "Sorry. I'm sure you're all working really hard." She gave them a tight smile. "You just have to work harder."

"Do you know anyone who'd want to hurt you and Charlie?"

"I'm a cop. She's a lawyer. We both piss people off from time to time. But we've had no threats. No one's been hanging around, so far as I know."

Archer could barely hear her now.

"Has she mentioned an Antony Creed?"

"I don't think so. God, I wish I could think…"

Joan's eyes closed. Her breathing became rhythmical.

"Should I call a nurse?" Dan asked.

"We'll tell them she's sleeping. I'm sure she's as well as can be expected."

"Maybe I should stay with her. Be here when she wakes up."

She saw the strain on his face and felt a rush of affection for him. His wife was pregnant, and horrendous memories, coming back to haunt him once more, were already taking their toll. Yet here, at this moment, all he could think of was supporting Joan.

"I think her parents will want to do that, Dan. We need you on the case."

"But… in case she remembers something?"

"They can call us. Come on." She stood up and headed for the door.

He stood too. "But she could drift off again in the time it takes for us to get here. At least let's station Jason here."

She paused by the door, thinking for a moment. Jason was a valuable resource, yet he was closer to Joan than anyone on the team.

"Yeah, okay. For now. Give him a ring."

He made the call as they walked the corridors leading back to reception and the exit. Out in the car park, the air was still. In the distance, thunder rumbled. It felt like an omen. And not a good one.

*

Charlie didn't need to use the torch to have a pretty good idea how deep the water had become. Kneeling, it lapped around her backside. Although it would need to rise an awfully long way before she had serious cause for alarm, she was already feeling a prickling of unease. She'd known a lot of rain was forecast. And, it seemed, the more it rained, the more water would get in here.

She supposed there was some way for the level to go down, or it would have been over her head when she was first brought here. But it was equally apparent that the water must recede a damn sight slower than it rose, for it to have ever reached that tide line. She'd didn't know for sure if it was raining right now, but she'd be happier if it just stopped altogether and the level started going down. It was quite bad enough thinking of this underground room as a cell. She didn't want to start thinking of it as a coffin.

When she'd been left here, cuffed to the floor, she couldn't believe this was what was planned for her. Not for rising rainwater to drown her. A slow death from starvation and thirst, maybe...

She mustn't think that way. They were coming back. She was a prisoner, that was all. She'd even managed to persuade herself that the water and cereal bars hadn't been deliberately placed so far out of her reach. Maybe that had just been a mistake. She was meant to be able to get them, to keep going until they returned, perhaps with more provisions.

Perhaps to release her.

But when were they coming back? Did they even know that, with persistent, heavy rain, this place would ship water so badly?

At least the rat seemed to have deserted, doubtless seeking somewhere drier.

The fear was constant, but out and out panic seemed to come in waves. She'd calm herself, try to be positive. Take herself to places she'd been with Joan, things they'd done together. Tell herself this was temporary. That she wasn't intended to die in this dark place, that she'd be freed eventually.

But then the chilling, negative thoughts would keep crashing back in, no matter how hard she tried to build walls to protect herself from them. And perhaps the most frightening of all was that, even if she did somehow get out of here, she might never see Joan again. That she'd finally found the love of her life, only to lose her to a single punch.

The thought had even occurred to her that, should she die here, and if there was something else afterwards – she could never quite decide what she believed – but, if there was, then maybe Joan would be waiting there for her, wearing the smile she knew and loved so well, arms opening to embrace her.

It was such a comforting, seductive notion that she knew there was a risk that she might surrender to it. That this daydream of death would detract from her determination to cling onto life.

She knew too that such thinking was close to giving up on Joan; that yearning to meet her in some afterlife made the possibility of her death more real.

So, for now, she pushed those thoughts away again.

Since her Fitbit battery had expired, she had no way of keeping track of time, although she was as sure as she could be, in this perpetual darkness, that it was still Monday. She'd actually removed the fitness tracker and attempted to use the casing to wear away at the concrete surrounding the metal ring to which she was shackled. She couldn't say it was making *no* impression, but the soft plastic was going to rub away long before the concrete did.

But then she'd realised, cursing her slow wits, that she had something tougher

Her belt buckle.

Clumsily, encumbered by the handcuff, she'd unbuckled the belt once more. She'd hoped the chunky steel buckle would be tough enough to wear concrete away, although she hadn't a clue how long it would take before it relinquished its hold on that metal ring.

Making sure the torch was secure and clear of the water, she'd reached down, fumbled around, and found the ring. She'd found where it was embedded in the concrete and applied the buckle, making sawing motions.

She wished she'd studied physics at school, or at least paid more attention in general science. Then maybe she'd know if damp concrete was any easier to erode than dry. Whether attempting to erode it under water was any sort of a hindrance.

But, in the absence of any such information, she'd just kept plugging away. Because, right now, all she had was a steel buckle and an indeterminate amount of time.

She set to again, sawing with fresh enthusiasm, praying that the water didn't reduce the friction. She had some vague notion it might be working in her favour, lubricating her makeshift tool and preventing it from heating up.

A sharp pain in her middle finger told her she'd grazed herself on the concrete. Again. She had to be careful. If she ended up rubbing her fingers raw, it would just make her task even harder.

That the water was cold didn't help. She fancied that, when night fell, the temperature might plummet now there was so much water.

But then, for all she knew, maybe night had fallen already.

What she did know was that, if the rain persisted, and the water kept on rising, it must eventually reach that ominous tide mark.

"Never mind that now," she hissed. "Just concentrate on the job."

She sighed. When she and Joan had set out to celebrate her birthday on Friday night, this situation couldn't have been further from their minds. Kneeling on concrete, her knees aching, up to her bum in water and repeatedly rubbing her nice belt buckle on a hard, unforgiving surface. Gradually shredding her fingers.

"Wow, Joan," she whispered, "you certainly know how to show a girl a good time."

The absurdity forced laughter to bubble out of her, and when she started laughing, she couldn't stop. It echoed off the walls, off the water. She had to force herself to stop it, stop the hysteria, only for violent sobbing to overtake her.

She wanted Joan. She wanted her mum.

She wanted this nightmare to end.

"Please," she whispered. "Please, God. Please help me."

26

"Well," Phil Gordon said, "I don't think we need worry about any mess we made. The place looked as if it had been ransacked before we even started."

Amir Rashid, standing on Antony Creed's tiny driveway, next to his unkempt postage stamp of grass, was inclined to agree. The suspect's home looked like an exaggerated stereotype of a bachelor pad. Dirty crockery sat in and by the kitchen sink, and tabloid newspapers made an untidy pile by the threadbare sofa in the living room. In the bedroom, clothes had been deposited on the floor. He didn't actually seem to own anything resembling a laundry bin.

A couple of well-thumbed porn magazines sat on Creed's bedside cabinet.

"Blimey," DC Natalie Chen had said, flicking through one. "I'm amazed anyone buys wank mags in this day and age, with what's out there on the web." She'd dropped it back where it came from. "Pretty tame stuff, too. And owning them doesn't make him a killer, does it?"

The whole search spoke to a sad, rather depressing existence. Rashid thought *he*'d be angry at the world if this was representative of his life.

"So you're taking away anything that bears further examination, Phil?" he said.

"Computer and tablet, obviously. Shoes, just in case there are soil samples suggesting burial sites. His tool box, in case he's used any of the items to dismember a body."

"Wow," Natalie said, "always the ray of sunshine, Phil. I bet it's a laugh a minute around the Gordon dining table."

"Oh, aye. Especially when I start doing me magic tricks."

"Do you know any?" Rashid was suddenly intrigued.

"Well, you should see me make the wife's sticky toffee pud disappear."

Natalie laughed. "With custard?"

"Of course."

"Anyhow," Rashid said, enjoying the banter, but keen to get on, "we'll leave you to it for now, Phil. We're going to knock a few doors while we're here. See if anyone's seen or heard anything of interest."

The detectives decided to split up. The houses were all pretty much identical: maybe ten years old, narrow, and with a little porch over a white front door. Creed's was second from the end of the terrace, so Rashid took the end house and Natalie the other side.

It was late afternoon, and the likelihood was that most residents would still be out at work, so he wasn't overly surprised to get no response to the doorbell. Making a note that someone should come back later, he walked back past Creed's door, intent on leapfrogging Natalie. She was in conversation with a woman in a long cardigan and jeans.

"Just a sec, Amir," she called.

He turned and walked up the woman's drive to join them.

"Would you mind telling my colleague what you just told me, Ms…"

"It's Mrs. My husband died a few years ago, and I've downsized. I thought the kids could do with the money now, not wait until I'm gone. I'm Anna Lewis. Make it Anna."

"You were saying you saw Mr Creed on Friday evening?"

"Yes. We don't exactly see much of each other. I like to keep myself to myself, and so does he. We nod, exchange a few pleasantries. The weather and the like. He was putting some rubbish in the bins. So what's going on? Is he okay?"

"What time would that be?" Rashid asked.

She fiddled with a stray strand of light brown hair. "Well, let's see. The news was finished and I'd turned over to *Newsnight*. I like it on a Friday, 'cause they do an arts review. I always call my cat in before it gets properly going. Usually about a quarter to eleven. As I came out, he closed the lid on his wheelie bin – I didn't notice if it was the general waste or the recycling – and he went indoors. I don't think he even noticed me."

Rashid looked over at Creed's bins, lined up like soldiers about a foot to the side of the front door. "When do they get emptied?"

"Friday, as it happens, and it was the green one last week."

"Did you see or hear anything untoward on Friday or since?"

"From Antony? No, he's very quiet."

"How do you find him?"

"In what way?"

"What sort of person is he?"

"Oh, I don't know. All right. A bit strange, maybe. Stares at you when he's talking. Feels a bit too intense for my liking. But we're all different, aren't we? I'd rather him than someone playing loud music, or a couple always screaming at each other."

"Did you notice what time he got home on Friday night?"

"I didn't. Although his car wasn't there, I don't think, when I got in from work around five. Nothing unusual about that, though. He usually gets home after me."

"Would you be prepared to put all that in a signed statement?"

"Well, yes, of course. If you think it would help with whatever this is about."

She was a chatterbox, but a good witness, Rashid decided. He wouldn't be surprised if she was a bit of a busybody, but then the police rather liked busybodies. They noticed things.

They thanked Anna Lewis and heard the door close behind them as they walked back down her drive. Rashid was already pulling on latex gloves.

The green general waste bin contained one cheap white bin liner. He checked the recycling bin for good measure. Papers, cardboard boxes, plastic bottles and packaging. The same dross you'd find in any set of bins up and down the country. The food caddy seemed similarly innocuous.

"One thing's for sure," Rashid said. "If he was here, dumping rubbish in his bin, when Joan was attacked then, whatever else he might have done, he had nothing to do with that."

*

Jason Bell had arrived at Stoke Mandeville to find Joan's parents at her bedside. He'd made his presence known to them and found a chair in the corridor.

The truth was, he was feeling conflicted between wanting to be here for his friend and wanting to be out and trying to catch whoever had put her in here and find out what had happened to Charlie. Privately he feared the worst, and he suspected he wasn't alone.

As he sat fiddling with his phone, he was aware of a figure standing over him. He looked up to see a nurse, her hair as red as his own. She was smiling.

"You're a colleague of Joanne's, right?"

He was confused for a moment.

"You mentioned it at reception, when you were asking where she was?"

"Oh," he said, "yeah. I'm DC Bell. Jason."

"Well, I'm going to grab a coffee and wondered if I could get you one."

He realised he hadn't had a drink in ages. "That'd be great..." he checked out her name badge, "Holly." He pulled out his wallet. "Let me get them though."

"Don't be daft. What would you like?"

"Flat white, please. No sugar."

He watched her walk away. She seemed nice. He found himself looking forward to her coming back. It was a while since he'd practiced his chat up lines.

He immediately felt guilty for even thinking about a distraction. Now wasn't the time to be thinking about his non-existent love life. Or his totally tame social life, come to that.

He returned to checking his emails on his phone. When a shadow fell upon him again, he looked up, expecting to see Nurse Holly with his coffee, but it was Joan's parents.

"We thought we'd go and get a sandwich," said her dad, Paul. "Are you okay to sit with her for a while?"

"Of course. You go and get something to eat."

He'd seen Joan briefly over the weekend, when the signs were encouraging but it wasn't clear when she might wake up. He couldn't decide if she looked any better. Maybe a little?

He sat down in one of the chairs by her bedside. "Hi, Joan," he said. "It's me, Jason." He reached out, took her hand and squeezed it. She squeezed back and her eyes fluttered open.

"Hello, mate," she said groggily. "Where's Mum and Dad?"

"Popped to the canteen. So you're stuck with me."

"Huh. Just my luck." But she was smiling, or at least attempting to. "Any news?"

He shook his head. "Sorry. But we're pulling out all the stops."

He'd agreed with Lizzie and Dan that there was no need to rush into telling her someone who might just be a serial killer was a person of interest.

"I know you are," she said. She frowned. "Jason?"

"Yep."

"I've had this... I don't know if it's a dream or a memory. A flashback?"

The door into the room opened and Nurse Holly entered with a Costa coffee cup. She held it out to him. "There you go, Jason." She looked at Joan. "How are you feeling?"

Joan grimaced. "Dunno. Crap. Better than earlier, I think."

"Do you need anything?"

"Not at the moment, but thanks."

"Fair enough. I'll see you later. Enjoy your coffee, Jason."

"Cheers, Holly."

She departed.

Joan rolled her eyes. "I never knew you were such a fast worker."

"What?" It sounded defensive, even to him.

"*'Enjoy your coffee, Jason.' 'Cheers, Holly.'* You're in there, I reckon."

He felt the familiar heat rising to his cheeks, mentally cursing its betrayal. "Yeah, right. So what was this flashback?"

She looked serious. "I suppose it must have been just a dream. I still can't really remember anything about Friday, but, I don't know, it's happened twice now."

"What has?" He took her hand again.

"We're in the town. I'm with Charlie. We're cutting through on our way home. You know where I mean?"

"Yeah. It's where you were attacked."

"Sorry, yeah, they said. Well, it's dark. I hear footsteps coming up behind us. Fast. I turn around, and this person's there in a balaclava."

"And?"

"And nothing. That's it."

He searched her face. "Could this be the man who attacked you? Was he tall? What sort of build?"

Her eyelids drooped. "I dunno. Taller than me or Charlie, I suppose. It's all just an impression, really. Ah, it must have just been a dream."

He wasn't so sure. "Or maybe it *is* a flashback. A fragment of a memory. Can you think of anything else about this guy, maybe something distinctive?"

She squeezed her eyes shut. "Just this balaclava. But Jason?"

"Yeah?"

"I dunno, there's something about him. I can't quite put my finger…"

She'd drifted off again.

Bell sipped his coffee. What was he supposed to make of this? A figure in a balaclava, confronting them – not quite, but coming up behind them. The head trauma had caused her to lose her memories, not only of the attack but of much of the day leading up to it, yet she seemed to possibly be recalling a snippet of memory from just before she was injured.

Despite her insistence that it was probably a dream, he wasn't so sure. He'd come across something a bit like this way back when he was in uniform: the victim of a hit and run, a teenage boy. What had the doctors called it? Not amnesia: confusion. Post-traumatic confusional state. The lad had remembered nothing of the accident, yet could describe the car that hit him well enough that it had helped solve the case.

Maybe, given time, Joan's recall would become sharper. Maybe even give them something useful they could work with.

Would it be in time to save Charlie? He had no idea. But he prayed it might.

27

The news that Antony Creed had an alibi for Friday night he didn't even know about, from a neighbour happy to make a signed statement, had effectively knocked him out of contention for the attack on Joan and Charlie.

But not for the Invisible Man. Assuming Carol Eustace had any credibility left at all.

Creed remained the only suspect they'd scrutinised at the time of the killings that bore re-examination now, but that was on the say-so of an ex-wife whose story was increasingly all over the place.

"Right," she'd said to Lara, twenty minutes ago, "you and me and Ms Eustace. We're going to get to the bottom of her story once and for all."

So now they were back in that shabby, airless interview room with Eustace and her brief, both of whom had asked after Charlie.

"I can't talk about the case," Archer said. "I'm sure you'll understand why. Now, Ms Eustace… look, is it okay to call you Carol?"

"Of course." She seemed very nervous.

"Carol, we're really struggling with your story. We just can't get it straight in our minds. That's why I've decided to do this interview. A fresh pair of eyes and ears, you know?"

"Okay."

"Good. So, just to recap. Back in 2001, you backed up Antony Creed's assertion that he was in probation appointments with you when two high-profile murders were being carried out. You were, in fact, having a very ill-advised relationship with him at the time, which you omitted to mention. Is that right?"

"Mmm."

"For the tape, was that a yes?"

"Yes."

"Thank you." Archer did a doodle on her pad. The interview was being recorded, but she'd found that appearing to write things down imparted an extra layer of gravity to proceedings.

"So," she continued. "You subsequently left the probation service, married Mr Creed, and later you were divorced."

"Yes. As I said, he—"

"No, I don't need the details," Archer said with an encouraging smile. "Not for now, anyway. But that's another yes?"

"Yes."

"So fast-forward to this week, and suddenly it all gets a bit fuzzy. A retired policeman, fact-checking for a book about the Invisible Man, contacts you about the evidence you gave back then, and you retract it, saying you lied for him. Since then, in your conversation with us, it's got vaguer and vaguer. You're no longer sure you lied on those occasions. You were in the habit of lying for him and, oh golly, you can't remember what was truth and what was lies now."

"Y-yes."

"So Mr Creed *might* have been at those meetings with you, or he might not? Yes?"

"I guess so."

"You guess. You see, that's just more obfuscation, isn't it? And you know what? I don't believe a word of it."

"Now hold on," Eustace's waif-like lawyer protested.

"No." Archer injected iron and a hint of menace into her voice. "You hold on. Because it just won't do. You're an intelligent woman, Carol. We're all intelligent women in this room. So please don't insult our intelligence any further. In 2001, we were hunting for a maniac who ended up killing six women and at least five children."

She paused for a beat.

"You were asked about your boyfriend's, your *client*'s movements at the times when some of those women and children were being murdered. Now, either he was with you, or he wasn't. You knew which it was at the time. So you either lied, or you didn't, and you knew it. So don't pretend now that you don't remember which it was. Because something like that does not slip your mind." She spat the last five words out like nails.

Eustace's tongue slipped out, moistening her lips. A wild, panicky look had entered her eyes. "I, I…"

"My client has no comment," the lawyer said, "at this time."

"I see," Archer said. "No comment. And what are we supposed to make of that?" She made eye contact with Eustace. "Do you agree with her? That it's no comment? Even though you set this hare running in the first place."

"No comment," Carol Eustace squeaked.

"That's it," Lara interjected. "I've had enough of this. What shall we charge her with? I mean, there's several options."

"I think we'll go for the lot," Archer replied. "See which ones the DPP fancies running with. But it's jail time for sure, if we get a conviction. Anything from three or four years, right up to life. And the more you mess us about, the worse you're making matters."

"You're intimidating my client," protested the lawyer.

"No," Archer said, "we're waking her up. Let me level with you. I really don't want to be doing this right now. I want every officer I can spare helping me find your colleague, Charlie Ward. But your bloody client said what she said, and we have to follow it up. So I just want the truth, so we can either try and identify what Mr Creed was really doing on the dates in question, or accept that he really was with Carol here and stop wasting our damn time."

"Oh, God." Eustace put her head in her hands.

"Still no comment?" Lara demanded.

The pale-faced woman pulled herself together and sat up straight. "All right. I'll tell you the truth."

Her lawyer flashed her a look, leaned across and whispered in her ear.

Eustace shook her head. "No." She looked at Archer. "Look, I've always been proud that, when Antony showed his true colours, when I realised he was possibly going to kill me if things carried on the way they were going, I left him. I got out of the marriage and, when he started coming after me again, I dealt with that too.

"But don't think that means I've just got on with my life. I still have nightmares. I have trust issues. I doubt I'll ever be able to commit to a relationship again."

She and her brief had been given a glass of water each. She sipped from hers.

"I've spent years hating him for what he did to me. Fantasising about hurting him back. And then someone I thought was police came and asked me about those alibis. It was a moment of unpremeditated madness. Antony *was* with me those times, just like he said he was, like I confirmed. But I suddenly found myself saying he wasn't. Call it a rush of blood. And then it all started getting out of hand. I should have admitted straight away that I'd told a silly lie, but instead I kept on digging."

"Let's be clear, then," Archer said, a feeling of sick disappointment settling in her stomach. "You're going back to square one. Antony Creed could not have committed those four murders, because he was with you at the times in question?"

"That's the honest truth. He may be a lot of things. I wouldn't even put murder past him, to be honest. But he didn't do those, no." She started to cry. "I'm really, really sorry. What are you going to do?"

"I know what we should do," said Archer, seething inside. "And Mr Creed might not want to let it drop either. Although it might not be in his interests to make something of it and run the risk of some unsavoury publicity. You can go for now. We'll let you know what we decide."

"When will we hear from you?" Eustace's solicitor asked.

"We'll be in touch," Archer said. "All I can say for now."

*

Jason Bell returned to the station with news that Joan might be beginning to remember the attack, and Lizzie decided to call an impromptu briefing to get the whole team up to date. In the ten minutes leading up to the meeting, Lizzie broke the news to

Baines: Antony Creed was out of the frame for the Invisible Man murders as well as Charlie's abduction.

Baines didn't know whether to laugh or cry.

There was just about time to call Mac and put him in the picture before the meeting started.

"Och, I'm really sorry, laddie," his old friend said. He sounded almost as crushed as he had that day Baines had found him crying in the gents'. "So I've got your hopes up and it's all dead ends. Oh, well…"

There was a difficult silence on the line. Mac had articulated exactly what Baines felt. He also felt angry, but he contained that.

"Anyhow," Mac said, "I've got to be heading back North tomorrow afternoon, it seems. There's a new cold case with my name on it, and I've more or less done what the lovely Claire wanted. The rest we can do by phone and email."

"That's a shame." He realised that, in spite of everything, he still felt regret that he hadn't seen more of his old friend these past few days. "I'd suggest meeting up, but God knows when I'll have a spare second."

"By the way, I tried to speak to Robin Watson about those parent groups. That Amy lassie was really helpful. Gave me his number. Sounds like he's not changed. If he can get out the office, he'll do so, and he takes his own sweet time getting back. Anyway, I called him, but he didn't pick up, so I left him a message. Bit of a busted flush now, isn't it, with Creed out of the frame? Anyhow, he hasn't got back to me yet."

"Did you say what it was about?"

"Aye, I said it was to do with the Invisible Man case and those groups he did the talks to. Maybe he's ignoring me, maybe he's actually busy for a change. I guess I'll try again and tell him not to bother. I might leave a message for him with Amy too."

"Belt and braces?" Typical Mac.

"Aye. Well," he said, "I guess you should wish me bon voyage."

"Yeah. It was good to see you, Mac. Safe journey."

"And if you're ever up my way, look us up."

28

The briefing started out as a dour affair. Joan's possible recollection of a balaclava-wearing attacker seemed of limited practical value; even if her memory grew sharper, she wasn't going to be able to identify an assailant whose face she hadn't seen. That, plus the evaporation of the possible Antony Creed lead meant they were nowhere further forward in the search for Charlie.

The only chink of light was that, if Joan really was remembering a third party assailant, the possibility that Charlie herself had struck the blow that put Joan in hospital could be ruled out.

"I don't think any of us ever really quite believed it," Archer said, "even though her ex-partner, Vicky Weaver, did hint at an aggressive side to Charlie's nature when they were together."

"I never believed it," Jason declared.

"What was that name again?" Will Tyler piped up. He was frowning.

"What name, Will?"

"The ex. Charlie's ex."

"Vicky. Vicky Weaver."

His brow furrowed. "Hold on. That rings a bell."

"In what sense?

"Ibrahim and I have been going through CCTV in and around the area where the attack happened, as you know, boss. Noting registration numbers and getting owners' names from DVLA." He turned around in his seat. "Ibrahim? Didn't we have a Weaver?"

"I'm not sure. Possibly."

Archer's pulse raced. "Will, you're saying Vicky Weaver was in the area where Joan was attacked, around the time it happened?"

He shook his head. "I can't be sure about that. It's a lot of cars and a lot of names. But Weaver, yeah, that's definitely familiar. I can't remember the first name, or even if it was a woman."

"Right," Archer said, "let's pause the meeting and reconvene when you've checked it out. How long will it take you?"

"Ten minutes max," Ibrahim said. "Maybe a bit more if you want a bit of background data from DVLA. Say twenty minutes altogether?"

"Make it fifteen," said Archer.

Dan and Lara joined her in her office while they waited.

"You know," she said, "I'm thinking about Antony Creed and Carol Eustace, both giving different versions of their marriage. Each saying it was the other that instigated practices they found abhorrent."

"What's that got to do with this case?" Lara wondered.

"Well, what if Vicky was twisting the truth? What if, instead of Charlie being the violent one, it was Vicky? What if Charlie left her?"

Baines saw her point. "It could certainly explain why she developed a passion for domestic abuse cases soon after the breakup."

"Makes sense," Lara agreed. "Of course we don't hear nearly so much about violence or abuse in same-sex relationships. I don't know if it occurs less frequently or just gets reported less. But still, it's not unheard of."

A quarter of an hour later, there were new additions to the board: a note of the registration number of Vicky Weaver's ten-year-old white Citroen Picasso; and CCTV images taken in Aylesbury in a window stretching from one hour before Joan and Charlie were attacked to one hour afterwards. They showed Vicky's Citroen, first in the vicinity of La Salute, where the couple had celebrated Charlie's birthday; and later, close to the site of the attack.

"It can't be a coincidence," Dan remarked.

"Pity there are no cameras in the actual road where the attack happened," said Jason.

"Can you track her, Ibrahim?" Archer prompted. "See where she might have gone afterwards?"

"I'll get on it right away."

"Dan, speak to our contacts at Oxford and get Vicky picked up and brought here. Sort out a warrant to search her room. Will," she jabbed a finger at Will Tyler, "get Phil Gordon and his team ready to do their stuff as soon as we've got the warrant. They need to check over her car, too."

She turned to Lara Moseley. "Lara, can you get people checking out any connections Vicky might have in or around Great Missenden, Princes Risborough, anywhere out that way?"

She felt the familiar buzz in her blood: she sensed that the hunt was really on this time.

"And Jason? Get back to the hospital. Find out what Joan knows about Vicky. And whether there's any possibility that the figure in her flashbacks might be a woman."

It was just short of a week since Maisie Albright and Lauren Black had been targeted by a troubled, but vicious, homophobe. They'd got a result on that one, which had to be a source of great satisfaction.

Everything else had proved a struggle.

And she so wanted, against all the odds, for the mystery of Charlie's disappearance to have a good outcome.

"Remember, we've wrong-footed ourselves enough times this week, so let's not jump to conclusions," she said.

But she could see her own excitement reflected back in several pairs of eyes.

"Anything else?" No hands shot up. "Let's get to work, then."

*

Jason Bell found Joan sitting up in bed, eating toast and talking to her parents. Paul and Sarah were reluctant to leave her side so he could talk to her, but Joan waved them away.

"You could do with a break from me," she insisted.

As soon as the door closed behind them, she rolled her eyes.

"I love them to bits," she said, "but it's exhausting. Mostly they just sit looking at me, as if they expect me to relapse at any moment. Or break like glass. And, I swear, if they ask me if I'm all right one more time…"

"You can't blame them," Bell said. "They've been so worried. We all have."

"I know," she said. "I'm sorry."

"Hardly your fault." He smiled slyly. "So, anyway. Are you all right?"

"If I wasn't starving, I'd throw this toast at you." The smile faded from her lips. "I'm guessing you still haven't found Charlie?"

She was still very tired, and only able to concentrate for so long, but her intuition and her mental organisation seemed largely intact. He thought she was amazing. If he'd not long come round after several days unconscious, to be plunged into mind-numbing worry about someone he loved, he doubted he'd be able to function.

"No. But we're following a new line of enquiry and we need something from you."

"What new line?" she immediately looked more alert.

"Here's the thing," he said. "That dream or flashback of the attack. We're wondering, could it be a woman behind the balaclava?"

"A *woman?*" She leaned back. Stared at the ceiling. Closed, then opened, her eyes again. "You remember, I said there was something about them. I couldn't put my finger on it, but yeah. That could be it, now I think about it. Something in the bearing. But what made you think of that?"

"We had a lucky break. Or lucky if it pays off, anyway."

He explained how Vicky Weaver had been questioned on the off-chance she knew anything useful; and how the name had come up on a list of vehicles caught on camera close to the attack.

She gawped at him. "You're looking at *Vicky?*"

"What do you know about her?"

"Next to nothing. I never met her. No reason I should. And Charlie didn't talk about her much. I never asked, for that matter

– well, you don't ask about your girlfriend's exes, do you? Well, I don't." She made a face. "I'm prattling. Point is, she never mentioned her, except to say she'd lived with someone for a while; and that it hadn't worked out. I just thought there was nothing much to tell."

Bell knew what he had to tell her next, and he realised he was dreading it.

"That first time we spoke to Vicky? One of the things we were trying to establish was whether Charlie had ever been aggressive or violent towards her. She implied she had. We thought she was playing it down. Now I wonder if she was just being subtle."

"Hoping I'd die? Or at least not remember? Shit, Jason. You didn't think she was lying, even when I said Charlie was never like that with me?"

"No. Exaggerating maybe. It never occurred to us that she might have been the attacker. Now we think *she* was the aggressive one and, for some reason, she chose Friday night to come after Charlie."

"It was her birthday. Maybe that was it."

"Could be," he agreed. "It could make a twisted sort of sense. Anyhow, we're bringing her in for formal questioning."

Joan's face twisted. He couldn't tell if she was angry or miserable. Probably a bit of both. "You know, I tell Charlie everything. I thought it worked both ways. Fuck." She shook her head. "But that's not important now. You really think it might have been Vicky, don't you?"

There was a knock on the door and Nurse Holly breezed in.

"Oh," she said, her skin taking on a slightly pinkish hue. "Jason. Hi. How are you?"

He felt his own colour rising. "Good, thanks, Holly. You?"

"Yeah, yeah." She was checking Joan's stats and making notes. "Coffee?"

"Oh, no, you've work to do."

"Oh, it won't take a minute. Got to keep the thin blue line going."

"Great then. Flat—"

"Flat white. I remember. How are you, Joan?"

"Getting there. In fact," she looked at Bell, "I ought to get up and get back to work."

"Nice try," Holly beamed. "You'll leave when the docs say you can." She smiled at Bell, dazzling him, making him blush deeper and curse himself for doing so.

"Blimey, Jason," Joan said when she'd gone, "get her number."

"Eh?"

"You like each other. Get her bloody number. Or do I have to get it for you?"

"Oh," he protested, "no, no. It wouldn't be right, what with—"

"Mate, however this turns out, I'm not going to hate you if something good happens for you."

"Well, thanks." He didn't suppose he'd do anything about it though. At least, not for now. "I don't even know how you can think about that at the moment."

"Nor do I." Her lip wobbled. "Anything to stop me thinking, imagining. I think, if I fall apart, I might never…" She took a deep, ragged breath. Tears rolled down her face and she batted them away angrily. Recomposed her features. "I'm going to go mad in here. I've got to *do* something.

"You can still help," he said. "In fact, that's one of the reasons I'm here. You say you don't know anything about Vicky? But does Charlie still see anyone who knew them both?"

"A few. I've got their numbers in my phone. Where *is* my phone?"

"We've got it. I can probably bring it in next time."

"Well, try Sami Jelf – that's as in Samantha – and Mary Young, and Angus Sewell."

He made a note. "Got it."

A few minutes later, Holly came back with his coffee. She winked at Joan on her way out.

Bell put the paper cup aside to cool. He saw Joan eyeing it.

"Did you fancy one yourself?" he asked.

"What? Oh, no. But you might want to keep that cup."

He looked at her, bemused. "Why?"

"Because it's got what looks like a mobile phone number written on it."

*

DC Steve Ashby drew his sleek Audi up outside Vicky Weaver's home, turned to DS Amy Petrescu in the passenger seat, and gestured to the dirty and slightly battered vehicle in front of him,

"That's her car. Let's hope she's at home."

A marked patrol car pulled in behind him. He spoke to the occupants, then he and Amy walked up to the house and rang the bell.

One of Vicky's housemates, a young man with one of those man-buns that Ashby despised and a zip-up cardigan, answered the door. They showed their ID.

"Vicky?" He scratched his stomach. "I dunno. She was in, and I haven't heard the front door go, but I've been playing music…"

"We know the way," Ashby said, brushing past him. Amy followed in his wake as he climbed the stairs and halted outside Vicky's door, rapping on a panel with his knuckles. He heard movement inside, then the door opened to reveal the suspect, in the act of pulling off a set of headphones.

She blinked. "Inspector?" She flashed a smile. "Back again?"

"It's DC Ashby actually. This is DS Petrescu."

Vicky looked Amy up and down, then smiled again. "Hi." She turned her attention to Ashby again. "More questions?"

"More questions," he confirmed. "But this time we need you to come to Aylesbury with us for a more formal interview."

The smile melted away. "Formal? What, am I a suspect now? Am I under arrest?"

"We'd rather not have to."

She shrugged. "You'd best come in."

They followed her into the room.

"And we'd like permission to search your room, properly this time, and your car," said Amy. "We can get a warrant if we have to, but…"

She flapped a hand. "No need for that." But there was something forced about her airiness, and Ashby had seen panic in enough suspects' eyes to recognise it in Vicky Weaver.

"If you could just grab what you need and let us have the car keys then," he said. "I'm afraid we'll have to take the car away. One of my colleagues will drive it."

She left the door ajar as she pulled on an electric blue puffa jacket that had seen better days, then sat on the bed to pull on boots.

"So I'm assuming you haven't found Charlie yet," she said as she stood up, picked up a shoulder bag from a bedside chest and rummaged inside it.

"We can't discuss the case," Amy said.

"Well, as I've said before, you're wasting your time here." She pulled out a set of car keys and moved towards the door.

Amy held out a hand. "I'll take the keys."

Vicky made to hand them over, then shoved Amy into Ashby before bolting out the door. Ashby heard her footsteps pounding on the stairs as he disentangled himself from Amy and gave chase.

The front door barely slowed her down and Ashby heard the beep of a car's central locking as she hurtled into the street.

She was fast, but so was Ashby. As she reached the Citroen, he laid a hand upon her shoulder, only for her to spin around and kick him in the testicles in one smooth movement, the mask finally slipping as her eyes glittered with glee. Sick agony surged through him as he doubled over, clutching the injured area.

Vicky was already in the car. Amy brushed past Ashby and yanked on the passenger door, but the fleeing suspect had already re-engaged the locks. The Citroen's engine started and it roared away, Amy letting go to avoid being dragged over.

She turned to the patrol car, its occupants gawping. Visibly furious, she waved them after the speeding Citroen. As the patrol car sped off, sirens screeching and blue light flashing,

Ashby wordlessly handed his car keys to Amy and hobbled to the passenger door. Seconds later, they too were in pursuit.

The road was on a slight incline and so he could see Vicky's car ahead, traveling at frightening speeds. An oncoming van was forced to take evasive action. Ashby knew she'd have to stop or slow down at the junction with the main road, and the patrol car was steadily gaining on her.

"She won't get far," Amy said, her eyes fixed on the road. "All she's doing is confirming her guilt."

"I've never known an innocent person to run," Ashby agreed, his eyes still watering.

"Nor to assault a police officer in the process."

Vicky was almost at the junction. Ashby was expecting her brake lights to come on at any second. Was surprised they hadn't already.

Realised she had no intention of stopping.

At the last moment, the brake lights did blink, but only for an instant. A sense of horrified inevitability washed over him as the Citroen barrelled into a left turn with no sign of reducing speed. He saw the rear end fishtail, then right itself.

Then an oncoming lorry ploughed into it. Even at this distance, the sound of the impact was immense, like a small bomb exploding.

29

Outside the station, thunder rumbled in the distance. It was as if the weather was drifting around, confined by the Chiltern Hills, searching angrily for a way out. The tense atmosphere in the briefing room felt even more charged.

The sense of shock was palpable. Archer had to force herself not to think back a few years to when she'd had little time for Steve Ashby and would have been prepared to assume he'd made a mess of what should have been a simple enough job. But Ashby had changed, and she knew he and Amy were as desperate for Charlie to be found as were her own team.

It happened. Suspects sensed that the game was up and, perhaps not thinking straight, made a run for it. Sometimes they took you off guard. Usually they didn't get very far.

But Vicky Weaver had made it to her car. Now the Citroen was a mangled heap of metal and Vicky was in Oxford's John Radcliffe Hospital, fighting for her life. Apparently her chances of pulling through were 40-60 at best.

Now it was a waiting game. In the meantime, forensic experts had begun searching Vicky's house, the bins, what was left of her car, her clothes. Archer was confident that if there was any trace of Charlie Ward, or Joan for that matter, they would find them.

"There's already some very interesting news," she told the assembled team. "CSI found a Sainsbury's bag in the bin, containing a black balaclava. They've also found traces of blood on Vicky's steering wheel. Hair and fibres in the boot of the car."

"Obviously, it's all subject to testing," Phil Gordon said, "but if the balaclava has Vicky Weaver's DNA on it; if the blood is a match for Charlie or Joan; and if the traces in the boot or on any of her clothes can be matched to Charlie…" He made an open-palmed gesture.

"I want everything fast tracked," said Superintendent Stowe. "Cost is immaterial."

"There's a couple of other things," Phil added. "Hot off the press." Archer sensed excitement in his voice.

"First of all," he said, "we found some medication. It's the kind used to manage psychotic disorders and, judging by the date on the packet, the dose, and the number of tablets left, it's pretty clear she hasn't taken them as regularly as she should have."

Archer took this in. "If Charlie knew anything about this, surely she'd have shared it with Joan?"

"Not if she felt it wasn't for her to share," Jason said. "It seems Charlie didn't say much to Joan about Vicky at all."

"If Charlie even knew," Dan said. "Could she have had the disorder back when she was with Charlie and somehow managed to conceal it?"

He was looking at Phil, who smiled and shook his head. "You'd have to ask an expert. I'm just a humble crime scene manager."

"Okay," Archer said. "Phil, there was something else?"

"Miss Weaver's keys," Phil continued. "Most of them what one would expect: house keys, room key, car key. But there's something else. Why would she have what looks very much like a handcuff key?"

Archer met his eyes. "Any actual handcuffs?"

He shook his head. "I mean, the search goes on, but no sign so far."

"So where are they?"

"This is how I read it," he said. "I think the blood, hair and fibres are going to nail Vicky Weaver to the attack on Friday night. She struck Joan and she fell, striking her head."

"Agreed."

"I'd say maybe she didn't mean to hurt her so badly. Maybe she panicked and abducted Charlie as the only witness. Except, I reckon she had the handcuffs with her, which I reckon suggests some degree of premeditation."

"So maybe abduction was the plan all along." Her gaze travelled around the room. "So maybe this is good news. If we're right in her thinking, then chances are Vicky's holding Charlie somewhere, and she's alive."

"But at risk," Baines pointed out.

"Very much so," she agreed. She stole a glance at Vicky Weaver's photograph on the board. "We'd better pray Vicky pulls through. And quickly."

*

It was gone midnight when Archer got home, tired, hungry and dispirited. Not all of the news was bad. Superintendent Stowe had leaned hard for the fast-track testing of DNA samples from the wreckage of Vicky Weaver's car, and the results had been promised for early tomorrow morning. She strongly suspected they would confirm that Vicky had recently got Joan Collins's blood on her hands and transferred it to the steering wheel; and that Charlie had been in contact with the inside of the car's boot.

A receipt from a sex shop for the handcuffs had also turned up.

Before sending them home to get some sleep themselves, Archer had caught up with the rest of the team. Jason Bell had gone through Joan's phone and picked out the three contacts she knew through Charlie who went back to her time with Vicky.

All three had admitted to sometimes sensing a tension in the relationship and domineering tendencies in Vicky. Two of them hadn't seen her since the couple split up. Only one, Angus Sewell, had kept in sporadic touch. About six months ago they'd had coffee together and she had mentioned that Charlie was in a new relationship.

"How did she seem to be taking it?" Jason had asked him.

"She said she wished her luck, but she wasn't fooling me. I thought she was upset. She said it wouldn't last."

"You've got a good memory."

"It was the way she said it," Sewell told him. "Not just a throwaway thing. She said it with complete conviction. I said something like, 'You never know,' and she just gave me this funny smile and said, 'Trust me.' It was all a bit weird."

Had Vicky Weaver been merely expressing a hope that her ex-partner's new love would flounder? Or was she already signalling an intention to do something about it?

The three contacts had also been asked about other buildings she might have access to. No one knew of any such place.

Asked what sort of person Weaver was, all three had used the word 'obsessive'. She adopted an interest, often something quite extreme, and it dominated her. She'd dabbled in skydiving, rock climbing, wild swimming... and cajoled Charlie into trying them all. Archer wondered if 'bullied' would probably be a more accurate description.

"So," she'd addressed the team, "we're assuming she was still obsessed with Charlie. What's her thought process?"

"I reckon she'd find it hard to accept the breakup," suggested Amir. "Maybe she'd try to win her back."

"And if that failed?"

PC Sue Dyson raised her hand. "Maybe she'd move onto a new obsession at first, but then she has the chat with this Angus guy. That might spark her jealousy all over again. Or maybe just the thought that Charlie's birthday was coming up."

"Perhaps she even started stalking her and Joan," suggested Will Tyler. "Maybe just watching them together at first. Then she decides, if she can't have Charlie, no one will."

"So you're thinking, what exactly? That Charlie's dead?"

"That's the logic." Will's expression was sombre. "If there's nowhere she's likely to be keeping her..."

Archer had sensed a darkening of the mood in the room. "I think you're probably right," she admitted quietly.

There. She'd said it. Having done so, she felt sick. Had to remind herself who she was and that leadership was what was needed now.

"Just one thing though?" Jason looked pensive. "Why attack them both? Why not get Charlie on her own?"

"Oh, I can think of a couple of reasons," said Dan. "I tend to agree that Charlie's birthday might have had extra significance. Secondly, why not go after the person who stole Charlie from her, as well as Charlie herself? Maybe she actually intended to kill Joan in front of her. Maybe she thought she had."

Archer was sickened by the thought, but made herself embrace it. "So why not kill Charlie there and then?"

Dan had looked appalled by his own thought process. "Too quick, maybe. Perhaps she'd want to make it last, to make Charlie really suffer. But it doesn't mean she took her to any premises. Could be she took her deep into a wood, or somewhere else remote, and tortured her before she killed her."

"You might be right," she accepted. The weight of responsibility was like a stone on her shoulders. Because this was too personal, too close to home. "Okay, everyone. We all need sleep. Tomorrow we start a full-scale search for her body. Not a stone left unturned. We'll draft people in from across Thames Valley. Neighbouring forces too, if they can be spared."

Now, locking her car on her drive, she saw that an upstairs light at Dominic's still burned. She had her own key, so she let herself in.

"Only me," she called up the stairs as Barney wound himself around her legs.

Moments later, Dominic appeared on the landing in his tee shirt and boxers.

"You look terrible."

"Wow, you know how to give a girl a lift, Newman."

"Have you eaten?"

"No, but I'm past caring. I'll just make myself a sandwich, if that's okay."

"I'll do it. Ham and cheese?"

"Whatever. Is it all right if I sleep here? I really don't want to be on my own tonight."

By now he had come downstairs. He held her close. "Of course. Just to sleep?"

"Do you mind? I'm so fucking tired."

He kissed her forehead. "Do you want to talk about it?"

She sighed. "It's Charlie."

He held her a little tighter. "Oh, no. Is she…?"

"We don't know for sure, but it's not looking at all good. As of tomorrow morning, we're searching for her body. I mean, we're still hoping against hope, but that hope is fading. Poor Joan. Jason says she's holding it together incredibly well."

"I can't begin to imagine what she's going through. If you were missing like that, I'd be out of my mind."

His words and his embrace gave her a rush of comfort and love.

"I'm so lucky I've got you," she said.

He gave her a quick squeeze. "Go on, up to bed. I'll be up with something to eat, and a drink, in a mo. Hot chocolate?"

"Yeah, go on. I love you."

"Love you too."

She went upstairs, used the loo, got undressed, and fished her nightdress out of what had become 'her' drawer in the bedroom chest. She sat up in bed, listening to the persistent drumming of rain on the windowpane. She sent up a silent prayer that Charlie was alive and being held captive somewhere, and not lying dead in the darkness somewhere, covered by undergrowth or soil, rain splashing on her dead, staring eyes.

The mental image, once conjured, seemed to burn itself onto her brain. She couldn't stop seeing it. By the time Dominic came up with a plate and a mug, she was lying down, covers pulled up to her nose, shivering. She wondered if she was coming down with something, but she knew it was more likely a reaction to the case, getting deep under her skin. This was a friend. It was personal.

She ate and drank on autopilot, then snuggled down again. She was asleep before Dominic joined her in bed, a sleep infested with dark and twisting dreams.

A sleep she was ripped from by the pealing of her phone.

Groggy, disorientated, she answered it, vaguely noting that it was approaching 4am.

The news was as bad as it could be. Vicky Weaver had died of her injuries. She'd never regained consciousness.

30

Baines and Lizzie had arrived at the station at more or less the same time. Vicky's death was a shattering blow to their hopes of finding Charlie alive, and neither could sleep. So they'd come to work, even though there was nothing they could do at so early an hour.

Baines could see Lizzie was as exhausted as he was. Sometimes, only pure adrenalin kept you going.

He had no doubt at all now that Charlie's former lover was responsible for what had happened to her and Joan. But she'd fooled him and Jason when they'd questioned her in her home. If she'd been in the midst of some form of psychotic episode at the time, she'd appeared to be functioning normally enough. But then they didn't know what her 'normal' looked like.

"We didn't exactly miss it, Lizzie," he said, as they sat in her office drinking coffee. "We just couldn't see it. I think now, from the moment she knew Charlie had found someone else, she decided she wasn't having it. So she starts planning what she's going to do about it. I think she decides to do it on her birthday, out of some sick sense of irony. And she's so convinced she'll get away with it, she doesn't bother to remove evidence from the car, not even after our first visit. She even disposes of the balaclava in her own bin."

"And now the only person who knew what happened to Charlie is dead." Lizzie looked haggard. Grey-faced, formidable bags under bloodshot eyes. She'd not done her make-up, nor taken much care over her hair, which was as unruly as he'd seen it. The scar she usually took such pains to conceal was clearly visible. He doubted she was even aware.

"Doesn't sound good, does it?" she said. "But I'm damned if I'm having another bloody Jessica Winter. Not on my watch."

Baines knew the case, one that went back to her days at the Met. Jessica was known to be the victim of a pair of serial killers but, like Baines's son, Jack, her body had never been found. Lizzie hadn't worked the case herself, but she'd seen how the guilt of failure, the obsession with finding Jessica, had devoured her old boss, DCI Nick Gibson, from the inside. It hadn't destroyed him – he was too strong for that – but it had haunted him in the same way the Invisible Man still haunted Baines and Mac.

When Lizzie spoke of Jessica Winter, Baines guessed she was thinking also of Jack, and of the countless other murder victims whose loved ones had never had the closure of a funeral. Of knowing where their remains were resting.

Yet, as they sat there in her office, sharing coffee, exhaustion and the darkest of thoughts, he found himself wondering.

"That detour Vicky made, after she took Charlie. Out Great Missenden way. At least we know that's where we should concentrate our initial search effort. It has to be where she killed her and disposed of her body."

"I think you're right," she agreed. "We've really given up all hope, haven't we?"

Baines turned the question over. Even when he'd finally, finally, accepted the logic of Jack's death, a little hope had somehow remained, a spark that had briefly flared into flame when he'd imagined seeing him outside the Waterside Theatre, before the realisation that it was simply that same old ghost, conjured back into his mind by Mac's return to the Vale.

"I haven't actually," he decided. "Not completely. But then I've always let my heart rule my head too much."

She held her hand out to him, across the desk. After a moment, he took it and squeezed gently. She looked so tired and vulnerable.

"That's good," she said. "I need to kick myself up the arse and find some hope too."

*

The misery was overwhelming. Charlie didn't see how much longer she could hang on. For once, the weather forecasters seemed to be on the money. On Friday – however long ago that had been now – they'd said there'd be little let-up in the rain for the coming week, and that much of it would be heavy. And that prediction was being borne out by the steady rise in the water level around her, now the best part of a meter deep, waist-height on her imposed kneeling position.

She was wet and cold. She'd tried to do some form of physical exercise, within the limitations of her confinement, to try and keep some degree of warmth in her cold body. Scraping away at the metal ring to which she was cuffed burned a few calories. Squats and sit-ups, shuffling around on her knees, moving her free arm in a circular motion – she did these regularly, mindlessly. All to try and ward off the inevitable onset of hypothermia. But she knew it was a losing battle. That it was already setting in.

Her skin felt cold to the touch, and she could barely feel her hands or feet. She was growing ever more sluggish, drowsy and lethargic. When she dozed, she would dream, and she was finding it harder to distinguish between the dreams and reality. At one point, she'd been convinced the door to the exit shaft had opened, light streaming in and burning her eyes. Joan's face had appeared, her smile radiant, and then she'd rushed in, sloshing into the water, grabbing Charlie in an embrace.

"We found you!" she'd cried joyfully.

And Charlie had jerked awake, cold and wet in the darkness. Her howls had echoed off the walls.

She realised now just how much she'd been clinging to the hope that Joan was alive, and Joan would somehow find her. Now, at last, she realised how unlikely that was.

There was no reason why anyone would suspect Vicky of something like this. Not even Charlie herself would have thought it possible.

It was true that the loving person she had first been so attracted to – had fallen in love with – had turned out so unpredictable. She could also be stiflingly possessive, prone to wild accusations and dark moods. For a while, she'd found herself making allowances. In denial, she'd supposed afterwards.

It hadn't been until the first time Vicky hit her that she'd finally woken up and walked out, going back to live with her parents while she looked for somewhere else. But she'd simply told her family and friends – and later Joan – that the relationship hadn't worked out. Why hadn't she told anyone just how bad things had become before she had finally walked away?

Maybe she'd just felt a fool for being so blind to the kind of person she'd fallen for.

It had taken a while for Vicky to accept that it was over and to stop trying to contact her. Now, Charlie realised too late, she'd accepted nothing of the sort. And only now did she realise that what lay behind her mood swings and that first crossing of the line into violence was some sort of illness. For all the terror and, yes, the hatred she felt for Vicky plunging her into this nightmare, there was shame, too.

Had she just been too wrapped up in her career to see the warning signs? It was evident now that Vicky was unwell. Charlie had walked out on her when maybe she should have been much more supportive.

At least she thought she could guess why Vicky appeared to have left it so long before exacting this revenge. Once Joan had come out to everyone who mattered to her, Charlie had changed her social media status to 'in a relationship' and had even posted a few photos of them together. If Vicky had been stalking her online, she would have known about it for a while. But it seemed she'd deliberately bided her time until Charlie's birthday.

The reason was appallingly obvious.

Last year, for Charlie's first birthday after the breakup, Vicky had sent a card and a present. Charlie had returned them with a polite note, imploring her not to contact her again. Perhaps that was when Vicky had determined that this year's birthday would be like no other.

Maybe even the last she would see.

Because, from that single punch – from what they'd taken for a passing jogger, in a balaclava, sending Joan crashing to the pavement – to Vicky abandoning her here, she had spoken just three words, other than barking instructions.

As she walked away, ignoring all the pleas, curses and questions, she'd paused at the door to the entrance shaft. Turned and smiled.

"Happy birthday, darling."

And then she had left, not saying whether she intended to return.

It was looking increasingly unlikely that she would.

Once more, she reached into her mind for Joan, telling herself again that she was alive; that she would somehow know, deep down, if that was not the case. And, even if that was pure fancy, Charlie was sure she wouldn't want her ever to give up, not until the last breath left her body.

She'd continued to use the torch sparingly, but she turned it on now, illuminating the door beyond which lay that metal ladder up to the hatch. Beyond that, freedom. It seemed to taunt her.

She needed to get free of that handcuff.

Working at the concrete around the ring was futile, she knew that in her heart. Hypothermia would finish her, if drowning or pure exhaustion didn't do the job first. Thoughts of picking the lock returned. If only she had something small enough to fit inside those locks. But she had nothing.

Happy birthday, darling.

The realisation that hit her like a thunderbolt, and she cursed herself for not thinking of it before. She'd thought she had nothing. Had her mind been so fogged, so clouded with terror?

How could she have forgotten the beautiful sunflower brooch Joan had given her for her birthday?

She remembered the anxious look on her partner's face as she'd watched Charlie first unwrap, then open, the red faux leather jeweller's box to reveal the gift over dinner at La Salute. She remembered lifting the brooch out, fingering the tiny petals, holding it so it caught the light.

"Well?" Joan had asked. "Do you like it?"

She'd kissed her on the mouth, then hugged her close. "No, I don't *like* it. I bloody *love* it!"

She'd wanted to try it on there and then. Had held it against her black silk top. The fabric showed the silver sunflower to its best advantage, but Joan, ever the practical one, had been concerned that the pin and the weight of the brooch would ruin the fabric. So Charlie had zipped the box safely inside her jacket pocket, saving it for a more suitable garment.

The top was almost certainly ruined anyway now, but maybe the brooch's fastening pin could save her life.

She turned on the torch and clamped it between her teeth once more. Training its light as best she could, she removed the box from her pocket and then lifted the brooch out, fumbling with icy cold fingers that felt like sausages, almost dropping it.

Holding the opened pin between her right thumb and forefinger, she stared through the murky water at the handcuff, trying to remember how Joan had bent the paper clip. It wasn't easy with her brain so fogged, but her powers of recall were good, and she'd paid attention because she'd found the lock-picking fascinating.

Her hands were shaking, either from cold or nervousness. Maybe both. Having to do this under water was hardly helping, either.

As she inserted the pin into the lock, she could almost hear Joan's voice giving a running commentary on what she was doing as she picked open a handcuff on their little kitchen table:

You've got to push it in halfway. If it goes all the way in, you won't be able to bend it right. Now I'm bending it to the left. You want a ninety-degree bend.

The pin was much harder to bend than a paper clip. In one way, she thought that was no bad thing. Joan had said the pick needed to be strong enough to apply sufficient pressure to the mechanism. But she also thought it might be less forgiving. Get it wrong, and she might not be able to straighten it properly again. She could end up with a useless picking tool.

So she might only have one shot at getting this right.

She paused, dipping into her memory for more of Joan's commentary.

Now I'm inserting the paper clip again, this time halfway past the first bend. I need another ninety-degree bend to the left. It gives me a sort of 'S' shape.

She withdrew the pin carefully. As far as her memory allowed, she didn't think it was too bad a replication of the paper clip pick Joan had fashioned.

She hesitated. Joan had said something about a single lock and a double lock. The police used double locks, to stop the cuff from ratcheting tighter through, for example, the prisoner struggling. Too tight, and the handcuffs could cause nerve damage or loss of circulation. The wearer could also tighten the cuffs deliberately so an officer would have to loosen them, providing a chance to attempt escape.

Yes. With a single lock, you had to press the pick one way. With the double, the other. But which was which? And, since these were probably not police issue handcuffs, she couldn't be sure what kind they were anyway.

She worried about it. Did it matter? She could try both ways: with and against the cuff's direction of travel. Hopefully, her pick – if she'd even fashioned it right – would be robust enough to withstand one wrong attempt, so long as she didn't force it.

Wherever Vicky had got the cuffs, they looked a good quality. And she'd tried to pull her hand through a few times, hoping the water would lubricate it, or that she'd lost a little weight down here that might make her wrist slimmer.

The cuff hadn't tightened, so it was probably double lock. But that didn't help her decide which way to press first. And her recollection of how exactly to manoeuvre the pick was hazier than her memory of how to make it.

She calmed her breathing. Cleared her racing mind. Reached for Joan's voice again.

For a double lock, you insert the pick into the upper cut-out of the lock, pointing it away from the cuff's direction of travel.

Away? Was she really remembering this?

Intuition? Or clear, genuine memory? She couldn't shake the notion that Joan was somehow talking to her, helping her. She followed the instruction in her head, slipping the pick into the cut-out.

You have to manoeuvre the pick under the handcuff housing and turn it away from the direction of travel, the way the key would turn to release the lock.

She tried, gingerly. Nothing happened.

Her jaws hurt from holding the torch. She felt that her front teeth might snap against the cold, hard casing.

The double lock takes a bit of pressure to move, so you do need some tension against the pick to press the bar inside and release it.

The fear that the pick might actually snap or get caught in the mechanism was almost unbearable, but she didn't see she had a lot of choice. She gradually increased the pressure. Just as she was becoming convinced that she was actually going the wrong way, she felt the resistance go and the cuff sprang open.

The relief was unbelievable. For the first time in God knew when, she was able to stand up straight. But she didn't do so until she had extricated her precious brooch from the lock and secured it back in her jacket pocket.

As she rose and straightened, muscles and joints that had been constrained for too long shrieked in protest. Her hips, knees and lower body felt like part of a ninety-year-old.

Finally she was upright, heaving a sigh of exquisite pleasure.

That was when her teeth lost their grip on the torch. As panic knifed through her, it plummeted into the water with a splash.

"No!" she cried. "No, no, no…"

Even as she bent those stiff, screaming muscles to retrieve it, it dimmed. As her hand closed over it, it went out.

"Fuck," she said. "Fuck, fuck, fuck."

She was free of the cuff that had secured her wrist to the floor and standing upright, the water suddenly feeling less deep and threatening than it had a short while ago. But now she was in utter darkness. She turned the torch off, turned it on again. Tried shaking it. Took the battery out, shook it, did her best to dry it with the least damp parts of her clothing. Put it back and tried again.

Nothing.

She supposed it was a cheap torch, not built to be watertight. But so what? All she had to do was find the door to the shaft where the ladder was, climb up and open the hatch. It might be dark outside, for all she knew, and she wasn't entirely sure where she was. But she'd be free.

One step at a time. The first thing to do was climb the ladder. She knew where the door leading to it had been in relation to where she stood, but she could easily have turned herself around. That didn't really matter. All she had to do was find a wall, and work her way along it until she found that door. It might take time but, now she could see an end to this nightmare, a few more minutes didn't really matter. And it wasn't as if this room was exactly palatial.

She sloshed through the water, the sound it made eerie in this dark, echoey space, her arms stretched out in front of her, moving slowly, anticipating contact with the painted brickwork. When it came, she suspected it had taken less time than it seemed.

She calmed herself again. She thought she might have veered off to her right at some point, and that the door had originally been to her left. So she turned herself to the left and began feeling her way along the wall. Once her foot contacted some sort of debris and she almost stumbled.

It seemed to take an age, but then the texture under her palms changed. It had to be the door. Where was the handle? She tried to envisage it. About halfway down, to the left of the door? She groped around and almost sagged with relief when she encountered it.

Relief immediately gave way to doubt and fear. What if Vicky had had the means to lock the door?

Oh, but what would have been the point? As far as Vicky was concerned, Charlie could stay secured to the floor for eternity. She wasn't going anywhere. Heart in mouth, she tried the handle and it turned easily, the door opening outwards. It sounded like water flowed out of the shaft as it opened, suggesting that this might be where the rain was coming in. Likely the hatch wasn't watertight. Indeed, she could hear it pouring down from above, splashing in the water below.

Inside the shaft, the sound of running water was louder. She easily found the ladder, its metal rungs icy to the touch. The notion of climbing it in almost total darkness was scary, but there was no choice. At least now her hands were free. She tried the torch one more time, but it remained dead. Maybe she could try again to dry it out, but she was just impatient to get out of this hell-hole now.

She climbed slowly, carefully, hand over hand, dragging herself up with tired arms, regularly pausing to feel around above her. The last thing she wanted to do was discover the hatch by striking her head on it. She imagined herself knocked unconscious, plummeting...

She forced the thought away, reaching for fresh positivity. Up a couple of rungs, feel above. Repeat.

When her fingertips found metal instead of air above her, she felt like cheering. Instead, she calmed herself, regained focus. Climbed up until she could get a palm underneath the hatch and push.

She met only resistance.

"No," she moaned.

She pushed harder. Climbed one more rung, leaned in close to the ladder to maximise her balance, and attempted to shove with both hands. All that happened was that she almost fell. She had to grab at the ladder with both hands, panic stabbing her heart. She clung on, gulping in stale air until the terror subsided.

She had to face the facts. She might be free of the handcuffs, in no serious danger of drowning. But she was still trapped here in the cold and the dark, her body's reserves and her food and drink all but exhausted.

If help didn't come soon, she was going to die here.

31

Superintendent Stowe had arrived at 6.30am, surprising Archer, and he'd had her straight into his office for an update.

Attempts were still being made to track down a next of kin for Vicky Weaver. She was an only child whose parents had died a few years ago, and so far no contacts had been identified who might be an uncle, aunt or cousin. It was unlikely to help them find Charlie. She reiterated her plan to embark on a full-scale search for a body today.

"I'm really sorry to hear that," he said. "Do we think there's no hope at all?"

"Dan's still hoping for the best," she said, "but I'm damned if I can think where Charlie's being held if she's still alive."

"I'm afraid that was my feeling at the outset," Stowe said, nodding. "And that feeling's only grown stronger with the passage of time. It's not going to end well, I'm afraid. Does Dan base this hope on anything concrete?"

"He cares about Joan," she said simply. "We all do."

"I know." He sighed. "I know we don't know each other well yet, and I know I can seem a bit intense and maybe over-focused. But I've seen how tight this division is, and how you all look out for each other. That's at least partly down to your leadership."

"It's eating everybody up."

"I know it is. So let's do our best to find her, one way or another. Then at least Joan, and everyone else who loves Charlie, will be on the way to some sort of closure."

Now it was 7.30am and the team were gathered in the briefing room. A lot of work had been done overnight, especially on the forensics, at doubtlessly eye-watering cost. There was no lingering doubt that Vicky Weaver was indeed Joan's attacker and Charlie's abductor.

They were halfway through hearing a specialist Police Search Advisor's proposals for an area-wide search, focused first on Great Missenden and the immediate surrounding area, when the briefing room door opened and a familiar, if shaky, figure walked in.

"Joan," Archer said, stunned. "What the hell…?"

"I discharged myself," Joan said. "I belong here, not in bed. So what's going on?"

"Don't be so daft," Jason Bell said. "Let me run you back to the hospital."

"Or at least home," added Dan. "You shouldn't be here."

She was pale, still bruised around the nose, but there was also that set of her jaw that Archer knew well.

"Have you found Charlie?" she demanded.

The awkward silence was deafening. Joan looked around, registered the search advisor. "Fuck me, you've given up on her, haven't you?"

"No," Archer protested, "but—"

"Please don't lie to me, Lizzie."

"We haven't given up. But it's time to—"

"To search for a body." Her face twisted in misery. "But why? What makes you so sure—"

Stowe was out of his seat, striding up to her. Archer braced herself but, with unexpected gentleness, he laid a hand on Joan's shoulder.

"Come on," he said. "You shouldn't be standing. Come and sit at the front."

He offered her his arm. It was an old-fashioned gesture that Archer was sure Joan would refuse but, after a moment, she took it, accepting the support. He escorted her to the seat he had vacated, got others to budge up, and sat next to her.

"Someone get some water," he said. Jason was quickest off the mark.

"We've not given up on Charlie," said Stowe. "But we're running out of options and we have to look at everything. We're still hoping she's alive somewhere, and we're doing everything possible to think where that might be."

She received the plastic tumbler of water from Jason and took a sip. "Has Vicky come round yet? We need to question her."

Archer felt herself wince. This briefing, with everyone watching, was not the right arena for answering that. And yet trying to take Joan somewhere more private was likely to cause serious ructions. She exchanged a glance with Stowe, who nodded.

"I only wish we could, Joan," she said. "I'm afraid Vicky died in the early hours of this morning."

Joan looked as if she had been slapped. Her lower lip wobbled. "Oh, Christ. Then how will you..." She lowered her face into her hands. "Oh, Jesus," she mumbled. "She could be dying somewhere, and you haven't got a clue."

"Well," Dan said, "we're pretty sure, if she is being held, it's not any property Vicky owns, or has access to. Ibrahim's examining her computer. Maybe that'll give us a clue."

"Look," Archer said decisively, "there's two main tasks here, and it doesn't need all of us pontificating on it. There's the wider search, and there's trying to identify where Vicky might have been holding Charlie. So Dan, Jason, Joan: why don't you three go in one of the smaller meeting rooms and try to pull together what we know, and see if there's anything we might have missed? Anything we've overlooked, any questions we ought to have asked. I'll come and see you as soon as we're done here."

Joan looked at her challengingly. "You'd better not be managing me."

"You know me better than that."

Joan glowered at her, then nodded and heaved herself to her feet. Jason was there in an instant, offering his arm as he had seen the Superintendent do.

"Anyone would think I'm a fucking invalid," she muttered as she accepted it.

"After days in a coma?" Jason said. "Why would anyone imagine that?"

*

Baines's phone rang just as they were sitting down in the meeting room. Mac. He let it go to voicemail. He had no time for that now.

He knew that, perhaps for the first time since her promotion, Lizzie was really feeling the weight of her added responsibility. And he knew why. This case was personal, and they had nothing. Even the disappointment that Mac had unearthed nothing new seemed inconsequential compared to the tragedy playing out here and now.

He didn't need to imagine the hell Joan was going through. He thought it must exactly mirror the agony he'd suffered in the early days after Jack's abduction, the not knowing a constant torture.

"So Joan," he began. "I know Jason's spoken to you about this before, but think hard: did Charlie ever mention anywhere that might have had special significance for her and Vicky?"

Joan screwed her eyes shut, concentration lines furrowing her brow.

"No," she said at last. "I mean, it's not so unusual for people not to say much about their ex, is it? No one wants to think they're being compared, right?"

She had a sort of point, he supposed, although he could remember in his teenage days going on a date with a girl who'd gone on and on about the guy she'd previously been going out with. He hadn't called her again.

"Jason," he turned to the Scot. "You spoke to people who knew her. I know you didn't get much of use out of them, but was there anything at all that might help?"

"As I said before, she seems to have had her fads about extreme sports," Jason said. "But I don't suppose that's much use."

"Extreme..." Joan's eyes widened. "Hang on a minute. That's right."

"Yeah," Jason said. "All sorts of stuff you wouldn't get me doing. Wild swimming skydiving, rock climbing."

"And urban exploration," Joan said.

"Yeah. That too."

Baines stared at him, seeing the source of Joan's excitement. "That's where people get into abandoned buildings and the like, right?"

"Yeah," Jason said again. "They often trespass on private property. I think they go down storm drains and sewers too."

Baines gave him a hard look. "You didn't think this was worth mentioning before?"

Jason blushed, mumbled an apology.

"My God, yes," Joan was suddenly animated. "One of the few times Charlie did talk to me about Vicky, she talked about being dragged out with a bunch of 'urban adventurers', I think she called them. They got into some old art deco cinema that hadn't been in use for donkey's years. It creeped her out, and she was pretty sure it wouldn't do her legal career a lot of good if they got caught."

Baines stared at her. "So where is this cinema?"

"No," she said, "it's since been done up and is back in use. All swanky armchairs and tables. But what if it's somewhere *like* that? Or even," she shuddered, "a drain?"

Jason looked out the window. It was raining heavily yet again, coming down in stair rods.

"Dear God," he said, "I hope not."

"But there must be dozens, maybe hundreds of sites," Baines said. Then he checked himself. "I wonder what there is around Missenden though."

"Missenden?" Joan demanded.

"Sorry," he said, "you're out of the loop." He briefly explained how CCTV and ANPR had tracked Vicky's car after the attack, and the mysterious detour from her obvious route home.

Meanwhile, Jason had been busy with his phone. "There's websites that map abandoned places in Buckinghamshire," he said. "First one up lists sixty-three. There's another website… ah, it's a forum where people can pool information." He looked up. "There could be quite a lot."

"There's a map?" Joan said, leaning in. "Can you pull it up?"

The map was dotted with various icons, and there was a key to what sort of place it was: architecture; urban; transport; and more. He zoomed in and managed to focus on Great Missenden and the area around it.

"No icons there," he said. "Maybe we're on the wrong track."

"But that forum," Baines said. "Maybe Vicky found something through that. Or maybe she found something herself that no one else knows about."

"Please don't." Joan was crying. "We're clutching at straws. She could be anywhere. We'll never find her, will we?"

"Let me call Ibrahim," Jason said. "If there's anything online, he'll find it much quicker than I would."

"And ask him if he's had any joy with Vicky's computer," Baines suggested.

While Jason made the call, Baines looked at Joan, uncertain whether to offer comfort. He was sure she didn't ought to be here. At the same time, he doubted any hospital could have held him for long if it was Karen who was missing.

"How's your head?" he asked her, knowing it was a lame question.

"Still a bit muzzy. And, apart from that balaclava flashback, or whatever it was, I can't remember a bloody thing about last Friday evening. It's like a chunk of memory's just been wiped."

"Ibrahim's coming round, and he's bringing the laptop," Jason said as he closed the call. "He's got something to show us."

"Something good, I hope," said Baines.

A couple of minutes later, the IT man was seated at the table, Vicky Weaver's laptop open in front of him, the others clustered around him.

"We've looked through her recent emails," he said. "It's amazing how little correspondence she had. The usual scams and spam, the odd online purchase, including that balaclava. Nothing social for months. She really does seem to have been a bit of a loner. But it's her browsing history that's interesting. Stuff like how long a person can survive without food or water and how much of each a person needs per day to keep going."

"Oh, Jesus," Joan whispered.

"No doubt at all that she took Charlie, then," observed Baines. "And she'd got it all planned."

"But the really important thing is this," Ibrahim went on. He pulled up a website.

"Subterranea Britannica?" Jason read.

"Yeah. It's a UK-based society for people interested in underground structures and spaces, as in man-made, and what it calls man-used. Everything from Neolithic flint mines to nuclear bunkers. It's got over a thousand members, believe it or not, and links with the likes of the Council for British Archaeology, English Heritage and similar organisations elsewhere in Europe."

Baines felt a stirring of excitement. "Does it list the sites?"

"Well, there are quite a few documented on the website. Apparently, some can be quite easily visited. Others need specialist training or equipment, and some no longer exist. But there's one type she's seemed especially interested in."

"So tell us."

A few clicks, and they were looking at a list of sites in Buckinghamshire, accompanied by a map with a series of red flags.

"You'll see quite a few – most, in fact – are ROC posts," said Ibrahim.

"ROC?" Baines repeated.

"I looked it up. Stands for Royal Observer Corps. A civil defence organisation. Goes back to 1925 and stood down in the mid-nineties."

"So what are these posts?" Baines demanded.

"Made of reinforced concrete and waterproofed with bitumen. Twenty-five feet deep, the whole structure covered with compacted soil. You got in via a steel ladder in a vertical shaft leading to a single room. Pretty basic. They must have been cramped, cold, and damp."

"And Vicky was looking at these?" Joan's voice was wobbly.

"Yeah. I was about to crash Lizzie's briefing when Jason called about this urban exploring thing. Similar sort of interest, I thought. Too coincidental, wouldn't you say?"

"Yes, I would," Baines agreed. A nasty thought crossed his mind. "How did they breathe down there?"

"Yeah, I looked all that up too. Air was circulated from grilled ventilators at both ends of the post and electricity was provided by a battery, which they charged occasionally with a petrol generator."

"And was Vicky looking at any particular sites around here? Especially near Great Missenden?"

"Oh, yes, all around here. And as you can see from the list here," he went back to the Subterranea Britannica site, "there are a few candidates in the area we're interested in: Great Missenden itself has a centre, there's one at Princes Risborough. But the one she kept going back to was this one."

He clicked on a flag between the towns of Chesham and Amersham. "Little Rissingham. It's pretty remote." He clicked 'more' and some text came up. "Closed since 1990. In the middle of a field, just at the foot of a hill. It says it's locked and the landowner doesn't allow visits, although I doubt he'd be aware of anyone sneaking out there at night. There's a few pics."

He clicked 'images'. There was a shot from the top of the shaft of the ladder going down, and a couple of pictures of a grim-looking room with a couple of bits of very basic furniture, the floor strewn with rubbish. There were also a couple of pictures of the outside: one showed what looked like a rectangular metal chimney rising from the ground, with the hill in the background; the other was looking down on a metal hatch at the top of the chimney-like protuberance, evidently the entrance to the shaft. In the picture, it was secured with a padlock.

"We need to check all three of these sites," Baines said, "but, if she's been looking at this one the most, then it could well be where Charlie is." He looked at Ibrahim. "You said they were built from reinforced concrete. So it's possible you could yell your head off down there and no one outside would hear unless they were right on top of it."

"Not that there are likely to be too many passers-by," Jason said. "All the rain we've been having, and it's absolutely chucking it down out there."

Baines thought again about that field, that must be a swamp by now, and a hideous thought struck him. He hoped the bitumen waterproofing was still effective after all these years. Because this heavy rain could run off that hill quite quickly, and the bunker, or whatever you'd call it, was right in its path.

32

With her left arm hooked around the side of the ladder, Charlie took another sip from her last bottle of water. The thirst had become all-consuming, and she knew she had begun to hallucinate. Shadows had formed themselves into terrifying, misshapen monsters and although, even now, she had enough self-control to be able to assure herself that they weren't real, they still scared her, and she feared it was only a matter of time before she lost touch with reality.

Rain was hammering a staccato on the outside of the hatch.

Being free of the handcuffs, only to find that the hatch was locked, had been devastating. Vicky must have had a padlock with her, although, why she'd feel the need to lock it with her prisoner secured to the floor of the structure was anyone's guess. Maybe just to deter some random, inquisitive passer-by from taking a look inside.

At least she was out of the water. She'd thought she might even have dried out a little in the stuffy atmosphere.

She could tell it was daylight outside, as a little light was filtering in from a chink between the hatch and the shaft. Water was trickling in too, but that wasn't the real point of ingress. It was pouring in through a more significant gap in the shaft wall, perhaps where the top of the shaft emerged from the ground.

She could just about make out the water level below. She was convinced it was continuing to rise. She'd made the right decision to stay up here, although her arms would get tired from hanging on and she had to keep switching arms.

She had no idea how long she could hang on like this. Sleep was threatening to overwhelm her and both her arms ached like fire. And she was beginning to wonder if hanging on wasn't futile anyway.

Hanging on for what? For who? No one knew she was here. Wherever 'here' even was.

Her eyelids drooped again. This was no position in which to sleep, clinging to a ladder at least twenty feet up. But the pull of sleep was ever more seductive.

She hoped Joan was alive. And she hoped she knew how much she loved her.

She regretted now the cross words she'd spoken when, even on her birthday, Joan hadn't been able to tear herself away from work at a reasonable time. It had been selfish and unreasonable. They both loved their jobs, were both committed and conscientious, and she'd known from the beginning that Joan's work was never going to be a comfortable nine to five.

The fact was, she'd had a difficult day at work herself, and had imagined Joan making a point of coming home early for a romantic evening. When it hadn't gone according to script, she'd taken her frustration out on the person she loved.

But Joan had been so contrite, her anger had melted away and she'd apologised for acting like a child. It had all blown over and been forgotten by the time they'd set off for the restaurant. With all the rain that had been falling, Joan had offered to drive, but Charlie had suggested they walk, taking advantage of the forecast let-up in the bad weather to get some much-needed fresh air.

It must have afforded Vicky the perfect opportunity. If only she'd agreed to taking the car.

Oh, but now she was heaping hot coals on her own head, finding things to reproach herself with, as if her predicament was somehow her own fault.

There was only one person to blame.

Her eyelids sagged once more. The dull ache at the back of her skull had intensified, and she fought feebly against her body's insistence on shutting down.

This time, her body won the argument. Sleep washed over her. How long it lasted, she didn't know, but when her eyes snapped open again, she was falling. She dropped like a stone, hitting the surface of the flood below, the air being driven out of her lungs.

The ice-cold water accepted her into its embrace with the greed of an ardent lover.

33

Archer had moved quickly when Dan crashed back into the briefing room.

"We need to get over there," she agreed after listening to him. "Ibrahim, work with Will. Get hold of the landowners for all three of those ROC places and tell them to be ready for us, with any keys they might need to get us in. Dan, Jason, you're with me."

"And me," Joan protested.

Archer sighed. "Joan, that place we're starting with is quite a trudge across a field that's likely to be a quagmire, in pouring rain. You've only just – rather foolishly – discharged yourself from hospital. Let us do our jobs."

"Let me at least wait in the car," she'd pleaded.

And Archer had relented. Now they were hurtling along roads like rivers. Potholes had become ponds, whilst dips where the storm drains were blocked or inadequate resembled mini-lakes. Dan's wipers, even at full speed, were barely coping. Over the years, she'd learned to trust in his driving, even though it was often too quick for her liking. But this was a real white knuckle ride. She found herself gripping her door pull like grim death as he slewed around bends. Joan and Jason sat behind them, silent. The tension inside the vehicle was palpable.

After what felt like hours, Dan stopped the car with little ceremony next to a soggy field. Through the epic deluge and the grey of the day, Archer recognised the bulk of the hill from the Subterranea Britannica photograph. The field was lined with a hedge, but Will had relayed information from the farmer about a gap he'd been meaning to do something about. Even in these semi-apocalyptic conditions, Dan's eyes had picked it out.

"What do you reckon?" he said. "It'll be like wading through a swamp, but quicker than driving around to the farm."

"Yeah, let's go this way. Joan, before you argue, you're not coming, but make yourself useful. Ring Will and make damn sure the farmer's waiting by the hatch with that key. Of course, if Vicky's been there, she'll have most likely broken or cut through any locks, but even if she hasn't we'll still want to check inside. Just in case."

As Joan concentrated on her phone, the others set off.

It wouldn't normally have taken too long to cross the field but, in these conditions, it was slow progress. Feet slipped. Twice Archer's foot sank in mud that came up almost to her knee. The second time, the sucking mud pulled off her wellie. Jason managed to pull it out for her and empty the worst of the mud and rainwater out, but the inside was now soggy, squelchy and unpleasant. The men fared little better.

Rain poured off their waterproofs. Even with hoods up, it drove into their faces. Archer's eyes stung and she had to resist wiping at them with now filthy hands.

They were nearing the hill.

"Where exactly is that fucking observer post?" Archer demanded.

"And where the fuck is the bloody farmer?" Dan wanted to know.

Jason's mobile rang. Archer could only half-hear his brief conversation. When he'd finished, he looked grim.

"That was Will. The farmer's been there once, but he says the padlock's been changed. It was an old-fashioned one with a key-turn lock. He found it cut through and discarded. There's a new one with a combi-lock. So he's gone back to the farm to get some bolt cutters. In fact," he added, "this must be him now."

Coming across the field from the far side was a pair of headlights, their beams slicing through the rain.

"Come on, come on," Archer muttered impatiently. "She's in there, isn't she?" she voiced her thoughts.

The vehicle halted about a hundred yards away and the three detectives headed towards it. Its shape resolved into that of an ancient Land Rover. Two men had already clambered out. Archer could see the protruding access to the underground chamber. By the time they got there, one of the men was already working with what looked like bolt cutters.

The other man, in his sixties, raised a hand in greeting as they reached him. "Stan Noakes. You must be DCI Archer. My son, David, will have that open in a jiffy."

"Did you bang on the hatch? Call out?"

"Of course. Not a peep, I'm afraid. You really think there's someone in there? Because that thing can flood. Normally not much, but this weather isn't normal."

Archer marched over to the man working on the lock.

"What's the problem?"

"It's a good quality lock," he said, not looking up, "and these cutters have seen better days."

She pounded on the metal hatch. "Charlie? Can you hear me? It's Lizzie Archer. Charlie?"

She fancied she just might have heard some sort of response but, with the rain pounding on the hatch, it was impossible to be certain.

"Oh, damn these things!" David Noakes bellowed in frustration. "I told Dad we needed new ones."

"Give 'em here," said Stan. "You haven't got the knack."

As David handed the cutters over, Archer hammered again. "Charlie? Charlie?"

"Please," the answer was faint but unmistakeable. "Please help me. I'm so cold."

"Oh, God," moaned Jason. "It's her."

Stan Noakes applied the bolt cutters to the hasp of the padlock, twisted them slightly, made a sawing motion, then grunted with exertion as he forced the two handles together. There was a clunk as the thick metal loop parted. Stan flung the cutters aside and quickly removed the padlock before heaving open the hatch. David, Jason and Dan all shone their flashlights inside.

Charlie hung from the metal ladder like a drowned rat, connected to a rung by her belt, which she'd had the presence of mind to use as an anchor. She was shivering violently, her skin grey and waxy-looking even in the torchlight. Water cascaded into the shaft. Archer couldn't judge how deep it was at the bottom, but it was enough to make her thankful Charlie had managed to get to a higher position.

"How are we going to do this?" Dan said. "We can't have her fall. And she will if she undoes that belt."

"If she even can," Jason added.

"Look," said David, "I know you guys are the pros and all that, but we're forever rescuing sheep who get themselves in fixes. I suggest I squeeze down the outside of the ladder, then one of you follows and gets a hold of her. Actually, one either side would be better. I'll get behind her and undo the belt and, between us, we can manoeuvre her out."

Dan looked at Archer. "Any better ideas?"

"No," she decided. "But I don't like it. Worst case, all four of you fall. I shouldn't let you do this, David."

"We're wasting time," he said. "She looks pretty awful to me. Why don't you call an ambulance while we're doing it? Dad, there's some blankets in the Land Rover that should be fairly dry. Can you get them ready?"

Archer wasn't going to argue further. She seemed to have been relegated to the woman who did the admin while the men did the heavy lifting. And, for once, she didn't mind.

34

Stan and David Noakes had driven a blanket-swathed Charlie back to their farmhouse. Stan had phoned ahead to his wife, who promised to have plenty of towels and some dry clothes standing by. Lizzie had gone with them, while Baines and Jason trudged back to the car, where Joan was frantic to see her partner. Jason had called her the moment they'd got Charlie out of the shaft to reassure her that she was alive, albeit not in a good way.

When the ambulance arrived, paramedics had confirmed she was suffering with hypothermia as well as dehydration and malnutrition. Joan had gone with Charlie in the ambulance, leaving the other three bedraggled detectives enjoying a welcome cup of coffee and some hefty slices of Mrs Noakes' homemade fruitcake. The family had given them their cosy parlour, complete with an open fire that Stan had got going, to talk and make some calls while they took their refreshment.

Baines thought Lizzie took a little too much wicked pleasure in informing Phil Gordon that he and his team had a badly flooded crime scene to process in this inclement weather. Meanwhile, he checked his own phone. He'd been vaguely aware of some alerts while they were getting Charlie out of what had almost become a watery grave, and now he saw that he had more missed calls from Mac. Wondering if his old friend had changed his plans, he called him back.

"No, no, laddie. I'm just doing a few bits here, then I'll be heading north. But I wondered if you'd heard about Robin Watson?"

"What about him?"

"Apparently he's missing."

"Missing?" His pulse quickened.

"Aye. Young Amy called me about an hour ago asking if I'd managed to speak to him. But, as you know, he didn't answer my call. I left him a voicemail, saying I wanted to talk to him, and why, but he never called back. Now it seems he never got home last night. At first, his missus thought it was just a work thing, even though he usually let her know if he'd be late. I mean, come on, Dan, Watson working late? You ever hear of such a thing?"

"So why did Amy call you?"

"Like I say, they knew I was trying to get hold of him, and they wondered if I had, and what time."

"Sounds odd. I hope he's okay. This weather, if he's come off the road…"

"Aye, he might have slithered into the undergrowth or something. But I've been thinking."

"Thinking what? I mean, I'm sorry and all that, Mac, but it's been a bit of a nightmare here."

"Did you find that missing lassie?"

"Yeah. I think she'll be okay."

"Good, good. Well, here's the thing. Remember all the Invisible Man's victims belonged to groups Watson saw on his security roadshow jolly?"

"Yes."

"And Watson was always swanning off somewhere, remember? By all accounts, he hasn't changed much."

The back of Baines's neck prickled.

"After all this time," Mac was saying, "I doubt anyone can say precisely where he was when those murders happened. What's the betting he'd found some excuse to be out and about every single time, Dan?"

"What are you saying?" But Baines knew full well where this was going. And it was ridiculous.

Wasn't it?

"And there's another thing," Mac said. "How many times was Watson one of the first on the scene? Normally, we'd wonder about something like that. But not when it's a copper and everything's happening at once."

"Hang on, Mac," he said, "aren't you getting a bit carried away here?"

"You think so? Well, maybe. This case has sat on my shoulder for the best part of twenty years, and *I* didn't even lose any family like you did. Don't you see? It's been under our noses the whole time. We suspected the Invisible Man had good forensics knowledge…"

Baines had got up and taken the phone to a corner of the room, staring out the window as they spoke. The rain might be easing off a little.

"By 2001, half the world had good forensics knowledge, Mac, we knew that. All those TV cop shows. I know they exaggerated what was possible, but they contained a lot of detail about how to cover your tracks. Anyone who watched them—"

"Who are you trying to kid? Yeah, yeah, there was a lot of forensics stuff on TV, but I think someone might have half-joked that the killer might be a cop. We should have taken it seriously."

Baines's stomach was in knots. He didn't know whether to rubbish what Mac was saying, or to get excited. He had a hunch that the latter was going to win out.

"You're seriously thinking the Invisible Man was a cop?"

"Not any cop. Robin Bloody Watson. He had the perfect means to select his targets through that roadshow of his. He could watch their habits, pick his moment, and turn up on their doorstep, a friendly face they recognised, maybe offering some sort of security check. Once he's inside, the mask slips. But he's forensically aware. That's why we find no trace of him. And, Danny boy, there's one other thing."

And Baines knew what it was. "The nickname. He said 'Invisible Man' in earshot of the press."

"Aye. We thought the killer had seized on the headlines to taunt us with those drawings, but we were wrong."

And Baines found himself nodding. "He *wanted* the press to broadcast the name, because he wanted an excuse to leave the drawings."

"I think so. All part of his sick game. And, laddie?"

"What?"

"I think it's no coincidence he's gone missing as soon as he finds out I'm poking around in the case and want to talk to him. Whatever the reason he stopped killing when he did, he's had an awful long time to wonder if he'll ever get caught. An awful lot of time for the doubts to set in. Hell, he's a cop. For all we know, he knows he made some slip-up that we missed at the time, and he's been stewing about it ever since."

"Okay," Baines said. His heart was thumping so loud, he was amazed the others hadn't heard it, but he was trying to think rationally. "It's a theory, and one we should take seriously. There are still two things I don't get."

"Why he did it?"

"And why he stopped."

"When you find him, you can ask him."

His emotions were a jumble. It wasn't the first time in the past week he'd wondered if they were onto something, but it was the first time he'd felt something akin to elation. Yet even that instinct was muted. If Watson hadn't chosen now to go missing, he would have dismissed the theory as circumstantial nonsense. That the sergeant *had* vanished at this precise moment was maybe just too much of a coincidence.

And that was the other reason his guts were twisting and, actually, his overriding sensation was that he was close to vomiting. Because, if it really was that simple, how on earth had he and his colleagues not seen it at the time? Ploddy, lazy, inept Robin Watson. He'd never come close to their radar. How many lives might have been saved?

"Will you stick around?" he asked. "See how this pans out?"

"Ah, I really wish I could, but I can't not do this job."

"Won't it wait?"

The Scot's voice was tinged with regret. "I don't think they'd be impressed and, to be honest, I need the money. That's why I took Claire King's job. Teenagers like my lad don't come cheap to run these days. Besides, I ought to make sure Peter's been behaving himself." He paused. "But I'll try and come back down as soon as I'm able. Who knows, maybe you'll have a result we can celebrate."

"Okay." He was disappointed.

"Oh," Mac said, "I got a wee present for the baby. Karen works from home, right?"

Her employers had been forced to cut back drastically on office space, and homeworking was a better bet than the redundancy that had been hanging over her head.

"Yes, but you shouldn't have," he said, although he was desperate to end the call.

"Aye, well, I'll drop it off and say goodbye to her. Good luck with finding Watson."

He ended the call and returned to the others. "We need to get back to the station."

"You okay?" Lizzie asked. "You look a bit queasy."

"I am."

"Eat some cake," Jason suggested.

The very thought made him taste bile. "You have it."

Jason needed no second invitation, moving the cake from Baines's plate to his own and breaking off a large chunk, which he pushed into his mouth. But Lizzie was regarding him anxiously.

"What's going on?"

"Can we talk, just the two of us?"

Jason looked from one to the other, chewing. He swallowed his mouthful. "I can easily leave you the room."

"If you would," Lizzie said.

With no sign of rancour, the Scot carried his coffee and cake out into the hall, nudging the door closed with his knee. Baines recounted his conversation with Mac.

She listened in silence, her face giving nothing away. He began to wonder if she suspected him and his old colleague of feeding each other's obsessions. Of having completely lost the plot in a desperate, delusional attempt to finally find someone, anyone they could pin the Invisible Man murders on and give themselves closure.

When she did finally speak, she came pretty close to saying as much.

"Dan," she said gently, "you're sure this isn't just about wish-fulfilment, like those visions of Jack you've started having again?" Her eyes never left his face. "I mean, your old mate comes down, itching to have another poke around in the case, and suddenly—"

"No," he forestalled her. "At least, I don't think so. The thing is, if he's running, he might even try to leave the country."

"But you said he had a wife."

"Who knows? Maybe she's had a very lucky escape. Or," another thought struck him, "or maybe she's in on it. He's confessed all, she's persuaded, I don't know, that he was mentally ill at the time and is better now. Maybe this is some long-planned exit strategy. She plays the worried spouse, sorts out whatever financial plans they have, then disappears herself and joins him somewhere."

"I don't know." He'd never seen her look quite so troubled, or indecisive. "You almost had me convinced about Antony Creed. I got the Super onside there, and I think he's still pissed off about it."

"But this really *works*," he persisted. "Christ, he was even one of the first on the scene at my house when…" He swallowed hard. "When I called it in. How often has a killer been the one to 'find the body'?" He made parenthesis with his fingers. "Or been an apparently casual onlooker in a crowd at a crime scene?

The more he thought about it, the more it made sense. All except the motive. And surely that would come out once they started grilling him and digging around in Watson's past.

"Okay, then," she said. "Let's get back to the station. I'd hoped to nip home and get out of these damp things, but it'll have to wait. Back to the station, and I'll update the Super on Charlie and then tell him our thoughts about this Watson."

Our thoughts. She was on his side. Again.

"I'll ring Amy," he said. "Put her in the picture and get her to pull the wife in. Then we need to issue an all points bulletin—"

She held up a hand. "Whoa. Don't do any of that yet. One thing at a time. We need the Super onside and, if we set a load of hares running before we've done that…"

"Okay," he said, frustrated, wanting to spring into action. "Fair enough." He realised he was trembling. Maybe they could make Watson talk. Tell them where Jack's body was.

Because, if Watson was the killer, then the likelihood that he still had Jack alive, had even raised him as his own, evaporated. All the time Watson had worked with him, he'd never had children. Had claimed they couldn't have them. Maybe that was even part of his warped motivation.

A psychopath hiding in plain sight in a police uniform.

Jack was dead. He knew that now, for sure. Strangely, it seemed to give him some sort of comfort, as if the burden of not knowing had eased from his shoulders a little. They'd track down Watson, bring him to justice, whatever it took. He promised it to himself, to Louise and to Jack.

And then Baines and Karen could get on with their future, a future that included the child they had made together.

"Earth to Dan?" Lizzie said.

"Sorry. It's just a lot to take in. Do you think the Super will listen?"

"I'll make sure he does."

They thanked the Noakses for their help and hospitality on their way out.

35

Charlie still couldn't decide if she was hallucinating. Everything was so strange and confused. She couldn't keep her eyes open, but every time she closed them, she was back in that place, certain she was going to die in the dark.

When she'd dozed off and fallen from the ladder into the water below, the urge to give in, to let it take her, had been almost overwhelming. Yet something had made her fight it, made her break the surface again, coughing and spluttering, find her way back to the ladder and climb to comparative safety. She seemed to remember using her belt to strap herself to the ladder, before a deeper darkness claimed her.

Her rescue, people finally coming and getting her out of what she'd been almost convinced would become her tomb, was confused. Everything was confused.

Except when she opened her eyes and saw, right in front of her, the reason why she'd never given up.

Joan.

She seemed to look a little older, as if time had passed more quickly outside of that prison. She exuded exhaustion. Her nose was bruised and slightly crooked. But the love and concern that burned in her eyes seemed to warm Charlie.

"You're with us again," Joan said.

"Hi," whispered Charlie. "Have I told you you're looking like shit?"

"You might have mentioned it, yes. But thank you, darling. You're not exactly the *Vogue* cover girl yourself."

She looked, for the umpteenth time, at the tubes and wires attached to her. Felt her eyelids drooping again, but fought the urge to sleep.

"Did I dream it?" she asked. "Or did someone tell me Vicky's dead?"

"I did," Joan replied. "She can't hurt you again."

In spite of everything, Charlie felt a hollowness inside her, and a wave of sadness and regret broke over her.

"I can't be glad. I loved her once. Or I thought I did. We had problems, but I never dreamed she'd do anything like this."

"It's not your fault."

Charlie sighed. "I suppose. She was lovely, you know? When we first got together."

"You never really talked about her."

"I guess I wanted to put it behind me and forget. She took everything way too fast. Desperate for us to move in together. And, when we did, more and more possessiveness and jealousy. Rages. The violence was the last straw."

Joan shrugged. "You moved on. But it seems she didn't. She got worse."

Guilt gnawed at her. "She was really ill, wasn't she? Why didn't I see that? Why didn't I make her get help?"

Her partner squeezed her hand. "Hindsight, eh? You've nothing to blame yourself for. I'm just glad we're both still here, and we're going to be okay." She looked anxious. "We are, aren't we?"

Charlie tried to squeeze back, but found she didn't have the strength. Sleep was beckoning again, and this time she couldn't refuse its siren call.

"Yes," she murmured as she drifted off. "Yes, I think we are."

*

Baines was at his desk, in an agony of frustration. He kept checking his watch, but it was as if the minute hand was moving in slow motion. How much longer was Lizzie going to be with the Super? The inactivity was killing him.

The new life that Baines and Karen had somehow come together to build didn't alter what Watson had stolen from them in one terrible afternoon. In his mind's eye, he kept seeing the man's face: the cheeky winks, the roguish grins. The laughter. All masks, concealing the face of a monster.

And now the monster had to pay.

Lizzie hadn't yet told him he couldn't be part of the manhunt that was about to be unleashed, but he had no doubt that she would. Would he, could he accept it?

Perhaps he should. Maybe, if he found himself within reach of Watson, he wouldn't be able to control himself. When his mind conjured up Watson's face, the urge to start punching it was overwhelming, but he was still capable of enough rational thought to know that would help nobody.

Nevertheless, sitting here at his desk, doing nothing, was doing his head in. He'd called Amir and aborted the search for Charlie, filling him in on the good news. And he'd agreed to Jason heading off to the hospital to check on Charlie and try to persuade Joan to get herself readmitted.

Lizzie had counselled – no, instructed – Baines not to speak to anyone, not even get back to Mac, about the Watson theory until she'd finished talking to the Super.

What was keeping her?

He got up and headed down the corridor to her office. The door was closed, which only ever happened if she was out, or wanted privacy. Even so, he knocked. There was no reply, so he opened the door and stepped inside. The room was empty. He sighed and walked around her desk to look out the window. At least you could see some sky from this office. It had stopped raining, and there were even a few chinks of blue. It seemed like a symbol of hope.

Telling himself to have more patience, he turned around to leave. As he passed her desk, he unconsciously read the cover of the file on Lizzie's desk top.

The Invisible Man case.

He'd known she planned to get hold of the files. This one was particularly fat.

The sight of it flipped his stomach over. All the details of the case, collected at the time of the murders. Was there something in there that should have pointed them towards the truth at the time? Something they'd missed, or not understood the significance of?

Knowing he shouldn't, that it would probably do him more harm than good, he found himself sinking into Lizzie's chair and pulling the file towards him.

*

Karen had really got the baking bug since she'd joined the WI. Not just the cakes that were the organisation's trademark, but also savouries. She was especially proud of her quiche, as authentic as she could make it, with double cream and gruyere cheese. It had won first prize in this year's village show.

She'd just taken one out of the oven and set it to cool beside the cherry and almond tray bake she'd made earlier. Mac was supposed to be dropping by, and she thought she might offer him some of each to take home with him to share with his son.

Dan had feared that Mac's reappearance would cause the horrors of the past to resurface in a negative way. Karen had thought it might help bring some sort of closure. It hadn't worked out that way, but she'd really liked Dan's old mate and mentor when he'd come to dinner the other night, and it was nice that he wanted to say goodbye properly. He'd assured them of a warm welcome if they were ever in his neck of the woods, and a trip to Scotland some time sounded appealing.

Of course, she'd keep most of her fresh-baked treats for herself and Dan, and she knew she'd probably devour the lion's share. After all, she was eating for two now, or so she told herself. She was loving the experience of a new tiny person growing inside her, knowing how he or she was developing. She and Dan were determined not to know the baby's gender ahead of the birth. They genuinely cared only that their child was healthy.

It was strange. She'd never been bothered about having children in her first marriage, and her husband had been keen to wait a bit longer while they concentrated on their careers and became a little more financially stable. Even Jack's birth hadn't made her in the least bit broody, despite the strong bond that existed between the twins.

But, as her relationship with Dan had grown and deepened, the seed of the idea of a child, their child, had planted itself. After the honeymoon, they'd discussed their hopes and plans for the future and realised that this was what they both wanted.

In need of a drink, she filled the kettle, looking out the kitchen window at the garden she'd put her own beautiful stamp on. The drizzle had started again, just as she'd hoped the wet weather was about to break.

As the kettle started to boil, she popped a herbal teabag in a cup. She missed coffee, but she'd sworn off caffeine for the duration of the pregnancy.

Maybe a slice of tray bake with it. Why not?

The doorbell rang. It must be Mac. She wiped her hands on a towel, scraped renegade strands of hair back from her face, and went to let him in.

When she opened the front door, she saw a stranger standing there.

*

Baines flipped through the file, some documents still remembered, some photographs still recognised, too many of them grim and upsetting, even after all this time.

He was only skimming the file; to attempt to read everything would take hours. But, as he turned over the pages bearing photographs from the Richardson house, he knew what was coming next.

He'd been taken off the case, of course, when his own family had fallen victim to a seemingly unstoppable killer. He hadn't seen the crime scene photographs from his own home. Hadn't wanted to, not then. Did he really want to see them now?

Swallowing hard, he kept turning the pages, and suddenly there was a scene that had kept coming back to him in nightmares and flashbacks for years: two bodies, one much smaller than the other, lying on his living room floor, their heads encased in cling film. An inner coldness knifed through him. He felt the blood draining from his face and a film of cold sweat breaking out on his forehead and upper lip. Just for a moment, the world turned grey.

He closed his eyes, opened them again, and proceeded with his trip down the most horrific of memory lanes.

Even as he continued, he asked himself why was doing this. As it was, if Lizzie caught him reading a file he knew he wasn't meant to see, she'd be less than amused. And simply turning those pages was unlikely to enlighten him in any way. But still he turned on, past those photographs and on to other typed material. He hadn't got much further when he realised that something was niggling him. He turned back through the pages, looking through the photographs again, puzzled now.

He'd half-hoped to see something everyone had missed at the time. Something that should have told them what he now knew, leaping out at him now the intensity of the case had receded. But what was bothering him now was not so much something there in plain sight. More like something that ought to have been there and wasn't.

He'd lingered long enough, and he didn't want to irritate Lizzie. He closed the file, returned it to something like its original position, and left her office, returning to the open office and his own desk, while he turned the puzzle over in his mind. The more he dwelt on it, the more he tried to fit it in with what they'd already determined about Robin Watson, the more disquiet he felt.

He opened his phone, extracted a piece of information, and jotted it down. Then he went to a website on his desktop computer, entered the details he'd noted, and hit 'search'. It didn't take long. What he'd never expected to find, doubted even existed, was there on his screen. It seemed impossible. Yet he could see now how all the jigsaw pieces finally fitted together, making a complete picture at last.

A picture that took his breath away, terrifying him.

He stood up, and he thought for a moment that his legs were about to give way. He leaned on his desk, controlling his breathing, trying to ignore the roaring in his ears as he swept up his phone and car keys. It was all he could do not to run over to

Will Tyler's desk. He needed to appear in control, not like the madman he was in danger of presenting.

"Will," he said, "I need you to listen carefully and not ask questions. Can you do that for me?"

Will looked surprised, but nodded gravely. "Sure, Dan. What do you need?"

Baines told him, made him repeat it back.

"But what are *you* going to do?" Will asked, eyes wide.

"I'm going over there right away. I can't wait for the cavalry." He stared hard at Will, fighting down rising panic. "Why are you still here?"

By the time he hit the car park, he was running full pelt, his heart pounding as if it would burst.

36

No sign of any strange cars outside the house, but that came as no surprise to Baines. It didn't mean the Invisible Man wasn't here already. Back when they'd been investigating the case, they'd been convinced he parked some distance away from his targets, so the same vehicle didn't keep turning up in the vicinity of crime scenes.

He'd driven here like a maniac, lights and sirens going until he'd reached the top of the road, even badly jumping a couple of red lights, scaring other drivers. He prayed he'd got this impossibly, stupidly wrong. If he had, and Lizzie had done what he'd asked, via Will, he was not just going to look ridiculous. He could find himself back in uniform, busted down to PC, and driving a squad car. Either that, or pensioned off on mental health grounds.

He didn't care. He'd almost welcome that, and more, if it was the price of having this all wrong.

Please, he silently prayed, *please let me be wrong.*

He moved slowly, quietly up the drive, door key in hand, but he didn't need it. His front door wasn't properly closed. Inside his house, he could hear the murmur of voices. Two he recognised, but the third was that of a stranger.

The knot had tightened in his stomach as he'd tried first his home number, then Karen's mobile, without response. At least the voices confirmed that he wasn't yet too late.

As quietly as he could, he walked along the hallway to his living room. The tableau that greeted him was as bad as anything his mind had manufactured.

Karen was on her knees in the middle of the floor, her hands behind her back, evidently secured there. She was white with terror.

A young man, perhaps nineteen or twenty years old, stood beside her, plastic booties on his feet and latex gloves on hands that held a roll of cling film, a couple of feet of it already unwound. He wore a dark, waterproof coat, the hood pushed back.

The figure standing a few feet off to the younger man's right, holding a knife with a large, serrated blade, was similarly attired.

Mac.

Karen saw Baines first. "Dan—" she gasped.

"Shut up," Mac said harshly. Then he smiled. "Welcome to the party, laddie. You're just in time to see how this plays out. Although, I must say, you've complicated matters a wee bit."

The younger man was regarding Baines strangely. Mac gave him a hard look.

"What are you looking at? Get on with it." He grinned at Baines. "My boy, Peter. A real chip off the old block, eh?"

Peter stepped closer to Karen with the cling film. She shrank from him, whimpering. "Don't... please..."

Baines also stepped forward, but so did Mac, blocking his way and raising the knife.

"I wouldn't, laddie. Unless you want the last thing your lovely wife sees to be you, gutted like a fish. But I must admit, I'm curious. I mean, have you just come home early? Or have you somehow worked it out?"

"Oh, I worked it out, Mac. Something you said the other night. You compared our kitchen here with the one in my old house, even though you'd never been in that house. Not even when it became a crime scene."

The Scot smiled. "True. But I thought I'd recovered rather well."

"Saying you'd seen the kitchen in the crime scene photographs? Yes, and I took it at face value at the time. But in the end, that was the trouble. You see, I've just been looking through the case file. My boss retrieved it in the context of Antony Creed. And there's only one picture taken in the kitchen: a close up of that 'Invisible Man' sketch, pinned to the fridge door by a magnet. You can't get any sense of the size of the kitchen."

Peter McNeill hadn't moved. He was watching the exchange with interest.

"Still," Mac said. "Just one little slip of the tongue..."

"An obvious lie."

"Maybe. You won't be around to argue the point. I'm genuinely sorry about that, by the way."

"You mean to kill me?"

"I can't not, can I?"

Baines shrugged, managing to keep himself calm. "You can try."

"Two onto one, and I've got the knife. You're nae Superman, Dan." He made a twirling gesture with the knife. "And afterwards, there's all that evidence stacked against Watson."

"Yes and no. That 'slip of the tongue' got me thinking. Nothing's black and white, is it? I mean, yes, Robin Watson mouthed off about us seeking an Invisible Man, that's true. But it was you coined the nickname in the first place, at a briefing, then quickly said how we'd better not start using it. Maybe you were *hoping* some fool would manage to let it slip in the wrong place?"

"It's true. And Watson didn't let me down, did he? It could have been anyone, but I wasn't surprised it was him. It allowed me to introduce the calling card. That was fun, but it was also a handy distraction. It made our job – sorry, *your* job, I suppose – more complicated."

"But why, Mac? Why did you do it?" He risked a glance at Karen. She was silent, watching this play out. He wondered if the trauma would harm the baby, but he couldn't dwell on that. "Why are you doing *this*?"

A strange smile played around the ex-cop's lips. "You wouldn't begin to understand."

"Try me."

"No. It'd take too long, and you still wouldn't get it. Let's just say I've felt things that other people don't even dream of."

"Killing for kicks?"

"Och, that trivialises it, son. You should try it some time. Doing the unthinkable, just because you can. Watching the light go out of a person's eyes as the soul leaves the body. Except you won't be trying anything now, will you?"

"But why these killings, here? Mothers and their children?"

Mac uttered something between a cough and a laugh. "Why? Because it amused me, being part of a team running around like headless chickens. Why do you think I went out of my way to create a unique signature? And, even though I say it myself, that weekly interval, that race against time, really were a master stroke." He smiled again. "Of course, I can't take all the credit. It was that stupid outreach programme that gave me the idea. And it was easy enough to get a hold of Watson's programme. All I had to do after that was be around when they were turning out, identify likely subjects and follow them home."

Baines was appalled. "But those weekly intervals with the children. Between the abduction and the killing. They were still alive for a whole week. Where were they?"

"I had them well enough looked after. A drug-addicted prostitute, who'd do anything for a fix. When I had no further use for her, I sort of helped her to the overdose that had always been inevitable. No one knew of our connection. I'm a very clever man."

One more murder.

Karen spoke at last. "And my sister? Dan's wife? Why were there no more after her?"

"Why?" Mac grinned. "Well, that was difficult, I grant you. Believe it or not, I really do have a soft spot for him. But a happily married detective, actually on the case, with a family that fitted the profile so perfectly? Being part of the team, seeing the aftermath? It was too delicious. But I'd always known I'd have to stop somewhere. You can't be a cop without knowing that even the cleverest bad guy's luck runs out sooner or later. Complacency breeds carelessness. Louise and Jack were the perfect final flourish. It was like the final chapter of the book had been written."

He looked pleased with himself, and Baines remembered that night – was it really only a few days ago – when Mac had come to dinner. He'd laid this out as his theory of why the Invisible Man had stopped when he had. Only it hadn't been just a theory.

"You were right," Baines said. "I really don't understand you at all. But even more so, I don't get this. Why are you doing *this*?" He gestured towards Karen.

Mac sighed. "I really did take Claire King's offer mostly for the money. But I must admit, I also didn't want anyone else digging around in the case. I didn't think there was anything to find, but better safe than sorry. Then I come down here, and I see just how like Louise Karen really is. And I find that she's pregnant. It was irresistible. But how to get away with it? And then I realised how easily I could frame Watson. The complication with Antony Creed also came in handy, because it helped show I wanted to solve the case. Who would suspect I'd been the real killer all along?"

"And where's Robin now?" Baines wondered.

"Smart, aren't you, son? You always were. He's in the boot of my car, doped up to the eyeballs with something that won't show up on a standard tox screen. It'll look like my phone call triggered one last, ironic kill – the twin of his last victim. You showing up has complicated matters, but it still works. I'll make sure your people believe you interrupted Watson and became collateral damage. Watson himself will appear to have gone into the woods nearby and hanged himself. I still remember that lonely place where that teenager killed herself in 1999. I'm going to try and get him to write a note, but it doesn't matter if I can't. The facts will speak for themselves. You did tell someone we suspected Watson, didn't you?"

"Lizzie. I left her talking to our Super about it."

"And did you tell her you suspected me? I'm guessing not, or you wouldn't be here alone."

"I had to be sure." He didn't want to tell Mac reinforcements would be here soon. He might decide to rush the job.

"Excellent." His old friend seemed to believe him.

Baines looked at Peter McNeill, still beside Karen with the cling film ready. He'd made no move to use it.

"Peter," he said, "I can only assume your dad's convinced you of his cause, or whatever he says it is." *Brainwashed, no doubt.*

"He knows what I did and why," Mac answered for him. "He was happy to get a train down when I called him. I thought it was right for my son to help me out with this little post script."

Baines shook his head and looked at Peter again. "And you're really okay with this? Killing a pregnant woman and her husband, and murdering a cop just to frame him for your father's crimes?"

"Stop talking to him." A harsh note entered Mac's voice. "And don't think I don't know what you're doing, stalling for time. Maybe you lied. Maybe the cavalry won't be too far behind after all. But they'll be too late." He fixed his gaze on his son. "It's time, son. Let's get on with it."

Peter looked at Karen, then raised the cling film.

37

At first, Archer had been none too impressed when Will Tyler had interrupted her meeting with Superintendent Stowe, especially as it was proving a difficult enough conversation already.

"Let me get this straight," Stowe had been saying. "We spent valuable time, when we were supposed to be finding Charlie Ward, turning over the traces of the Invisible Man case, all because a vindictive ex-spouse decided to make trouble for her former husband?"

She'd felt the sting of criticism. "That's putting it a bit simply, sir."

"But those are the bald facts, yes? And then you decided no, no, perhaps he was Joan's attacker instead?"

"He was known to have been angry with Charlie in the past."

"So why didn't we arrest the exes of every client she's ever had?" He shook his head. She'd seen his gentler side. Now she was seeing what he looked like when he was seriously pissed off.

"And now, all of a sudden, an officer is missing in Oxfordshire, and now DI Baines is saying, no, no, *he*'s the Invisible Man, not Creed. I mean, you know Dan Baines, Lizzie. Is he all right?"

"He's fine, sir." It felt like a lie. "And there is a logic to what he says. A cop the victims would have known through that outreach programme…"

He sighed. "Well, I suppose it will do no harm to speak to him, but I'm not going to treat him as a suspect for now. It's only a year since we had a case right here that reflected badly on the force, so I think caution is justified. Just tell Oxford we'd like to see him if and when he turns up. Offer to help find him. But that's all."

That was when there was a tap on the door and the Super's PA looked in.

"Sorry to disturb," she said. "I've got DC Tyler outside, needing to talk to Lizzie. He insists that it's urgent."

"Can't it wait?" Stowe was visibly irritated.

"He says not."

He sighed again. "It had better be important. You'd better deal with whatever it is, Lizzie. Then come straight back."

Will followed her to her office. She shut the door.

"I hope this is good, Will."

"It's Dan," he said.

Her heart sank to her boots. Of course it was. What now?

"It doesn't make much sense to me," Will said, "but he was obviously in a bit of a state. He said to tell you, it's not Watson."

"Not Watson?" Oh, for pity's sake. "Couldn't he tell me that himself?"

The DC looked nonplussed. "I don't even know who Watson is, boss. But he said to tell you it's Mac, and he thinks Karen may be in danger."

Her mind had reeled. Dan was in a worse way than she'd imagined, and she'd already had her worries. She was glad this conversation wasn't happening in the Super's presence.

This obsession, seemingly fed by that damned book and Mac re-entering his life, had really taken flight now. This time, Mac himself was the killer, making three prime suspects this week.

"And where *is* Dan?"

"He's on his way home now. He wants you to scramble an armed response unit. I asked him if he didn't want to wait for backup, but he said there was no time, and just to tell you."

He stood there, waiting for her response, while she processed this. She cared deeply about Dan and Karen. They were almost like family. But calling out armed police felt like reckless overkill and risked someone winding up shot in response to the craziest hunch yet. This chopping and changing of suspects smacked of a damaged man trying a little too hard for closure.

"It's way too soon to mobilise an ARU," she decided, "but get one on standby for me. Just as a precaution."

"What are you going to do?"

What could she do? "I'm going over there myself."

"Are you sure? I can come with you?"

"No, Will, just talk to firearms, ask them to stand a unit by and await instructions. And Will?"

"Boss?"

"Keep this to yourself for now."

As she left her office, she grabbed her bag and pulled out her car keys and phone. She speed-dialled Dan.

"Are ARU on their way?" he said before she could speak.

"Where are you?"

"Five, ten minutes from home." She could hear the panic in his voice.

"I'm on my way. But why do you think it's Mac? And why would he target Karen?"

"I don't have time to explain. I hope I'm wrong. But he said he was going home today, and he said he'd visit Karen before he left. And now she isn't answering her home phone or the mobile."

"There could be any reason for that. Look, wait and I'll catch you up."

"I'm not waiting," he said, and hung up.

Damn. She was no wiser. Her instincts told her Dan wasn't well, and she certainly wasn't about to make a fool of herself over this. But she owed it to him to go after him.

As she hurried across the car park to her car, she met Amir Rashid coming the other way.

"Good news about Charlie, boss," he began.

She'd hesitated, then made a decision. "You've done the police driving course, right?"

"Sorry?" He looked momentarily fazed. "Oh, yeah."

"Good. Well, you're with me. And you're driving."

He recovered fast. "Okay. Where we going, boss?"

"Little Aston," she said. "Let's leave it at that for now."

*

As Peter McNeill moved the cling film towards Karen's face, she flinched away.

"Please don't do this," she begged. "My baby…"

Baines knew he had to do something, yet if he got himself stabbed to death, he'd be no more help to her than if he waited a little longer for the right moment to act.

If such a moment was ever going to come.

Yet Peter seemed to be hesitating. And, as Baines watched him, the sensation he'd felt when he'd first laid eyes on the lad seemed to grow.

"I don't know, Dad," Peter said. "I don't know if I can."

"You can," Mac urged. "You have to. Do it for me, like we agreed."

"I know, I know. It's just…" He looked at Baines, hesitating. "I *know* you, don't I? I mean, I've seen you?"

"Yes," Baines agreed, "I think you have. Outside the Waterside theatre the other day."

"That's right. I saw you looking at me. But I'd seen you before, I think."

There was a strange look in his eye, and Baines was filled with the certainty that he was talking about numerous dreams, about looking at Baines through the window of a house overlooking a beach. The very house Baines had found on Google Earth after keying in Mac's postcode.

The notion was beyond impossible. Crazy. Yet it had confirmed his suspicions.

He'd not mentioned this last bit to Lizzie when she'd called him on hands-free on his way here. It would have sounded as insane to her as it seemed to him. He had no idea how it was even remotely possible. But nor did he have any doubt what it meant.

"Look," he continued, "this might not be the ideal time for a Darth Vader moment. But I think I'm your father, Peter. I think you're my son. Your real name is Jack."

The young man looked from Baines to Mac and back again.

"My *father*?"

"Don't let him mess with your head, son," Mac said. "We don't have time for this. We've wasted enough already."

Karen was looking at the youth. "Dan? You really think this is *Jack*?"

"Enough talk now." A harshness had entered the Scot's tone. "Wrap the cling film around her head, Peter."

"He can't help it," Baines said. "Your dad's not well. It's not his fault."

And he meant it. Since Louise's murder and Jack's disappearance, he'd entertained such dark fantasies about what he might do to the Invisible Man if he ever caught up with him. But now he looked at Mac and he no longer saw a faceless predatory monster. He knew a thing or two about mental illness from first-hand experience. He didn't believe people were born evil. Something had happened to the man he'd counted as a friend, something that had twisted and deformed him. If Baines could yet talk his way out of this, then maybe Mac could get the professional help he plainly needed.

And yet, perhaps Baines himself hadn't been mentally ill at all. Those dreams, those visions…

I know you, don't I? I mean, I've seen you?

Mac barked a harsh laugh. "You think I'm nuts?"

"I don't think what you did – what you're *doing* – is what I'd call rational."

"Enough talking. Do it now, Peter." He brandished the knife for emphasis.

"Think, Peter," Baines persisted. "Why did he need you in on this? Why does he want to make you into a killer?"

He could see the uncertainty in the youngster's eyes.

"She's your aunt," Baines said. "Your mother's identical twin. He wants to make you kill a woman who looks exactly like your real mum. To kill your mum again, if you like. Ask yourself why he wants *you* to do it. To become a killer like him."

Mac laughed again. "Oh, laddie, laddie, you're way off beam. You think this'll be his first killing?"

Baines reeled. "What are you talking about? You stopped."

"Who said that? Just because the Invisible Man stopped, doesn't mean *I* did. And his modus operandi was only ever part of the game. I didn't need to stick with it. But enough talk. If you don't do it, Peter, I'll slit this man's throat and then do her myself. We've got to get out of here."

"I'm sorry," the younger man told Baine. "But I think Dad's right. He's always right."

He began to wind the plastic film around Karen's head, across her face, she started to scream, the sounds quickly muffled. Mac's eyes momentarily shifted from Baines to the boy's action and Baines, seeing his one chance, launched himself across the room at him. As he impacted with the older man, he felt a sharp, burning sensation, as the blade sliced into his side. Then they both crashed to the floor, Baines punching the side of his opponent's head. He felt Mac's fist thudding into his side, bringing renewed pain, and he guessed each blow must be a stab, inflicting catastrophic damage.

But he was wrong about that.

"Peter!" Mac screamed. "Grab the knife for me!"

The weapon must have flown from his hand when they went down.

Baines had some twenty years advantage on Mac, but the man was still as hard as Scottish granite. Their two heads were close together as they grappled. Baines drew his own head back and then butted Mac as hard as he could, full in the face. There was a crunch as the nose snapped. Mac's grip on Baines loosened and Baines sprang to his feet, Mac beginning to rise too, but more slowly, blood pouring from his nose.

Baines kicked him in the chest, flooring him again, then looked at Peter, who was bending to pick up the knife. Baines felt his clothes sticking to him, soaked with his own blood. He saw Karen, cling film across her face, just like Louise must have looked as she died, struggling in vain, her eyes wild, the film going in and out as she tried to breathe.

He knew her brain, starved of oxygen, would begin to suffer damage within just a couple of minutes. What was it doing to their baby?

Help her, or fight Peter for the knife?

The young man stood between him and his wife. Time slowed down as he staggered across the carpet, blood-loss already weakening him. Peter's hand had closed on the knife.

Baines aimed a kick at his hand, missed, and then somehow barged past him, dropping to his knees in front of Karen, clawing at the cling film across her gaping mouth, trying to open an airway for her. He made a small hole, was about to attempt to enlarge it, when an arm snaked across his chest, pulling him away from her. He felt the knife blade against his throat.

"We've wasted enough time," he heard Mac say. "I'm sorry, Dan lad, but we can't leave you behind. Give me the knife, Peter."

Grab the knife for me. Give me the knife.

"You don't want him to finish me off himself?" Baines panted, never taking his eyes off Karen. Her face was puce, but he hoped that small hole was giving her enough air that she could hold out a little longer. "Or is making him kill his own father too much even for you?"

"Dad?" Peter's grasp relaxed a fraction. "Why's he keep saying that?"

"I told you. He's messing with you. Now give me—"

"What happened to Jack then, Mac?" Baines asked.

He saw Peter eyeing his father, questions burning in his eyes. Mac shrugged.

"I killed him, of course. Buried his body."

It rolled too glibly off his tongue.

"Yes? But you would have been waiting until the following Friday to kill him. Your little ritual. If you had the next murder and abduction planned. But you said Louise was always going to be the last. So why would you still go through with killing Jack, if you weren't going to leave him at another murder scene? It just doesn't make sense. You could have just let him go. He was two years old. Too young to be any use as a witness."

"Dad?"

Doubt in the young man's voice.

"I don't know exactly how you pulled it off," Baines said, "but I think you and your junkie nursemaid kept him until you left the force and went back to Scotland. You wound up at Aberdeen, the poor woman murdered by then. You told me you'd married a widow with a young son. She'd died and you'd adopted the lad. But I think you arrived there with Jack, telling the locals he was your own son, a little older than his real age, his mum already dead. Maybe in the kid's own mind, the woman who'd looked after him *was* his mother."

"Stop talking."

"You're a cop. You'd know all about wangling fake legal documents good enough to fool the authorities. Hell, we do it all the time for undercover cops. All these years, and you've been raising my son as your own and, by the sound of it, drip-feeding him your sickness."

He could see Karen was breathing, but she was struggling. The air hole was too small for her to breathe freely. Her breath was coming in whistles.

"In dreams," Peter said. "I've seen you in dreams. I'm looking out my bedroom window, and there's a stranger, looking up at me from the beach. I think it's you. But how can that be?"

Baines found himself almost overwhelmed by layer upon layer of emotion. The impossibility of him and his son being somehow truly connected through that dream. Those dreams of a house on a cliff had somehow been shared: the house was real, the face at the window had been looking back at him through the eyes of a young man who now held a knife to his throat.

The horror that his Jack was alive but – unless Mac had lied again – had been turned into a killer.

The knowledge that Karen and the baby could die if he didn't help her soon.

"Give me the fucking knife," Mac snarled. Baines heard running feet, then the knife nicked his neck as Peter's arm was ripped away from his chest. He leaned forward, tore a bigger hole in the cling film, then forced himself to rise, feeling weak and groggy. A few years ago, he'd been shot and lost a lot of blood. There was a sense of déjà vu.

Mac and Peter were grappling for the knife. Baines hesitated to get involved. Someone could get hurt, and things were bad enough already.

"I want the truth, Dad," Peter said.

"Mac," Baines said, his voice seeming to be fading, "think. That knife's going into one of you if you don't stop this. Do you want to kill Peter? Do you want him having your death on his conscience?"

The Scot stopped struggling. He stepped away from Peter. "Come on then, son. If you believe he's your real dad, and your old man's just some sick psycho, then use that knife to put me out of my misery."

The young man looked at him, looked at the weapon in his hand, then threw it into a corner. Baines's knees sagged. Whether it was from relief or blood loss, he wasn't sure.

"You can't do it, can you, son?" said Mac softly. Peter sobbed and pulled him into a rough embrace.

And that was when a familiar voice said, "Police! Everyone stay exactly where you are."

38

Archer sat with Karen in the same café at Stoke Mandeville Hospital where she had spoken to Joan Collins' parents not so very long ago. Dan was going to be fine. He'd lost a fair bit of blood, but paramedics had staunched the flow and there was nothing much wrong with him that stitches and a few days' rest wouldn't put right.

The stitches were being administered now. Archer would make damn sure he took the rest.

He wouldn't be allowed anywhere near the interviews with Mac or the lad who still thought of himself as Peter McNeill, and he was fine with that. After what Karen had gone through, all he wanted was be with her and reassure himself that she was okay.

"He's going to stifle me," Karen said. "You watch. I can see it now. He'll treat me like I'm made of glass. He won't let me lift a finger. It was bad enough when we first found I was pregnant. After this…"

"You can hardly blame him," said Archer. "Someone tried to kill you. Nigh on succeeded. I must say, you seem pretty calm about it all. You're sure you and the baby are all right?"

"That's what they say. And I'm probably calm right now for Dan's sake. When I saw all that blood, I thought we were both going to die." Her face folded and she covered it with her hands.

Archer reached across the table and put a hand on her shoulder. "Maybe you should be home in bed. Be kind to yourself and the baby. There could still be a delayed reaction."

"I know. I've been warned what to look out for. But me and Dan'll go home together. We'll both take it easy and look after each other. I'll get us some ready meals."

"Just give me a list and I'll get them in for you." She grinned. "Well, Dominic will, I'm sure."

"You've got a good man there, Lizzie. Don't lose him."

"I won't."

"Do you know how Joan and Charlie are doing?"

"Physically they'll be fine, I think. I looked in on them before I came to find you. But, like you and Dan, they've been through a lot. With Joan and Dan, I'm going to be missing a couple of my best officers for a while, but we'll cope."

"Good." Karen frowned. "Speaking of your team, did I see Jason Bell in the corridor?"

"Yeah." Archer couldn't help grinning. "Ostensibly to check on Joan too, but she tells me there's a nurse here he's finally found the bottle to ask out."

Karen giggled. "I bet he looked like a beetroot. Did she say yes?"

"She did. Maybe a few personal bed baths are what he needs to finally overcome this shy Scot thing he's got going."

"Well, thanks for putting that image in my head, Lizzie."

The two women laughed. It felt good.

Archer sobered. "When we were arresting Mac and his boy, Dan asked the kid if he'd take a DNA test, and he said he would. So I guess you're going to find out for sure if he's Jack. How do you feel about that?"

"Strange. Apprehensive. I mean, we've always talked about what we'd do if Jack turned out to be alive. We knew it would be complicated, but this?" She shuddered. "This is the person who wrapped cling film around my head. I'll never forget what that felt like. The panic."

There was a haunted look in her eyes. "I'm sure he's been damaged by whatever Mac's filled his head with," she said, "probably for most of his life. But can I ever forgive him, or trust him? I just don't know. We've only scratched the surface of the truth and, quite frankly, I wouldn't believe one single word Mac says, ever again."

She toyed with her untouched smoothie. "Besides, it's not like he'll be coming to live with us. At least, not any time soon. I'd imagine he'll be in trouble for this. Will he be bailed, do you think?"

"I can't see it. He's going to have to spend time with psychologists for assessments before any decisions are made, as will Mac. But in Peter's case, or Jack's, if you like... at best, he'll need to be under some sort of supervision for the immediate future. For all we know, he's a danger to himself, let alone anyone else."

"Mac said there'd been other killings, evidently more recent. That Peter – sorry, I can't think of him as Jack, not yet – that *Peter* carried out at least some of them, or at least helped."

"We're looking into that, obviously, although whether we get any more information out of them remains to be seen. They've both got legal representation now, and I'm sure their briefs will be strongly advising them to keep schtum on that. Mac might say it was just bravado, something he said to hurt Dan. I don't think he'd have said half of what he did in your house if he'd thought you or Dan would be alive when they left."

"Sometimes I hate the bloody police," Karen said. "Nothing personal, but the force arguably got Lou killed and Jack taken away. Maybe even got him turned into a killer. Certainly badly messed up. It got you that scar. It got Dan shot. Now this."

Archer privately wondered how differently things might actually have played out if Dan hadn't been a cop. Mac would still have been on his twisted mission. He might still have targeted Louise and Jack through that parent and toddler group.

And maybe he'd have kept in touch with Dan, the grieving widower and still visited him when he returned to the Vale last week. He'd still have learned of Karen's pregnancy, triggering the attempt to kill her and frame Robin Watson.

Watson himself had been recovered from Mac's car boot and was also in the hospital, doing fine. The receptionist had joked that, if the trend continued, they would need to build a dedicated police wing.

"There was one thing Peter said that seems unbelievable," Karen was saying. "Peter said, more than once he'd seen Dan before, and then he started talking about a dream he'd had."

"A dream?" This hadn't come up when she'd spoken to Dan before his surgery.

"Lizzie, there's no way he could have known about Dan's dreams, but it's pretty obvious they've been having the same one, maybe even at the same time. How can that be? Can you fathom it?"

Archer shook her head. "Two people who don't know each other, hundreds of miles apart, sharing dreams? It sounds like something out of the *Twilight Zone*. And yet," she said, "it makes some sort of perfect, crazy sense too, doesn't it? I'll have to ask Dominic. He knows some weird shit."

"You know," Karen said, "there's something else that's been bothering me. A few years ago, I persuaded Dan to come with me to a mediumship evening in Aylesbury."

"Isn't that psychic stuff, where they're supposed to get spirit messages for people in the audience?"

"Basically, yes."

"I've always assumed they were all frauds. What did you make of it?"

"Yes, Dan was very sceptical too. I had to practically drag him. But then the guy had messages for Dan that he said were from Lou."

"I bet he did." She'd always considered Karen pretty down to earth. "Did you believe it? I thought it was all about informed guesswork and intuition. Subtly getting stuff out of the mark that they can use to look authentic."

"Dan thought so too. I was more agnostic. I thought we had nothing to lose. But this guy knew stuff he couldn't possibly have. Dan insisted on seeing him backstage afterwards – I'm afraid he even flashed his warrant card. First he accused the guy of faking it, then he wanted to know exactly what Lou was supposed to have said to him."

"And did he say?"

"Yes. He said Lou sounded scared. She warned him not to look for Jack. That no good would come of it. And now we find he's been alive all these years, and quite possibly at least an accomplice to murder." She blinked. "I can't help wondering if that's what the medium meant."

And Archer found she had no answers.

*

All in all, it had been a hell of a day. The rescue of Charlie. Arrests finally made in the Invisible Man case. Injury to Dan. The likelihood that Jack Baines was alive, but was either a killer himself or an accomplice to murder – although, as Archer herself had predicted, neither Duncan McNeill nor the boy he still called his son were saying anything more about that.

There had been one other spot of news of sorts. Young Liam Gunner had been picked up just over the Oxfordshire border last night, supplying drugs out of the boot of his BMW. She asked the local cops to lean on him about Tuesday night. She wouldn't mind betting that was why he had been 'driving about' near Stoke Mandeville around the time Lauren and Maisie's flat was being desecrated.

The past week had tilted the world on its axis for two of Archer's best officers. She herself had snatched maybe three hours' sleep in the past two days. She was entirely exhausted, yet way too wired to think of sleep. As she pulled up on her drive, she knew where she wanted to be.

Dominic grinned at her when he opened the door. "Slacking, are we? It's not even nine o'clock."

"Got any wine open?"

"Nope, but it can be arranged."

They kissed and then she followed him into the kitchen and pulled up a stool. Barney sprang up onto her lap, and she stroked his soft fur, listening to him purring.

"I hoped I'd see you," Dominic said as he unscrewed a bottle of red. "I've been listening to the news, of course, and following it online too. What a day you must have had."

"Yeah, but do you mind if we don't talk about that for now?" She slipped off her suit jacket. "I don't want to think about police things for a while."

"Sure. But I'm glad Charlie's okay. And arrests in connection with the Invisible Man? Dan must be pleased."

"It's complicated," she said.

He handed her a glass. "Well, we'll talk about it when you feel like it. Do you want feeding?"

A warm glow that had nothing to do with her first mouthful of wine spread over her.

"You're too good for me. I don't deserve you."

You've got a good man there, Lizzie.

"You're worth it. What do you fancy?"

"I don't mind. Something quick and easy."

"Omelette?"

"Perfect."

She watched him cracking eggs and grating cheese.

Don't lose him.

"Thing is," she said, "I've been thinking. About us."

He froze, putting down the grater. "Don't tell me you want to finish it?"

"What? *No!* Quite the opposite. It's just we're practically living together, here and next door, and I know we're not exactly love's young dream, but I'm happy. Are you?"

"Yes," he said gravely. "I am."

"Well, then, I was wondering if we should, you know, get a place together. I know we said we'd take it slow, but I think I'm ready, if you are."

"Wow," he said. "You mean, actually be like a proper couple?"

"We can even get married, if you like."

There. She hadn't meant to say that. But now she had.

He wiped his hands and walked over to her. "Are you serious? I know it's not a leap year, and it's not Valentine's day…"

"Don't take the piss."

"Sorry." He took her glass and set it on the worktop. Removed an indignant Barney from her lap. Then he took her hands in his. "Just tell me you mean it."

She was bone-tired and emotionally drained, but she knew that wasn't clouding her judgement.

"I can't think of anything I want more."

He dropped to one knee.

"Get up," she giggled. "There's no reason to be a tit."

"No, no," he insisted. "Gotta do things properly. Lizzie, will you marry me?"

He was still holding her hands. She stood up and pulled him to his feet.

"Yes, you idiot," she said. "Now shut up and kiss me."

THE END

AUTHOR'S NOTE

If you've been following the Archer and Baines series from the beginning, you'll know that this book has finally resolved a mystery that has overshadowed Dan Baines's life since long before the opening scenes of the first book, *The Scars Beneath the Soul*.

I hope you enjoyed *Die in the Dark*, maybe enough to tell your friends and even post a review. Can I beg a favour though? If you could keep what this book reveals under your hat, then it will hopefully come as a surprise to other readers, as I hope it has to you.

Of course, everything still isn't all nicely tied up with a satin bow. But that's for the future.

Dave Sivers

ACKNOWLEDGEMENTS

I owe huge thanks to my brilliant beta readers, Debbie Porteous and Chris Sivers, who read this book during its development and made invaluable and insightful comments. Thanks too to Helen Baggott for helping me knock it into its final shape.

Thanks are also due to several people who helped me research all the stuff I needed to know for this story, especially Clare Houston, Paul Brennan and Ed Combes. As always, any mistakes are entirely mine.

Huge respect to the amazing Jessica Bell for yet another stunning cover design.

I'm indebted to so many in the writing community for their ongoing friendship, support and inspiration: Carole Matthews and Lovely Kev; long-standing comrades in crime, Bob Barker and Janet O'Kane; Carolyn Gillis and the rest of the Fab Four – Caroline England, Sam Carrington and Libby Carpenter; Christina Jones, Alison Gray, Alison Bruce, Nic Parker, Louise Mangos, Jane Risdon, Liz Mistry, Chris 'The Guru' Longmuir, Anne Coates, Jane Isaac, Susi and Jamie Holliday, Rebecca Bradley, Vicky Newham, Linda Huber, Vic Watson, Simon Bewick and Sumaira Wilson; my mates at Chiltern Writers; and many, many more. Anyone I've missed is a function of age.

Thanks too to my forever friends: Dave, Mandy, Rob, Maggie, Kim, Les, Eileen, Paul and Kate, just for being there. And above all, thanks to my wonderful wife, Chris, and my phenomenal dad, for their constant love and support.

Buckinghamshire, 2021
www.davesivers.co.uk
Twitter: @davesivers
Facebook: @davesiversauthor1

Printed in Great Britain
by Amazon

81530768R00171